Gustavia Browne

❧

A novel

To my Reader,
with Love and
appreciation,

[signature]

OTHER BOOKS BY ALENE ROBERTS

Fragrance of Lilacs
A Rescued Heart
A Butterfly in Winter
It's Bliss
Pipit's Song
Heart of The Rose

Gustavia Browne

a novel by
ALENE ROBERTS

BONNEVILLE BOOKS ™

Springville, Utah

ISBN: 1-55517-758-1
e. 1

Published by Bonneville Books
Imprint of Cedar Fort Inc.
www.cedarfort.com

Distributed by:

Cover design by Nicole Cunningham
Cover design © 2003 by Lyle Mortimer

Printed in the United States of America
10 9 8 7 6 5 4 3 2 1

Printed on acid-free paper

Library of Congress Cataloging-in-Publication Data

Roberts, Alene.
  Gustavia Browne : a novel / by Alene Roberts.
      p. cm.
  ISBN 1-55517-758-1 (pbk. : alk. paper)
1. Young women--Fiction. 2. Grandparents--Fiction. 3. Loss (Psychology)--Fiction. 4. Friendship--Fiction. 5. Boston (Mass.)--Fiction. I. Title.

  PS3568.O2367G875 2004
  813'.54--dc22
                    2004000235

AUTHOR'S NOTES

Though I hadn't even started my writing career, the seed of inspiration for this book came about in 1986 while I, my husband, Elliott, and our twenty-one-year-old son, Whit, were in Hull, England visiting a dear friend, Fred Hopkins.

It was truly a memorable experience visiting with this valiant, gentle man who, when his wife left him, raised his children alone. During the conversation, we were surprised and disheartened to learn that Fred had been put into an orphanage at age seven—Hesslewood Orphanage. He shared with us how worthless and insecure he felt during much of his time there.

Our visit lasted till dark and Fred invited us to stay the night. Not wanting to put him out, we thanked him and told him we needed to leave.

After saying reluctant goodbyes, we searched for a hotel. We found one on the Humber River, but it had no vacancies. The manager told us of another one that was being completed and might have a room. Following his directions to the adjoining town, Hessle, we located it.

We were greeted by a man dressed formally in black who assured us that though this magnificent old mansion was being remodeled into a luxury hotel, they did indeed have a room.

While climbing the wide, curved stairs to our room, we were surprised to see wooden perpendicular pegs pounded into the bannister every 15 inches. When I asked about it, he explained that the building used to be an orphanage, Hesslewood Orphanage. We were stunned. Goose pimples rose and tears stung our eyes. It was one of those pivotal moments that strikes deep into the heart, never to be forgotten.

ACKNOWLEDGMENTS

I thank J. D. Hicks for the fascinating information he collected and made into the book, *Our Orphans,* and the assistance from the Board and staff of the Hull Seamen's and General Orphanage, the staff of the Humberside County Record Office, the Hull City Council Record Office and the Hull Local History Library. In my research, I was fascinated at how well, on the whole, the orphans were treated.

I thank the Hull City Archives for the time and information they so graciously gave me.

I acknowledge our valuable visit to Ludlow and its wonderful cemetery. I appreciate David Lloyd and Peter Klein for their book on the historic old town.

I thank my 'walking encyclopedia'—my husband, Elliott—who can answer almost any question I ask him! His input about the weather, as well as other remembrances of Hull and Grimsby, where he spent two years, was invaluable. I thank him for the hours and hours he spent reading and rereading the manuscript, giving me wonderful suggestions, which greatly enriched the story.

I thank my three, wonderful, but ruthless readers: Whit, Lisa, and Christie. They made valuable suggestions, which significantly improved the book.

I thank my teen-age granddaughters, Morgan and Lauren, who, wistfully longing to live in a different century where the clothing was beautiful and feminine, made and wore lovely empire-styled dresses like Jane Austen's Emma wore. They, as you will learn, inspired an integral part of the book.

I thank my granddaughter, Leah. Because of her fascination with costume and clothing design, she has collected many books on the subject, which she has generously shared with me.

Last, but not least, I thank all my other granddaughters who are old enough to be aware: Erin, Heather, Jamie, Catie, Callianne, Eliza and Amber, who confirm to me that there are really heroines in this world—like Gustavia.

DEDICATION

In remembrance of our beloved friend, Fred Hopkins,
and his life in Hesslewood Orphanage

&CHAPTER 1&

BELFORD, MAINE, APRIL 2001:

He first saw her after he had closed Ada Redmore's tall wrought iron gate and stepped out onto the sidewalk. She was a block away standing motionless, her profile to him, gazing across the street. He blinked a couple of times staring through the late afternoon drizzle. For a moment it was as if he were in the 1890s. A silhouette against the steel gray sky, she held an umbrella over her dark Gibson-girl-type hair style and waisted-in dress of deep wine, its skirt sweeping to the ankles.

Mesmerized, he had to consciously will his legs to move, hoping to advance toward her unnoticed. He had to get a closer look! Just as he took his first step, she turned abruptly and walked rapidly toward town.

He too walked swiftly, not wanting to lose her. His long strides quickly closed the distance between them, but by then she had turned the corner. He ran. Rounding the corner he halted abruptly, for only a few yards away she had stopped to look into a store window. Before he could scrutinize her, she moved on to The Flower Shoppe next door. Through the window she gazed at the potted plants and flowers, oblivious to the stares of the passing pedestrians and motorists. He wondered if they too felt as though they had momentarily caught a glimpse of the past.

Next she entered the Boutique Shop. He stood under an awning, to wait. Feeling the water trickle down the back of his neck, he realized he hadn't taken time to put up his own umbrella.

When she came out, he was only a few feet away. He drew in a sharp breath. It was her! She moved on, unaware of him or his intense gaze. As he continued to follow her—drawn by the sight of her graceful movements window shopping, entering and exiting shops—he could almost hear a flute playing Gaubert's beautiful and mystical *Fantasie*.

Remembering suddenly his pressing errand for Miss Redmore, he reluctantly crossed the street, turned in the opposite direction and headed for his law office on the corner.

&

It was 5:40 when Gustavia remembered to look at her watch. Cousin Ada had informed her that dinner was promptly at 6:00 P.M.—not a minute sooner, nor a minute later.

The rain had stopped, but the lower part of her skirt was damp, making it harder to run. She chastised herself for not wearing her father's raincoat, the only coat long enough to cover the dress. Having left Ada's house in anger, she had forgotten. As her anger cooled, curiosity led her to investigate the quaint town of Belford.

She turned and ran through town and up the two long blocks to Cousin Ada's elegant old Victorian home. Breathlessly slamming the gate shut, she ran up the steps and into the house, dropping the umbrella in the brass holder just inside. Glancing at her watch, she realized it was exactly six o'clock when she stepped to the entrance of the dining room. The tall imperious figure of her cousin stood behind a chair waiting, her thin lips tightly pursed in obvious displeasure.

"You're one minute late, Gustavia. As I said, I expect you to be on time."

Gustavia's chin rose in obstinacy. "Well, then I guess we'll have to synchronize our watches, Cousin Ada, for mine says exactly 6:00."

"Move yours up one minute." Her words were clipped and sharp. "Shall we dine?"

It sounded to Gustavia more like an order than a question. Apparently, it was natural for Ada to speak in commands. She fought back resentment over Ada's cruel insinuations earlier—which sent her out of the house with only an umbrella. Breathing in deeply, she told herself once more that she had to make the best of the situation—no matter how Ada acted. Straightening her shoulders, she forced herself to look pleasant, then took a seat across from her cousin.

Presently, the cook brought in small bowls of hot cream of asparagus soup. The thick warm liquid felt good going through her chilled body. Early April here in Maine didn't feel like spring—more like the cold springs in Hessle, England, where she had lived as a child.

"Well, how did you like the big metropolis of Belford?" Ada asked matter-of-factly.

"It's rather enchanting I would say. Kind of like a picture book of the olden days," she added wistfully.

"About like you're dressed, Gustavia," she stated with disdain. "I suppose people stared at you in that . . . that costume."

"As I told you before, Cousin Ada, it isn't a costume. These are the kind of clothes I wear." *When the whim comes over me*, she added to herself. And today was one of those times. Why she felt in the mood to wear the cumbersome 1890s dress this morning to drive from Boston to Belford, she had no idea.

"To get attention I suppose," she heard Ada say.

Looking up, Gustavia noted the frown on her cousin's face.

"You don't seem to be listening, Gustavia. Answer my question. Did people stare at you?"

"I wasn't aware you asked a question. I don't really know if people stared at me." She paused as though considering the possibility. "I didn't notice."

Turning to her food, Gustavia allowed her mind to wander. Her study of the history of fashion was a precursor to her profession, costume and clothing design. She had designed and made clothes from several eras—from the 1890s through each significant era to modern-day. She avidly watched the current fashion trends, fascinated at how they had evolved in the fashion designers' minds—recycling from fashions of the distant past, the immediate past—the mid-twenties influencing the fashions of the early sixties, then back to the thirties. She was intrigued that during the seventies Yves Saint Laurent focused on the forties with new respect. The forties themselves were full of Victorian details! Throughout the eighties, designers explored and re-explored the fifties and sixties and ad infinitum.

She often ignored the latest styles and wore whatever fashion year she was in the mood to wear. Of course people stared. That was the downside of her predilection for wearing different and unique clothing.

Realizing that Ada had been talking to her, she directed her attention to what she was saying.

"Edgar warned me that you had turned into an eccentric—which is very odd for one so young."

"I'm not so young. I'm thirty."

"Hmph, as you might suppose, that's young to me, Gustavia."

"How old is your brother?"

"Edgar is seventy-two. Now, I suppose you want to know how old I am." At Gustavia's nod, she said, "I'm seventy-four and going strong."

Gustavia smiled. "That's one of the first things I noticed about you today—your strength and determination. I thought you must be in your sixties."

Pleased, though not disposed to show it, Ada lifted the cup to her lips and sipped the tea carefully.

The cook removed their empty bowls and returned with a cart. She placed on the table between them a bowl of seasoned rice and chicken, lemon buttered broccoli and a plate of fresh fruit.

Gustavia watched Ada's long bony hand reach out and take servings of each, then she helped herself. She was starving after her walk. If lunch was any indication, Ada had a good cook. Everything was as she expected—delicious.

She looked around the large, extravagant dining room. Its opulent crystal chandelier and brocade drapes were as overdone and oppressive as the large floral paintings hanging on two of the pale blue walls.

She wished she were back in Boston in her own apartment. Instead, she was in this stiff and formal atmosphere, sitting across from her unapproachable cousin! Gustavia's shoulders tensed as she thought of the events that motivated her to make the life-changing move from her homeland to the United States, then unexpectedly to Belford and to Ada's home.

Six years ago in Cornwall, England while standing at her mother's graveside, numbly accepting condolences from the line of friends and neighbors, she suddenly became aware of two strangers scrutinizing her. Introducing themselves as Ada and Edgar Redmore, the man announced that they were her father's first cousins, that her grandmother, Fanny Sullivan Browne, was their mother's sister. In her grief and desperate long illness, she could only gaze at them in confusion. Why hadn't she known of them before? Why hadn't they made themselves known? As far as she could remember there was only her and Mum. They hadn't been aware of any existing relatives—so how did Ada and Edgar learn of her mother's death?

Gathering what presence of mind she could, she had managed to blurt out the most pressing question. "Did my father know that he had an aunt and uncle and cousins?" Ada's answers had been vague and confusing. Nevertheless, feeling completely alone in the world, Gustavia was thrilled to find out that she actually had relatives, and close relatives at that! She eagerly reached out to them, but was rebuffed by aloof condolences, leaving her deeply disappointed and more confused than ever.

Because of their distant attitude, Gustavia found it strange that Edgar had requested she keep them informed of her whereabouts and activities at all times. She had shoved their address into a pocket of her dress, fully intending to ignore his request and dispose of it once she arrived home. Instead, she tossed it into the back of a drawer and promptly put it out of her mind.

Periodically, she found herself reflecting upon the strange circumstances of two unknown cousins coming into her life, but only after her mother's death. Why then? Why not before? *Are they really who they say they are?* she had once asked herself, then promptly forgot her doubts.

Then a year ago, her desire to find out what the Redmores knew about her father's parents began to occupy her mind to such an extent, she gave in and went searching for their address. When she found it, she composed a letter to them, purposely leaving out questions about her family and making it as interesting as she could.

After some time, she was surprised to receive a letter from the Redmores with a return address of Belford, Maine! It was from Ada. She explained that three months after they attended her mother's funeral, she and Edgar moved to the United States, but retained their home in the fishing port of Grimsby, Lincolnshire, hence her letter had to be forwarded by an employee. Eagerly, she read on, her hopes rising, only to be dashed. Its contents were brief and lacked the warmth of sincere interest in her or her activities. However, she blamed herself. After all, she hadn't kept them informed as Edgar had requested five years before. Even so, because of their remoteness in person and by mail, she was concerned whether they would be willing to answer questions in a letter. It was then she decided that she would have to live closer to them in order to ferret out the information she needed to know. Hence her decision to move to America—closer to the Redmores.

She applied for a professorship in costume history and design at Boston University. They offered her a position as an assistant professor with the possibility of a full professorship in the future. She gratefully accepted.

The first thing she did when she arrived in Boston was rent a mini storage unit to house all her design paraphernalia, and her sewing machines. Since she didn't know the city, she talked a home owner in the Cambridge area into letting her rent a small furnished studio apartment for one month only.

Friendless and lonely in a strange city and new country, she had called Ada sooner than she had intended. She listened for some indication that her cousin was glad she had moved closer. Instead, Ada sounded shocked, then promptly reproved her for not writing and informing them beforehand that she was moving to the U.S. Before hanging up, she briskly requested Gustavia's phone number and address.

Rebuffed, but still determined, she went ahead with her present plans, which included purchasing a small car and getting acquainted with the city.

On the day she was to finalize the contract with the university, she was startled to hear a loud insistent knock on the door of her apartment. Opening it, she was surprised to see Edgar standing on the doorstep.

He greeted her cordially, as if it had been only a week since he had seen her rather than six years. Appearing much older now, he was a tall, austere-looking man with a small steel-gray mustache above his thin upper lip. His brown eyes were deep-set under hooded gray brows.

It had taken her a moment to summon presence of mind enough to invite him in. He removed his English cap, leaving his full head of gray hair tousled, then stepped in. Looking and acting very uncomfortable, he accepted her offer to be seated while delivering his message.

"Miss Gustavia," he began awkwardly, "Ada has mentioned she would like someone to write her biography. Since you're family, I would like you to do it."

Gustavia blinked in surprise. "I . . . uh, may be family, but we hardly know each other. A stranger could do as well."

"Nevertheless, I would like you to do it."

"Why?"

"Because we are family, we need to become . . . uh, closer."

Since that was what Gustavia also wanted, but had about given up on, she took a few moments to think it over. *Maybe I might come across something in Ada's biography that would answer some questions about my family,* she thought. "All right. If you'll give me the information, I'll work on it as I can."

"Not here. I want you to live in Ada's home while you work on it, and I would like you to start right away."

The message was delivered concisely, dispassionately. Shocked, Gustavia could only stare at him and wonder if a smile had ever relaxed his stoic features. The only emotion he betrayed was manifested by the continuous kneading of his cap.

"But I've just signed a month's lease on this apartment," she had blurted out in frustration, "and I'm committed to sign the university contract today. I'm looking forward to the position they've offered me."

"I will reimburse you for any loss you might incur breaking the lease. And you'll be paid far more than your salary at the university."

Gustavia could scarcely believe Edgar's audacity. How could he expect her to give up her job to do Ada's biography? "If I don't sign the contract today, I'm certain I'll never get another opportunity to work at Boston University," she had stated firmly.

Edgar's demeanor softened. He leaned forward, his eyes beseeching hers. "I want Ada's biography written by *you,* Gustavia—for her sake. It's my hope that she'll open up to you. Before I have to step in," he added quickly.

"What do you mean?"

Edgar stood up as if the matter we re settled. "I can't reveal that just yet."

"Cousin Edgar, the reason I've moved to America and applied at Boston University was so I could be near you and Ada. I need to find some answers about my father's family." She got up and stepped over to him, her voice rising in frustration. "I don't need anymore secrets! I want answers!"

Edgar's right hand stopped kneading his cap and patted her gently on the shoulder, his brown eyes kind. "Be patient, Gustavia. I promise you that if you move into Ada's home and write her biography, much of what you want will be given you."

"Why can't you give it to me now?" she demanded.

He studied her in silence, then in a gentle voice he replied, "I hope to help you understand—later." He paused. "I suppose you have Ada's address. In case you have misplaced it during your move, here it is."

And that was that, and here she was—in Ada's house as Edgar had requested, but only after some grueling self examination. She looked over at Ada and was struck, as she had been when she arrived today, by the fact that she had hardly aged. Her pale skin, pulled tightly across high cheek bones, prominent nose and chin, was amazingly free of wrinkles. And her light brown hair, cut short and slightly turned under, was devoid of any gray. Ada's eyes reminded her of brownish-gray dishwater, her high eyebrows the same. She was altogether a colorless woman, especially when one considered her clothing—drab shades of brown and gray.

Gustavia finished her dessert of vanilla custard. "Please excuse me, Cousin Ada, I need to unpack," she said, anxious to escape to her room.

"You're excused, Gustavia, but be ready to work in the library tomorrow morning after breakfast promptly at 8:00." She stressed the word "promptly."

As Gustavia slowly climbed the stairs, she remembered how intrigued she had been by the turret tower on the right when she first saw this big old clap-board Victorian house. After lunch, when Ada had led her upstairs to the small dark room where she was supposed to stay, she had asked about the turret room. Ada had informed her that she saved that for special guests only. At Gustavia's insistence, Ada had reluctantly showed it to her.

"This is the room I want to stay in, Cousin Ada," she had stated firmly.

"As I said, I save this only for . . ."

"I'm one of those special guests wouldn't you say, Cousin Ada?" she asked in a tone that dared her to disagree. "It will cheer me up and help me accomplish what Edgar has asked me to do."

"It wasn't my idea to have you come and do my biography, Gustavia. In fact, I was totally against it, but Edgar . . . " She stopped herself, glaring at her cousin.

"I didn't want to come either, Ada, but I still want the turret room."

Ada let out an impatient breath. "All right, have it your own way. I see you have some of the willful qualities that your grandmother Fanny Sullivan displayed so scandalously."

Shocked at this information, Gustavia asked, "What do you mean?"

"Fanny's behavior is something my mother refused to discuss, and I'm certainly not going to discuss it with you."

"Why?" Gustavia challenged.

Ada's silence answered her.

Infuriated, Gustavia's voice had risen several decibels. "Mum never knew anything scandalous about grandmother!"

"Of course not. Your father knew nothing of it," Ada answered smugly. Turning her back on Gustavia, she exited the room.

Gustavia, shocked and angry, had run out of the house into the rain.

Bringing her thoughts back to the present, Gustavia found herself breathing faster. She moved from the hallway into the turret room and found the bags where she had left them earlier.

Locking the door, she immediately stepped over to the delightful round alcove of the turret. A blue padded window seat encircled it. Pillows of blue, lavender, and pink were propped under the four elongated rectangular windows. Seating herself, she leaned back in comfort.

Weighed down by troubling thoughts, she asked aloud, "Why was my father raised by strangers? Why didn't Ada's parents take him in?" Unless they had a terribly good excuse, Gustavia felt that this was far more scandalous than anything her grandmother could have done! She shook her head, knowing it was useless to dwell on it any longer. It was Ada and Edgar who held the answers to questions that surely must have haunted her father and which now bedeviled her.

Edgar had asked her to be patient, but she hoped that as she compiled the information about Ada's life for her biography, she might find out something—clues which might help her unravel the mystery surrounding Josiah and Fanny Sullivan Browne.

This thought lifted her spirits. She turned and looked out at the front garden and the tree-lined street. The rain had melted the few patches of snow that had stubbornly remained in the garden, resisting the coming of spring. Suddenly, an enveloping cloak of excitement hugged her heart. She could almost hear the words her mother had spoken to her often: *Gusty dear, your ability to find enjoyment in any situation you're in will be your saving grace.* Gustavia was certain that this was because her mother had read to her out of the Bible almost every day of her life, and from this she learned how God loved His children. She felt particularly loved by Him. Why, she didn't know, but she did know that the security this gave her made it possible to look outside herself and enjoy this wonderful world and everything in it.

Gazing at her new surroundings, her eyes were first drawn to the blue oval rug which covered most of the dark-stained oak floor. Then she noticed the bed. Spooled rungs of dark oak made up the headboard. The bedspread was white with a two inch border of lavender and blue flowers. The white pillow shams were edged with the same border as well as the curtains at the window on the other side of the bed near the dresser. A small oak table by the bed held an old wind-up clock and a blue and white vase filled with delicate, pink silk flowers. The large old walnut dresser with a wide beveled mirror and abundance of drawers gave the room a finished, homey feel. *Ada must have had some help decorating this room,* she thought. *It's the most pleasant room in the house.*

The comforting clank of the radiators meant they were warming up, reminding Gustavia that she was still slightly chilled by the damp dress. Quickly changing to her flannel nightgown, she slipped on warm house slippers and began to unpack.

Later, as she lay in bed watching the clouds disappear and the moon-light flood the room through the turret windows, she wondered what tomorrow held for her, tomorrow and the days after that.

❧CHAPTER 2❧

While Ada retrieved records and piles of papers from a cupboard under one of the book shelves, Gustavia gazed around the large room which Ada called the library, noting that it was quite utilitarian. Across from the double door entrance was a single large window. Maple book-shelves and cupboards flanked each side of it. The two adjacent walls were paneled in the same warm maple. Against these two walls, closer to the entrance, stood two large L-shaped computer desks upon which were up-to-date computers and printers. Closed cupboards covered the wall on each side of the doorway. Wall-to-wall light green, low-pile carpet covered the floor.

Presently, Ada, carrying the material across the room, opened a cupboard which housed filing cabinets and pulled out several large folders, adding these to the rest.

"Gustavia, this is your desk," she informed her, walking over to the one on the right of the entrance and placing the formidable pile of material on it. "It's Edgar's old computer. Now—come and sit down while I explain in more detail what I want you to do."

Ada moved over to a conversational grouping of furniture in the center of the room, which consisted of a small brown leather couch and two chairs. She seated herself in one of the chairs and directed Gustavia to take the other one.

Gustavia, her eyes stilled glued to the pile of material, edged herself over and sat down. The chair was surprisingly comfortable.

"First of all, as Edgar told you, your salary will be generous. Much more, I'm certain, than for the job you gave up. Much of my biography will include detailed accounts of my successful business career, which of course will include Edgar. I've placed on your desk all the records you need at the moment. I want you to organize them and begin."

Gustavia couldn't help but compare this arduous task to the interesting job she had given up at the university. *Besides*, she wondered, *who will read the biography?* Ada had never married, and neither had Edgar.

"Why are you looking at me like that, Gustavia?"

"Well, since you have no descendants, I was wondering who will read your biography."

Ada bristled. "You wouldn't know of course, but the city of Grimsby where we lived for years has requested this. I've done a great deal for that community, and they want it in the archives as part of the history of Grimsby. And . . . it's possible you'll marry, Gustavia, that is, if you'll stop being so odd and dress normally—in which case your children should be interested."

Still smarting over Ada's refusal to explain what she meant by her scathing remark about her grandmother, Gustavia blurted out, "How long have you known about my father?"

Ada refused to respond.

"Somehow," Gustavia continued, "I think you've known for some time! And if so, why didn't you try to get to know him, my mum or me?"

"I'll ignore your raised voice, Gustavia. You may begin to organize the material now. If you'd like, you may join me for mid-morning tea. Lunch will be served at 12:30 . . . not a minute later."

Tears of helplessness trickled down Gustavia's cheeks as she watched Ada leave the room. She wiped her cheeks impatiently. "Neither Edgar nor Ada know how I ache for family. Nor how great my need to feel connected to grandparents, and great-grandparents. I never would've come otherwise!" Information about her father's side of the family was nonexistent as far as she knew. She was hanging on to Edgar's nebulous promise. On her mother's side, all she had were stories she had written down when her mum had told her about her life as a child, and the names of her mother's parents and grandparents. Beyond that—nothing—the flu epidemic took her mother's parents and siblings when she was only twelve. A kind, distant cousin had taken her mother in and raised her, but the cousin was no longer living.

She got up and went over to her desk and sat down. Distractedly, she picked up a pencil and paper and sketched out a small pedigree chart of her father's side.

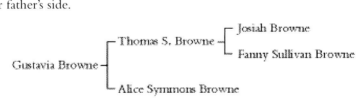

"Pathetically small," Gustavia muttered. Restlessly, she got up, went to the window and looked out. The bushes and the two chestnut trees were still bare-limbed. *Soon,* she thought, *little buds will be poking their heads out*

with new life. Recalling the moment of excitement she felt the evening before, her hope returned—hope that being here working for Ada would, in the end, provide the answers she was seeking and maybe also turn out to be an interesting adventure. Cultivating this kind of optimism was the only way she had managed to get through life and be happy.

Ada walked in. Seeing Gustatvia staring out the window, she cleared her throat.

Straightening her shoulders, Gustavia turned and moved quickly to the desk to begin the daunting task Ada had thrust upon her.

The next two hours were spent just glancing through each page, trying to find a place to start, but she had barely made a dent in the stack of material.

When Ada stood up to go to tea, Gustavia remained. Her mind reeling over how complicated the project was going to be, she placed her elbows on the desk, her hands covering her face.

"Good morning, Gustavia."

Gustavia's head swiveled toward the voice—the man who was responsible for her present predicament. "I wouldn't say it was a good morning."

"I didn't say it would be easy, Gustavia. Come and sit down. I would like to ask you some questions."

"And I would like to ask you some," she retorted, getting up and plopping herself down in one of the leather chairs.

Edgar seated himself across from her. "I hope you find your accommodations to your liking."

"So far that's all I find to my liking."

Edgar cleared his throat. "I would like to know more about your immediate family, Gustavia. Tell me about your father."

"Why? Why don't *you* tell *me*?"

"Miss Gustavia, there's no need to be testy. I told you to be patient and much of what you want will be given you. But I know very little about your mother and father."

Gustavia gripped her hands tightly, her eyes gazing intently into his. "You may know that my father's parents, Josiah and Fanny Sullivan Browne were mysteriously killed. Surely, you must also know why my father was raised by strangers rather than his aunt and uncle—your parents."

Edgar returned her gaze unflinchingly. "No, I don't. But it's a damnable shame, it is."

Her indignation deflated, she let out a heavy sigh. "Oh. Well, he was raised by an older, childless couple by the name of Beddows. Fanny and Josiah moved into a small flat next to them in London when he was two-and-a-half-years old. The Beddows told my father how much they liked his young parents and that immediately, they had fallen in love with their little Thomas.

"Unfortunately, all my father learned about his parents' deaths from the Beddows was that a week before, his parents had seemed worried about something and had asked them if they would consider being guardians to their little Thomas if anything should happen to them. The Beddows readily agreed."

Gustavia watched Edgar closely. "You know nothing about this?"

"No. What happened next?"

"The Beddows told my father that his parents always took him everywhere with them, but that one morning they seemed a little uneasy and they asked if they could leave the baby with them for a couple of hours. Fanny and Josiah never returned."

"Terrible!" Edgar said, shaking his head "Terrible. Did they find out what happened?"

"From what the Beddows could find out from the law, some men had killed them. The chief inspector could find no clue as to who they were."

"Tell me more about your father."

"I barely remember him. He died when I was only two. But Mum told me many wonderful things about him. He was going to the university where he met Mum. When they married, he had to quit until he had enough money to support themselves and save for his education. Mum interrupted her own education to work. When she became pregnant with me, Dad had to find a job that paid higher wages. Because of his previous experience, he got a job as a North Sea pilot on a large fishing trawler. He had just about saved enough to start back to school when he was drowned off the coast of Norfolk."

"I'm sorry, Gustavia." He paused, his face grave. "What did your mother do then?"

"She stayed home to care for me for a while, until the money started to run out, then went to work as a seamstress in a clothing factory. She took me with her and hid me under the sewing machine. This went on until the foreman discovered it and fired her. For two years she eked out a living here and there in several different cities until in Hull she was hired to be a live-in cook and housekeeper for a Mr. Charles Fretwell."

Edgar looked down, his face troubled, his hands wringing his cap. "I . . . I'm sorry," he muttered, his eyes on the floor, "that your young mother had to work like that."

Curious, Gustavia studied him. "Thank you, Edgar."

He looked up. "How did you manage, Gustavia?"

"Even though it was just Mum and me, I've had a wonderful life. We were very close. It was difficult to leave her to attend Cambridge University, but she insisted."

"How did your mother pay for your education?"

"Mr. Fretwell helped out."

"I'm glad to hear that . . . glad to hear it."

Edgar's last remark came with a breath of relief. More so than Gustavia would have expected, though she barely heard him. Her mind was far away. "One weekend in my fourth year at the university, I left to visit my mother and found her very ill with viral pneumonia. It had come on quickly, and in just three days, she was gone." She blinked back tears that always came when she remembered the shock of losing her mother so abruptly.

"I'm sorry, Gustavia."

"The next thing I knew, you and Ada were at her graveside announcing that you were my father's first cousins."

"I know."

"How did you find out about my mother's death?"

"I asked you to be patient, Gustavia. In time you'll know."

"Then what do you know about Fanny's scandalous behavior?"

"What?" he asked surprised.

"Ada said I had the 'same willful qualities that Fanny Sullivan displayed so scandalously.' What was she talking about?"

Edgar's jaw tightened. "I don't know."

"Why are you here, Edgar?" Ada demanded as she entered.

"I came over to say hello to Gustavia and ask if you could come over to my office. We have some business to discuss."

⚮CHAPTER 3⚭

Ada and Edgar Redmore had spent their growing up years working in the family fish merchant firm in Grimsby, Lincolnshire at the mouth of the Humber on the North Sea. Also, they were often taken to Ludlow, Shropshire to learn the workings of their parents' stone quarry. Their mother had insisted they learn the businesses, leaving them little time for social life, thus neither had married.

Ada, the business mind of the two, was always looking for places to invest their wealth. She had learned about a large lumber mill for sale in a small town in Maine. After much investigation, they visited the States and purchased the mill, which was on the outskirts of Belford, as well as a paper mill. The Redmores also purchased the only gourmet grocery store in Belford which had a connecting drugstore/pharmacy, both of which catered to the wealthy summer residents. Their businesses provided jobs for the small community and for many who commuted from Augusta.

Edgar was good at managing and organizing. He had an office near the lumber mill where a number of employees worked for him, helping him manage the myriad and complicated details their businesses engendered. Edgar also had a way with personnel and, unlike Ada, managed to get the best from them at all times.

Edgar hadn't wanted to expand, reminding Ada that they were both advancing in years, but she was in denial. Ada was restless and needed to be kept busy, so to keep her happy, they took on the responsibility and pressure of trying to manage businesses in two different countries.

On the way to the office Edgar's brows hovered over his eyes in concern. He wasn't quite sure of the exact date Ada had begun to change for the worse, but it was near the time they had attended Alice Browne's funeral and met Gustavia. He had asked her why angry moods would come upon her at unexpected times. Her only reply was that he was imagining things. Then he began to notice a pattern. His suspicion that Ada was hiding something from him increased after talking with Gustavia this morning.

Parking, he entered his office on the side entrance of the building. He hung his cap on a hook, went over to his desk and sat down. He could hear the busy activity on the other side of the inner door where his employees worked in a bank of three offices on each side of the building. He rubbed his tired eyes and waited for his sister.

Fifteen minutes later, Ada bustled in and sat down across from him. "All right, Edgar, what is it you want to discuss with me?"

"Ada, why did you tell Gustavia that her grandmother, Fanny, had behaved scandalously?"

"Because she did."

"How did you find that out?"

Ada paused, weighing the question. Her upper lids lowered slightly over her eyes. "Mother mentioned it once."

"I never heard her."

"Well, I did," she replied quickly. "And apparently, Gustavia has some of her willful qualities."

"What are you hiding from me, Ada?" he asked carefully.

Ada flushed. "Hiding? Why would you think I would hide anything from you, Edgar?"

"It's obvious you're carrying around a lot of anger, but I realize now that whenever the subject of Gustavia comes up you get angrier. Why?"

"You should know why, Edgar!" she stated emphatically. "I didn't want to attend Alice's funeral, I didn't want to keep track of her daughter, Gustavia, and least of all you know I didn't want her in my home. You know it's dangerous."

"Ada, because of the circumstances, you agreed that we should help her in any way we can, and how can we help her unless we know what she needs?"

"We can find out without her living with me."

"We've already settled this, Ada, remember?" he reminded her.

"I don't want her here!" Ada exclaimed, standing up.

Edgar stood and faced up to her. "She's staying, Ada. Don't say another word about it. If you don't abide by this, I'll have to take action."

Ada's lips trembled. Her brother had never stood up to her like this until Gustavia Browne came into the picture! She turned and headed for the door, speaking as she went out. "It will be your fault, Edgar, if she finds out what we . . ."

Edgar didn't hear the rest, but he knew what she said. The sense that she was hiding something from him was even stronger. "But what?" he asked himself, feeling bone tired, as he often did when dealing with his difficult sister, the sister he loved nevertheless.

∾

He found her cross-legged on the floor facing the large window. Papers were strewn around her in piles. Still an illusion from the past, she was dressed in old fashioned clothing: a white puff-sleeved blouse and long black skirt. Her thick shiny black hair was piled up off her neck, allowing slightly curly tendrils to escape along her neckline. He almost questioned if she were real—as he did when he followed her yesterday.

He took in a slow breath and let it out. "Hello," he said.

Startled, she turned her head, then sprang to her feet. She looked up at him with wide eyes, the color of bitter chocolate. Her face looked small and a little on the narrow side framed by all that black hair. Every feature was exquisite, from her large pixie-shaped eyes to her full, up-turned lips and cameo complexion.

"Who are you?" she asked.

"I'm Paul Camden, Ada's attorney. And from the small photo Ada showed me, you must be Gustavia."

She held out her hand, smiling. "Pleased to meet you, Mr. Camden."

Her smile, so child-like and joyous, took his breath away. He took her proffered hand, swallowing it in his. "Pleased to meet you. It's good to have some fresh air in this stale old house. I must say you do light up the place."

"Thank you. I was about to stop for tea. Would you like to join us? "

"Yes, thank you. I have some business to transact with Ada."

Ada looked up as they entered the dining room. "You two have met, I see."

"We have," Paul replied. "I brought over the papers for you to sign."

"Sit down, Paul. I'll sign when I'm through with tea. Would you join us?"

"Yes, thank you and I'll have one of those oatmeal biscuits," he said as he seated himself next to Ada and reached for one.

Gustavia exclaimed with delight. "Oh! Real English oat biscuits. Where did you find them here in the States?"

"I order them directly from England, from a shop in Ludlow." She turned to Paul. "What do you think of my young cousin here?"

"You didn't warn me that she slipped in from the past."

"Humph!"

Paul smiled. "Do you have a reason for dressing like you do, Miss Gustavia Browne?"

Gustavia only smiled and sipped her tea.

"To get attention, that's what," Ada retorted.

Paul Camden watched Gustavia's reaction to Ada's scathing remark.

She seemed remarkably unperturbed by it. "I see you don't want to answer that question, but my curiosity is getting the better of me."

"You wouldn't understand if I told you," she stated flatly. "No one does."

"Try me. I might."

"All right. I was born in the wrong century," she answered flippantly, flashing a challenging glance at each of them.

"What?" Ada exclaimed.

Paul Camden studied her quizzically, then laughed.

Irritated, Ada shot him a glance. "Don't encourage her, Paul."

"I'm sure nothing I do or say will encourage or discourage her, Ada." He smiled at Gustavia. "I'd like to hear more about that sometime."

"Show me the papers you want me to sign, Paul," Ada said, trying to change the direction of the conversation.

Gustavia grabbed a couple of biscuits. "Excuse me, but I need to get back to work."

Paul watched her leave.

"Don't gape, Paul," Ada stated irritably.

Paul's head swivelled back to Ada. One eyebrow rose. A smile twitched at his lips. "I'm sure you've caused a few gapes in your lifetime, Ada."

Not allowing Paul to see how his remark had salved her lonely heart, she replied, "I'm not paying you a cent more for that flattery. Now, open that briefcase of yours and let me sign the papers."

Paul walked out of the dining room, but before leaving for his office, he backtracked to the library for one more look at Gustavia. He caught her sitting on the floor with her face in her hands, rocking back and forth. She groaned.

"That was a large groan from one so petite."

She visibly jumped. "Mr. Camden! That's the second time you've startled me. Can't you warn a person?"

He grinned. "Sorry, but how can I warn you without speaking?"

"I don't know. Maybe it's your deep voice I'm not expecting."

"Why the groan, Miss Browne?"

She shook her head and spread her hands out indicating the papers on the floor. "I don't know how I'll ever get this all organized. I don't know why Edgar thought I could write her history in the first place."

"I understand that you're well educated. Why couldn't you write her biography?"

Gustavia considered his remarks a moment. "I guess education helps, but it certainly doesn't help me organize all this information. It looks rather daunting to say the least." She paused. "However, if and when I do, I suppose it will be more interesting to write since she's a cousin. Do you have relatives, Mr. Camden?"

Sitting down on the floor in front of her, his arms on his knees, he replied, "Lots."

Wistfully, she asked, "What includes 'lots?'"

"A mother and father, one younger brother, two older sisters, aunts and uncles and grandparents on both sides."

Gustavia sighed, her dark eyes soft, she murmured. "How nice for you. I only had a mother growing up. No grandparents on either side, no aunts or uncles and the only cousins I have are Ada and Edgar." Paul Camden's smoky blue eyes seemed to gaze at her with an unusual amount of sympathy. Not wanting his sympathy she hurried on. "At least," she smiled, "I had my best friend. But he was worse off than I. He lost both his parents. My Mum and I lived next to the orphanage where he lived."

"Oh? What was his name?"

"Freddie Finch. I believe his name was Frederick. Frederick Finch." She always added this hoping someone might know him or perhaps have heard of him.

"Do you keep in touch?"

"No. I've lost track of him."

"Well!" came Ada's sharp voice from the doorway. "I'm paying you both to work, not to loll around on the floor and visit."

Unaffected by her tone, Paul replied, "Don't fret, Ada, I was just trying to mollify your young cousin here. I'm afraid the many things you've accomplished in your life have made the organization of all this material difficult."

Ada remained unmoved. "That isn't what I'm paying you to do."

"All right, Ada, I'll get back down to the office. Maybe you can give her some encouragement." Leisurely he stood and picked up his briefcase. "Good luck, Miss Browne, and goodbye to both of you." He strode out.

The displeasure on Ada's face remained. "I hope you don't require hand holding, Gustavia."

"Don't worry, Ada . . ."

"I've asked you to call me *Cousin* Ada, Gustavia. I demand respect from you at all times." She turned and left the room.

Gustavia released a heavy sigh and began to sink into one of her blue funks, as her mother always called it. She hadn't thought of Freddie for a while and when she did, it always disheartened her. *Where is he? What's happened to him?* she asked herself for the millionth time. She was only two-and-a-half months shy of turning five when she first met Freddie, but it was as clear as if it were yesterday.

When they first arrived at their new home where her mum was going to work as a cook and housekeeper for Mr. Fretwell, she vividly remembered how excited she had been over the "castle" close to Mr. Fretwell's house. She knew all about castles and the kings, princes and princesses who lived in them. She was just about to ask if she could go see the princess when they heard the pandemonium.

Gustavia smiled as she recalled her first encounter with the incomparable Freddie Finch.

❧CHAPTER 4❧

HESSLE, ENGLAND, MAY 1975:

Riding in the back seat of Mr. Snelby's motorcar with her mother, four-year-old Gustavia gazed out the window, her eyes wide with excitement. They were going to live in Mr. Fretwell's house which had a real backyard!

Mr. Fretwell, being unusually busy that day, had requested that Mr. Snelby, his assistant watch repairman, drive his new employee and her daughter to his home. Alice Browne was grateful that she didn't have to find her way to his house on the bus.

Though thrilled that her daughter would, at last, have a yard to play in, Alice was also feeling a bit apprehensive. She had accepted employment as a cook and housekeeper with a widower, Mr. Charles Fretwell, owner of a watch and jewelry shop on Queens Street in Hull. He was a humorless man in his late fifties with thick brown brows fanning across his wide forehead. Underneath, thick wire-rimmed glasses hung on the bridge of his nose, and he spoke with thin-lipped abruptness. She was concerned how secure the job would be since he had never had children and wasn't used to being around them.

They entered Hessle from Motorway 62, then turned onto Ferriby Road. Gustavia let out a squeal of delight. "Look, Mum, there's a castle!"

Alice gazed at the magnificent structure they were approaching.

Mr. Snelby smiled at the child's remark and explained. "That mansion was called Hesslewood House, Mrs. Browne. As you can see, built in the true Georgian style of architecture, it has a number of dormer windows whose sloping roofs peak into ornamental spires, which a child might construe as a castle."

Alice studied the large white brick structure with stone dressings. It stood in a picturesque park of many acres situated near the Humber River. Facing south, it commanded a splendid view of the river.

Gustavia asked again, "Can I go see the princess who lives there?"

Alice smiled at her precocious four-year-old. "I have a princess sitting right beside me, little love."

"You do? Where?" Gustavia asked, looking on the other side of her mother.

"Right here," Alice replied, leaning down and kissing her on the forehead.

Gustavia giggled. "I don't mean me. I mean the princess in that castle," she said, pointing to the palatial building they were passing.

Before Alice could respond to her little daughter, Mr. Snelby said, "Hessle is a good-sized town with many nice homes and some very handsome residences."

"Hesslewood House is certainly one of them, Mr. Snelby."

"Yes. It has now been turned into an orphanage, Hesslewood Orphanage. It used to be the country manor of Joseph Robinson Pease, Esq., a prominent banker in Hull," he said, turning left into the driveway of a home situated on a small parcel of land that bordered Hesslewood. "Here we are, Mrs. Browne."

Gustavia, wide-eyed and incredulous, whispered, "We get to live next to the castle?"

Unaware of Gustavia's question, Mr. Snelby continued his explanation. "The land around Hesslewood used to be much larger, but the Pease family sold off parcels of land which contained a fine quality of chalk. There used to be steep chalk quarries on two sides of Hesslewood, but these were covered up long ago. One thing you should keep in mind, Mrs. Browne, there's a railway line that travels behind both Hesslewood and Mr. Fretwell's house—so keep the little one inside the yard."

Alice was disappointed to hear this, but nevertheless, she still felt grateful for the opportunity of working and living here.

Mr. Snelby turned off the motor, got out and opened the door for his passengers.

"Thank you, Mr. Snelby.

"This is so pretty, Mum!" exclaimed Gustavia, scrambling out of the car.

"It certainly is, Gusty."

Mr. Snelby had just opened the boot of the motorcar and picked up a box and a satchel when Alice protested. "Please, Mr. Snelby, Gustavia and I can carry in our own things."

He smiled kindly, but refused their help. Alice was concerned about Mr. Snelby carrying her belongings. He was round-shouldered, pale and a little weak-looking, probably from years of leaning over performing the meticulous task of repairing watches.

She and Gustavia followed him as he came and went until he had deposited everything inside. They thanked him and waved goodbye as he backed out and drove off. They turned and gazed in awe at the house that was now their home. Alice could hardly believe their good fortune. It was a nice looking one-story red brick with a rounded bay window in the front.

Alice took Gustavia's hand and led her around the side of the house toward the entrance of their quarters, but before entering, they eagerly examined the yard. A neatly trimmed privet hedge enclosed the yard on one side and all across the back. The other side of the yard was bordered by a rock wall, behind which Hesslewood Orphanage rose majestically. One tall old horse chestnut tree towered over Mr. Fretwell's yard of sparse green grass.

Gustavia clapped her hands in glee. "Look Mum! We have some pretty yellow flowers in our yard."

Alice studied the few hardy blooms springing up along the wall. "Why I believe we have daffodils, Gusty. And look, there in the corner are some white flowers called snow drops."

Gusty ran over to the snow drops. "Can I pick one, Mum?"

"Why don't we leave the flowers in the yard. They brighten it up, don't you think?"

"They do, Mum. Now can we go see the princess in that castle?" she asked, pointing.

Alice opened her mouth to explain what the building was when a cacophony of noise emanated from behind the wall—created by a group of children, all talking, laughing and yelling at once.

Gustavia's eyes were wide with surprise. "What's that, Mum?"

"Those are children, Gusty. They live there."

"They do? They live in that castle?" Her eyes were wide as pence bits. "Can I see them?" she asked eagerly.

Alice's first impulse, to rush Gustavia into the house, was quickly replaced by understanding. Gustavia yearned for friends, never having had any to play with because of their circumstances and where they'd had to live. She softened. "Come and I'll lift you up to look over the wall for just a second, Gusty."

Alice lifted her up and Gustavia gasped at the spectacle of so many children together all at once.

"Who are you?" a surprised boy on the other side of the wall blurted out.

Alice immediately set Gustavia back down. "You mustn't talk with the . . ." Before she could finish the sentence, the young boy was on top of the wall looking down at them, openmouthed.

"Hi," he said finally, grinning at the strange little girl. "Who are you?" he asked again.

"My name's Gustavia."

"Gus who?"

"Me mum calls me Gusty most of the time."

"Oh. Hi, Gusty. My name's Freddie Finch. Are you going to live here?" he asked, his blue eyes incredulous.

"Yes. We're moving into Mr. Fretwell's house and Mum is going to cook and keep house for him."

"Wow! Well, look out. He's mean. He doesn't like children. He always says we're too noisy, so we call him Mr. 'Fret-a-lot.'"

Alice laughed. She was taken with the charming little sandy-haired, freckled-faced boy. She and Thomas had always wanted a boy. "I'm Mrs. Browne, Freddie. We're glad to meet you, but won't you get into trouble sitting on the wall?"

"Naw, just as long as I don't go over it. Some older boys have climbed over it to run away. Some have gone over it to see friends, and some have gone over it to see their mother, but I don't have friends or a mother or any family, so I just sit on the wall."

Gustavia gasped in disbelief, "You don't have a mother?"

"Gusty," her mother interceded quickly, "we must get unpacked and check out the kitchen so we can prepare dinner for Mr. Fretwell. Maybe we'll see you another time, Freddie."

"Okay."

"Bye, Freddie," Gustavia said, smiling and waving while her mother pulled her toward the house. "See you later!"

"See ya later!" he yelled back, his face reflecting the eagerness in his voice.

Reaching the private entrance of their quarters on the other side of the house, they found that Mr. Snelby had put their belongings just inside. Mr. Fretwell had informed her that these two rooms had been added on for the late Mrs. Fretwell's two sisters.

The bedroom contained two single beds covered with floral bedspreads, lace curtains at the windows and a tall old oak chest of drawers. A tall narrow mirror hung on the wall beside it. One oak rocker and a large mahogany armoire were the only other pieces of furniture in the room. A faded green rug covered an old oak floor. It looked so good to Alice, she almost cried. The flats she and Gustavia had lived in were rat-infested, drafty and ugly, with little or no real furniture.

"This is so pretty, Mum! Which bed do you want?"

"Which one do you want, little love?"

"The one by the window so I can see the stars at night."

"It's yours, Gusty. We haven't seen the other room. Let's go see it now."

The small connecting room was furnished with one deep green, horse-hair couch and chair. An old trunk in front of the couch was covered with a large lace-trimmed doily which held a glass bowl filled with pink plastic flowers with green leaves. The rug was the same as the bedroom, faded green. The doily, the pretty bowl of flowers and the lace curtains, gave the room a soft homey feel.

"Are we rich now, Mum?" Gusty asked in awed tones.

"It feels like it, love, doesn't it?"

Gustavia smiled and nodded, her dark eyes sparkling with happiness. "Let's go put up our things," she said running back into the bedroom.

Delighted to have so much room, Alice savored the unpacking. When she told Gustavia she could have the two lower drawers of the tall chest all by herself, Gustavia could hardly contain her excitement.

When they were through, Alice sat down in the rocker and sighed. Gustavia climbed onto her lap and together they rocked, both feeling a contentment that had long been missing in their lives. Alice silently thanked the good Lord, for she felt with all her heart that He had brought them here.

Wriggling out of her mother's arms, Gustavia announced, "I'm going out to play with Freddie now."

"Gusty, you can't play with Freddie."

Her small face clouded up. "Why?"

"Come, get back on my lap, love, and I'll tell you."

Pouting, she climbed up.

"First of all, Gusty, that building over the wall isn't a castle. It looks a little like a castle, but it's only a magnificent big home that used to be called Hesslewood House. Now, it's called Hesslewood Orphanage."

"What's an orphage?"

Alice repeated the word slowly and had Gustavia repeat it until she could say it right, then explained. "An orphanage is a place where children live when they don't have a mother or a father, or like Freddie, who doesn't have either a mother or a father." Alice had heard that nowadays, orphanages were beginning to house more neglected and abused children than orphans, but it was easier and less painful to explain about orphans.

"Why don't they have mothers and fathers?" Gusty asked, bewildered.

"Some of the children in the orphanage are children without a father. Maybe a few of them drowned at sea and went up to heaven like yours did."

A look of fear crossed her small face. "You won't leave me and go up to heaven, will you, Mummy?"

Alice hugged her tightly. "No, little love, I won't."

Reassured, Gustavia hopped off her mother's lap. "Maybe Freddie's sitting on the wall. Can I go see?"

"Not now, Gusty. Even if he is, the orphanage may not let any of their boys and girls play with neighbor children."

"Why not?"

"I don't know, but maybe it's because they have so many children to keep track of."

Gustavia's chin quivered with disappointment.

"Let's go in Mr. Fretwell's kitchen and see if we can find something good to eat before supper. I'm hungry, aren't you?"

Gusty nodded, her eyes wide and eager. "Yes! Let's go look."

"And you can help me decide what to fix for supper. Maybe we can fix Mr. Fretwell a nice dessert."

Gustavia squealed with delight, took hold of her hand and together they left their bedroom to go find the kitchen.

◈CHAPTER 5◈

AUGUSTA, MAINE, APRIL 2001:

Paul Camden was employed by Pinkham, Myer and Shanks, one of the largest firms in Augusta. Not yet a partner, he was nonetheless considered by the firm to be one of their best and brightest corporate tax attorneys.

A little less than a year-and-a-half ago, Paul had become aware of the Redmores and their considerable holdings. A couple of months later, it came to his attention that they had fired their third attorney. Quickly gathering some references, he made an appointment with them and offered his services, as well as the resources of his firm. After the Redmores checked on his references, they interviewed him; then Ada, the business brains of the two and the more tight-fisted of the siblings, had tried to hire him away from his firm at a much lower figure than Paul had quoted. He politely turned it down. After interviewing several other attorneys, Ada, in desperation, gave in and hired Paul at the firm's fee.

Even though the Redmores had retained an accounting firm to handle their taxes, Ada found Paul's expertise in this area invaluable. Doing business in both the States and in England presented special tax challenges for them.

Paul had been sent to England twice by Ada to check on legal problems that had arisen because of poor business decisions made by the local management. While on his second trip to England he accidently discovered something the Redmores hadn't expected anyone to find out. In checking further, the records revealed something so astonishing he could only stare at it for a moment, unable to believe his own eyes! Then realizing the full impact of this discovery, he smiled. The power and control this gave him was heady.

Since Ada's *modus operandi* seemed to be based on intimidation—she already had twice threatened to fire him—the ball was now in his court! He could tell that Ada perceived a subtle shift in his attitude, and though outwardly nothing had changed, he sensed it had slightly unsettled her.

Even with all this, Paul found working with Ada tedious and difficult, and he dreaded the time he had to spend with her, that is, until Edgar convinced the delightfully unique Miss Gustavia Browne to come and write Ada's history. Now he was trying to find excuses to be at Ada's library office more often.

The Redmores, two of the firm's most wealthy clients, demanded so much of Paul's time, the firm had arranged for him to open a small satellite office in Belford where he could service them easily and also serve clients from the surrounding area. He had to spend a couple of days a week in Belford, usually on Tuesdays and Thursdays.

Today was Wednesday and as usual he was working in Augusta. Realizing he could be through by 4:00, Paul decided to go to Belford, hoping to entice Gustavia into spending some time with him this evening.

Ada frowned in disapproval. "Is it necessary for you to spread out all the papers on the floor, Gustavia?"

"It isn't if you'll let me spread them out on the dining room table."

"I can't have clutter in there."

"It will only be until I can organize everything."

Ada paused, deliberately letting her irritation show. "Oh, all right, go ahead."

After several trips, Gustavia had everything spread out on the lower half of the long table. Standing over it, she organized the material by dates and subject matter.

A deep, resonant voice spoke from the entrance of the dining room, startling her. Looking over her shoulder, she saw Paul Camden. "Don't you ring the doorbell, Mr. Camden? You frightened me once again."

"I'm sorry. Ada and I have an arrangement to have me walk right into her office when I come. I saw you on my way there. I see you've found a more convenient place to organize."

"Yes. Ada wasn't too happy about it, but she gave in."

Paul entered, pulled out a chair and sat down across from her, noticing that today she had on a green striped cotton dress with a fitted waist and full skirt. "I'm curious, Miss Browne," he began, a half-smile on his face, "what era of clothing are you wearing today?"

There was a lilt in her teasing laugh, "This is a lot closer to today's fashion. I've come all the way up to the 1950s."

He chuckled. "Where in the world do you get your clothes? Surely, you can't purchase them."

"I've studied fashion and dress design. I make them myself. Actually, I have purchased several old relics from individuals, but I wear those only rarely because they're delicate." She smiled, sat down and changed the subject. "What kind of an attorney are you, Mr. Camden?"

"A corporate tax attorney."

"Don't clients usually go to the attorney's office?"

"They do." He grinned. "But Ada is willing to pay extra so she doesn't have to gather up her material and drive three blocks. So—like doctors in the past, I make house calls."

Gustavia chuckled. "I'm glad. You relieve the monotony."

"Oh? Well in that case I'm going to get right to the point, Miss Browne. Are you dating anyone?"

Her brows rose in surprise. "That's a little personal, Mr. Camden."

"I meant it to be because I want to take you out."

"No. I'm not dating anyone, but I don't know you."

He gazed at her with amusement. "Isn't that the purpose of dating . . . to get acquainted? You do date don't you?"

"I have in the past, but . . ." She stopped, contemplating how much to tell him.

"But what?"

"But since it can't go past that, I don't think I'd better."

Puzzled, Paul asked tentatively, "Why can't it go past dating?"

"I don't know you well enough to tell you why."

"Oh? Well then Miss Browne, I'll keep hounding you until you give in and tell me, or go out with me. Preferably both."

"I really have to get back to work, Mr. Camden. If Ada catches me, she'll chastise me again."

"All right. May I see you later tonight?"

"No."

"Then you had better tell me now why you don't intend to get married."

"I didn't say that."

"It certainly sounded like it."

Gustavia let out an exasperated breath. "All right, I'll tell you. Actually, I'm betrothed."

Paul squinted, wondering if he had heard correctly. "You mean . . . you're engaged?"

"No. Betrothed."

The word hung in the air between them. "Betrothed? That's an archaic word, Miss Browne. What do you mean by it?"

"That I've accepted a proposal."

Disappointment sliced deep. "Then you *are* engaged?"

"No, I'm not."

Paul stood up and walked away scratching his head. Turning, he asked. "When were you betrothed?"

"When I was nine years old."

Relief washed over him like a breeze of spring air, and he let out the breath he had been holding. "When . . . you were . . . nine years old?"

"That's what I said, Mr. Camden. Now, I really must return to my work."

"A relative arranged it?" he asked carefully.

"No. Please . . . Ada will . . ."

"I'll leave when you tell me who you're betrothed to."

Resigned, her words rushed out clipped. "Freddie Finch. I told you about him. Now may I return to my work?"

There was a short silence; then Paul Camden smiled, the smile erupting into a laugh that resounded from deep inside.

Gustavia gazed at him, her dark eyes snapping with anger. Before she could open her mouth to ask why he found that amusing, he addressed her. "I'm off to see the dragon lady. See you later, Miss Browne."

The cook brought dishes and utensils into the dining room to set the table for the night meal. Surprised to see Gustavia there with papers taking up half the space, she hesitated.

Gustavia smiled at her. "Hello. I'm sorry we haven't been properly introduced. I'm Gustavia Browne, Miss Redmore's cousin. And you are?"

"I expected Ada to introduce us when I first served you. My name is Carol . . . Carol DeWulf."

"I'm glad to meet you, Carol. Your cooking is excellent."

"Thank you."

"Does Edgar eat here with Ada?"

"He does once in awhile, but he has stomach problems so he cooks for himself in his own home most of the time. Well, I guess I'd better finish. Dinner has to be on the table right on the dot of 6:00."

"Yes, so I've been told."

Gustavia glanced up from her work as Carol came and went, preparing the uncluttered end of the table, guessing that she was probably in her late forties. She was a trim, pleasant looking woman with a ready smile. Her reddish hair was cut and trimmed closely around her face.

Ada, with Paul Camden, entered the dining room two minutes early. Gustavia stood up and went to her place at the table and was surprised to see three places set. She hadn't noticed. Ada's place was at the end of the table with Gustavia on her right and Paul on her left. He smiled across at her as he stood behind his chair. Refusing to return his smile, Gustavia's eyes slid away.

Paul waited until Ada seated herself. Only when Gustavia was also seated did he sit down. "Thanks for inviting me to eat dinner, Ada. Carol's cooking is much better than my own."

"Don't expect this to be a regular event."

"I wouldn't dare." The three ate in silence for some time, then Paul looked across the table at Gustavia. "Miss Browne, do you have a middle name?"

"No," she answered not looking at him.

"Since we'll be running into each other often, don't you think it would be easier to be less formal and use first names?"

"Not necessarily."

Ada frowned. "I agree with Gustavia, Paul. It isn't necessary."

"I would find it more comfortable, Ada. Would you mind, Miss Browne?"

"If you're more comfortable with first names, it's really of no conse-quence to me."

He nodded and smiled. "Thank you, Gustavia. But do you have a nickname? Gustavia is quite a mouthful."

Gustavia stopped eating, her dark eyes snapping again. "Then, don't use it."

"Don't get me wrong," Paul said hastily, "I like the name Gustavia. I was asking if you had a nickname more out of curiosity than anything else."

Repenting of her snappish behavior, she relented. "About half the time Mum called me 'Gusty.'"

"Hmph! How ridiculous," Ada remarked.

"How charming," Paul replied, "especially for one so beautiful."

"Paul!" exclaimed Ada. "I don't appreciate you . . . uh, dallying with my cousin."

Carol brought in three small bowls of sugared white grapes, and cleared off the plates.

"Since the dessert is light, may I take you both downtown to The Ice Cream Parlor and buy you a bowl of their famous maple nut ice cream?" Paul asked.

"I hired Gustavia to work, not socialize. I'll thank you to remember that, Paul."

Gustavia bristled. "I thought slave labor was outlawed in the United States, Cousin Ada. I assumed that after work, I could do as I wish."

Paul couldn't have been more pleased.

Ada for once was at a loss for words. Gathering her composure, she only addressed Paul's invitation to her. "Surely, you must know that I don't socialize with my hired help."

Paul grinned. "Well, Gustavia, your cousin has just put us in our place. Maybe the hired help—you and I—can go get an ice cream. How about it?"

Gustavia, feeling a perverse pleasure at annoying Ada, accepted the invitation.

❧

The small ice cream shop held only eight booths. People occupying two of the booths stared at Gustavia, eyeing her unusual attire as she walked in. She wore a soft white shawl over her blouse to protect her from the cold evening.

Paul led her over to a booth and pointed to the short list of ice cream flavors on the wall behind the counter. "They make the ice-cream right here and it's great. When the wealthy summer residents arrive, their kids, together with the local kids, line up out the door to buy cones."

One of the two women working behind the counter came over and took their orders. Soon, they were each enjoying the specialty of the house.

"This is delicious, Mr. Camden, I mean, Paul. Thank you. Actually, it's a treat to get out of Ada's house for a while. I'm used to coming and going as I please, but I've felt a little intimidated by her."

"To the first part, your welcome. As to the second, you certainly weren't intimidated by her tonight. You were very adept at putting her in her place." He chuckled. "She couldn't think of a thing to say to your remark about slave labor."

"At times I can speak my mind, but deep down, because there was just Mum and me, much of the time I feel a little vulnerable when it comes to the only two relatives I have in the world."

"You and your 'mum,' huh? That reminds me, your English accent is beautiful, high class."

"How do you know?"

"Because Ada and Edgar have holdings in England and I've had to go over there twice since I started working for her. By the way, how did you get acquainted with your—uh, friend, Freddie?"

"I told you we lived next to the orphanage," she began, eager to talk about him. "Well, the first day we arrived at Mum's employer's place, she lifted me up to look over the wall so I could see the children who lived there. And there he was right by the wall. Before we knew it, he hopped up on top of the wall and asked my name." She stared past him and smiled. "Mum told me years later how captivated she was by his inquisitive blue eyes, sandy hair and freckles."

Paul turned thoughtful, a faraway expression in his eyes. It was a few moments before he spoke. "How do you know he isn't married by now?"

"I don't. But somehow I have to find that out. He simply seems to have disappeared. I've even had someone try to locate him on the Internet, but with no luck."

Paul noted the sadness in her eyes, and it looked for a moment as though she were going to cry. "I'm sorry. I'm sure you'll find him."

Gustavia blinked in surprise. Studying him, once more she saw empathy in his smoky blue eyes—penetrating eyes that seemed to look deep inside her. They're kind eyes, she thought. "Thank you. For some reason, you've given me hope."

He smiled. "I'm glad. Now, since you've told me you were betrothed, I'm going to ask you if I can take you out—until you find Freddie." Then as Gustavia was about to protest, he added quickly, "I promise you, I won't expect anything more from you than friendship—unless of course you change your mind."

"What do you expect? As a . . . a friend, I mean?"

"I won't expect anything. I would just like us to do things together, maybe go to dinner, a play, or a musical, or maybe just a walk. If you don't want to do anything with me, maybe we can just talk."

"Why do you want to be friends? You don't even know me."

He smiled. "Because I find you intriguing."

Gustavia looked down, contemplating his remarks. She had never thought of herself like that, nor had any other man told her that. Her gaze refocused on him, studying his face. She had begun to think of him as the 'man with the smiling eyes' for they always seemed to be smiling whenever he looked at her, just as he was at this moment. Then she realized part of it was because a half-smile always accompanied the expression.

She remembered how after he had startled her that first day in the library, her spirits lifted when he smiled. His whole face took part, from the crinkles fanning out from the corners of his eyes to the creases spreading out from the fine lines under his eyes, resulting in a wide smile that was joyfully irresistible. His face was open and pleasant. Above brown, straight brows, his expansive forehead was framed by light brown hair, parted on the side. A firm chin balanced his attractive face. Noticing him fidget under her long gaze, she smiled. "Have you ever been married, Paul?"

Surprised at the question, he stumbled." Uh, no. I've come close once, but something was missing, so I couldn't go through with it."

"Maybe you're afraid of commitment."

"I hope that isn't the case. There's nothing I want more than a wife and family."

"All right, Mr. Cam . . . I mean, Paul. It would be nice to have a friend. But since you want a family, hadn't you better be on the lookout for a wife?"

A small smile tipped his lips to one side. "You better believe it. I'm not getting any younger."

Gustavia thought she detected something deeper in his remark than mere agreement.

❧CHAPTER 6❧

Alice stood before the tall mirror brushing her short brown hair, grateful for the little bit of natural curl on the ends. She stared at her image. Sad eyes reflected back, her heart heavy with loneliness for Thomas, a loneliness that never left her. She was too young to be a widow! *So many years ahead of me without him,* she thought with anguish. *I suppose I could marry again.* The thought was repugnant. Nevertheless, she studied her face with that as a future possibility for Gustavia's sake. Thomas had told her many times that she was beautiful. Her eyes were blue, set into an oval face with even features. She sighed. "I guess I'm pretty enough," she murmured aloud. But she looked nothing like her beautiful dark-eyed child. It was her handsome Thomas who had the dark hair and dark eyes. Placing the brush disconsolately on top of the chest of drawers, she went into the kitchen.

Even though it took a while to learn and remember Mr. Fretwell's likes and dislikes, Alice was feeling more and more comfortable in her new position. To Alice's relief, Mr. Fretwell, though not fond of children, did not seem to mind having a child as part of the household as long as she stayed out of his way. He preferred eating alone in the small dining area, which was an extension of the living room. She was grateful that she and her daughter could eat in the kitchen by themselves.

At first, Gustavia would hide behind her mother's skirt when Mr. Fretwell entered the room, afraid of the frown between his dark brows, and the magnified eyes behind the wire-rimmed glasses. Alice had explained that it wasn't really a frown, only deep lines that had become permanent from squinting at the tiny mechanisms of watches.

Having a yard for Gustavia to run and play in soon changed her cheeks from pallid to rosy. And at last, she had a friend—Freddie. Everyday he climbed the wall to visit with her. Since he was not allowed to venture further, he would whistle for her, and she would come running out of the kitchen door.

At first, Alice wondered how these two children could play—one on the ground and one on the wall. But she watched their imaginations soar with the challenge. Almost daily they came up with new ideas and ways to have fun. They would play catch with whatever they could find, laugh and tell stories, riddles, guessing games, pantomimes and many other creative ideas.

Alice often wished Gustavia had the opportunity to also play with a little girl from the orphanage. But since she only knew Freddie, she wished that he would be allowed to come into the yard where they could really play. And she found herself becoming more and more attached to the boy. It amazed her that he was basically a happy child in spite of his circumstances. How she wished she could adopt him.

In between her chores, Alice read to Gustavia, who was already recognizing words. Mr. Fretwell had a wonderful library of books lining one wall of his living room. She was going to use them to help educate her precocious child.

Gustavia was looking through a book when she heard Freddie's whistle. Gleefully, she ran outside and over to the wall. "Hi. What's that in your hand, Freddie?"

"A magic stick."

"Magic? Looks just like a plain ol' stick."

"But, Gusty, it isn't. Honest. See how it has three tiny limbs sticking out at this end. I point them to the sky and make a wish. I've done it twice and both times my wishes came true."

"They did?" Gustavia asked, her eyes wide with wonder. "What did you wish for?"

"The first one was today at dinner. I wished that I could have an extra helping of roast beef and mashed potatoes cuz I'm always hungry. The boy next to me had been working in the kitchen and had sneaked so many mouthfuls while they were fixing dinner that he was too full to eat all of his, so I got what he couldn't eat. The second wish is the best one. The band master said I was too young to play a musical instrument, but I made a wish and kept hangin' around him today, hoping. Then, a little while ago he told me he had an instrument I could practice on by myself until I was old enough to be in the band."

"What is it, Freddie? What is it?" wheedled Gustavia, jumping up and down.

Freddie grinned and pulled it out of his pocket for her to see.

Gustavia wrinkled her nose. "What's that?"

"A harmonica!"

Gustavia was mystified. "What's a . . ."

Before she could say another word, Freddie was blowing on it, in and out while sliding his mouth from side to side. "See? Isn't it great?"

"Oh! It is. Let me go get Mum so she can hear it." Soon, Alice was being tugged outside toward Freddie. "Oh listen, Mum," Gustavia exclaimed with excitement. "Play it, Freddie."

Freddie performed admirably, the notes issuing forth in no particular order, and when he was through, Alice laughed and clapped her hands. "Where did you get that, Freddie?"

"From the band master." His face was all eagerness. "He's going to show me how to make notes on it, so I can play tunes."

"We're happy for you, Freddie." Alice wished she could fetch him down off that wall and hug him. *How mature he is for five*, she thought. Even though Hesslewood Orphanage had a reputation for taking good care of the children, some of them were troubled and difficult. Freddie had to look out for himself and grow up quickly. Even her own Gusty didn't have the childhood she should have and had to grow up too soon.

As the days wore on, and the noise from Freddie's harmonica continued unabated, Alice sometimes wondered how much more she could stand. Then one day, the noise began to assume a more pleasing pattern— Freddie was actually playing tunes.

☙

SEPTEMBER 1975:

Both Gustavia and Freddie had birthdays in August. Freddie turned six and Gustavia five. All the children in Hesslewood and the surrounding community attended the Church of England school which comprised both an Infant and Primary school. Gustavia and Freddie were enrolled in the Infant school, which took students ages four to six years.

Alice walked her child to and from school each day and soon Freddie, much to the delight of Gustavia, joined them rather than walk with the children from Hesselwood.

Amazed at how well her daughter was reading, Alice asked Freddie one day if he could read.

"Yes. I learned how last winter in school. The teachers say I'm a good reader."

"If you have a favorite book, maybe you could bring it to the wall and you and Gusty can read to each other."

Gustavia clapped her hands. "Yes! Yes! Let's do, Freddie." Thus began a daily ritual: first, time for play, then the joy of reading together while Freddie sat on the wall and Gustavia sat on a wooden box on the ground.

When the weather turned cold and rainy, which it often did, their time of play had to be shortened and the reading time eliminated.

One day Gustavia came running inside to her mother. "Mum, Freddie's crying 'cause he lost his magic stick!"

Alice slipped on her coat and went outside to Freddie who was trying his best to be brave. The minute he saw her sympathetic face, he had a renewed attack of grief.

"There, there, Freddie," Alice said, patting his leg. "Tell me why the stick is magic."

Tearfully, Freddie told her the story of his two wishes.

Alice's heart broke. That he had to rely on a stick was more than she could bear. "Freddie, as soon as you quit crying I want to tell you something." Immediately, his tears dried up. "The stick didn't bring you good luck. It was God who was looking after you. Do you say prayers before you go to bed?"

"Some times they tell us about God and prayers, but I forget to pray 'cuz I don't know if God listens to me. I'm just an orphan."

"Oh Freddie, He'll listen to you even more because you are an orphan. He loves all his children, and He particularly listens to children—no matter who they are."

His eyes were wistful. "He does?"

"Yes. I'm sure that He's the one who put it in the heart of your band master to give you that harmonica." Then Alice thought of something. "Stay here Freddie, I'm going into the house and get something for both you and Gusty."

His eyes lit up. "All right."

"What, Mum? What are you going to get?"

"You stay here with Freddie and I'll bring them out."

In the bedroom, Alice pulled out a wooden box from the top drawer. Tenderly she rubbed her hand over it. The few items in it were precious to her, items that belonged to her mother and father. She withdrew two small Bibles. One belonged to her mother and one to her father. She couldn't believe that she had such a strong feeling to give her father's Bible to Freddie. She had treasured it for so long. Her mother's she would give to Gustavia.

Carrying them both in her hands, she went outside to the children. Eagerly, they watched her walk toward them trying to see what she had in her hands. She put them behind her back.

"Little loves, I'm going to give you each something that is very precious to me, something I've been saving for a long time. They've had very good care and when I give them to you, you must promise me that you'll take good care of them for the rest of your lives—and never lose them."

"We promise! We promise!"

"Before I give them to you I have to explain why they're so important." She brought her hands forward. "These are two small Bibles. One belonged to my mother and one belonged to my father. They are very old and you have to turn the pages carefully."

"They are so little and cute!" Gustavia cried.

"Righto!" Freddie agreed enthusiastically.

"Gusty, do you think it's important to read the Bible?" her mother asked.

"Yes, Mum."

"Why?"

"'Cause it tells us all the time how much God loves us."

"It does?" Freddie asked, his eager little face wanting it to be true.

"It does, Freddie, love. And He wants you to read His words from the Bible, and He also wants you to talk to Him everyday. In other words, He wants you to pray often in your heart and at least once or twice on your knees if you can. When you're lonely, afraid or sad, pray to him and He'll comfort you. After a while you won't think twice about that stick you lost."

❧CHAPTER 7❦

The organization of Ada's material was completed and placed in fold-ers in chronological order. Gustavia had cleared the dining room table of everything and had transferred it all into the library where she placed it carefully on a shelf. Though she had only been able to scan the material, she realized that something was missing.

"Cousin Ada? Could I speak with you a moment?"

Her head bent over the desk, Ada replied distractedly. "Can't it wait, I'm in the middle of something very important."

"I can't proceed with my work until you give me more information."

Annoyed, Ada took off her glasses and looked up. "I'm very thorough, Gustavia. I gave you all the information."

"You've given me only sterile facts. I need to know personal stories, information about your parents, grandparents. A biography needs feelings and reflections about things you've experienced."

Her face closed. "That is no one's business but mine."

"But plain, boring facts don't make up your life, Cousin Ada."

"You're not here to tell me what makes up my life. Write from what I've given you."

Gustavia was deeply disappointed. Gleaning anything from Ada's his-tory that might clear up the mystery surrounding Fanny would be diffi-cult if not impossible. "All right, Cousin Ada, but I assure you that your history won't be fit for anything but the dusty old archives of Grimsby."

"How dare you talk to me like that, Gustavia. Leave this room!"

Gustavia shot to her feet and stared at the rigid, angry woman. "All right!" She turned on her heal and walked rapidly out, turning in the direction of the stairs. Reaching them she lifted her skirt and took two at a time. Pacing the floor of her room, growing more and more agitated, she decided she couldn't stay in Ada's house a moment longer. Throwing on her father's old winter coat, she ran back down the stairs and out the front door.

The sharp wind took her breath away. "When is it ever going to feel like spring?" she muttered as she ran down the steps. Ducking her head to avoid the wind, she opened the gate and shut it furiously. Taking a quick step forward, she bumped into Paul Camden.

"Hey, where are you off to with a frown on your face?" His attention was drawn to her dark hair. The wind was whipping it loose from its restraints.

Gustavia blinked in surprise. "What are you doing here on a Monday?"

"I came to see if you'd like to ride to Augusta for dinner tonight."

"Oh yes! Thank you. Anything to get away from Ada."

Paul chuckled. "You mean you'd do anything—even go out with me—to get away?"

A smile erased Gustavia's frown. "I didn't mean it that way at all. Ada and I had words."

Her smile was like a ray of sunshine bursting through a cloudy sky. "Oh? That sounds interesting. Not many people dare have words with her. Shall we go?"

"She'll probably fire me if I go without telling her I won't be home for dinner."

"Do you care?"

"No. Yes."

He laughed. "Okay. Why no and why yes?"

"No, I don't care. I want to leave, but yes for two reasons. One, I've lost my job at the university as well as my apartment. Two, I'm truly interested in Ada's history. Since she's a cousin, it's kind of my history, too." She was careful not to cast any aspersions upon her grandmother Fanny by telling Paul of Ada's unkind insinuations, and her search for the truth.

"I understand."

Gustavia could tell by the expression in his eyes that he did. "Let me go tell Ada where I'm going."

"I'll go with you and protect you from the dragon lady."

Gustavia laughed. "Thanks."

Ada looked up as the two of them breezed in. "Why are you here, Paul? And where do you think you're going, Gustavia?"

"You told me to leave the room. So where I go should not concern you."

"Why you impudent . . ."

"Calm down, Ada," Paul soothed. "I've asked her to drive to Augusta with me for dinner tonight."

Ada's distrustful eyes looked from one to the other. "Are you two con-
niving against me?"

"Why would we want to do that, Ada?"

Uncomfortable under Paul's penetrating gaze, and unable to answer
his question, she spoke sharply. "Never mind. Just leave."

"I'll be back to work in the morning, Cousin Ada. That is, if by then
my banishment is over."

As they walked toward the front door, Gustavia stopped. "May I
change and comb my hair, Paul?"

"Of course, but I like your hair just as it is."

Paul waited at the foot of the stairs. He watched her graceful energy
as she ran up. Transfixed by the sight, he was hardly prepared for her return.
Her beauty took his breath away. Her dark hair and eyes looked even dark-
er in the wine colored old-fashioned dress, the same one she was wearing
when he first saw her. But he hadn't fully realized how attractive her figure was.

She held a coat and scarf in her arms. Paul took the coat and helped
her into it, then studied her quizzically.

"That coat swallows you."

"It was my father's coat."

"Your father's?"

She nodded while putting a protective scarf over her hair and tying it
under her chin. "It's the only coat long enough for this dress."

Amusement in his eyes, he said, "You're what my mother would call a
fashion society dropout."

Gustavia smiled. "That's exactly what I am, but I've never heard it put
quite that way."

He opened the door for her. "Shall we?"

Out on the sidewalk, Paul took hold of Gustavia's hand and together
they ran against the wind for two blocks and on across the street to his
office where his car was parked.

Breathlessly, Gustavia waited for Paul to unlock the car door. When
they were both inside, they grinned at each other.

"That was fun, Paul."

"It was. But isn't it a little cumbersome running in a long dress like
that?"

"Yes it is. It's hardly a practical style for that sort of thing." She
grinned. "I hadn't planned on being banished and going for a run in the
cold wind with you."

"I must say, I like that dress on you. It's hard to believe you made it
yourself. You're good."

"Thank you."

"What else are you good at?" he asked, backing out of the parking lot and onto the street.

Gustavia looked over at him, wondering. These weren't perfunctory questions. She had never experienced this kind of interest from a man. "Why do you want to know?"

He glanced at her, his eyes smiling. "I just do, that's all."

"I have too many interests to be good at anything but sewing, and that was because Mum had a sewing machine and taught me when I was young." Suddenly curious about him, she asked, "Where do your parents live, Paul?"

"In San Diego, California."

"How nice. From the pictures I've seen, California is a lovely place. But why are you way out here? If I had family, I wouldn't move so far away."

"When I graduated from law school, I didn't have many options. Too many lawyers just out of school were looking for jobs, so I accepted the only offer I got. It was with a firm in Washington D.C."

"That sounds exciting."

"I thought so too—for a while. I did 'grunt' work for a pittance, but I learned a lot. I saved a little here and there and took advantage of some of the investments that came to the firm's attention. After three years, I realized I wasn't going to be made a partner. After interviewing with several firms, I was most impressed with the one I'm with now."

"How did Ada and Edgar become clients of yours?"

The Redmores came to my attention when they fired their third attorney. I made an appointment with them and gave them my credentials. Luck was with me. I was able to acquire their account."

"I doubt that luck had anything to do with it. You wooed Ada into retaining your services I'm certain. I've noticed how smooth you are at handling her."

He raised an eyebrow and glanced at her. "You have?"

"I have. But she may still fire you. She's a little unpredictable."

"She won't fire me." he replied with a confident smile.

"You seem rather sure."

"I am." He changed the subject. "From what Ada told me, you recently moved to Boston and had just acquired a job with the costume department at Boston University."

"Yes. I was going to sign the university contract the day Edgar appeared at my door and requested I give up my job and move to Belford to write Ada's biography."

Paul chuckled. "What kind of a trade-off did he think that was?"

"Apparently, he has some information that's important to me."

Paul's face turned grave. "Did he tell you what it is?"

"No. He told me to be patient. And, for some reason, he also thinks I can help Ada in some way. I'm rather puzzled how I can do that. But I'm hardly 'patient' as Edgar wants me to be. I can't get the history done fast enough."

While Paul weighed this latest information, Gustavia's attention was drawn to the scenery. She had noticed that there were forests everywhere—between the communities, alongside the highways and in many backyards.

"There are so many trees," she murmured.

"Yes," Paul replied. "Maine harvests more lumber than states twice its size. And what's interesting is that Maine's small woodland ownerships generate more than 40 percent of Maine's wood industry."

"That's very interesting."

Almost as an afterthought, he added, "America's made up of so many large conglomerates and chains, it's refreshing to live in a state where there are so many small businesses and individual farms."

Gustavia contemplated this, then looked out the side window. "Most of the forests look so green. There must be a great many evergreens."

"There are. Because Maine has such an abundance of the valuable eastern white pine, it's known as the Pine Tree State. The white pine contributes a lot to its economy."

"I suppose Ada and Edgar's lumber mill and paper mill are successful then."

"Very."

"I love trees," she mused.

Paul smiled at her. "I do too."

Arriving at the outskirts of Augusta Paul said, "The heart of Augusta actually runs on both sides of the Kennebec River. One of the streets running along side of the river is called Water Street. It's quite a beautiful little city."

"I'm looking forward to seeing it."

Before entering the city proper, Paul took a road that led them into a wooded area to a small restaurant behind an old abandoned mill. It was on the water's edge of the Kennebec. He pulled into the parking lot and turned off the motor, then led her to the Mill on The Kennebec. It was cozy and intimate, conducive to conversation. After they were seated and had been given the menus, Paul said, "This restaurant has some of the best lobster, salmon and haddock I have ever eaten, not withstanding the fish I've eaten in England."

"That sounds good. I was raised on the best fish in the world. Fish right fresh off the trawler."

When the waitress came, she took their orders of haddock, corn and exotic mushroom salad. "Do you miss England?" Paul asked.

"A little. I mainly miss my mother. I miss my friend, Freddie, now and then too. Actually, at times I find that a bit odd since it has been years since I've seen him."

"I can understand you missing your mother. How long has it been since you've seen Freddie?"

Gustavia hesitated to tell him, feeling he would probably react like others who had asked the same question. Why should I care how he reacts? "When I was nine and he was ten." She studied him closely and was surprised. He was silent, the expression in his eyes unfathomable.

She returned his gaze questioningly. "Well?"

"You want a reaction from me?"

"I just want to know what you're thinking. This isn't the typical response I get."

A slow smile spread across his face. "I can imagine the reactions you get."

"So you think I'm foolish? You think I'm idealizing Freddie?"

"Those are the responses you get?"

"Yes." She waited for his answer, but his eyes slid away, focusing somewhere on the floor behind her. "Excuse me, are you going to answer my question?"

His gaze returned to her, one side of his mouth tilted up. "Why do you want to know what I think?"

"I'm not sure. Just curious I guess."

"And I'm curious about you being betrothed at such a young age. How did that happen?"

Gustavia was silent.

"Aren't you going to answer my question?"

"That's private between Freddie and me. As I asked you before, do you think I'm idealizing Freddie?"

"All I can say is I think some guy—Freddie, or any other man—who wins your heart in the end, will be a very lucky man. You're the most loyal and honorable woman I've ever known."

Gustavia was speechless. After a long pause she replied, "I understand the loyal part, but I don't know why you called me honorable."

"Because you want to keep your word to Freddie. I hope he's just as honorable. Or do I?" he added, grinning.

❧CHAPTER 8❦

HESSLE, ENGLAND, MAY 1976:

It was when Freddie fell off the wall into Mr. Fretwell's yard that things changed. He was showing off and lost his footing. Horrified, Gustavia stared at her surprised little friend lying on the ground. She gasped. "Did you hurt yourself, Freddie?"

He got up grinning. "Naw. Just scared me is all."

Alice had been hanging out clothes when it happened. Running over to him, she asked the same question. Though he hadn't been hurt, this brought Alice to a decision she had been toying with for some time. "Go back over the wall and into the yard with the other children, Freddie. I'm going to take Gusty and see if I can meet with your superintendent."

"What for?" Freddie asked tremulously.

"I'm going to ask him if you can come into the yard here and play with Gusty."

"Oh." His eyes were round as saucers. "They never let kids out to play. I better say a prayer."

"Good. You do that, Freddie, and we'll say one too."

They watched Freddie grab the stones of the wall with his hands, placing the toe of his shoes on the edge of others and scramble up like a little mountain goat. Once he was over safely, they said a quick prayer.

Alice, gripping Gustavia's hand, marched purposefully to the front sidewalk and turned toward Hesslewood. Entering the gate, she pulled Gustavia along briskly and knocked on the front door. No one answered. She turned the knob slowly. Surprised to find it unlocked, she entered, closing the door behind them. She looked around the wide entry for an office of some kind.

Gustavia gasped at the sight of the tall curved stairway to the left. "Look, Mum!" she exclaimed, pulling her over. "It does look like a castle in here."

"It does at that, love."

"But what are those things sticking up all the way up the stair rail, Mum?"

A strange, curt voice behind them answered. "Those are pegs in the banister to keep the children from sliding down it."

They turned to see a woman who was looking very displeased at their presence.

Gustavia frowned. "Why? It would be fun to slide down the banister."

"Madam," she began, ignoring the child's disapproval, "you can't just walk in here and expect us to take your child. She has to be approved by the Board of Management."

"Oh, I'm not here to leave my child. I'm here to talk with the superintendent about something."

The woman hesitated, but agreed to go get him. The two of them waited nervously. Presently the superintendent appeared and Alice was relieved to see that he had a kind face.

"I'm Mr. Torr, the superintendent of Hesselwood Orphanage. What can I do for you, Madam?"

"How do you do, Mr. Torr, my name is Mrs. Browne. I work for Mr. Fretwell next door. You have an orphan here by the name of Freddie Finch."

He smiled. "Ah yes. We do. And a nice lad he is too."

"I wholeheartedly agree. He's a charming little fellow. I do hope I won't get him into trouble by telling you that he climbs up on the wall between Hesslewood and Mr. Fretwell's yard."

"I'm aware of that. Is he bothering you?"

"Quite the opposite. Due to circumstances in the past, my daughter Gustavia here has never been able to have friends. Freddie climbed up on the wall to speak to us the first day we moved in, and since then he and my daughter have become good friends."

Relief registered upon the superintendent's face. "That's nice. You see, Freddie has been with us from infancy. Since he has no family at all that we know of, we give him a few privileges that the other children don't get."

"I'm happy to hear that. Might I ask you for one more privilege for him?"

"What's that, Mrs. Browne?"

"If I come here everyday at a time acceptable to you, could I take him over to our place, so the children can play together?"

He frowned and rubbed his chin. "Now that would be setting a precedent that could cause problems with the other children, Mrs. Browne."

"Do the other children have to know about it?" Alice gave Mr. Torr a smile that would have melted the heart of a Scrooge. "There are so many of them, would he be missed?" she asked in a mischievous tone.

"Oh please, Mr. Super, Freddie's my best friend," Gustavia pleaded.

The superintendent gazed at the lovely child, and was moved by her dark persuasive eyes. He scratched his head. After a few moments, he said, "All right, Mrs. Browne. I shouldn't, but . . . Freddie is such an unusual boy, he deserves some good fortune."

Gustavia squealed. "Oh thank you, thank you, Mr. Super!"

"Yes, thank you, Mr. Torr," Alice added. "You're very kind."

Alice and the superintendent agreed that during the summer, right after dinner midday was a good time for Freddie to be picked up and then returned for supper at 4:45.

Returning home, Gustavia anxiously waited in the yard for Freddie to show up while Alice finished hanging up the wash.

Smiling at her happy little daughter, whose excitement wouldn't allow her to stand still, Alice returned to the house and watched through the kitchen window. It wasn't long before Freddie hopped up onto the wall. Gustavia jumped up and down as she told him the good news. His little face looked incredulous, then he broke the rule and jumped off the wall, grabbed Gustavia's hand and danced with her round and round like a spinning top. Alice could hear their exuberant cries of happiness, then Freddy scrambled back up the wall like a little monkey and obediently assumed his proper position on top. He pulled out his harmonica and played what could be interpreted as a happy tune, while Gustavia did a little dance of her own. Alice said a prayer of thanks to the good Lord who had softened the superintendent's heart.

From then on, the two children played together everyday on Mr. Fretwell's property. Sometimes they imagined they were characters in the books which Alice read to them. Always, Freddie brought his harmonica and played a semblance of tunes that Gustavia would dance to; other times she sang to the tunes, making up the words as she went along. They played spy and rocket ship. Sometimes they chased each other around the tall old horse chestnut tree and in and through the gaps of the privet hedge.

Once in a great while Gustavia coerced Freddie into 'playing house' with her—she as the mama and he as the daddy. Using old pieces of glass she had collected for dishes, she created elaborate mud-pie meals for him. Then there were the detailed, but mostly one-sided discussions of their imaginary children. To Gustavia's dismay, however, Freddie could only stand to play this game for a short time.

When it rained, Alice let them come into the sitting room and play quiet games.

Freddie was beside himself with happiness. For the first time in his life he felt as though he were part of a family.

The summer went by joyfully for Alice and the children. By August, Gustavia had turned six and Freddie seven and their school situation changed. Freddie graduated to the Primary school while Gustavia remained in the Infant school, and they had less than two hours to play each day. Though Gustavia developed friendships at school, Freddie remained her favorite.

Alice helped Gustavia with her lessons in the evening and she progressed rapidly in her reading. Freddie was also doing well in school. He loved to read, and he reported that he read faithfully out of his little Bible. Alice almost felt as though she had the little boy she and Thomas had always wanted. Freddie was affectionate, and let her hug him. When the three of them sat reading together on the couch, her arms around each, he remained quiet, soaking up all the love he could get. Gustavia began to pretend that her best friend, Freddie, was also her brother. It was a 'time in the sun' for all three of them.

❧CHAPTER 9❦

BELFORD, MAINE, MAY 2001:

April moved cautiously into May. The buds on the trees in Ada's front and backyards, and between the sidewalk and the curb all along the street were opening. The clean, fresh air would soon be filled with the fragrance of spring blossoms. The sun released some of its warmth upon the winter-laden state, bringing more smiles, and more neighborliness among its inhabitants.

Instead of taking breaks for tea mid-morning and mid-afternoon, Gustavia meandered out into the front garden or up and down the sidewalk, breathing deeply the health-giving air and giving in to the joy of spring.

She desperately needed a daily respite from the dry facts she was trying to put together for Ada's biography. All that kept her interest alive was the hope of finding a hidden fact or two about her grandparents. She did find out that Ada's parents were Melissa and Sir John Redmore. It felt strange to think of them as Aunt Melissa and Uncle John, but that's who they were. Whenever she had asked for more information or for a pedigree chart of the family, Ada had put her off. Why had Ada carefully omitted anything of a personal nature other than meticulous details about Sir John Redmore's status, and the education and academic achievements to which she and Edgar had attained? Why hadn't she mentioned her mother's lineage as she had her father's? Edgar's promise held her to the burdensome task, but without the knowledge of and cohesiveness of family relationships, such information in the end would be an incomplete and sterile history.

Often, Gustavia wondered what joy Ada could possibly get out of life living only to run her businesses. It seemed like an excruciatingly boring and empty existence.

Paul had taken her on several walks and several drives through the countryside. She looked forward to these outings with him. And though Ada was not good company, Edgar was proving to be a kind and caring man. He had dropped in now and then asking her how she was and how she and Ada were getting along. Though disappointed to learn that Ada's attitude toward Gustavia had not improved, he remained optimistic.

When Paul entered Ada's library office Tuesday morning, he was surprised to see only Ada. "Where's your biographer, Ada?" he greeted.

She swivelled the chair around, her lips pursing. "She's ten minutes late from tea break, and I'm not going to have it."

Paul's brows rose in surprise. "She didn't come back in here with you after tea?"

"She didn't have tea. She hasn't taken tea with me lately, just spends time outside in the garden or goes for a walk, then loses track of time."

A smile twitched at his lips. "Getting a little fresh air, Ada, should clear her mind and help her with the writing."

"I hardly think you're an authority on what would help her write, Paul."

It was at that moment they heard a door slam, and soon Gustavia entered breathlessly. "I'm sorry, Cousin Ada. I guess I have spring fever because I keep forgetting to look at my watch."

"I will not have you walk in here late one more time, Gustavia."

Hello, Paul," Gustavia greeted, ignoring Ada's ultimatum.

"Hello, Gusty," he grinned.

Not accustomed to being ignored, color suffused Ada's pale cheeks. "Gustavia! Did you hear me?"

"I did, Cousin Ada. And what will you do if I walk in late one more time?"

Though angry, Ada did not respond to the challenge. She had made it through life by rigid discipline, and she expected the same from others.

Gustavia smiled at her cousin. "Would you like to go for a walk with me sometime, Cousin Ada, you know, take time out to 'smell the roses' as they say?"

This only added to Ada's vexation. "Will you please get back to work, Gustavia? I'm much too busy for such a useless exercise."

"I'm sorry you feel that way," Gustavia said, sitting down at her desk, as though dismissing the whole affair.

Paul smiled and commenced his business with Ada.

Ada, still smarting over Gustavia's defiance, began reading the first draft of the six chapters that had been handed to her for proof reading. She read it with a jaundiced eye, and when she had finished, she protested rather vehemently, "Gustavia!"

Startled, Gustavia swivelled around. "Yes?"

"This is trash! I thought you could write better than this."

Gustavia's dark eyes smoldered. "Trash?" Then quickly recovering, she smiled. "You're calling your life trash, Cousin Ada?"

"How dare you twist what I said."

"Unless you tell me specifics, that's the only interpretation I can make."

"You have made my accomplishments seem insignificant and meaningless by the way you've expressed them."

"You gave me only facts. I asked for more, but you refused. What do you want me to do with the facts, embellish them? Speak in flowery, complimentary adjectives when stating them?"

Ada lifted her head high and spoke imperiously. "You say that with disparagement, Gustavia, but that's exactly what I want you to do. When people work hard and make their businesses grow and provide jobs for many people, making the community better, that's to be commended, no matter who it is. And since we're related, I would think that writing about those accomplishments in a favorable manner would be a high priority for you."

Gustavia realized her impatience to get the history written had to be squelched. If she didn't do it as Ada wanted, it would take much longer. "All right, Cousin Ada." She got up, took the papers from her and spoke evenly. "I'll revise it and do my best to write it in a way that is worthy of what you've done with your life."

Surprised at her cousin's acquiescence, Ada replied, "That's a much better attitude, Gustavia."

A loneliness descended upon Gustavia. The promise of spring now and then brought it on when she was least expecting it. Whenever this happened, she felt a great need to be alone, a phenomenon most people would probably find odd. The two most satisfying ways for her to disengage herself from society were to frequent antique shops or attend a symphony. It was Saturday morning and the Augusta newspaper, the Kennebec Journal, announced that the Kennebec Performing Arts was presenting a Mozart symphony to be performed this weekend and next in St Mary's Catholic church.

She wondered briefly if part of the reason she felt lonely was because Paul had not asked to spend any time with her this week. Shrugging her shoulders, she put the thought out of her mind. Free to do as she wished, she called for a last minute reservation to the symphony. She decided to leave right after lunch and browse antique shops in Augusta, grab a bite to eat somewhere, then attend the symphony.

Going through her wardrobe, she chose a 1920s "Flapper Girl" dress of leaf-green, finely woven cotton with a low waist. It was still cold at night, so she threw over her arm the only dressy period coat she owned— a short black velvet coat with fur-trimmed collar and cuffs. This she had purchased from the costume department at Cambridge. It was one of several replicas of an antique piece they had acquired.

Gustavia had never followed the period hair styles except for the Gibson Girl. She liked long hair because it was easier to get out of her way with a clip, or one long braid in the back. Clipping her hair back, she left it long under the warm cloche hat associated with the 1920s. Never attempting to wear the uncomfortable period-style foot-wear, she slipped on comfortable shoes, then left her room.

Running into Ada as she descended the stairs, she informed her of her plans.

Ada eyed her up and down critically. "I thought you were supposed to have been born in the nineteenth century, Gustavia," she remarked sarcastically, "Now you're in the twentieth?"

"If I had been born in the late nineteenth century, Cousin Ada, I probably would have still been living in the twentieth wouldn't I?" The question didn't require an answer, so she quickly moved to the back door to retrieve her car. "Good afternoon, Cousin Ada. I won't be back until late."

A covered walkway led her to the detached garage where Ada allowed her to keep her car. On the way to Augusta, she contemplated, as she had now and then, her desire to dress as the mood struck her. For some unfathomable reason, since she had been at Ada's, she felt more drawn to the late nineteenth and early twentieth centuries. She was fascinated by fashions of all the eras, so why was she beginning to feel emotionally attached to this period of time? For that was the way it felt.

Unable to answer the question, she turned her attention to the scenery and noticed that the bare trees interspersed among the pines were turning several shades of bright green gracing the forests with a variety of rich verdancy.

Arriving in Augusta with a map and a list of addresses of antique shops, she found her way to the first shop on her list in an older area. She parked in front of the store. It was a lovely old street with brick sidewalks and flower boxes in front of the stores. The buildings were three and four story red and tan brick, rich with history as was Augusta itself.

Leaving her coat in the car, Gustavia went into the store and looked around, noting with excitement that it had a magnificent selection.

Immediately engrossed, Gustavia was startled by the woman's question.

"Pardon me?"

"I said, may I help you? I'm Mrs. Tisdale, the owner of the shop."

"Oh. Not today, thank you. I would like to browse and get acquainted with what you have."

"Certainly. If you have any questions, just ask."

"Thank you."

Mrs. Tisdale, her mouth slightly open in awe, couldn't help but watch this mysterious young woman who seemed to have literally dropped in from the past. As she watched her move about, Mrs. Tisdale had the strange sensation that she belonged with this furniture and bric-a-brac of yesteryear.

Gustavia, meandering around, stopped and examined each piece that interested her. She came upon an old, armless, rose-cream velvet-cushioned love seat. Its ivory painted legs were curved, tapering gracefully to the floor. A long tube pillow of the same fabric, but with a patterned center of rose and pale gold, graced it's back. Gustavia gazed at it for a long time. It reminded her of chamber music, violin concertos, carriage rides, and red roses. She sighed and moved on, stopping at an old bureau with a hand-planed surface, a table with a hand-rubbed stain and a rocker with a worn paint finish, all hinting of past travels and fabled histories.

So deep in the days gone by that when Gustavia stepped outside the shop into the sunshine, she blinked, almost feeling shock at being in the world of modernity that hummed noisily along the street.

Inside St Mary's, Gustavia was guided by an usher to her reserved spot in the less expensive seating. She sighed with pleasure as she watched people filling the seats all around her.

Soon the lights went down and the concert began. It was only then that she could feel far away from the world. She had never attempted to explain this to anyone except her mother. Having other human beings—strangers—all about her as the beautiful music filled the space, enveloping her body and soul, she could—in the darkness—weep with happiness, loneliness, sadness or let her imagination carry her into the realms of her deepest and innermost dreams. At present, the music aroused loneliness for her mother and for the father she had never known.

After the intermission, Mozart's marvelous composition immortalized her love for Freddie, romanticizing it with tender violins, lamenting their separation with melancholy clarinets, and shouting their love to the world with the crescendo of drums, symbols and horns, ending with the plaintive cry of the oboe, kindling in her an aching desire for knowledge of what Freddie was like as a grown man, to know if he was well and happy—and to know most of all if he might be looking for her.

On the drive home, Gustavia examined how the music had aroused romantic feelings for Freddie. Ordinarily, knowing how music affected her emotions, she would have put it into perspective—but her thoughts had been focused on Freddie more since arriving at Ada's. Not only that, but her desire to meet him as a grown man had become more intense. Why at Ada's of all places? Why?

❧CHAPTER 10❧

HESSLE, ENGLAND, FEBRUARY 1977:

When Alice and her husband, Thomas, moved to Grimsby, the largest fishing port on the North Sea, to his new job on one of the fishing trawlers, she was content, but she could never get warm. The damp cold from the sea seemed to pierce her to the bone. Even in the summer, much of the time it wasn't warm enough for her.

Mr. Fretwell's house being close to the Humber River added to the biting cold every bit as much as the sea itself had. She longed to live in a warmer part of England. Mr. Fretwell had several times mentioned retiring one day and taking her and her daughter with him to a warmer climate. How pleasant this sounded! But what about Gustavia's friendship with Freddie? And she, herself, had become very attached to him. Since Mr. Fretwell had indicated that he wasn't ready to retire for a while, she decided to put this dilemma out of her mind.

The winter had been excessively rainy and cold. Freddie and Gustavia had to remain inside most of the time, and it was harder to keep them happily occupied. Freddie was getting quite accomplished on the harmonica, and Gustavia was still enjoying singing and dancing to his music. On the days they had to remain indoors, this activity kept them busy for at least part of the time.

One day after work, Mr. Fretwell entered the kitchen where Alice was finishing preparations for supper, announcing that he was thinking of selling the house and moving into town closer to his shop. Gustavia let out a howl of disapproval. Quickly shushing her, Alice suggested she go play in the bedroom so she could talk with her employer.

Mr. Fretwell explained. "The Board of Management of Hesslewood Orphanage has been talking about making a hotel out of Hesselwood. The board says that because the new Humber Bridge has its northern abutment on part of the former grounds of Hesslewood, they're sitting on a gold mine. Since this may be the case, Alice, my property value has gone up accordingly."

"How soon will you be selling your house?" Alice asked, concerned.

"The Board hasn't made a decision yet, and until they do, I won't consider moving. I just wanted to prepare you, Alice."

"Will you still want me as your housekeeper?"

"Of course."

"I was hoping to stay here because you have a yard for Gusty to play in."

"I'll try to find a place with a small yard, Alice, but I can't promise. Besides, this isn't the safest place to live because of the railway behind the house."

"I know, but . . ." her voice trailed off. Even though Mr. Fretwell knew that Freddie came over to play, she didn't like to bring it up for fear he would change his mind about allowing it.

Later, Alice placated Gustavia as best she could, telling her that Mr. Fretwell was just talking about it and not to worry. But Alice worried. If only Mr. Fretwell would let her adopt Freddie. He had softened toward Gustavia, but there it ended. His interest was only his work, good meals and relaxation at the end of the day, and Alice knew that having another child in the house would, in his mind, interfere with the latter.

OCTOBER 1978:

It was a beautiful, warm October, and Alice and the children spent as much time outside as possible. The fears of Mr. Fretwell moving had long been put aside since he had not mentioned it again.

In August Gustavia had turned eight and Freddie nine, and the superintendent told Alice that Freddie was old enough and trustworthy enough to just climb over the wall when his studies or chores were over, that she didn't have to go get him and bring him back each day. He had explained to the other children that this was allowed only for Freddie since he was the only child who had lived there all his life.

Gustavia and Freddie each had excelled in their studies and Freddie had become well known in Hull for his harmonica playing. Requests for his performance at weddings, funerals and programs had become a regular thing. The Board felt this spoke well for the orphanage and so allowed it if a small donation to the orphanage was made each time. This had long been the custom when the Hesslewood band performed.

It was also in October that Alice noticed a change in the relationship between Gusty and Freddie. They were even closer and enjoyed each other more. However, of late, Gustavia had come into the house several times looking very disgusted. And today it happened once more.

"What is it, Gusty?" her mother asked.

"Freddie's acting mushy!"

"What do you mean?"

"He says he loves me. Ugh!"

"Of course he loves you. You love him, too."

"I know. But this is different. He says he wants to marry me."

"Oh. Well, that's nice."

"No it isn't nice, Mum. It's mushy!"

"Where is Freddie?"

"I guess he's outside. I told him I wasn't going to play with him when he talked silly like that."

Alice turned her back to finish preparing supper, smiling at the new turn of events.

Secretly, Gustavia liked Freddie to say he loved her, but at the same time feeling awkward about it, she protested with the appropriate histrionics. It wasn't long before she went back outside to see if he had repented. He had—long enough to play ball for a while.

Freddie's repentance lasted for a few days, then one day he gave her a love note and told her not to read it until he was over the wall.

She opened it and read it. "Freddie!" she screeched. "Come back over the wall!"

Only his head appeared. "Yeah?"

"Why are you being goofy again?"

"That's not being goofy, Gusty. I can't help it if I love you," he said, hopping on top of the wall.

"The answer is no. You can't kiss me on the cheek!"

"Okay then, let's play soccer."

"Okay."

A few days later, Gustavia was inside when she heard Freddie playing his harmonica. Looking out the kitchen window she saw him sitting on the wall. Running outside, she sat down on the back porch and listened. She loved to hear him play.

When he was through, he yelled. "I love you Gustavia Browne!"

Gustavia stood up, put her hands on her hips and yelled back dramatically, "I *hate* you, Freddie Finch!"

Unruffled, he began playing a beautiful and mournful song. She remained standing, glaring at him all the while. When he was through, he again announced, "I love you Gustavia Browne!"

"I hate *you*, Freddie Finch!" she exclaimed again, then stomped into the house. Running to the kitchen window, she watched him. He continued to play his harmonica. She wanted to play with him, but couldn't when he was yelling his embarrassing declarations! Then an idea came to her. Trotting back outside, she went up to the wall, waiting until he was through playing the song.

He grinned. "I love you Gustavia Browne."

"If you love me," she smirked, "you'll play house with me. You be the father and I'll be the mother."

"Awe, Gusty, that's baby stuff. We're too big to play that anymore."

"No we're not."

"Can we play soccer instead?" he pleaded.

"Only if you'll stop being mushy."

"Okay!" He jumped off the wall and they began to play, back to their old selves, competing furiously, laughing and hollering.

❧CHAPTER 11❦

HESSLE, ENGLAND, 1979-1980:

The warm weather of October continued through to the end of November, then the rains brought bitter cold, much to Alice's dismay. It didn't seem to affect the children. Their blood coursed through their veins in a healthy rush, bringing roses to their cheeks.

Freddie the precocious ten-year-old harmonica player was still in demand all over Hull. Alice took Gustavia on the bus to as many performances as she could, to the delight and happiness of both Gustavia and Freddie.

December came and went. Freddie got a new harmonica for Christmas from a well-to-do benefactor in Hull. Excited at the quality of sound produced by his new instrument, he practiced more than ever.

Once again Freddie turned 'mushy' and Gustavia put on her usual indignant front. On a biting-cold January day, Freddie sat on top of the wall and played his harmonica. Gustavia threw her coat and hat on and went outside.

When the song ended, he yelled, "I love you Gustavia Browne!"

She yelled back, "I *hate* you, Freddie Finch."

Turning on her heel, she went back into the house and waited for him to quit his silly prattle. This time she didn't go back outside. When he came to the door, she refused to play with him.

Not wanting to miss one day of enjoyment with his beautiful little friend, from that day on, Freddie held his boyish infatuation deep inside him, that is, until the end of the first week in February.

Freddie and Gustavia had an especially good time together all of January and the first week of February. They read David Copperfield together, each taking turns. Alice had been encouraging the reading of books together to help pass the time during the cold winter.

It was on February 5th that Alice received the news. Gustavia was in bed for the night and Alice had just put away her book to join her when she heard Mr. Fretwell knock on her sitting room door. "Come in, Mr. Fretwell."

He opened the door and stepped in. "Alice, I would like to talk with you a moment."

"Please come in and have a seat, Mr. Fretwell."

"Thank you, Alice." He coughed. Pulling out his handkerchief, he covered his mouth as he coughed several more times.

A slice of fear went through Alice. She had been worried over his health of late. What if something happened to him? What would become of her and Gustavia? She studied him. He couldn't be more than sixty. His hair, though sparse on top, was still brown. The only wrinkles in his broad face were two very deep lines between his dark brows.

"I've been concerned about that cough, Mr. Fretwell."

Gazing at her thoughtfully through his thick glasses, he replied, "The doctor is too. He feels I need to spend a month or two in a warmer climate. I've decided to do that. Mr. Snelby will look after my shop while I'm gone. Mr. Snelby's son has been apprenticing with me, and he can help out."

"Where will you be going, Mr. Fretwell?" she asked, in a small voice, wondering what was going to become of her and Gustavia.

"I have a cousin who has a cottage in Cornwall which he uses now and then when he wants to get away from the city life in London. Will you accompany me, Alice? I'll need someone to cook and clean for me there. Of course I expect you to bring your daughter. There are two bedrooms and two baths. It's a luxurious place. My cousin is quite well-off."

Relief flooded through her. Warmer weather sounded good to Alice, but she wished she could take Freddie with them. Gustavia and Freddie had been friends and constant companions for almost five years. They had never been separated for even one day. *This will be hard on them*, she thought, *especially Freddie*. She and Gustavia were the only semblance of a 'family' he had ever known.

"Is there something wrong, Alice?" Mr. Fretwell asked, concerned over her silence.

"I fear that Gustavia will miss her friend, Freddie Finch," she ventured, hoping he might offer a solution that would make them all happy.

"In all likelihood, we'll be gone only thirty days at the most. Gustavia's young. The time will go by and before she knows it, we'll be back."

"When will we be leaving?"

"Day after tomorrow. The doctor wants me to leave as soon as possible."

"All right, Mr. Fretwell. I'll pack our things and be ready. The food we have left that won't keep can be taken over to the orphanage, so it won't go to waste. Do you need any help, besides washing and ironing your clothes?"

"No. I'll do my own packing. I appreciate your willingness to go with me, Alice. I've come to rely on you rather heavily."

The next day after school when Freddie came over to play with Gustavia, Alice called them to come into the sitting room. Requesting they both sit down on the small couch, she knelt before them.

"Little loves, you've been good friends for a long time, haven't you?"

They grinned at each other and nodded.

"True friendship lasts forever Freddie and Gusty. Sometimes friends have to be separated for a while, but when they get back together, their friendship is even stronger."

Their faces turned solemn. Alice could see the fear hovering at the edge of Freddie's eyes.

"Mr. Fretwell isn't feeling at all well. The doctor says he has to go to a warmer climate for a short while. You, Gusty, and I are going with him, so I can continue to cook and clean for him. We'll return when he feels better.

Immediately, the new adventure intrigued Gustavia, but almost as quickly, the idea of leaving Freddie brought a frown. "Can Freddie go with us?"

"I wish he could, but no. Mr. Fretwell says the cottage we'll be staying in doesn't belong to him."

Freddie listened in silence, his face ashen.

Alice sat beside him and put her arms around him. "Freddie, if you study hard, and practice on your new harmonica every day, time will go by faster than you think. I hear that you have more programs to play for, so that will make time pass quickly, also."

Still silent, he nodded.

"How about we go into the kitchen, love, and have some cookies and milk?"

Ordinarily, this brought a big smile to Freddie's face, but today his smile was a small pathetic one.

"We'll be back, Freddie, I promise," Gusty reassured him. She took hold of his hand. "Come on, let's go have some cookies."

"Okay," he said, smiling faintly.

❧

After school the next day, Freddie came over to play, but Alice and Gustavia were busy packing and getting things ready for their trip the following day. Freddie followed them around forlornly. Finally, he sat down on the couch, pulled out his harmonica and began playing the saddest songs he could think of.

Gustavia's excitement at packing and going on the very first trip she could remember kept her happy for a while, then Freddie's songs started to make her feel bad. She ran into the sitting room and scolded him. "Freddie! Don't play another sad song. Play a happy one."

"Oh, okay." He played all the fun bouncy songs he could think of, making himself feel better, then stuffed the instrument back into his pocket, went into Mr. Fretwell's parlor and looked at the clock. It was almost time for him to go back to the orphanage for supper. All his sadness returned. He found Gustavia in the kitchen. "Gusty, I've gotta go now."

Alice smiled at him. "First, I need to give you a hug goodbye, Freddie, because we're leaving early tomorrow morning." Freddie clung to her with all his might, then let go. "We'll see you sooner than you think, Freddie. Take care of yourself while we're gone, will you?"

"I will, Mrs. Browne. Thanks for being so nice to me, for being," he swallowed hard, struggling with his feelings, "my family."

Alice felt a painful knot in her heart. She hugged him again, holding him tightly until she had successfully blinked back the tears. "Thank you for being like the little boy I never had."

When Alice let go of him, he looked up at her with tears in his blue eyes. "I wish I was your little boy."

"Then you couldn't marry me if you were my brother, Freddie," Gustavia teased.

Freddie blinked. "Oh. That's right. Brothers and sisters don't marry do they?"

"No, silly." Gustavia giggled.

Freddie laughed too, then turned very serious. "Then you'll marry me when we grow up, Gusty?"

"I didn't say that."

"It sounded like it. I gotta go, Gusty, it's time for me to leave. Are you going to marry me or not? I have to know before you leave."

"Why?"

"I don't know. I just feel I gotta know, that's all."

"All right," Gustavia sighed in resignation, "I'll marry you."

"You promise?"

"Oh, Freddie!" she exclaimed in exasperation.

"Do you promise?"

"Okay! I promise."

Alice shook her head, not quite sure how she felt about this promise extracted from Gustavia. As an orphan, Freddie knew nothing about families—whole families. Even hers was incomplete. In many ways he was beyond his years, did he have any idea what he was asking of Gustavia?

Certainly, Gustavia didn't realize what she had promised. Even though they were only childish promises and could easily be forgotten, Alice was a little apprehensive. She stood by silently watching them as Freddie opened the door and stepped out onto the porch.

Gustavia, a panicky expression on her face called him back in. "Freddie! Can I hug you goodbye?"

Freddie's face lit up. "Sure!"

The two friends hugged each other hard. Then Freddie, with an air of desperation, ran out the door, his jaw tightly clamped. Gustavia stood on the porch, in the bone chilling winter, waving. Freddie turned and waved at her every few feet, and continued to do so while furiously blinking back tears—until he disappeared over the wall.

ᵏᵒCHAPTER 12ᵏᵒ

CORNWALL, ENGLAND, FEBRUARY 1980:

Alice was delighted with the cottage. Never had she been in such a nice home, let alone cook and keep house in one. Perched on a hill at the edge of the picturesque coastal town of Port Isaac, the cottage overlooked the beautiful rocky coast of Cornwall.

Though the mists from the coast rose up every morning and sometimes turned to fog giving off the familiar damp cold, the sun came out late morning or afternoon and warmed the countryside.

Mr. Fretwell stayed inside during the damp mists, but on the days it warmed up, he sat in the sun, and his health slowly began to improve.

Since Alice and Gustavia had no private quarters, Gustavia had to stay in their bedroom or go play outside so as not to be a bother to Mr. Fretwell. However, the lovely spacious bedroom was more like a sitting room and bedroom combined. It had a couch and chair on one side of the room in a cozy alcove overlooking the coast.

Gustavia was delighted with her freedom to explore. A day never went by that she didn't wish Freddie were there with her. "Wouldn't he just love it here, Mum?"

"He would, love. He would at that."

It wasn't long before Alice enrolled Gustavia in school for the short time they would be there, making it possible for her to become acquainted with other children in the village, and for the first time she developed a friendship with someone other than Freddie. Back in Hessle, her only desire had been to get home and play with Freddie. Here she formed a fast and close friendship with one girl in particular, Enid.

Each day after school, she and Enid would descend the hill and explore the rugged paths along the coast. They found wind-blown estuaries, and sheltered tree-lined creeks and their imaginations took flight. One day they would pretend to be searching for a lost treasure. The next they would pretend they were grown up with handsome suitors chasing them. Each excursion brought new fantasies.

Accompanying her mother to the market in the village was also an adventure to Gustavia. She loved walking through the narrow streets, passing the pastel colored, slate-slung houses to the cobbled alleys and fish 'cellars.' Sometimes her mother allowed her to meander through the dress shop. During these special times, she imagined herself wearing the prettiest ones. Afterward at home, she drew them from memory, then began to design many of her own fanciful dresses.

By the end of February, Gustavia was pining for Freddie. "If we don't go back soon, Mum, Freddie'll be scared. He'll think we aren't coming back."

"I'll ask Mr. Fretwell when he thinks he'll feel well enough, Gusty."

After Gustavia was in bed, Alice went into the front room where her employer was reading. "Excuse me, Mr. Fretwell, but do you have any idea when we'll be returning to Hessle?"

He was thoughtful for a moment. "I need to go now, but I'm not quite myself yet. Maybe a week, maybe two. Is there any reason you're asking?"

"I was just wondering."

"Please sit down, Alice. I need to talk with you about something."

Surprised, Alice did as he asked.

"My illness has given me pause to think. Lung cancer runs in my family and several males on my side of the family have died in their sixties with it. Fortunately, all I've had at this time is a stubborn lung congestion. When I pass on, I have no children to leave my estate to. As I've told you before, my wife has two sisters and I intend to leave something to each of them, but they both have husbands who are good providers. The cousin who is letting us use this cottage, as one might presume, doesn't need my inheritance."

Alice was quite astounded at this personal information. Mr. Fretwell had at all times been kind and cordial, but always concise and impersonal.

"Living next door to Hesslewood Orphanage," Mr. Fretwell was saying, "has caused me to ponder on something. A few of the children there have widowed mothers who are living, but can't take care of them because of the number of other children they have at home and their inability to provide for them. I would hate to see that happen to you, Alice. I've noticed how close you and your daughter are."

Charles Fretwell nervously cleared his throat. "My marriage was not a satisfying one so I've never wanted to remarry. You've been with me for almost five years now, Alice, and have been a good help to me. I would like to leave something to you in my will. However, in the event of my death, my sisters-in-law would be most unhappy about me leaving something to my housekeeper and I'm afraid they'd try to break the will—unless," he cleared his throat again, "unless . . ." He looked away. "Unless," he began again, "we were to marry," he finished in a rush.

Alice's astonishment over the whole narrative ended with a loud gasp at this last pronouncement.

Charles quickly added. "Of course, it would be a marriage in name only. You're only in your thirties and I'm in my sixties. Everyone will look askance at such an alliance, but it won't bother me, if it won't bother you, Alice."

At this point, the awkwardness he felt caused him to lean toward the fireplace, briskly rubbing his hands together as though for warmth. He waited, hoping she had taken his offer in the spirit in which he intended it.

When Alice's presence of mind returned, she felt profoundly touched. "How kind of you, Mr. Fretwell, to want to assure my financial security. My first impulse is to accept your offer, but it's so much to accept. I . . . "

"There's something you must consider before you decide, Alice," he stated before she could complete her thought. "And that is, a young man may come along whom you may want to marry. I'll put in the contract that you may annul the marriage under such circumstances, or for any reason you wish."

"Oh, Mr. Fretwell, you have simply thought of everything. How kind, how generous you are."

Charles flushed slightly, unused to such accolades. "Thank you Alice. Then you accept my offer?"

"I do, Mr. Fretwell. Thank you. When did you want to get . . . " her voice trailed off, unable to say the word 'married.'

"When we return to Hessle."

The next day Gustavia announced to her mother that she had to write Freddie a letter so he wouldn't worry. Alice found some stationery in a desk and handed it to her. She promptly sat down and wrote to him. Ten days passed as she waited anxiously for a reply. When none came, she wrote another, then another. Still no reply.

"Why isn't Freddie writing to me, Mum? Do you think he got my letters?"

"He must have. Be patient, Gusty. You should be getting one any day now," Alice said, trying to believe it herself. She was more concerned than she let on to Gustavia. It wasn't like him not to be excited about receiving letters from her, then answering them promptly. She also missed him and his smiling freckled face.

The end of March arrived and still there was no letter from him. Alice had an uneasy feeling in the pit of her stomach—afraid that something had happened to him. The whole week before, she had kept her daughter as busy as she could and saw to it that she played with her friend Enid as much as possible in order to keep her mind off Freddie. Nevertheless, Gustavia dissolved into tears at least once a day, begging her mother to ask Mr. Fretwell when they were going home.

Alice didn't want to seem anxious to leave for Hessle until her employer felt he was well enough, but for Gustavia's sake she couldn't wait another day. After she kissed Gustavia goodnight she went into the front room to do as she had promised. Before she could pose the question, Mr. Fretwell informed her that she should make preparations to leave in two days.

Alice immediately went in and informed Gustavia, who jumped up out of bed and hugged her mother. Alice smiled, careful not to betray the vague uneasiness she felt.

❧CHAPTER 13❧

Mr. Fretwell, not wanting to overdo it, took two days to motor back to Hessle. When they arrived home it was afternoon and Gustavia begged to go see Freddie immediately.

"Just as soon as all our things are inside and Mr. Fretwell is settled, we'll walk over to see the superintendent."

Gustavia helped as much as she could. When Mr. Fretwell had taken his bags inside, he informed Alice that he was going to the shop to check on things.

"Don't worry about supper tonight, Alice," he said. "I'll pick up some fish and chips."

"Thank you, Mr. Fretwell. That will be of great help since I won't be able to go to the market until tomorrow."

Gustavia danced around with eagerness until Mr. Fretwell left, and then grabbed hold of her mother's hand. "Let's go, Mum."

"All right, love," she said, trying to sound cheerful, hoping her fears were unfounded.

When they walked through the door of Hesslewood, the atmosphere of the place felt different to Alice. It wasn't long before a woman they had seen several times before saw them waiting.

"May I help you?"

"We've come to see Freddie Finch."

She looked surprised. "Freddie? I'm sorry ma'am, but that dear little lad hasn't been with us for about six weeks now."

Puzzled, Gustavia looked up at her mother. "What does that mean, Mum?"

"What do you mean?" Alice asked the woman.

"Why, he's been adopted. It was hard for those of us who've been here a while to see him go. It was hard for the other children, too. We'd all grown quite attached to the boy."

Gustavia's eyes were wide and troubled. "Who adopted him? Where do they live?"

"I don't know that, young miss."

"Could I speak with the superintendent please," Alice asked.

"Yes. I'll get him."

A tall austere looking man entered the hall. "May I help you?"

"I need to speak with the superintendent, please."

"I'm the new superintendent. Mr. Torr had to retire because of a sudden heart ailment. I've just recently heard that he passed away."

Stunned, it took Alice a few moments to react. "I'm so sorry to hear that. He's been very kind to my daughter, Gustavia, here. He let Freddie Finch come over every day to play with her. They became fast friends. We've been away for two months and we didn't know he'd been adopted."

"Oh yes. I've heard a lot about that young man. It was nice he could be adopted. That's rare at his age."

"Could you please give us the name and address of the people who adopted him?"

"I'm sorry, ma'am, but that's against regulations."

"What's that mean?" Gustavia asked fearfully.

The tall man looked down at the dark-eyed child. "That means I can't tell you."

"Why!" she demanded.

"It's the rule, that's why," he returned sternly.

Not used to unbending sternness, Gustavia's chin quivered and tears pooled in her eyes.

Alice intervened. "Mr . . . uh . . ."

"John Gee, madam."

"Mr. Gee, could you then just tell us about the circumstances surrounding the adoption of Freddie?"

"I'm sorry, madam, but it happened just before Mr. Torr took ill and I know nothing but the bare facts."

"Could someone . . . I mean, is there someone here who could relate how it all came about?" Alice pleaded.

John Gee's features gave no evidence that he was about to give out that information.

"Please, Mr. Superintendent," Gustavia begged. A tear escaped and rolled down her cheek.

John Gee fidgeted uneasily, then with a sweep of his arm pointed to his office. "Step in there and have a seat. I'll go find someone."

"Oh, thank you!" Alice exclaimed with emotion. Gripping Gustavia's hand tightly, she led her through the magnificent mahogany doorway into the spacious office and sat on the wooden chairs placed in front of a large old mahogany desk. Alice tried to smile reassuringly at her forlorn-looking little daughter, but could hardly muster one herself, her heart was aching so. *We should be happy for Freddie*, she thought, but at the moment it felt too agonizing to lose his company so abruptly.

Presently, Mr. Gee returned, followed by a plump, middle-aged woman with a round face and kind eyes. "This is Mrs. Mullin, my assistant who knew Freddie Finch very well and knows some of the circumstances concerning his adoption. Mrs. Mullin, this is Mrs. Browne."

Mrs. Mullin stepped over to Alice and held out her hand. "I'm so glad to meet you, Mrs. Browne. And this must be Freddie's friend, Gustavia," she said turning to her. "I would recognize you anywhere. Freddie said you had eyes that looked like big, sparkling black diamonds."

Her smile tremulous, Gustavia asked, "Where's Freddie?"

Mrs. Mullin pulled up another chair and sat by Gustavia, and Mr. Gee seated himself behind the desk.

"Freddie called you Gusty most of the time, didn't he?" Mrs Mullin asked, smiling.

Gustavia nodded solemnly.

"Well, Gusty, my dear child, I wish I knew where Freddie was. Many of the children also want to know as well as many of the grownups who work here. Everybody loved Freddie."

"I wrote lots of letters to him while I was gone. Did he get them?"

Mr. Gee swivelled his chair around, opened a drawer in a cabinet behind him and pulled out a small stack of letters. "Here they are," he said handing them to her.

Her forehead crimped in distress. "He didn't open any of them."

"Little Miss Browne," Mr. Gee said more kindly, "The first one came right after Mr. Torr took ill and had to leave. Because I had to take over rather quickly, everything here was in a state of confusion." He spoke to both mother and daughter. "There was no time for him to tell me anything or acquaint me with procedures. I had no idea where to forward the letters, so I just kept them until I found out."

"Do you know now, Mr. Gee?" Alice asked.

"No. From what I understand, the couple who adopted him were living in London at the time, but apparently had informed Mr. Torr that they would be moving right after the adoption."

"You can't tell me their names?" Alice persisted.

"No, it has been too soon. We have to protect all concerned until we know that the adoption is final."

"Why? Gustavia is just a friend who wants to write to him. It will help him adjust to his new situation, I'm sure."

"Mrs. Browne," he began impatiently, "you'll have to take that up with the Management Board. Mrs. Mullin, go ahead and tell them what you know."

"I would be glad to, sir." She smiled warmly at Freddie's friends. "From what I understood from Mr. Torr, a couple of weeks before he became ill, this couple who had not been able to have children were touring England and happened to go to the Music Hall on Jarratt Street where Freddie was playing his harmonica that night with a music group. He played several pieces. Apparently, it was announced that he was from Hesslewood Orphanage, and I guess the couple was taken with young Freddie and requested to meet him. After visiting with him a while, they liked him even more and decided to try to adopt him. Freddie wasn't aware of this. Mr. Torr didn't want to get his hopes up and then have them dashed. Mr. Torr said he was impressed with the couple.

When all the legal work had been taken care of, he was going to approach Freddie and have him meet with them. This happened rather quickly and the meeting with the couple was on a weekend when some of us weren't here. When Monday arrived, we found Freddie gone. Mr. Torr said that the couple took him to London, but promised Freddie they would bring him back so he could say goodbye to everyone. It was the next day that Mr. Torr had to leave. The couple never brought Freddie back to say goodbye as they promised, and we were all devastated."

Alice could scarcely breath. Her words came out hoarsely. "D-did Mr. Torr say how Freddie felt about being adopted and leaving here—leaving Gustavia?"

"None of us got to talk to Mr. Torr again and he was the only one who knew, except some day-help and they haven't been back."

Not quite understanding it all, Gustavia clung to her mother's arm, fearful and on the verge of tears.

"Mrs. Mullin, do you know anything about the circumstances that brought Freddie here to the orphanage?"

"Only a little. Apparently, his parents were ill or something because a nurse brought him in with a note that said he wasn't to be adopted, that his parents would be back to get him. When no one came back to get him, they had the police look for people by the name of Finch here in Hessle, in Hull and even Grimsby, but they couldn't find anyone by that name. The board didn't dare put him up for adoption for fear the parents would come for him eventually."

A woman in an apron appeared at the office door. Her face was flushed. "Excuse me, Mr. Gee, but we have a problem with a couple of the children."

Mr. Gee stood up. "We must excuse ourselves, Mrs. Browne."

"Yes. I understand. Thank you for your time."

Mrs. Mullin hugged Alice and whispered in her ear. "I'll try to find out the names of the couple who adopted him."

Alice nodded gratefully, giving her a squeeze in return. Gripping Gustavia's hand tightly, she smiled encouragingly at her, then led her out of the building quickly. On the way home, Alice told her what Mrs. Mullin had whispered in her ear. "So you see, love, we'll probably find Freddie before very long."

For several days, Alice talked with Gustavia about how happy they should be that Freddie now had a mother and a father. This kept Gustavia's spirits up for a short time, then one day Alice found her huddled up in a little ball on her bed, sobbing. Nothing her mother said would console her.

Everyday after school, Gustavia would go outside and sit with her back to the tall old chestnut tree and stare at the wall, hoping Freddie would miraculously appear. Everyday, Alice would have to go get her and coerce her inside because of the rain and cold weather.

One day, Gustavia woke up with a terrible racking cough and fever. Mr. Fretwell stayed home from work and took them to a physician. Returning home with medicine, Alice put Gustavia to bed.

"May I speak with you, Alice?" Mr. Fretwell asked as she emerged from the bedroom to the kitchen.

"Of course, Mr. Fretwell."

"I think it might be a good time to go ahead with our alliance. Is that all right with you?"

"Of course, Mr. Fretwell. After Gustavia gets well, you name the day."

One week later with Gustavia present, Alice Symmons Browne and Charles Fretwell were married. Beforehand, Alice had explained all about it to her little daughter as best she could, but as Gustavia looked on, she still couldn't understand why her mother would marry such a cross looking old man.

Gustavia soon learned that it didn't make any difference in their lives. The only thing that changed was her mother called Mr. Fretwell by his first name, Charles.

Though finally able to concentrate on her school, Gustavia kept asking the question that Alice had asked herself over and over. "Why isn't Freddie writing to me from where he is? He knows we were coming back here, Mum. Why?"

"I wish I knew, love, but it must be a very good reason. I have a feeling that someday we'll find out."

"Someday is a long ways off!" The tears started all over again.

Alice didn't know what to do to console Gustavia, until one afternoon, Mrs. Mullin came over with the name of the couple who adopted Freddie. She handed Alice the paper with names on it. "I wish I could find out their address, but they have moved as they said they were going to do. Please don't tell anyone I gave this much to you."

"I won't, Mrs. Mullin. I can't thank you enough for your kindness."

Gustavia was in the bedroom listlessly trying to read a book when Alice walked in with the names. She sat down on the bed and smiled. "Mrs. Mullin brought over the names of the couple who adopted Freddie."

Her eyes lit up and she bounced up and down. "Oh Mum! Who are they?"

"Their names are Robert and Sharon Banks."

"Where do they live?"

"Mrs. Mullin didn't know. She couldn't find out because as Mr. Gee said they were intending to move soon. But we do know that they lived in London. I'll ask Mr. Fretwell if he can help us."

Gustavia clapped her hands together and held her breath.

"Now don't get your hopes up too much, Gusty. We might not find them right away. We'll just have to keep praying like we have been, and someday you'll see Freddie again. I feel it here." She placed her hand over her heart.

After supper, Alice approached her employer. It was difficult to think of him as her husband even though legally he was most certainly that. "Charles, may I speak with you about some concerns I have?"

"Of course, Alice. I've had concerns also. You and your daughter have been rather solemn of late it seems. Are you unhappy about marrying me?"

"Oh no, Charles, I'm only concerned about Gustavia. She's listless and pale. She needs playmates, but she doesn't want to play with anyone but her friend Freddie. I'm afraid that living here by the orphanage and not playing with him is rather painful for her."

"That brings me to something I've been considering for sometime," Charles said. "It's something I haven't wanted to tell you because of Gustavia's friendship with the young boy from the orphanage. Since that isn't a problem now I'll tell you about it. I've been toying with the idea of retiring in the not too distant future, but now I find that my strength hasn't come back as I thought it would. I've put my shop up for sale. I felt much better in Cornwall, so I've approached my cousin about selling his cottage to me. He's interested because they have other homes they use more. He told me he would give me a good buy on it when my shop and my home sell."

Relief swept over Alice. "Oh, Charles, that would be wonderful. Gustavia had friends there, one in particular as you know. Going back there to her friend, Enid, will help take her mind off Freddie. I do hope the sales go through soon."

"I'm glad you approve."

It was then that Alice showed him the names of the couple who had adopted Freddie and told him that they had lived in London. "We need to find them so Gustavia and Freddie can correspond, and maybe someday see each other again."

"I'll ring up some friends in London and have them look for the couple."

"Oh, thank you, Charles!" She impulsively laid her hand on his arm, and was rewarded with a smile she had never seen before.

Charles Fretwell's home sold quickly because of the commercial value of the property and the prospect of Hesslewood being turned into a hotel.

Mr. Snelby and his married son, who had been apprenticing with Mr. Fretwell, bought the shop. Because Mr. Snelby had been such a loyal and dedicated employee for so many years, Charles sold it to him and his son at a reasonable price. He was relieved to find someone who would care about the shop as he had, giving good service and making it profitable.

Gustavia was thrilled to be moving back to where her friend Enid lived. Though Mr. Fretwell had not as yet been successful in finding the couple who adopted Freddie, he told her he would continue to investigate. So it was with this hope they moved with Mr. Fretwell back to the lovely cottage in Cornwall.

❧CHAPTER 14❧

BELFORD, MAINE, MAY 2001:

It was the last of May and Gustavia found herself looking forward more and more to Paul's visits. She enjoyed the few minutes he always took to visit with her. Admiring his appearance one day, she noticed how well his suits looked on his slightly angular frame.

Oftentimes when he worked with Ada in the office, she could feel his eyes upon her. Whenever she glanced in his direction, he quickly concealed whatever he was thinking, and with a wink or a smile, he would return to what he was doing. A couple of times, however, she caught the expression in his eyes before he could hide it. Puzzled, she tried to interpret what she had seen, but couldn't find words to describe it—only that he must have been feeling something deep and personal. He had certainly kept his promise about keeping their relationship on a friendship-only basis. *In fact,* Gustavia thought, *Paul Camden is something of a mystery.* And this aroused her curiosity. She found him very adept at sidestepping most of her questions—especially if they touched on his personal background.

Ada had accepted the last ten pages Gustavia had given her to read. Progress was slow, but she finally had learned a few phrases that pleased her cousin. It was a laborious effort to find ways and words to make her life and accomplishments illustrious when Ada herself made it impossible to really know her.

Her mind wandered to Maine's beautiful spring. Nature's annual miracle of regeneration was in full sway. Small leaves and early flowers magically appeared, surprising Gustavia daily. Ada's front garden would soon be beautiful. Bushes and flowers surrounded the flagstone courtyard. The tall elm at the corner of the house spread over part of the area, its limbs almost reaching the small dogwood tree. Long green fingers of perennials along the wrought iron fence were slow to bloom, and Gustavia was anxious to see what they were. Not that she would know when she saw them.

"Gustavia! Are you daydreaming again?"

"Actually, at one point I was thinking that if you let me know you better, writing this history would be easier."

"Do not mention that again. You'll find all you need to know in the material I gave you so quit allowing your mind to wander onto unnecessary things."

She stared at the blank computer screen and drummed her fingers for a few moments then began typing rapidly: "If Paul doesn't walk into this room right this moment, I might scream at Ada's narrow, empty outlook on life!!!!!!"

"Your wish is my command," a deep voice spoke from behind her.

Nearly jumping out of her skin, she giggled and quickly erased the sentence. Swiveling around, she looked up into Paul's grinning face. "Hi. Thanks for coming to my rescue," she whispered.

"You're welcome. How about us doing something tonight."

"By all means, let's!"

"Paul! Please don't interrupt that girl," Ada directed. "Her mind has already proven to be more of a sieve than a receptacle."

"How can you say that, Ada," Paul retorted. "I just read the most interesting sentence." Gustavia stifled another giggle.

"I'm not paying you to read what she's writing. Your job is over here," she stated, jabbing a bony finger at a document. "Another legal problem has erupted at the quarry."

His brows rose. "Maybe I'll have to go over and take care of it. The acquisition of the adjacent property seems to be getting more complicated than we anticipated."

Ada's and Paul's conversation was much more interesting to Gustavia than the material in front of her. She strained to hear as they lowered their voices.

It was just as well she couldn't hear them. It would distract her. It was difficult enough trying to write Ada's biography in an interesting manner and at the same time make her sound like an outstanding and benevolent citizen to the good people of Grimsby!

Paul and Ada worked until almost six, so Paul had invited himself to dinner. Gustavia was delighted, but it was soon obvious to her that something was troubling Ada. She was pensive, and Paul was unusually thoughtful—only directing a witty quip now and then to Gustavia, much to Ada's irritation.

"A smile once in a while wouldn't come amiss, Cousin Ada."

"Gustavia! Do not instruct me. You have no idea the burdens I carry."

After the dessert, Paul, with the usual one-sided tilt of his lips, asked, "Are you ready Gusty?"

"Ecstatically yes!"

Ada jerked her head up and glared at her cousin. "And what does that mean, Gustavia?"

"That I'm ecstatically ready to do whatever Paul wants me to do."

Ada glanced sharply at Paul. "This is most inappropriate, Paul."

"Well now, Ada," Paul grinned, "doesn't that depend on what I want Gusty to do?"

"Don't call her Gusty. That's a silly name her mother tacked onto her. It's hardly dignified."

"Neither am I dignified, Cousin Ada," retorted Gustavia. "Most of the time anyway. What are we going to do, Paul?" she asked, dismissing her cousin.

"How about a casual walk down to my office apartment, so I can change into hiking clothes—that is, after you change into yours."

"Hiking is exactly what I wanted to do," she stated exuberantly. "There's still plenty of daylight left. Excuse me." She scooted back her chair and moved quickly to the entrance of the dining room. She stopped and turned around. "Cheerio, Cousin Ada."

Ada glared after her, then transferred her gaze to Paul. "I don't want you to fraternize with my cousin anymore, Paul."

"What possible reason could you have for objecting to our friendship, Ada?"

"It's not a good thing for my help to . . . "

Paul's eyes turned hard. "You're a distrusting woman, Ada. Why is that?"

"I've lived a lot longer than you; therefore I've seen much dishonesty. The reason I've succeeded thus far is because I've made it a policy never to trust anyone."

"Why?"

"I've just told you the reason. Do not interrogate me."

"Well, I'm telling you that I'm going to continue to see Gusty as often as she'll allow it, so do not—do you hear me—do not raise your objections any more."

Ada drew back as if she had been struck. Her face turned crimson. "How brazen of you to order me, Paul. I've fired many attorneys in my life, and I'm not adverse to firing you."

His smile mocked her. "Okay. Fire me."

Ada's eyes flickered, her lower lip twitched. "I . . . I said I wasn't adverse to firing you. I'm not firing you yet."

Paul's silent gaze further unsettled Ada. He scooted his chair back and stood, his eyes still locked on hers; then he abruptly turned and strode out of the room.

Paul waited at the foot of the stairs. Soon Gustavia came running down dressed in jeans and a sweat shirt, her eyes shining like sunlit sable. Her dark hair was pulled back into one long braid down her back, enhancing the delicate bones of her face. He watched her, entranced.

He grinned. "Come friend," he emphasized, holding the crook of his arm toward her.

She took his arm and they left. She sighed as they moved down the sidewalk. "Thank you, Paul. I needed this."

"And so did I."

"You were left alone with the tigress. How did you manage?"

"I left her shaking in her shoes."

Gustavia laughed.

After Paul had changed, he led Gustavia back up along Ada's street, Federal Heights, on past her house. As they moved up the street, the homes became larger and more magnificent.

"I walk up here often and admire these homes, Paul."

He smiled. "The people who live in these summer homes are a spillover from Kennebunkport, the popular summer area for the rich and famous."

Federal Heights curved and when they reached the bend, Paul pointed to the most imposing and magnificent of the homes, the Belford Mansion built in the Federal style.

"The town is named after the Belfords. I've heard that they were tired of the tourists in Kennebunkport, so they bought acreage here and built this home. Others from their same social strata followed suit. The homes all have names. That one, built in the Georgian style," he said, pointing, "is called Wildwood Manor. The one across the street is Pinecrest Hall. The one next to it is called Falls Creek Villa, and so on."

"It sounds like quite an illustrious society," murmured Gustavia.

"Oh yes. A society Ada couldn't break into if she wanted to."

"Somehow I don't picture either her or Edgar being sociable enough to want to."

It wasn't long before they reached an uninhabited area. Paul took Gustavia's hand and led her to a path, almost hidden by wild bushes and trees."

"How delightful!" Gustavia exclaimed. "I didn't know this path was here."

"It's a shortcut to the river. These bushes are wild blueberry bushes. In Maine, the blueberry is king. I'll have to bring you here in August, and we'll go blueberry picking."

"How utterly delightful. I can hardly wait. Unless," she frowned, "I'm not here in August."

At that very moment Gustavia tripped and would have fallen if Paul hadn't grabbed her, pulling her to him.

"The woods are rather dense aren't they?" she managed, looking up at him, struggling to hide her confusion at the feel of Paul's arms holding her tightly.

Paul wasn't confused at all. The sensation of holding her in his arms was a bonus he was thoroughly enjoying. He wasn't in any hurry to let her go. "They are. The frequent rains keep things growing and green." When she squirmed, he took her hand and together they ducked under limbs and stepped around the foliage. He stopped suddenly and put his finger to his lips. "There's a red-winged blackbird on that limb over there," he whispered. While they gazed at its glossy black feathers and red shoulder patches, it sang. Its song, a liquid, gurgling *konk-la-reee*, ended in a trill.

"How lovely," Gustavia whispered.

When they reached the river, Paul studied it. "Much of the time the river is brackish brown, but tonight it's deep blue—just for us."

Paul let go of Gustavia's hand and they walked slowly in comfortable silence along the worn path on the bank of the Kennebec.

"The pine trees along the bank make the river so beautiful, Paul. But I see other kinds of trees interspersed. What are they?"

"That one over there is a basswood tree. And there's a maple and a poplar. The taller one is an oak."

"This state is as green as England I believe."

He nodded, appearing to contemplate the similarities.

Gustavia found her curiosity about Paul increasing daily. "Tell me more about your family, Paul." She could sense a slight tension, a tightening in him, then after a moment or two he seemed to relax, as if he had come to some decision.

"My father's a judge and is still working. My mother is at home working at trying to get my father to attend all the social functions. Equally important to her is arranging family get-togethers as often as possible."

"That's nice. Tell me more about your brother and sisters."

"I have two older sisters who're married and have children. I'm next in line. I have a brother thirteen months younger than I, and he's married with three small children."

"You're the only one in your family not married then?"

"I'm afraid so."

"Are you close to your brother and sisters?"

He was silent a moment. "I'm especially close to my brother. We've been best friends growing up, you might say."

"I guess one could say I had a brother who was my best friend."

"Freddie?"

"Yes."

"Hmm, how can you marry your brother?" he bantered, his eyes twinkling with mischief.

Gustavia smiled, her eyes gazing at the trees in the distance as she remembered saying that very thing to Freddie long ago.

"Do you mind me asking how you lost track of Freddie?"

"I do mind a little. When I allow myself to think about it, I always end up in the doldrums." She told him anyway, beginning with their trip to Cornwall. When she was through, she added wistfully, "I still have the letters I wrote to him that he never got."

"You do?"

Something in Paul's voice made her turn and look at him. The minute she did, whatever his expression, it changed to a smile before she caught it.

"I'd like to read them," he said.

"Why?"

"They would help me know what you were like as a child." When she didn't respond, he asked. "Did you ever find the people who adopted Freddie?"

"No. Mr. Fretwell tried to find them in London, but was unable to do so." She paused. "While we were still in Cornwall, Mr. Fretwell asked Mum to marry him so he could leave something to her in his will. His deceased wife's sisters wouldn't have allowed it otherwise. He told her it would be a marriage in name only."

"Did she marry him?"

"Yes, when we returned to Hessle. A short while later he informed her that because his health was not improving, he had decided to sell his home and shop. He bought his cousin's cottage in Cornwall. Mum told me that she was glad about this because living next door to the orphanage was proving too hard on me. I was becoming apathetic."

"You moved to Cornwall?" he asked surprised.

Again Gustavia looked over at Paul. "Why do you sound surprised?"

"For some reason I thought you had lived all your life in Hessle or near there."

"We lived in Cornwall from then on and Mr. Fretwell still kept looking for the people who adopted Freddie, but we never found them."

"Gustavia," Paul began hesitantly, "I've been wanting to ask you about your mother. Where is she?"

"She died of viral pneumonia when I was in my fourth year of college."

Paul grew silent. He rubbed his brow, clearly troubled.

"What is it, Paul?"

"I . . . I'm just very sorry to hear about your mother. You are alone in the world. I . . . I'm sorry that Ada and Edgar aren't better relatives to you."

Gustavia was touched by his sincere sympathy. "Thank you, Paul."

The sun dipped behind a grove of trees and fingers of pink spread across the gold horizon. Paul took hold of Gustavia's hand and they turned back. The Kennebec glistened gold and pink as it rippled beside them.

Gustavia felt a contentment she hadn't felt since her mother died. Paul was proving to be a caring friend. Still—she didn't really know him. Had she perceived something intangible in his reactions? His logical answers put them to rest, but—a prickle of uneasiness slipped into her flowering tranquillity like the thorn on the stem of a beautiful rose—you reach for the beauty only to prick your finger and protectively pull away.

❧CHAPTER 15❦

Ada was cold and aloof with Paul the following Thursday as they went over the legal problems in Ludlow. He smiled to himself as he remembered calling her bluff Tuesday. It was apparent she realized it would be disastrous to the business to change attorneys at this particular time. However, when things were settled, he had no doubt she would fire him. What she didn't know was it would be his choice whether he left or stayed. It was almost certain that he would have to fly to England to work out the Redmores' problems, and this was to his advantage. He had to get one more piece of information and he would have all the evidence he needed—then control would be in his hands.

His private investigation had been going on for several months. When Gustavia arrived, his impatience to finish it up increased tenfold. While in the same room, he could hardly take his eyes off her. He watched her every chance he could. And this afternoon, the only way he could describe her was adorable. Papers were spread out on the floor in front of her desk and she was sitting there reorganizing them. She wore another old-fashioned outfit of dark gray cotton with a white collar, on the front of which was a large red bow. Instead of a skirt, she wore the same color of knee-length bloomer-like pants. Shoeless, she wore black knee socks. Her hair was held in a bouffant by a clip allowing one long, thick strand to hang loose at the back of her head, gracefully curled over her left shoulder as she bent over the papers. Ordinarily, he only noticed the overall effect of women's clothes. Never had he examined them in detail until this dark-eyed nymph showed up wearing clothing from two different centuries.

She glanced up and caught him watching her. Her immediate smile lit up the whole room, lifting the heaviness that permeated everything around Ada.

Boldly, he asked, "Hey Gusty, how about dinner tonight?"

Ada looked up, her eyes shooting daggers. Before she could speak, Gustavia answered him.

"I would love to, Paul," she said, forgetting the twinge of ambivalence she felt two nights ago.

"Great!" He turned back to Ada. "Would you tell Carol we won't be here for dinner?"

"I'm going to tell Carol that you will never be dining with us again, Paul."

"That's cruel and unusual punishment, Ada," he replied. "Remember, I'm a poor bachelor who hates to cook."

"You're trying to elicit my sympathy when you've informed me that you intend to continue seeing my cousin despite my objections?"

Paul grinned. "Ada, you need to develop a sense of humor."

This only exacerbated her indignation. "I will not have you taking time out during our session to arrange your liaisons."

"You're right, Ada. Sorry. You see, when Gustavia smiles at me I can't help myself. Excuse me, but I must err one more time. "Tonight, wear what you have on, Gusty," he said. "You look enchanting."

Gustavia cast a glance at Ada, expecting a more caustic rebuke from her. Instead, an expression of a resolute nature appeared on her face and the muscles in her thin jaw rippled.

"Thank you for inviting me out tonight, Paul," Gustavia said as they drove toward Augusta. "It seems more stifling every day in that office with Ada. If it weren't for your presence now and then, I think I might suffocate."

"If it weren't for your presence, Gusty, I too might not be able to endure working for her, in spite of the lucrative fees she pays."

"How did you ever manage to extract anything resembling 'a lucrative fee' from my cousin?"

"She had no choice at the time she hired me. But I'm certain she'll soon put out feelers for a new attorney. For now, she has to put up with me."

"I hope you can at least stay until I'm through with her history."

"I will. You can be assured of that."

Gustavia looked over at him, surprised at the hard edge in his voice. "How can you be so sure? You're constantly baiting her and displeasing her."

Paul only smiled, and changed the subject. "Gusty, I find you enigmatic. Tell me about your life in Cornwall."

"I find you mysterious, Paul." Gustavia noted an evasive expression appear briefly.

"Oh? But I asked you first."

"All right," she answered hesitantly. "When we moved to Cornwall, my friend Enid helped me keep my mind off of Freddie. We were best of chums all through school. Living in Cornwall was wonderful. But I so often wished Freddie could have been there to enjoy it.

"I wasn't confined to Mr. Fretwell's small yard any longer. Enid and I had freedom to roam the coastal paths and seaside cliffs. It's so beautiful in the spring. The hillsides are covered with lush greenery, meadow grass and wild flowers. There are fields of daffodils, and sometimes when we were carefully stepping through them, flocks of skylarks flew over, trilling and warbling as they passed." She sighed and smiled. "We let our imaginations run wild. We were princesses living in castles; we were orphans trying to survive out in the wilderness; we were beautiful girls being courted by handsome, brave men."

Paul chuckled. "When you were pretending to be all these things, I was playing Batman, army spies, war and sabotage, and astronauts in rocket ships."

Gustavia smiled knowingly. "When Freddie and I played together, I tried to coax him into playing house with me. When I succeeded, I would be the mother and make him be the father. I was in heaven when he submitted to this, but always to my disappointment, it wasn't long before he got bored and wanted to play soccer or something."

Paul laughed long and hard. "I'm sorry," he said finally. "I think if I were Freddie I would have loved to play house with you."

Gustavia threw a skeptical glance at him. "You're speaking from a grown-up-boy perspective, aren't you?"

"Yeah. I guess you're right," he admitted. "Tell me where you went to college, Gusty."

"Enid and I attended Cambridge University together. We even took many of the same classes."

"What did you graduate in?"

"Costume history, then I got a Masters in costume and clothing design."

"Why did you begin dressing like you do now?"

Gustavia became thoughtful. "It's rather complicated, Paul. I don't know if I can explain it to you. There are many facets to it. From what I've seen the short time I've been in America, I believe England is even more fashion conscious. Mum used to say, 'Everyone follows Paris and London like a bunch of sheep.'"

Paul chuckled. "That's about the way it is here."

"You know," Gustavia mused, "everyone wants to feel included, and so we follow the latest fad. But, sometimes, I feel like being a bit naughty— just for a lark—and wear something different."

Paul laughed.

"I'm glad that amuses you," she said smiling. "I must say, you've been a good sport about putting up with it. Also I get bored wearing the same style day in and day out. Then—"

The pause that followed was so pronounced, Paul glanced at her. "Then what?" When she turned her face to his, he noted that her light-heartedness had disappeared.She sighed and gazed through the windshield at the fast moving scenery. "Then at times I would look at the latest style from Mum's eyes and realize that that particular style was not very becoming, especially on girls and women who weren't slender."

As if to herself, she spoke quietly. "During my years at the university, different styles came and went. Some I felt very uncomfortable wearing. Though I'm fascinated with the history of fashion, my preference is fashion design—more on the lines of what would enhance the femininity of all women."

Arriving at the restaurant, Paul parked the car and shifted in his seat to face her, but he stared past her, his eyes far away. "I once read a 1905 quote by an art critic, Samuel Isham. For some reason it seemed to strike a chord with me, so I memorized it. It went something like this: *The American people have no goddesses or saints . . . but something of that goddess, saint or heroine . . . they find in the idealization of their womankind. It is the grace of children, the tenderness of motherhood, the beauty and purity of young girls that they demand. The American girl is placed upon a pedestal.* Paul's eyes focused on hers.

Tears in Gustavia's eye's turned them into dark liquid pools. "You understand," she said simply. He nodded. "But that was in 1905," she added softly.

"Is that why you like to dress in . . ."

"Partly," she answered. "But not all. I've dwelt, at times, on the late 19th century and the early 20th century simply because I longed to live in a more gracious era where women could be women and men valued them as such, just as your art critic said."

She turned and stared out the window. "From my perspective, those times of the world seemed more gentle—not so coarse and immoral. But, of course, every age had its evils, so that's not realistic. I know that. At first, I thought those were the main reasons I've been more drawn to those eras than others, but there's another more indefinable reason, one I don't understand, which hovers all about me and deep inside." She gave him a sideways glance of bewilderment and shrugged her shoulders.

"Now you've really got me curious."

She studied him curiously. "I've never shared this with anyone, actually. What is it about you that lets me be myself?"

His smiling eyes contradicted his serious demeanor. "I suppose you sense that I'm your friend. Shall we go in?"

Gustavia admired the large impressive Senator Inn as Paul led her toward the entrance. After the hostess had seated them at a table, she looked around the room. Each table was covered with a white cloth, fresh flower center pieces and fancy folded napkins. Rose padded seats flanked the booths in front of the side windows.

She smiled at Paul. "This is what I call gracious dining."

"I brought you here because they have great desserts."

Her eyes twinkled with eagerness. "Maybe we should order dessert first."

Paul chuckled. "I've always thought that would be a good idea, especially when I was a boy."

After they had each ordered lobster, Gustavia said, "Now it's your turn to answer some questions."

"Not yet, Gusty. I'm not through asking you. I have a partial reason for why you dress like you do. Now, I want to know when did you start?"

Her brows crinkled in thought. "You know . . . it came on so gradually, I hardly know for certain. I think it was in my third year of college that I began wearing parts of such clothing now and then. I do know, by all the flack I got—calling me a bit of an odd ball and all that—that I was wearing them quite consistently during my fourth year."

Paul's half-smile spread into a charming wide one. "I would like to have been there and watched it all. I'd like to think I would have cheered you on. What did you do after you graduated?"

"You're very curious—for a man."

"It's more than curiosity, Gusty. I'm interested in what makes you tick."

"I don't think there's anything I could possibly tell you that would help you know that, but since you asked, I'll go on. Enid and I both got our masters in costume and clothing design. Mum had already passed away and I was having a difficult time. Enid tried to talk me into going to Paris with her and work in the fashion design industry, but I wanted to remain at Cambridge and work as a teacher's assistant in the costume design department and start working on my doctorate."

"How did you pay for college, let alone the expense your graduate studies incurred?"

"Mum had saved a little through the years. Mr. Fretwell passed away right after I graduated from high school and left Mum well taken care of, including the house in Cornwall as well as a college fund for me."

"How fortunate for you and your mother. How long were you at Cambridge?"

"After I got my doctorate, I spent a couple years teaching there. Enid begged me once more to join her in Paris, assuring me that I'd have a job. I was intrigued so I didn't renew my teaching contract and left for Paris the next summer. I got the job because the head of personnel was amazed that I had designed, made and wore such a variety of period clothing." She let out a small lilting laugh. "It seems in the fashion world it pays to be different—somewhat off-beat."

"How did you like working in the Paris fashion world?"

She let the question stand while she stared at the tablecloth with unfocused eyes. Almost inaudibly she began. "The atmosphere and lifestyle in the fashion design industry became rather oppressive to me." She lifted her eyes to his and saw what looked like appreciation.

He finally spoke, "A while back, Gusty, you asked me about my love life. Now it's my turn. Did you date anyone seriously while in college or consent to go out with any one of those Frenchmen who, I'm sure, were smitten the moment they saw you?"

"I dated in college and in Paris, but I chose to go out less and less because . . . oh, actually, Paul, my dating has not been eventful at all."

The waitress brought their lobster.

They concentrated on their food for a while. Gustavia swallowed a mouthful. "This lobster's delicious." Taking a breath, she said, "Now Mr. Camden, enough about me. I have a few questions to ask of you."

"Shoot."

"Have you had many girlfriends?"

"Bunches." He grinned.

"You said you were nearly married once. How long were you serious with her?"

"For a week or two."

"You're being evasive, Paul."

His eyes stared past her, far away again. "I think I became serious with her after we'd dated for about three months. I came very close to marrying her. But, as I said, I couldn't go through with it."

Her eyes were large and curious. "Why?"

He shrugged his shoulders. "Oh, I don't know. It didn't feel right for some reason."

"I feel sorry for her."

"Why?" he asked, surprised.

"I don't know you very well, but from what I do know, you seem to be what one would call—a catch." She grinned. "That makes you sound like a fish, doesn't it?"

He laughed. "Maybe a fish just waiting to be caught? Since you feel that I'm a 'catch,' do you think we could get past this friendship-only thing?"

"Oh, Paul. Really now. You said . . ."

"That I did. So . . . what shall we talk about?"

"Since I've missed most of Freddie's growing up years, tell me what you liked to do when you were eleven, twelve and on up?"

"That will take days and weeks. I guess we'll have to spend a lot of time together, won't we?" he asked, his eyes looking deeply into hers.

Gustavia blinked, then quickly looked down and rubbed her finger over the tablecloth. "I'm not sure it's fair to you, but I think I would enjoy that." She glanced up. "As you know, I look forward to spending time with you. It helps me get through the days with Ada."

"That's good enough for me, Gusty," he replied softly.

ᔓCHAPTER 16ᔓ

The dinner date helped Gustavia get through Friday and the week-end. She continued to work Saturday and Sunday hoping to hurry the project along. At the same time, she hoped Paul would show up and rescue her for a little while. Sunday was the loneliest day for her, and she found herself wondering what Paul did on the weekends when he didn't come to Belford.

Monday morning, Ada off-handedly mentioned that Paul had flown to England on Saturday to take care of a business problem.

"Oh. How long will he be there?" Gustavia asked, trying to sound casual.

"As long as he needs to, Gustavia."

Ada's house suddenly felt empty and lonely. She decided the only way she was going to survive the week without Paul was to throw herself into Ada's history with a vengeance.

Lately, she realized that no matter how she tried to hurry the project along, the more glitches Ada found in her work. An unsettling thought eased its way into her mind. *Is Ada finding fault with my work so she can tell Edgar it's not working out?*

"This just can't go on much longer!" she muttered to herself.

"What?" Ada asked.

"Oh. Nothing. I was just talking to myself."

"Don't. It disturbs me."

Thursday morning, during tea break, Gustavia restlessly looked through the bookcase in the library. Her eyes rested on a large Bible pushed up against one end, thinking how the size contrasted with the tiny Bibles her mother had given her and Freddie years ago. *Why haven't I noticed it before?* she wondered. Pulling it out, she sat down on the floor and opened it. On the first page in beautiful penmanship was inscribed, *The Sullivan Family Bible.* Her heart skipped a beat. Carefully she turned the worn page. She sucked in her breath as she gazed at an incomplete pedigree chart of John Sullivan and Sarah White—names she had never heard before! The cities and dates were indistinct. She could decipher the names, but the rest was blurred. Her eyes moved down to Fanny Sullivan and her sister Melissa Sullivan. John and Sarah Sullivan were Fanny Sullivan's parents! What a treasure! These should be included in Ada's history! *Why hasn't she given this to me? Mum didn't have any of this information!*

"What are you doing, Gustavia?" Ada asked, as she returned from tea.

"Ada! I mean, Cousin Ada, why haven't you given me this information?" She indicated the volume. "Surely, you would know that this would be important to me." The expression on Ada's face caused her to rush on. "Besides, this pedigree should be put in your history."

"It most certainly should not. I do not want anyone in Grimsby to know that I'm connected to the scandal surrounding your grandmother Fanny. Those things have a way of getting around."

"You keep referring to a scandal. I want to know about this so-called scandal."

"You will never hear it from my lips, Gustavia. Mother disavowed any relationship with her sister, Fanny."

Gustavia stood up, shoved the Bible back on the shelf and faced Ada, her voice low with anger. "If you've disavowed Fanny, why do you keep throwing her and her alleged scandal up to me?"

"To let you know that I'm actually doing you a favor by disregarding what happened in the past and acknowledging that you are a relative."

With all the willpower Gustavia could muster, she swallowed a scathing retort. She whirled around, went back over to the computer and began typing. The pages she typed were meaningless, something to keep her from acting rashly as she fought to get the anger under control.

Never able to hold on to anger long, Gustavia's mind returned to something more pleasant—the small pedigree chart in the Bible.

Time dragged by. At 4:30, she got into her car and went over to see Edgar, hoping he was still at the office. When she walked in, his face lit up as it always did, whether it was here or at Ada's.

"Gustavia! You just made my day brighter."

"I don't know if you'll feel like that when I tell you that my patience is getting thin. It seems Ada is harder to please lately and it's taking longer to write her biography because of it. I don't know why you can't tell me what you know—now. I promise I'll finish her biography."

Edgar rubbed his brow, suddenly looking tired. "I believe you, Gustavia, but it's a little more complicated than that. Please be patient. I have reasons for my delay."

"I found the Sullivan family Bible in Ada's library. I didn't even know our grandparents' names were John and Sarah Sullivan. Can't you at least tell me more about our ancestors?"

He looked puzzled. "I don't know much more than that myself, Gustavia. I guess all I've done is work from morning till night in the family businesses. My interests have been rather narrow."

"Then what in the world did you promise me? Wasn't it information on the family?" she burst out in frustration.

"It will be information about your family, but of a different kind. That's all I can say for the moment."

Disappointed, Gustavia sighed in resignation. "All right, Edgar. I'll keep working on Ada's biography, but what you have had better be worth it. Ada is unbending."

"I know, Gustavia," he said wearily, "I know."

Gustavia and Ada ate in silence. After dessert, Ada sipped her tea and read the paper while Gustavia excused herself and went for a walk. When she returned, Ada was no longer in the dining room. Moving quietly to the library, she saw Ada at her desk. Frustrated, Gustavia went upstairs to her room.

She took a shower and got ready for bed early, hoping that this would give Ada time enough to go to her own room. In her nightgown and bare feet, she left her bedroom and went down the stairs. Though a rug covered the steps, they creaked. She hadn't noticed it before. Hoping Ada hadn't heard, she slipped down the hall and peeked into the library. Ada was gone. She could see through the tall window that it was beginning to darken. Shafts of light from the curbside lamp shed light on the chestnut trees outside the window, softening the room.

She stopped and listened before she took another step. Why she felt the need to be secretive, she didn't know. Nevertheless, she quickly went over to the bookshelf, picked up the Bible, slipped out of the library, down the hall and up the stairs to her room. Locking the door, she got a pencil and paper, then sitting on the window seat, copied carefully every detail of the information she could decipher. Since the dates and places were virtually unreadable, she put down her best guesses. She sighed with satisfaction when she was through. What she was going to do with this wonderful information, she had no idea. Closing the Bible, she took it back downstairs and returned it to the shelf.

With the lights out, she lay in bed staring at the moonlight streaming through the turret windows and breathing deeply of the fresh air that floated through the right center one, the only one that opened. Before getting into bed, she had knelt and prayed. She thanked God for her marvelous discovery—for the incomplete, but tangible knowledge of her connection to the Sullivan family. She prayed to know that if there were any personal information about the Sullivans somewhere that she would find it, someway—somehow.

Tears trickled down her temples as she lay there. "Oh, Mum, if only you were here. We could search together." As she thought about it, hopelessness descended upon her. "How could I possibly find anything more?" Out of nowhere a memory flashed into her consciousness. She sat up in bed. "Yes!" One day when reading a newspaper, she had come across an article about the Mormon Church having the largest genealogical research facility in the world in Salt Lake City. They even had a Web site on the Internet! It seemed like a direct answer to her prayer!

Excited, she could no longer stay in bed. She paced the floor, thinking, then made a rash and impulsive decision. "I'll fly out to Salt Lake City tomorrow morning if I can get a flight." She flew out of her room, down the stairs and into the library. Turning on her desk lamp, she looked up airlines in the phone book, called, and made a reservation. It cost more than she expected, but she didn't care. As she returned to her room, Gustavia's heart pounded with adrenalin while she packed a suitcase, not allowing herself to think of Ada's reaction.

"You are what?" Ada almost shrieked.

"I'm catching a plane in Augusta this morning. I have some business to take care of."

"What business?"

"It's private, Cousin Ada. I'll work on another weekend to catch up. The work on your history won't suffer, I promise."

Ada studied her suspiciously. "Are you meeting someone? Is that it?"

"No, I'm not. You have nothing to worry about."

"I want you to know, Gustavia, that your work is not totally satisfactory. Also, you have disregarded my concern about associating with my attorney, and now this—leaving before my history is done—is unconscionable.

"I'm sorry, but I have to leave nevertheless. I have reservations to return Sunday evening. So you see, I'll be gone just a short time."

❦CHAPTER 17❦

Coming from the Salt Lake International Airport, the cab driver turned onto a street called West Temple, pointing out a large gray building in the middle of the block.

"That's the building where they do genealogy that you asked about. The Mormon Church calls it the Family History Library. Across the street, behind that gray wall is the area called Temple Square—so all the streets surrounding it are called Temple: West Temple, South Temple and so forth."

"Interesting," Gustavia said.

He turned right at the next corner onto South Temple, slowing down as he approached the Plaza Hotel. It was a fourteen story, cream colored building. Turning into the roundabout in front of the hotel, he said, "You wanted a hotel near the Family History Library and this is as close as you can get. It's just around the corner."

"It couldn't be more convenient. Thank you."

The driver got out and opened the door for Gustavia. She paid him, swallowing hard at the fee. She had already paid an exorbitant price for a one-day advance airline ticket. Picking up her small bag, she entered the hotel and found they had a room available. Luck was with her!

After registering, she took her bag up to the room on the fifth floor and freshened up. She changed from the pants she had traveled in to a skirt and blouse, then leaving her room, rode down to the lobby. Going directly to a restaurant on the corner called JB's, she ordered a sandwich for lunch.

Finishing her meal, she walked slowly next door to the Family History Library. She noticed that the street was lined with trees on both sides, and flowers were planted everywhere, even in the middle of the street! She caught a glimpse of a large dome-shaped building across the street, almost hidden by trees. Next to it she saw an older gray stone building that looked like an old church in England. These intriguing structures, enclosed by a tall gray stucco wall on a base of sandstone bricks, were the area the cab driver called Temple Square.

She walked past the Library to see what the building was next to it. On the front were intriguing bas-relief sculptures. It was called the Museum of Church History and Art. On an impulse she moved toward it then stopped, reminding herself of her mission and how little time she had. Set back in between the buildings was an interesting old log cabin.

Turning her attention to the History Library, she studied it. It was a large light gray building, maybe granite. Above the glassed entry were several stories of glass windows. Flowers were planted all around the center, the cabin and the museum.

As she walked toward the entrance, she noticed that flanking it on both sides were black and white banners with what appeared to be pictures of people from the 19th century. The bottom of each banner said something that spoke to her heart: *Discover Your Family*. When she entered, she stopped in her tracks—a huge oil painting covered the whole wall in front of her a few yards away. Christ in white was standing in the middle, and people were all around him portrayed in the most unusual ways.

Immediately, a very attractive mature woman with blonde hair approached her. "May I help you?" she asked, a beautiful and warm smile on her face.

"Oh, yes, thank you," Gustavia replied. She noticed the woman wore a black tag with a white name on it that said, Sister Hunt. *What an odd first name*, she thought. She told Ms. Hunt what she was there for, and was directed to an open room on the left to hear and see a fifteen minute presentation concerning how to do family history research. Ms. Hunt also told her that the British Isle research area was downstairs in basement Two.

Gustavia thanked her and was about to enter the room when she saw on the left wall a picture of a well-known American movie and TV star and her family tree above it. "Amazing," she muttered to herself. The room had twelve deeply cushioned benches. Seating herself, she saw pictures of families on the left wall accompanied by old letters and records. *This certainly is where I need to be!* she thought. To her right was a wall of glass revealing a large room with people at computers and tables. Behind them were rows and rows of books.

The presentation was so full of information it was confusing.

Taking the elevator down to basement 2, she entered a large room much like the one upstairs. It had forty computers, Ms. Hunt had told her. There were also rows of books and rows of machines that she later learned were microfilm machines.

Directly in front of her was a large circular information desk. Soon, a man with another black and white name tag offered his help.

She stared at his name tag and smiled at herself. "Upstairs, I thought the lady's first name was 'Sister,' but I see yours is 'Brother.' I think I understand now."

He smiled. "In the Church of Jesus Christ of Latter-day Saints, we believe we're all brothers and sisters. So at times we call each other that."

"So it appears." She showed him her small pedigree line taken from the Bible.

"You have question marks by where they were born." he stated.

"They were smudged with age, so I just guessed that they were born in Grimsby or nearby."

"Have you used a computer before, Miss . . . ?"

"Browne. Yes."

He smiled. "Good," he said, leading her to a computer. He then showed her step by step how to begin the search.

"Thank you," she breathed, her heart pounding with excitement.

Twenty minutes went by with no success, she looked around for help. Behind her, a young man was looking over her shoulder. Somewhat startled, she asked, "Is there something wrong?" she whispered.

"Yes," he whispered back. "That's my computer."

"Yours? I thought these belonged to the library."

"They do. But that's the computer I want to use."

Gustavia looked around and saw a computer that wasn't being used. "There's one over there that isn't occupied," she said pointing.

"I don't want to use that one. I want to use this one."

"You aren't serious, of course," she replied, smiling.

Though a spark of humor appeared in his blue eyes, he didn't return her smile. "I am serious."

"Well, if that's the case, all I can say is—that's your problem. Now, if you'll excuse me, I need to get back to my research." Sensing that the man had backed away, but was still standing behind her, she postponed getting some help until he left. She concentrated on her task, wondering if John Sullivan had been born in another part of the British Isles, maybe Wales, Scotland or Ireland. When she checked several cities in each, no John Sullivan name came up. Scooting back her chair, she stood up to go get help and almost bumped into the man who had accused her of using his computer. Standing firm, his arms folded.

"Excuse me!" she stated indignantly, then realized the volume of her voice was out of place in this room where people worked and talked quietly.

"You need help?" he whispered.

"Yes, I do. But not from you."

Before she could take a step, a silver-haired woman came over, her face warm and pleasant. "May I help you?"

"Oh, yes. Thank you. I can't call up the names I need. I thought they were born in England, but I can't find them."

"Are there other names you could try?"

"A sister named Melissa Sullivan."

"May I try?" the woman asked.

"Oh, please. Thank you."

She watched the woman start the search. Gustavia glanced at the man in irritation. He winked at her, exacerbating her annoyance, then walked away.

"Are you certain these dates are correct?" the woman asked.

"I copied them out of the Sullivan family Bible. I guess I could have copied them down wrong or read them wrong. The page was very old."

"Come with me, miss, and I'll show you where you can buy some instruction booklets on how to do research, and how to research in the British Isles."

"Thank you." She took a step, stopped and turned to the man. Her look shot daggers at him, daring him to usurp the computer, then followed the woman.

Gustavia returned, thrilled with the armful of booklets she had purchased and some free brochures. She found the man again standing behind her chair! She tried to keep her voice down. "Sir, I would think your legs would be tired by now. You see, I intend to use this computer for what is left of today, all evening, and all day tomorrow if it's available. You may have it as long as you want after that."

"Why won't you be using it after that?" he asked.

"Because I'm flying back to Maine Sunday morning."

"Maine? Hmm. You've come a long way. Well, good. I'm glad the computer will be free after that, unless I beat you to it tomorrow morning."

Placing her books down and seating herself, she looked up at him, puzzled now. "I suggest you might consider getting some professional counseling concerning your obsession with this computer."

The man laughed. "Thank you for the suggestion. What's your name?"

"Really now. That's none of your concern. Please, if you're intent on standing there, do not talk to me." She picked up a booklet and began studying it. So engrossed in what she was reading, she didn't notice when he left. Relieved to discover him gone, she experimented on the genealogical Web site and had a wonderful time until she realized she was hungry.

She gathered up her things and went next door to the convenient JB's and had a salad and a bowl of soup. On her way back to the library, she eyed the mysterious gray wall that encompassed Temple Square. Her curiosity grew, tempting her to stay a day longer to go see inside. Deciding she didn't want to incur more of Ada's wrath, she would return Sunday as she had promised. But with this decision, came another one voiced out loud. "But I'm not going to be held back by Ada much longer! I'll enlist Edgar's help if I have to, in order to finish it in a reasonable length of time." She was still talking to herself when she entered the library.

She found the computer she had been using occupied, but quickly discovered another available one. The rest of the evening she spent practicing using the Web site. In the back of her mind, she was determined to go back and find out from Ada one way or another where the Sullivans were born. The excitement of it all kept her going till the library closed at 10 P.M. The adrenalin which had raced through her left her depleted and exhausted.

As she stepped out the door, she gasped. The beautiful spires she had glimpsed through the trees, were now lit up. With regret, she headed toward the hotel.

Saturday morning, Gustavia didn't reach the Library until 9:30. She had been so keyed up the night before, she was unable to sleep, so she read her newly acquired material until 2:00 A.M. Hoping that the obtrusive man wouldn't show up today, she tentatively looked around. Relieved that he was nowhere in sight, she found only one computer available.

With more knowledge, she began searching for names she had known throughout her life. Finding success with Enid and her family, she was excited. Each time she explored, she learned more. At one o'clock she stopped for lunch.

Upon her return, she had to wait for an available computer. While waiting, she looked through the booklets she had purchased. At 3:00 a computer became available, and once more she began searching. Feeling someone behind her, she turned. Shocked to see the same man back, her dark eyes smoldered. "Why are you *here*? As you see, I'm not using *your* computer."

"Yes, you are. This is the one I want to use." Again, she saw a twinkle in his eyes, but no smile on his face.

Gustavia shook her head and let out a small quiet laugh. "What game are you playing, Mr. . . . uh . . ."

"Why should I tell you my name when you won't tell me yours?"

She stood up, placed her hands on her hips and looked up into his face, studying him. "Are you hitting on me?"

"Why would you think that?" he asked, raising his brows innocently.

"How else could one explain your ridiculous actions?"

"Maybe we can discuss it over dinner tonight?"

"You are hitting on me!" Heads around them turned and she put her hand over her mouth, then whispered, "Sorry."

"All right, so I'm guilty as charged," he whispered. "So will you?"

Gustavia gaped at him, then let out an impatient breath. "Sorry. I don't go out with strangers."

"I can be vouched for by that lady over there. She works here. She knows me and my family. I'm really a good guy, honest. Scout's honor." He held up his hand exhibiting the scout sign. "You know, honest, trustworthy and all that."

She couldn't help smiling. "Honest maybe, but a bit unconventional, I would say. I'm sorry, but I don't have time." Turning, she sat, trying to ignore him.

He stepped to the side of her and smiled. "Please, Miss . . . uh, . . ." She didn't offer her name, so he continued. "I want to take you to dinner at The Roof."

Her head swivelled toward him. "The roof? Isn't that a bit dangerous?" she teased.

He laughed. "It's on the top floor of a building on the other side of Temple Square. It looks out over the temple, and the food is great. Since you're a visitor here, I think you might find it something to go home and talk about."

It sounded wonderful to Gustavia, but she had been so irritated she had to think about it a moment. In the meantime, she studied him. His face had an open and honest appearance. In fact, it was boyish looking because of the freckles. It seemed foolish to trust him, but somehow she did. "I've been so annoyed at you, my inclination is to say no. However, it does sound intriguing."

"Great! What time will you be through here?"

"I would like to work until about 5:00. "I'm staying at the Plaza Hotel. Could you pick me up there in the lobby at 6:00?"

"I sure can! And—I'll quit bugging you now that I've accomplished what I set out to do the moment I saw you." He grinned. "What is your name?"

"Miss Browne."

"Formal, are we? Well, I'm not formal at all. My name's Artie. See you at 6:00, Miss Browne." He turned and strode quickly to the elevator.

Gustavia watched him leave. She inclined her head in thought, smiled and shrugged her shoulders, then returned to the computer. When 5:00

arrived, she was reluctant to leave even though she was looking forward to going to The Roof for dinner. *So why do I feel hesitant to leave the library?* After a moment she answered her own question. *It's because I feel peaceful in here. There's something special about the people who work here.* She sighed as she closed out and gathered her things.

❧

Gustavia put on a periwinkle button-front shirt and skirt with a white tank underneath. Glad that, though it was casual, it had a dressy air to it. She hoped it was all right to wear to The Roof.

Artie arrived on foot since he had parked his car elsewhere. What she had on was appropriate because he was dressed in a nice blue, long-sleeved cotton shirt and beige cotton pants.

"What a beautiful evening," Gustavia murmured, as they walked up the sidewalk toward their destination.

"It is, isn't it?" he grinned.

When they passed the entrance to Temple Square, Gustavia slowed down and looking in saw a breathtaking view of the spired building. "How beautiful. Is that what they call the temple?"

"Yes, it is. Have you been in Temple Square yet?" he asked.

"No. I've never even been to Salt Lake City."

"I can tell by your accent that you're English, Miss Browne."

"Yes I am. I've only been in America a short while."

"Are you a member?" he asked.

"A member of what?"

He chuckled. "I just assumed you were a member of The Church of Jesus Christ of Latter-day Saints, and that's the way we ask when we assume."

"Oh. Is that the same as the Mormon Church?"

"Yes. I take it by your answer that you're not a member."

"That's right. Are you a Mormon?"

He grinned. "'Yes, siree; dyed in the wool; true blue, through and through.'"

Gustavia smiled. "That sounds devoted."

"I am. But that's a literal quote from church history by a church leader when he was only nineteen years of age."

They arrived at the Joseph Smith Memorial Building. As they entered, Gustavia's eyes widened with admiration. "What a lovely place."

As Artie led her to the elevator, she caught sight of a large statue to her left. When she slowed down, Artie said, "We'll stop, and I'll explain who he is after we eat."

"All right."

The elevator opened on the top floor and Artie led her to the restaurant. They were greeted by the host and seated directly in front of a large window overlooking Temple Square. Gustavia gasped. "What a beautiful sight." She turned an appreciative gaze upon her escort. "Thank you for bringing me here. It was worth all the annoyance you put me through."

Artie laughed. "Then you've forgiven me?"

"I believe I have."

"In that case, let's go to the buffet and get our first fill-up," he said, standing and helping her scoot her chair back.

"We can have all we want to eat?"

"You bet," he said leading her up a couple of steps to the buffet.

"How nice. You see, I have a gargantuan appetite."

Artie looked her up and down. "You could never tell it."

"Thank you," she murmured as she eyed the array of wonderful looking appetizers, entrees and desserts. "I believe that already my eyes are larger than my stomach, as they say."

Artie laughed. "Well, give it a good try, anyway."

The evening passed delightfully for Gustavia. The conversation was kept light and she found herself laughing often at Artie's charming wit.

When Gustavia had all she could possibly eat, and swallowed the last bite of the delicious dessert, she smiled. "I'm literally stuffed! And now that I'm more than satisfied food-wise, I think it's time to satisfy my curiosity. What is your last name?"

"Banks. Artie Banks."

The name was familiar to Gustavia. "Banks. I've heard that name." Then in a shocking flash it came to her. Freddie was adopted by a Robert and Sharon Banks! She studied Artie. His face was covered with freckles just like Freddie! Also, he was blond and blue-eyed like Freddie! *Surely, it can't be!* She exhaled the breath she had been holding, and her breathing became rapid and short.

Surprised at her reaction, Artie asked, "What is it, Miss Browne?"

"Were you . . . were you adopted?" she asked breathlessly.

He inclined his head to one side, slightly incredulous. "Now why would you think to ask that? I was, as a matter of fact. My mother couldn't get pregnant. They were tired of waiting to get an infant from the adoption agency so they decided to adopt an older child, me. Then, miraculously, they had four children after that."

Gustavia's excitement increased. "My name is Gustavia." Breathlessly she watched his reaction, but was puzzled. "Does . . . does that sound familiar to you at all?"

He became silent, a bemused expression on his face. "Gustavia," he repeated. That's a most unusual name, but it doesn't sound familiar to me."

Refusing to believe his denial, she asked slowly, "Does Freddie Finch sound familiar?"

His brows drew together. "No. What's this all about?"

Gustavia's heart plummeted. She had gotten herself so worked up, she had to take several deep breaths to get hold of herself. "I, uh, have lost contact with a very dear friend by the name of Freddie Finch—and you look like him. He was adopted by a Robert and Sharon Banks. Do you know them?"

"Robert and Sharon Banks?" he repeated. "That's rather astounding. My father has a brother by the name of Robert and he had a wife named Sharon. I wonder if it's the same Robert and Sharon Banks?"

Gustavia's hopes returned. "Then you know them."

"I knew Uncle Robert when I was a boy. He frightened me a little for some reason. He left the Church and hasn't had anymore to do with the family since."

"Do you remember his wife, Sharon?"

"Not very well."

In her anxiety, Gustavia's next question came out almost in a whisper. "Do you remember your life before you were adopted?"

"He frowned. "You know . . . I don't very well, only a little here and there. I wish I did, but then maybe I don't want to remember. I don't know. I've had a happy life since I was adopted. I suppose I might have to come to grips with those gaps in my memory one day."

"Do your parents know what your life was like before?"

"The circumstances of my adoption are something my parents don't like to talk about, and for some reason neither do I."

Gustavia couldn't let it go. *He has to be Freddie! The coincidence of Robert and Sharon Banks is too great,* she thought. But disappointment that Artie couldn't remember very much weighed so heavily upon her heart she couldn't speak for a few moments.

"I see that you're disappointed that I can't answer all your questions. I'm sorry."

It came out in a whisper. "That's all right."

"Did your friend, Freddie, ever call you Gusty?"

She looked up at him shocked. "How did you know?"

"I didn't. It's a long name and I thought a good friend might shorten it to Tavia or Gusty."

"I need to go back to the hotel now, Artie."

"All right. Would you like to tour Temple Square on the way?" he asked hopefully.

She glanced at the now lit temple spires, and murmured. "It's beautiful." But her dejection and confusion were so great she shook her head. "Not tonight. Thank you."

Disappointment creased Artie's brow. "May I have your address then, Gustavia? I'll ask my parents if Uncle Robert and Aunt Sharon adopted a boy and let you know."

"Would you?" she asked, her face brightening. "If the answer is yes, do you think your father could find out where your Uncle Robert lives?"

"The last time I heard, my father didn't know his whereabouts, but maybe he can find out. I need your address and phone number. Do you have a pen and paper on you?"

"Yes." She opened her small purse and handed them to him, feeling a little more hopeful.

When they stepped off the elevator, Artie took her over to the statue of Joseph Smith and explained who he was. Seeing the preoccupation on her face, he pursued it no further. They walked back to the hotel in silence. When they arrived, Artie said, "This Freddie must have meant a lot to you."

"He did. I must go in now. Thank you for the delightful evening, Artie."

"You're welcome, Miss Gustavia Browne. You'll be hearing from me. I promise. Good night."

"Thank you. Goodnight, Artie." She watched him walk away, still wondering if he might be Freddie Finch. Her emotions were so scrambled that any option, no matter how far-fetched, could be made to sound plausible. *Maybe the adoption was so traumatic, he's suppressed the memories of his life in the orphanage, and our friendship.*

❧CHAPTER 18❦

Since Gustavia spent a restless night, she slept on the plane most of the way. But driving from Augusta State Airport to Belford, her mind flitted from the excitement of genealogical research, to the momentary exhilaration when she thought she had found Freddie, to the confusion when it appeared he might not be, and her need to find the proof one way or another. She sighed. *I hope Paul is back; I need a friend right now.* Though she had an early flight, plane changes caused her to arrive in Augusta late.

It was 11:00 P.M. when she walked into Ada's back door, just missing the incipient rainstorm. When she came to the library she saw the light on. She looked in and saw Ada at her desk. "I'm back, Cousin Ada."

"I heard you come in, Gustavia," she said, without turning. "Go on up to bed and be ready to start work in the morning."

"It's nice to see you too," she stated tartly. Ascending the stairs, Gustavia felt desperately lonely.

Quickly unpacking, she got ready, then lay in bed thinking as she listened to the thunderstorm. The rain fiercely beating upon the windows heightened her loneliness. It felt as though she had almost found Freddie. The 'almost' was painful. Her mind wandered back to another time of terrible loneliness. It was in 1986, the summer she turned seventeen. She and her mother had traveled back to Hessle once more to visit Hesslewood Orphanage hoping that somehow there would be a miracle and they could learn more about Freddie's whereabouts. In their hearts they knew it would probably be a wasted trip, but they had to try one more time.

It was dusk when they arrived at Hesslewood. Gone was the wrought-iron fence, leaving space for parking in front. It was apparently being remodeled. As they walked slowly to the front door, a flood of memories overcame them both—memories of Freddie. When they reached the entrance, a man dressed in black opened the door for them.

"May I help you?" he asked, smiling.

"Uh . . . yes. I see you're remodeling the orphanage," her mother replied.

"Orphanage? It's no longer an orphanage, ma'am. It's now the Hesslewood Hall Hotel."

"H-hotel?" Gustavia asked dumbly.

"Yes, miss. And when we're through remodeling it, it will be quite a luxurious place with elegant rooms each named after a famous person. We have an excellent restaurant also. If you need a room, we have a couple finished and ready for customers."

"Oh, uh . . . yes, we do need a room," Alice said. Charles had told her there were rumors that the orphanage might be closed and turned into a hotel, but still, her disappointment was great.

"Come over here and register and I'll show you up."

While her mother registered, Gustavia numbly stepped over to the winding stairs and gazed at the bannister, still with pegs of wood pounded into it every twelve to fifteen inches. Tears blinded her momentarily. Blinking them away, she remembered the disapproval she felt as a child when she saw the pegs, contrasting it with how she felt at the moment. Now, her heart was sad for the orphan children who had been deprived of the fun of sliding down the bannister, especially one orphan.

The man, noticing her study of the stairs, explained. "We have to keep the original stairs and bannister because of the restoration order, but we're going to take the pegs out so as to make it more comfortable for our customers. You see, they were put there to keep the orphan children from sliding down the bannister."

Gustavia nodded and her mother looked grim.

The man explained that he was the manager as he led them up to their room. He opened the door for them and with a flourish of his hand announced, "This is the Queen Victoria room. If you need anything, just let me know."

"Thank you," Alice replied.

Closing the door, they looked around. The room was very nice. There was a basket of apples on the mantle of the fireplace. Decorative dishes and silk flowers in several places gave it an elegant look. The tub in the bathroom was so long it brought a smile to Gustavia's face. "One could drown in this, Mum." Out of curiosity she turned on the faucet. Yellow water came out from the pipes. That and the draftiness around the toilet made them decide to bathe when they got home.

In the bedroom, Alice picked up a menu from a table. It looked wonderful, but they both felt too melancholy to eat. Instead they subsisted on the tea, hot chocolate and biscuits that the manager brought up to the room.

The memory of this last visit to Hesslewood only exhausted Gustavia's overworked mind, and soon she drifted off to a deep and forgetful sleep.

~

Gustavia awoke feeling a mixture of dread and excitement. Dread at having to get back to work on Ada's history and excitement at the possibility that Artie's Uncle Robert Banks was the same Banks who adopted Freddie. If so, it was possible to find Freddie—or clear up her suspicion as to whether or not Artie himself was Freddie!

In the meantime she would find a way to make Ada tell her where the Sullivans were born. A disturbing thought slipped in. She didn't have access to the Internet on the computer she was using for Ada's history. When she found out the information she needed, she couldn't search—unless she sneaked down after Ada was asleep and used her computer. With that thought, she bounced out of bed and quickly dressed for breakfast.

Ada was cold and distant, so breakfast was an ordeal. She escaped to the library as quickly as she could, knowing that if she asked if Paul were back Ada wouldn't tell her. She would just have to wait.

After her exciting and emotion-filled weekend, she could hardly keep her mind on the task before her. At 11:00 A.M., a call came for Ada. Gustavia's ears picked up when she heard Ada say Paul's name. She listened intently. Ada was speaking loudly because it was apparently long distance to England. In answer to some question, Ada said, "In that case you'll have to stay in Ludlow for another week to ten days."

Gustavia's spirits sank. How was she going to get through the week without Paul's presence? She said a prayer for help. Before long, ideas came to her, and she was actually able to accomplish much more than she had expected. In fact, she worked some on it after dinner, then retired to bed early.

Tuesday and Wednesday were more of the same; Ada's coldness cast a pall over the days, but Gustavia kept working and making good progress. She had almost enough pages for Ada to review.

After dinner Wednesday evening, Gustavia put on a pair of tan cotton pants, a blue T shirt, light matching jacket, and slipped out of the house for a walk. It was the first week of June, and the evening was beautiful. The trees were all leafed out, and flowers were blooming profusely in Ada's courtyard as well as in the other yards along Federal Heights. She breathed deeply of the fresh air, and basked in the waning sunshine, wishing she had company. Dreading to go back to Ada's dreary house, she didn't return until almost dark.

Feeling restless, she went directly to the library, picked out a book, and went upstairs to her room to read. Slipping off her shoes, she propped herself up on the bed and opened the book. Before she realized it, she was thinking about the likeable and charming Artie Banks and his unusual approach to get a date with her. She smiled. *I hope he remembers to ask his father the whereabouts of his uncle Robert Banks!* Why hadn't she gotten his address and phone number so she could contact him? *Of course he'll remember. He promised.*

↬CHAPTER 19↫

Both Gustavia and Ada were in the library when Paul arrived unexpectedly

"Paul!" Gustavia exclaimed. "I thought you were still in England."

He winked and smiled at her but greeted them in a business-like tone. "Good morning, Gustavia. Good morning, Ada."

Ada showed no surprise that Paul had returned from England earlier than instructed. Apparently he had informed her that he had been able to finish up in Ludlow sooner than expected.

He pulled up a chair beside Ada and got down to business. Gustavia tried to listen to their conversation, but she only picked up a word here and there. Their business so preoccupied them, Paul literally ignored her the whole day.

Because he never so much as glanced her way, her mind wandered to Artie Banks and her delightful weekend. She hadn't accomplished anything other than learning how to use the Web site to search for ancestors, meeting some nice people in the Family History Center and meeting Artie.

Her mind seemed to recycle the same thoughts as she relived the momentary excitement over the possibility that she might have found Freddie. She let out a tremulous breath. At least, through Artie she might be able to find him!

Promptly at 5:00 P.M., the doorbell rang.

"Go see who that is, Gustavia," Ada said, impatient at the interruption.

Glad for the respite, Gustavia went to the door. Opening it, she stared in disbelief. "Artie Banks! Wh-what are you doing here?"

"I came to see *you*, Gustavia."

Her dark eyes wide, her response was abrupt. "Why?"

Artie laughed. "That's putting it to me. Because I fell head over heels for you, and I had to see you again—soon—before you forgot me."

Gustavia was a bundle of emotions. Maybe he was here to tell her he remembered her after all and that he was Freddie or . . . No! She didn't want him here. What would Paul think? It would be embarrassing for them to meet! "Y-you're not serious of course."

"I'm dead serious. Uh . . . may I come in?"

She hesitated a moment. "Come in at your own risk," she said, stepping aside. "Cousin Ada is queen bee here."

"This is her home?" he asked, entering.

"Yes. I'm working for her temporarily."

"Gustavia!" Ada's shrill voice echoed through the hall.

"You see what I mean?" She took a deep breath and decided to get the meeting of Paul and Artie over with. "Come with me, Artie, and you may have the pleasure of meeting her. But beware of her stinger."

"Thanks for the warning."

Gustavia stopped at the library door. Her shoulders felt tense. Straightening them, she entered with Artie. "I have a guest, Cousin Ada." Ada swivelled her chair around and glared at the young man. "He's come a long way to see me. I would like you and Paul to meet Artie Banks from Salt Lake City, Utah. Artie, this is my cousin, Miss Ada Redmore, and Paul Camden, her attorney."

Artie nodded and smiled. "Glad to meet both of you."

Paul's shoulders stiffened. The astonished expression on his face changed to one of wariness. Nevertheless, he courteously stood up, stepped over to Artie and shook his hand. "Welcome to the beautiful state of Maine."

"Thank you, Paul."

Ada was not so cordial. "I'm afraid you've come a long way for very little time with Gustavia. You see, she has to work from 8:00 till 6:00."

"How long are you going to be here, Artie?" Gustavia asked before he could figure out how to respond to Ada's incivility.

"I'll be leaving Sunday morning."

"Well then, Cousin Ada, I'll have the evenings and Saturday free, won't I?" Her smile held no warmth.

Ada's lips disappeared into one tight line. Without acknowledging Gustavia's question, she spoke. "If you'll excuse us, Mr. Banks, my attorney and I must get back to work."

"Of course. Don't let me interrupt."

Gustavia took hold of Artie's arm. "I'll show you the way to the parlor." She glanced back at Paul, concerned at what he might be feeling. His eyes held hers for a moment, then he turned to his work with Ada.

Seated in the parlor, Gustavia smiled at Artie. "Now, Artie Banks, why are you really here?" she asked anxiously.

"I told you why."

"I . . . I thought maybe you had come to tell me . . ." She stopped in mid-sentence. What was she thinking? All the facts told her he wasn't Freddie Finch.

He leaned over. "Tell you what?" he asked quizzically.

"Nothing."

He looked doubtful.

"Really," she added.

He studied her interesting attire. "Now that's a style I've never seen."

"I've studied fashion history and design and I get a little creative with my designs." She saw his puzzled look. "Maybe I'm a romantic idealist . . . or something."

"Or an oddball," he grinned.

She smiled. "That too."

"Uh, hadn't you better get back in there to work?" Artie asked.

"No. Ada was rude to you, so I'm quitting for tonight."

"I see you have an independent streak."

"So I've been told. Well . . . what would you like to do tonight?"

"I'd like to take you out to dinner."

"That would be nice, but I need to change first." She started toward the door. "Oh . . . by the way, are we walking or riding?"

"Riding. I have a rental car. We're going to Augusta. There's a four-star restaurant there I'd like to try."

"That sounds awfully expensive. I hope you find it worth the trip," she teased.

"That depends," he said, smiling.

The expression in his eyes slightly flustered her. She turned quickly and said over her shoulder. "I'll be right down."

Upstairs—not in the mood to wear period clothing—she changed into a tan cotton twill jumper with small double straps over a white tee. After brushing her teeth, she took out the clip and let her hair fall loose.

Before she returned to the parlor, Gustavia went into the library and told Ada where she was going. Ada looked at her watch, then slowly lifted her eyes, displeasure written on her face.

"You look different, Gusty," Paul remarked cynically.

"And what do you mean by that tone of voice, Paul?"

"Take it however you choose."

She stared at him. "There's no reason to . . ."

"Have a good evening, Gustavia."

"Thank you, I will." Turning on her heel, she left. Reaching the parlor door, she said, "I'm ready, Artie."

He sprang to his feet, grinning. "You look great, Gustavia."

On the way to Augusta, Artie asked Gustavia about her cousin and the work she was doing for her. This led to a discussion of Gustavia's yearning to be connected to family—grandparents and great-grandparents, cousins, uncles and aunts.

Artie Banks fell silent as he thought of the two reasons he had come out to see Gustavia. He had told her the main reason—his infatuation with her. For that was how he thought of it. How else could he explain the ardent emotions he had felt so quickly? His common sense couldn't deal with the idea of love-at-first-sight. His parents couldn't either, and had expressed their concern about him traveling so far to see a young woman not of his faith. He had the same concern. But he had convinced himself that the second reason was the more compelling motive. Or was it? It occurred to him that on an emotional level they were inseparably connected.

They entered Augusta and Artie concentrated on finding the restaurant. "Oh, here's the street I'm looking for."

They entered the parking lot of a restaurant that Artie had picked from a well-known restaurant guide. He opened the car door, took Gustavia's hand and continued to hold it while entering the building. The hostess seated them and laid menus on the table.

"Even if a restaurant is rated four-star, I'm always a little nervous when I'm with someone special." His eyes locked on hers.

Gustavia quickly bent her head and stared intently at the menu. "The menu looks good," she said.

After they had ordered, Artie asked Gustavia how long she thought she would be working for her cousin and what she intended to do afterward.

Gustavia took a deep breath and answered his questions the best she could, then she asked what was foremost on her mind. "Artie, did you ask your father about his brother Robert?"

"I did. That's one of the things I came out to tell you. Dad said he used to live in Florida. He was a little skeptical of finding him because Uncle Robert quit jobs and moved often."

"Does your father know whether or not he and Sharon adopted a little boy?"

"My dad said he had lost all contact with them when Robert left the Church."

Gustavia was terribly disappointed, but there was still the possibility that Artie's father might locate his brother. She had to hang onto that hope.

The waitress arrived with the food. They ate silently for a while; then Gustavia courteously asked about his family. As he was talking, she couldn't help but compare the picture she had drawn in her mind of the grown-up Freddie with the man sitting across from her. They were so much alike!

Artie stopped talking and studied Gustavia. "I think I've lost you."

"I'm sorry. For a moment my mind wandered. I truly am interested in your family."

"Well, that brings me to one of the reasons I came out here."

A small smile appeared. "Oh, so I wasn't the whole reason you came after all."

"On the contrary, you were. I came to take you back to Salt Lake with me. I want my parents to meet you. And I want you to meet them."

This was the last thing Gustavia expected. Her own remark was intended only as a joke.

Artie could tell by Gustavia's expression that she was about to react negatively. He put up his hand. "Don't answer yet, Gustavia. Let's just enjoy our meal, then talk about it later."

"But, Artie, I . . ."

"Please think about it a little before you answer."

"All right."

❧

Artie found the park the restaurant hostess had told them about. The sun low in the west shed a gentle warmth upon the earth. They walked awhile then found a park bench.

"This is such a lovely warm evening. We had so few warm evenings in England. My poor mum suffered so with the cold. I sometimes wonder if it didn't just lodge in her bones causing her to die of pneumonia."

"I wondered if your parents were living."

"No. Neither one. The only living relatives I know about are Cousin Ada and her brother Edgar."

Though Artie had spoken of his parents, he hadn't mentioned their names. "What are your parent's names, Artie."

"Jonathon and Mary Banks."

"How old are you?"

"Twenty-eight." He noted the doubt on her face. "When my parents adopted me, they were told my age, but the people they adopted me from didn't have a birth certificate for me. Since it couldn't be located, my parents had to go to court and have one issued with the information told them."

"Is it possible twenty-eight isn't your correct age?"

"It's possible, but unlikely."

"How old are you, Gustavia?"

"Thirty."

A gray catbird in a nearby bush startled them when it burst forth with its melodious, nasal song, adding squeaky notes interspersed with catlike mewing sounds. They smiled at each other.

"Interesting sounding bird," Gustavia murmured, shivering.

"Are you cold?"

She shook her head. "I think I just need to get home, Artie."

"So soon?"

"Yes. I'm sorry."

"All right." Artie took her arm and together they walked to the car in silence.

When they arrived in Belford, Artie walked Gustavia to the door.

"Thank you for the nice evening, Artie."

"Your welcome. Thank you. Since you told the 'queen bee' that you would also have tomorrow night free, what time shall I pick you up for dinner?"

"Around 6:30."

"Goodnight then, beautiful maiden. See you tomorrow night."

Slowly, Gustavia got ready for bed, then plunked herself down on the window seat. Staring out into Ada's courtyard she thought about Artie. *Is it possible that the reason Artie's parents don't want to discuss his adoption is because they adopted him from Robert and Sharon Banks? If so, why didn't the name Freddie Finch sound familiar to him?* It didn't make sense.

There was something unusual about Artie. She had first seen it in his face at the restaurant in Salt Lake. What was it? Mentally she tried to describe it. It was a mildness in his expression or something akin to it—something that lit up his face.

She tried to think how she felt about him, how she felt about Paul, who had kept his promise about remaining only a friend, but had given hints that he felt more. Apparently Artie was beginning to feel something for her, too. *I don't want to hurt either one.* Emotionally exhausted, she left the window and crawled into bed.

❧CHAPTER 20❧

Gustavia's eyes scanned the page three times trying to present the material in a way that would satisfy Ada, but she couldn't concentrate. She was worrying how Paul felt about Artie coming to see her. She needed to talk to him!

Paul walked in briskly. "Where's Ada?" he asked without greeting.

Relieved to see him, she got up and walked over to him. "I don't know." His face looked a little haggard. "Didn't you sleep well last night?"

"Not very. Did you?"

"No."

Ada walked in before they could continue. Paul moved to Ada's desk and they quietly took up their business. This went on all morning until Paul went to lunch. When he returned, he and Ada resumed their serious discussion for the rest of the afternoon. Not once did he look in her direction.

The day was grueling for Gustavia. Her thoughts, like an endless reel of tape, played over and over the events of the weekend—Paul's sudden return with apparent serious issues to discuss with Ada, Artie showing up unexpectedly, and Paul suddenly seeming distant.

Disconcerted and unhappy, she watched the clock until it was time to get ready for her date with Artie. She got up and walked toward the door, glancing back at Paul, hoping to catch his eye and wave good night. Still, he ignored her.

During the meal, Gustavia and Artie conversed on many subjects, both avoiding anything serious. Since they were in a secluded section and the lighting was low Artie decided that it was a good place to continue their conversation of last night.

When they had finished their dessert and dishes had been cleared away, Artie asked, "Have you thought about coming to Salt Lake with me for a couple of days, Gustavia?"

"Yes."

"Well?"

"I can't."

"Why? Surely your cousin will let you have a couple of days off."

"It isn't that."

"What is it?"

"I'm promised to someone."

Artie frowned in concern. "You're . . . engaged?"

"No. I'm committed to marry someone else."

Artie's face was one of confusion. "You're in love with someone else?"

"No. Nevertheless, I'm committed. I promised."

"You promised to marry someone you aren't in love with?"

"It was many years ago. I couldn't have been in love at that age."

"How old were you when you made this promise?"

"Nine."

"Nine! Isn't that a little ridiculous, Gustavia?"

"That's what I've been told by quite a few men. Join the crew, Artie."

"How old was this young Romeo when he extracted that promise from an innocent little nine-year-old?

"Ten."

"Ten?" Artie burst out laughing. "You've got to be kidding!"

"Don't make fun of it," she said quietly. "You don't know the circumstances."

"Then tell me the circumstances."

"I'd rather not."

"Will you tell me this much? Is he holding you to that promise now?"

"I don't know. We both lived in England at the time and we got separated. I've been looking for him all these years. He's the friend I told you about, Freddie Finch."

"*The* Freddie Finch?"

"Yes."

"Do you still feel you have to keep that promise?"

"Yes, I do. At least until I find him, and give us a chance."

His expression turned grim. "Gustavia, this isn't right. It's unfair to you."

"As I said, you don't know all the details of our relationship."

Artie's shoulders sagged. "I care for you, Gustavia. I'm worried about you feeling beholden to a promise you made as a child to another child."

This whole conversation, she thought, *should prove to me that Artie is definitely not Freddie! But still, maybe the trauma of his adoption—No!* She quickly closed her mind to any more possibilities. She was being foolish!

"Please take me home, Artie."

All right," he said, hiding his dejection over trying to compete with a memory—a childhood promise. He stood up and led her out to the car. The ride back to Belford was strained, short conversations interspersed between long periods of silence.

❧

Gustavia said goodnight to Artie after he suggested they go on a picnic the next day. She opened Ada's front door, stepped in and leaned against the closed door, torn by contradictory emotions.

Down the hall, a soft light from the library dimly illuminated the rug. Ada didn't usually work this late. Knowing how her cousin felt about leaving lights on and running up the electric bill, Gustavia tip-toed to the library to turn it off. She stopped at the door, stunned. Silhouetted against the light of Ada's small desk lamp sat Paul, leaning over, concentrating intently on something. He hadn't heard her.

"Paul?"

He whirled around and saw her shadowed figure. "Gusty?"

"Wh-what are you doing here this late?"

He rose from the chair. "For two reasons. I told Ada I needed to work late in order to tie up some loose ends for her. And I also wanted to wait up for you." He walked slowly toward her.

She looked up into his face. As he was framed against the back-light of the small desk lamp, she was unable to see his expression.

"Where did this Artie Banks come from, Gusty? How did you meet him?"

Gustavia went to the book case and pulled out the large old Bible. "Let's go into the parlor and I'll tell you. It's rather astounding."

In the parlor Gustavia turned on the lamp. They seated themselves on the old blue velveteen couch.

His voice edged with sarcasm, he said, "All right, tell me this astounding story."

"Don't be like that, Paul."

"Sorry. Go on."

She told him how she had noticed the Bible. She opened it to the names inside.

He studied them intently. "Interesting!" he exclaimed.

She looked at him, curiously. "What do you mean?"

"Just interesting. That's all. What did you do after you found this?"

Gustavia told him of the visit to Salt Lake and the Family History Center and what she had learned there. "I met Artie there. He took me out to a restaurant with a view of the . . . "

"He's certainly a fast worker."

Ignoring his remark, she continued. "I went out with him because he seemed like such a nice person. The people who adopted Freddie were Robert and Sharon Banks. When I learned that Artie's last name was Banks, I couldn't believe it. When I looked at him, his freckles, his sandy blond hair, I realized he was almost the exact image I'd had of what Freddie would look like grown up. Oh Paul, I can't tell you how excited I got. I was sure he was Freddie. In fact, he was adopted when he was older, just like Freddie. Can you believe it?"

His brows furrowing, Paul shook his head. "An amazing coincidence."

"No matter how he denied that my name or Freddie's name were familiar, I couldn't accept it emotionally. I had gotten my hopes so high." A flicker of sadness crossed her face. "Tonight I think I was finally able to let it go."

Paul reached over and took her hand, his face troubled. "I'm sorry for your disappointment."

"Thank you," she said, warmed by his sympathetic response.

"How does Artie feel about you, Gusty?"

"It's really not important for you to know that."

"As a friend, it's important to me. So tell me."

"He wants me to go to Salt Lake with him and meet his family."

Paul's jaw rippled, a grim expression on his face. "How . . . how do you feel about him?"

She paused. "I'm not sure. There's something in his face, his eyes, that I'm drawn to." She saw pain cross Paul's face. "But I told him I was betrothed," she added quickly.

"What did he say?"

"What difference does that make?"

"It makes a difference to me," he said, a hard edge to his voice.

Put off by his attitude, she pulled her hand away. "He said it was unfair to ask an innocent child of nine to make a promise like that."

"Do you agree with him?"

"No. I told him he didn't know the circumstances."

Paul nodded, then stood up. "Well, I've got a big day ahead of me tomorrow, so I'll say goodnight. I have business with Ada tomorrow, so I'll see you."

She watched him stride out of the parlor to the front door. Disturbed at his attitude toward Artie, and his rather hasty departure, she turned off the light in the parlor and slowly walked upstairs.

"Why do things have to be so complicated?" she muttered. *If only I could find Freddie, I could resolve it one way or another and get on with my life!*

❧CHAPTER 21❧

A piercing shriek echoed through the halls and up the stairwell, waking Gustavia with a start. Dazed and frightened she sat upright. Her heart pounding, she jumped out of bed and flew down the stairs. Not sure where the sound had come from, she looked in the dining room first. Seeing no one, she ran down the hall to the library. The glow of dawn, streaming through the tall window, revealed Ada sitting at her desk.

"Cousin Ada, d–did you scream?" she uttered breathlessly.

Ada took her time answering. When she swivelled her chair around to acknowledge the question, Gustavia gasped silently. Never had she seen such hate and fury in anyone's eyes. Ada's low rancorous voice was a sharp contrast to the shriek she had heard a few moments ago.

"Gustavia, do you know that you've been fraternizing with a charlatan?"

"What! What do you mean by that, Ada?" she blurted out, purposely leaving off the respectful title of cousin.

"I mean just what I said. Paul Camden is a criminal, a crook!"

Gustavia felt as though she had been struck a blow; she could scarcely breath. "Ada, don't be ridiculous."

"I have the proof right here!" Ada barked. "He's a low–down black-mailer, that's what he is."

"I don't believe it."

"Well, you're a stupid girl if you don't. Paul is coming over here at 11:00 and you'll see for yourself. Now get out of that nightgown and be ready for breakfast on time." She swivelled her chair around, dismissing her.

Gustavia was so shaken, she had to hold on to the bannister to steady herself as she walked upstairs. *Ada has lost her mind*, she told herself.

Trying to relax, she took a long hot shower and washed her hair. Slipping on a pair of jeans and a T shirt, she dried her hair and slowly wound it into one braid down the back. Dreading breakfast with Ada, she made herself go anyway. All she could get down was a glass of orange juice and a half piece of toast. She excused herself while her morose cousin was still eating.

Leaving the house, she went for a brisk walk. It would be almost three hours before Paul would be there. An involuntary sob escaped as she walked up the sidewalk toward the mansions. "Oh Mum, I need you. I need your help. I'm so desperately lonely and confused." *Could Ada be right?* A sliver of doubt crept in. *Could he really be a blackmailer? No!* Everything inside her protested.

Exhausted and edgy, Gustavia returned about fifteen minutes before Paul was to arrive. She went upstairs, freshened up, and drank a cold glass of water. Saying a prayer in her heart, she slowly descended the stairs. Entering the library, she found no one. Troubled, she sat down on the couch and waited. It wasn't long before Ada walked in briskly, her jaw protruding determinedly, her eyes flashing with anger.

The doorbell rang, but Paul walked in without waiting for anyone to answer. He moved quickly down the hall to the library. "Good morning, Gustavia," he greeted, his face expressionless. Not speaking to Ada, he stood, waiting for the explosion.

Ada got up from her chair with a paper in her hand. Her whole body was trembling. "You left this on my desk last night."

"I did, Ada."

"How dare you! You are nothing but a blackmailer. I'll see that you're disbarred and sent to prison. I'm going to call the police."

"I think that would be a good idea. Why don't you do it? Right now."

Ada hesitated, the first glimpse of uncertainty touching her eyes. Her chin trembled slightly. "How dare you accuse me of anything—threaten to expose me." Trying to regain the upper hand she blustered, "You make one false statement and I'll sue you for libel!"

Paul ignored the threat. "I've been gathering the information for some time. My last trip to Ludlow furnished me with the rest of the details I needed."

Ada turned to Gustavia, shaking the paper in her hand. "Do you know what's on this? It's a threat! It says he'll expose me for some unnamed thing if I don't do what he asks."

Gustavia felt the blood drain from her face. *It can't be true!* She looked over at Paul, imploring him to tell her it wasn't true. "What-what unnamed thing?"

"I'm here this morning to tell you both."

"Tell us both? This is just between you and me, young man. Gustavia, go to your room."

"Gustavia is to stay, Ada. This concerns her as well as you."

"Leave, Gustavia. Do as I say."

"I think I need to be here, Ada. I can't believe Paul is a blackmailer."

Ada looked as if she were going to combust at any moment. Shaking visibly, she glared wildly at one, then the other.

"You'd better be seated when you hear this, Ada," he warned.

"I will remain standing."

"As you wish." He moved back and forth in measured steps. "About six weeks before Gustavia came to the U.S. you sent me on the second trip to Ludlow. While I was there, something came up concerning the legal ownership of the stone quarry. I had to go to the Ludlow City archives and look up how long the quarry had been owned by you and Edgar. I learned that the two of you were executors of the estate of a John and Sarah Sullivan. There was also a list of their descendants—Melissa and Fanny Sullivan."

He gazed into Gustavia's incredulous eyes for a moment, then turned to Ada. "The rest of the records were missing. I talked with the archivist and he said that they had just reorganized everything and some records must have gotten misfiled. He said he'd look for them." He noted the tight cords in Ada's neck relax a little.

Paul stopped moving and faced Ada. "After finding out that there were legal problems over the ownership of the quarry, and that you and Edgar had inherited the John and Sarah Sullivan estate, I began to have suspicions about your ownership of the quarry. I couldn't prove it, however, because of the missing records.

"Since John Sullivan was wealthy and owned a large fish merchant business in Grimsby, and a very profitable stone quarry in Ludlow, I wondered what part of the estate he had left to his daughter, Fanny."

Ada's hand shook as she grasped the back of the chair. She sank into it. This wasn't lost on Paul. He sat down next to Gustavia on the couch. "Needless to say, I was anxious for the next opportunity to go back to England. On this recent trip to Ludlow, I discovered the records had been found."

Gustavia held her breath, unable to guess what Paul could have found. It was obvious that whatever it was, Ada was frightened. She seemed to have shrunk now looking like what she was—an old woman who could see the end approaching.

"Not only was John Sullivan the owner of a fish merchant firm in Grimsby, and a quarry in Ludlow, but the owner of a small fleet of fishing boats as well. He was a very wealthy man. His wife died of typhoid fever leaving two daughters, a ten-year-old and a twenty-year-old. The older one, Melissa, married Sir John Redmore."

Gustavia glanced at Ada. Her tight-lipped face was a stone mask.

"Shortly after Sarah died," Paul continued, "John Sullivan went out on one of his fishing trawlers—why we don't know—and died at sea when a terrible storm struck the vessel. But your great-grandfather, Gustavia, was a man who was prepared for any eventuality. He left a will and an executer to deliver it. To his daughter, twenty-year-old Melissa, he left the fish merchant plant. To his young ten-year-old daughter, Fanny, he left the stone quarry in Ludlow. The fishing fleet was to be sold and the profit divided between the two daughters."

Gustavia gasped. "Fanny? Fanny Sullivan, my grandmother, owned the quarry?"

"Yes, Gusty," Paul replied grimly.

Slowly, Gustavia turned to Ada, only to find her face paper-white, and the expression in her eyes was one of fear. "You already knew all this, didn't you, Ada?"

Ada refused to answer, so Paul went on. "Melissa and Sir John Redmore were Ada's parents, as you know, Gusty. They only had two children, Ada and Edgar. After John Sullivan's wife had died, he added a codicil to his will stating that if anything happened to him before Fanny had reached her majority, his oldest daughter, Melissa was to look after her younger sister and see to it that she received her inheritance when she was of age. If anything were to happen to Fanny, her inheritance would go to her offspring."

"Then . . ." Gustavia began hesitantly, "by right, the stone quarry belonged to my father. Since he died, it would revert to my mother?"

"That's right, Gusty. In an addendum to the records, it states that Melissa held the inheritance because Fanny was too young to manage it. Another addendum dated eight years later said that Fanny had disappeared so the inheritance reverted to Melissa. The latter addendum was highly suspect. There was a question about the legality of it, therefore a question of the true ownership of the quarry arose."

A voice spoke from the doorway. "Paul is right, Gustavia."

Ada gasped. "Edgar! What are you doing here? This is a private meeting. You shouldn't be here."

"Why not, Ada?" Paul asked.

Thick silence settled over the room. Ada's throat convulsed, but there was no sound.

"I invited him, Ada," Paul said. "When I returned from England, I met with him first and told him what I had found out."

Ada tried to rally. "You aren't going to get away with this, Paul Camden," she said through clenched teeth.

"No, Ada. It's you and Edgar who aren't going to get away with it. I found more documents, one of which stated that Fanny Sullivan could not be found, and may have died on the boat with her father, John Sullivan. That, of course, was a lie. A lie spawned by your mother, Melissa. The ownership of the stone quarry then illegally reverted to Melissa Sullivan Redmore."

Paul noted the stunned expression on Gustavia's face, the incomprehension, the disbelief.

"But Fanny didn't die on a boat!" Gustavia cried.

"We know," Paul said. "We don't know what happened to her or where she was from the time her father died to the time that she married Josiah Browne, and had Thomas, your father." His gaze turned to Ada. "Whatever happened, we do know that Melissa stole Fanny's inheritance."

"I knew nothing about this," Ada stated defiantly. "I wasn't even born."

"But," Edgar interjected, "we learned about it after our parents died, and . . ."

"Edgar! Keep quiet! She leaned toward him, lowering her voice. "If you hadn't insisted on going to Alice's funeral and hadn't insisted on knowing where Gustavia was at all times and then insisted she live with me and do my biography, none of this would have come out."

"Ada, stop and think," Edgar gently urged, "Paul still would have discovered what he did, regardless, and I'm glad he did. I told Paul everything when he visited my office and told me what he had found, what he knew. We shouldn't have perpetuated the lies, and the theft of our aunt Fanny's inheritance—which now legally belongs to her heir, Gustavia."

"How dare you betray us like this," Ada hissed, her bony fingers restlessly clasping and unclasping. "You're a stupid man, Edgar. You know we both could be put in prison for this."

Sitting down heavily on the remaining chair, Edgar looked old and tired. "I know, Ada, but I've lived with the guilt of this far too long."

Paul broke into the recriminations. "I believe Edgar has something he wants to give to Gustavia."

"I left it in the hall, Paul," Edgar said, starting to rise.

"I'll get it, Edgar," Paul offered quickly. He stepped out and returned with a box, handing it to Edgar.

Ada gasped when she saw it. "Edgar, no!"

"We have to, Ada. We have no choice. I only wish we had given it to Gustavia before we were compelled to do so." His heavy-lidded eyes gazed sadly at his young cousin. "This was what I intended to give you when you were through with Ada's biography, Gustavia. It has information you need to have."

Before Gustavia could respond, Ada blurted out, "You intended to give this to her all along?"

Edgar nodded. "Most of it, yes."

"You betrayed me, Edgar," she rasped. "You're about to give Gustavia proof to send us to prison."

"I'm fully aware of that, Ada," he said quietly. Placing the box down beside him, he turned to Gustavia. "Our mother died five years after father died, leaving Ada and me to run the businesses. We put all their old records and personal things up in the attic, intending to go through them someday."

Edgar glanced at his sister. She sat rigidly, her arms tightly folded across her mid-section. Focusing downward, her lips pursed in angry disapproval.

Letting out a heavy sigh, he continued. "About eight months before your mother died, Gustavia, Ada and I decided to clear out the attic and dispose of unnecessary items and records. Ada began the process one day while I was attending to some pressing business. She discovered this box. We had never noticed it before. It apparently was one that was put up into the attic by our mother not too long before she died."

"When I came home, Ada showed the me the box and the shocking contents. We didn't know what to do with the information. How could we prove we hadn't known about it before? It was then I hired a private investigator to locate you and your mother, Gustavia. When he did so, I paid him to continue his vigilance in case something changed. Rather than the possibility of a court trial and prison, we decided to keep track of you and your mother and help you financially in any way we could. That's how we knew about your mother's death."

Edgar glanced at Ada. She hadn't moved from her previous posture. His hands, one gripping the back of the other, shook slightly. His watery eyes fastened on Gustavia. "After the funeral, we let six years slip by. I'm sorry for the part I've played in this deception and for any suffering it might have caused you, Gustavia."

Gustavia, still trying to absorb everything, could not respond.

"I intend to turn back the ownership of the quarry to you and pay you for the years of profit we've made on it. Also, we'll pay you half the profit from the sale of the fishing fleet with interest. I know this won't make up for the hard work your poor young mother had to do to support you. It . . . it's unforgivable that our mother turned a blind eye to your poverty." His voice cracked with emotion. "I'm an old man, older than my years because of the heavy burden I've been carrying around."

The doorbell rang, startling all of them. "Oh! It's Artie. Oh dear." Please excuse me," she said, walking toward the hall. "I'll be right back."

She opened the front door knowing that she had to break the date.

"Hi," Artie grinned.

Gustavia stepped out onto the porch and closed the door. "Artie, I don't know quite how to tell you this, but . . ." She stopped, feeling terrible about what she had to do.

"Go on," he muttered apprehensively.

"A crises has come up. Actually, I'm very distraught—and anxious. I'm going to have to cancel our date. I'm terribly sorry since you've come such a long way to see me."

His disappointment apparent, he was silent. He opened his mouth several times to protest, but ended up reluctantly accepting it. "All right, Gustavia. Is there any chance that later on tonight you'll feel better?"

"I think it will take several days before I'll be myself."

"In that case, I might as well try to get a flight out tonight. I'm sorry about your crises, Gustavia. May I call you in a week or two?"

"Yes. I'd like to hear from you."

He stepped off the porch. "All right. I've enjoyed the short time I've spent with you and hope to spend some more time with you in the future."

"Thank you for taking this so well, Artie."

He smiled, nodded and turned, walking rapidly to the gate and out.

Feeling regret, Gustavia watched him get into his car and drive off.

When she entered the library, Paul looked at her questioningly. "Where's Artie?"

"I canceled our date. He's going to try to find a flight home tonight."

Paul let out a quiet breath of relief. "Good. You need to be here."

The cook, Carol, knocked on the door frame of the library. "Excuse me, Miss Redmore, but lunch has been waiting. Would you like to eat now?"

Ada seemed unable to answer so Edgar took over. "Can you prepare lunch for all of us, Carol?"

"Yes, of course. It will be ready in about ten minutes."

"After lunch," Paul said, "we'll begin where we left off."

Ada stood up. "Edgar, tell Carol to bring lunch to me in my room." Without a glance at anyone, she left.

After lunch, everyone was back in the library. Paul resumed arbitrating. "Is there something else you wanted to do or say, Edgar?"

He nodded. His shoulders slumped in weariness. He gazed intently at his sister. "Ada, you know that I've asked you several times if you were hiding something from me. In looking carefully through the records and documents in the box once more before bringing it over here, I noticed two small words at the bottom of a document, put there in pencil by our mother, almost as an afterthought—perhaps a reminder of some sort. I had to read it several times because they didn't make sense by themselves. 'Fanny's diaries.'"

Gustavia gasped. "Diaries?"

Edgar went on. "Ada, you looked into the box before I got home. Did you find anything that resembled diaries?"

"You saw what was in there, Edgar," Ada replied curtly.

"That isn't an answer, Ada. Did you discover diaries in the box?"

Everyone's eyes were upon Ada, waiting. They saw the rigid woman's struggle to give up this last vestige of control. At length, she gave Edgar a slight nod. She stood up stiffly. Her head high, she held on to her dignity as she walked out of the library.

Gustavia looked over at Edgar. "Thank you, Edgar."

Lowering his eyes, he nodded.

Finally Ada returned with something in her hand. She sullenly thrust it at Edgar, then seated herself.

Edgar studied it, turned it over, then looked inside. Closing it, he got up and handed it to Gustavia.

Gustavia, holding her breath, slowly opened it. "It is a diary! It's Fanny Sullivan's diary!" Paging through it quickly, she looked over at Paul. "She began this diary at ten and ended when she was twelve. I wish there were more." Then something struck her as very puzzling. "Ada, you've mentioned several times about Fanny's scandal. How could she behave scandalously at ten or twelve years of age?"

"Ada," Edgar began rubbing his chin thoughtfully, "I believe mother wrote 'diaries,' plural. Will you please give Gustavia the *rest* of the diaries," he demanded curtly.

"You're a dull-witted man, Edgar! They could possibly give Paul further evidence to convict us with."

"So be it, Ada. As I said, I'm tired of living with the guilt."

Ada fumed, sending a hateful glare at her brother, then promptly waggled a bony finger at Paul. "If this meddling man here hadn't taken our pay to look into our private business, we could have handled the situation as we planned." Slowly, she exited the room.

"There are more diaries, Paul!" Gustavia said with excitement.

He smiled. Putting his arm around her shoulders, he gave her a squeeze. "I'm glad for you, Gusty."

Gustavia looked over at her dejected cousin. "Thank you, Edgar, for being so astute to find that little clue about the diaries and for insisting that Ada give them to me." She got up and kissed his distressed brow.

Edgar could only nod, his eyes a watery blur.

Paul's suspicions arose when Ada didn't return in a reasonable length of time. He was about to ask Edgar to go find her when she entered and dropped several ledger-like volumes into Gustavia's lap, then turned to leave.

"Don't leave this room, Ada," Paul said.

"You can't order me about, Paul Camden."

"I said, stay here."

Ada's eyes darted around, landing on Edgar, who slowly nodded, and fear held her fast. Jerkily, she walked over and sat in her desk chair, away from the group.

Gustavia hugged the diaries to her heart, tears glistening in her eyes.

Paul's head swivelled around to Ada, his voice low with anger. "How cruel of you, Ada, to keep this treasure from Gustavia all these years. More cruel than hiding the theft of her inheritance."

Gustavia looked over at Paul, her eyes tender with gratitude for bringing this all about.

Paul's anger left when he looked into Gustavia's face. He allowed her to glance through the diaries for a few moments then he spoke. "I'm leaving your employ, Ada. I am now Gustavia's lawyer." Gustavia looked over at him in surprise. "Though I'm not in criminal law, a lawyer in my firm is. We'll report the theft of the quarry to the authorities in England and give them all the documents of proof."

"Paul, no!" Gustavia exclaimed. "I don't want Ada and Edgar to go to prison."

Paul's half smile appeared. This was how he suspected Gustavia would react. "Are you sure, Gusty?"

"Yes, I am."

"Do you hear that, Ada?" Paul asked. "You don't deserve that kind of mercy." He saw no gratitude in Ada's face, only perverseness. On the other hand, Edgar was on the verge of breaking down.

"We'll need to transact the rest of our business at your office, Edgar," Paul resumed in a business-like tone. "We'll need you there for your signature, Gustavia. And of course, it goes without saying, Ada, you will be there also. After the transaction, I'll take care of the legalities in England."

The meeting in Edgar's office took nearly three hours. Edgar, eager and cooperative, couldn't do enough to help. Ada remained aloof and cold, unable to give in, to show any remorse whatsoever. Paul drove Gustavia back to Ada's, leaving her two cousins in Edgar's office to work out their business and personal problems.

Parking in front of Ada's house, Paul helped Gustavia out of the car. He opened the wrought-iron gate and, not trusting himself to be alone with Gustavia, was about to turn back to his car when she took his hand and pulled him to the garden bench. The dogwood tree was covered with yellowish white blossoms. Clumps of lavender forget-me-nots and baby-blue-eyes were blooming all along the fence. Foxglove and daylilies in and around the shrubs edging the house and parlor window were budding, but the zinnias were blooming bright yellow. Gustavia sighed. "Isn't this a beautiful garden?"

"Yes it is, Gusty."

Gustavia looked into the face of her friend. "How brilliant you are, Paul, to have discovered all of this. Though I'm finding it all rather difficult to absorb. How can I ever thank you for what you've done for me."

"Just seeing your happiness, Gusty, is thanks enough."

Gustavia, gazing into his smiling eyes, saw a depth of feeling that frightened her a little.

His eyes drifted to the flagstones for several moments and when he looked back, he had effectively concealed all emotion. "Gustavia, we have to unravel all of the legal problems incurred by the Redmore's deception. You'll have to go to Ludlow with me as soon as I can arrange it with my firm."

"I will?" she asked, surprised.

"Yes. Well," he said, standing up. "I'll be going. I know you're anxious to read your grandmother's diaries."

"Oh, yes I am, but uh . . ." she stammered following him to the gate. "When will you be back in Belford?"

"I'm not sure yet. I have to fly to Boston for a couple of days on a case I'm working on. Have an enjoyable time reading, Gusty," he said, opening the gate.

Gustavia watched him leave, feeling empty. She had missed him while he was in England, and the minute he got back, he had to spend two days with Ada, giving them no time to spend together. Why hadn't she told him that for the rest of the afternoon and evening she would rather visit with him than read the diaries? She stared at the daylilies thinking, then answered her own question. Even though it was apparent how happy Paul was that he was able to secure her inheritance and subsequently her grandmother's diaries, he still wasn't himself. He hadn't been since he had interrogated her about Artie.

She got up and disconsolately went inside. She stood in the foyer, feeling lonely and unsatisfied.

The diaries in one arm, the box in the other, Gustavia carried them up to her room and placed them on the bed. Removing the lid, she looked through the contents of the box in a cursory manner. Finding old bills, legal documents and so forth, she realized she needed Paul to go through it with her.

Next, she picked up each diary in turn and paged through it, looking at Fanny's writing as a child, then as an adult. These were priceless. *If only Dad had had these!* "It's a tragic shame, that's what it is." She closed them and placed them in a drawer, feeling too restless to begin reading the first one, and all because of Paul!

Hearing the phone ring in the library, she ran down to get it, not sure if Ada was back from meeting with Edgar. Just as she reached the door, she heard Ada say to someone, "I'm not taking calls for Gustavia Browne. You'll . . ."

"Ada, let me have the phone!" The fury in Gustavia's voice took Ada back, then in retaliation, she shoved the instrument at Gustavia, almost causing her to drop it. Speaking into the phone, she said, "This is Gustavia, just a moment please." Holding her hand over the speaker, she glared at Ada. "Don't you ever not take a call for me. If I find out you have, I'll change my mind about taking you to court."

Ada hid the fear, but not the hatred.

Gustavia took a couple of breaths to calm down as she watched Ada leave the library, each staccato clip of her heels on the oak hall floor echoing her feelings.

"Thank you for holding. This is Gustavia," she said, hoping it was Paul.

A familiar voice came through the phone. "Is anything wrong, Gustavia?"

"Who is this?"

"I'm sorry. This is Artie."

"Artie?" In Gustavia's distracted state it took a moment for the name to register. "Oh, Artie. Hi." There was a short pause. "Yes, there's something wrong, but something I have complete control of, so don't worry. I didn't expect to hear from you so soon."

"That's obvious," he chuckled. "I know you have a crisis, but I have a request to make. You remember I asked you before if you would come out to Salt Lake?"

"Yes."

I'm renewing that invitation. I want you to come out and meet my family—as soon as things get settled there for you."

Gustavia thought about this a moment. Even though Paul had distanced himself from her and was going to be in Boston, she couldn't even consider it. Still—she would like to meet his family! Refusing to give in to this desire—the desire to be around a close family, she replied, "Artie, it wouldn't be fair to you."

"Why?"

"I'd rather not discuss it."

"Will you come out?"

"If I came out, it would be giving you false hopes."

"I'm very aware of that. I'll continue to hope until you've made up your mind about this Freddie situation. I assure you, you needn't feel beholden to me or my family."

"Thank you, Artie, but I can't."

"Gustavia, even if you'd told me you had found your friend Freddie, I still would have invited you out. All my family have been rather vocal about not having had the opportunity to meet you."

In her lonely and unsettled state, this last inducement was her undoing. The old ache returned—the longing to see what a real family was like—a family with both a mother and a father, and siblings. Enid's family was far from ideal. She was the only child at home. Her one brother and sister were away and married and her parents were undemonstrative.

She and her mother were so close, she wondered if big families, traditional ones, could be that close. She wanted to watch a family in action—Artie's family. What harm would it do since he told her that she needn't feel beholden?

"Gustavia?"

"I'm still here, Artie. I'm arguing with myself."

He chuckled. "Who's winning?"

"My impulsive nature is winning out . . . I think."

"That's wonderful. When can you come?"

"The only time I could come is tomorrow morning. I would have only Sunday afternoon till Monday afternoon to spend with you and your family. Then I'd have to return."

"Great!"

"That hardly seems worth the expense of last minute plane tickets, Artie. Maybe I'd better come at a later date."

"No. Come now. I'm paying for the tickets. Even a short visit will be worth it. I'm thrilled it will be so soon. I'll call for plane reservations right now and call you back."

"Get me reservations at the hotel, also, will you?"

"No. You'll be staying with my family."

"With you? Oh, I couldn't do that, Artie."

"My mother won't hear of anything else."

"Well, if you're sure it's all right," she replied hesitantly.

❧CHAPTER 22❧

Sunday morning, Gustavia informed Ada that she would be out of town for two days and asked that she inform Carol.

"You need to clean your things out of that room and leave, Gustavia. I don't feel comfortable having you here any longer."

Gustavia stared at her in disbelief. "It's I who should feel uncomfortable, Ada. After all, you have accepted my efforts to write your history all the while knowing about my stolen inheritance and Fanny's diaries. Our business isn't finished, and I'm staying here until it is." With her suitcase, she walked toward the back door. "I'll be back Monday night," she called over her shoulder.

Before leaving Belford, Gustavia drove over to the lumber mill. Finding Edgar in his office, she left her grandmother's diaries with him, not trusting them in Ada's house while she was gone. He was more than eager to keep them safe for her.

Driving to Augusta State Airport, Gustavia, began to question her motive in accepting Artie's invitation. Was she being selfish by using Artie and his family to satisfy her need to see what a big family was like? The answer was yes.

Artie's call had come at a moment when she was feeling vulnerable. After accepting, she had argued with herself over the prudence of her rash decision until she convinced herself it was all right and, now, she had to convince herself all over again.

Sunday afternoon, Artie greeted her at the baggage claim with a big grin on his face. "Hi, beautiful. It's great to see you."

"Thank you. It's nice to see you." She really wanted to say, "Your ever-cheerful personality is just what I need right now."

In the car he turned to her. "Mom has prepared a big Sunday dinner for us. Most of my family will be there. My two married sisters and their husbands and children and my younger sister who still lives at home. The only one who won't be there is a brother who is on a mission."

"A mission? You mean like in the army?"

He smiled. "No, he's not in the army. When the young men in our church turn nineteen years of age, if they're worthy, they're called on a mission to preach the gospel for two years. They or the family pay for the mission. My brother earned and saved enough money to support himself, just as I did."

"That's rather amazing. I can't imagine a young man giving up that much time. I would think they'd have to feel as strongly about your church as you do, Artie."

"Most of us feel it in different degrees. Usually, while on their missions, the young men begin to feel even more committed to the work."

"Interesting."

"What church do you belong to, Gustavia?"

"I belong to the Church of England."

"Are you quite committed to it?"

"Actually, I've never thought about it seriously. Mum always taught me to read the Bible on a daily basis, and I've felt that was all I needed."

"Hm, that's interesting."

Artie turned into the driveway of a nice red brick home with a green lawn, tall old trees, and flowers planted in every space one could think to put them.

Gustavia was impressed. "What a beautiful home. The flowers are breathtaking."

"Yes, Mom could make any house look nice with all her flowers."

When they entered the house, they were suddenly surrounded by the whole family, all eager, and smiling. As Artie introduced her, each one responded with such kindness, such enthusiasm, she felt her throat constrict and her eyes moisten.

Dinner was delicious. Gustavia couldn't answer enough questions it seemed, they all were so interested in her. Mr. and Mrs. Banks were especially kind. But what was the most interesting to Gustavia, during the afternoon and evening, was the love and closeness between the parents and children. *So this is what a real family is like!* Of course everyone was putting on their 'best' because of her presence. She suspected that this family had their struggles just like any other family. Throughout her college years, she had questioned her friends about their families. From everything she learned, she realized there was no perfect family. But it seemed to Gustavia that, in the end, a family with parents who loved each other and who sacrificed and served, like her mum, would triumph over all the problems and still love each other and remain close.

It was a rash decision to come, but she needed to see this family—to know what a family could be. This was the kind of family she wanted to have when she married. She found herself wanting to belong to a family like this!

When his sisters and their husbands and children had said their good-byes and left, and the rest of the family had gone to their bedrooms, Artie led her from what they called the family room to the living room where they both settled themselves on the couch.

Gustavia finally had the opportunity to ask Artie if by chance his father had located his brother.

"No. He never knew his address, nor the company he worked for. As I said, he thinks he may have left Florida by now."

"Could he try to locate him on the Internet?"

"Dad seems hesitant to do that and has asked me not to. I think he must be afraid to find out what Uncle Robert is up to . . . or something."

Or maybe . . . Gustavia thought. Then just as quickly, she reminded herself that she wasn't going to entertain anymore maybe's.

A small newspaper caught Gustavia's eye. It lay open on the coffee table. In dark letters beside a picture of an elderly man at a pulpit, it said: *An amazing thing happens when people begin to trace their roots. They discover that they are not alone in the world.*

Gustavia's heart felt as though it had a knot the size of a bowling ball inside it. When she could speak, she pointed to the man in the picture. "Who is that man?"

"He's our prophet, the President of the Church. Or to be more accurate. He is the Prophet."

"You have a prophet . . . uh, like they had in the Bible?"

"Yes," he replied smiling.

"That's rather difficult to believe."

"Do you like what he said?"

"Yes." Not wanting him to know how greatly it had touched her she quickly added, "But then I've liked what a number of other religious leaders have said."

Artie changed the subject. "Well, what do you think of my family?"

"I think they're wonderful. They've shown me such kindness."

Artie put his arm around her shoulders and pulled her close. "How could they help it? You're a lovable and beautiful person."

She looked up at him. "Thank you, Artie. I needed to hear that."

Before she could turn her head away, his lips were on hers. It was a sweet kiss, and she couldn't help but return it.

"Oh Artie," she breathed, "this is a little soon."

"Not for me, Gustavia. I think I'm in love with you."

"How can you be? You barely know me."

"That's what I keep asking myself. But nevertheless, that's the way I feel."

"Artie, I . . . uh, I'm drawn to you in a way I haven't been drawn to any other man, but I'm afraid I don't love you."

"Though I was hoping otherwise, I knew it was too soon for you. I'll give you all the time you need."

"But as I told you, I didn't feel my coming out here was fair to you."

"I was willing to take the chance when I asked you to come. I still am."

"I don't want to hurt you, Artie. And I wouldn't want to hurt Freddie—if we ever find each other. Of course, that's assuming he's looking for me."

"What ever you do, Gustavia, don't feel obligated to either one of us."

"Thank you." She gave him a tremulous smile of appreciation. "I must say, Artie, there's something about you; I don't know quite how to explain it, but it's something in your eyes, the way you look. Your whole family has it."

"It's the gospel of Jesus Christ, Gustavia."

Gustavia contemplated this for a moment. "You mean the church you belong to?" At his nod she commented. "Interesting. I'll have to give that some thought."

Artie got up and went to a cabinet, pulled out a book and presented it to her. "I would like to give this to you. I hope you'll read it and pray about it."

Gustavia looked at the title: *The Book of Mormon.* "This is why you're called Mormons?"

"Yes."

"Thank you. I can't promise I'll read it, but I promise I'll think about it."

"That's good enough for now." He leaned over to kiss her again, but she pulled away.

"No, Artie. The kiss you gave me was premature."

"But you kissed me back."

"How could any girl help it?" She smiled. "Not only are you nice, but you're charming and good looking."

"Thanks. I guess I'll have to settle for that . . . for now."

"Please, Artie, don't have expectations. At the moment, I don't know how anything is going to turn out."

"I won't, Gustavia, I'll just hope."

❧

That night Gustavia lay in bed in the Banks' peaceful home thinking of Paul, of Artie and his parents. She couldn't sort it all out. It seemed almost impossible to stand back and be objective. However, she was certain about one thing—she would like to marry into a family like the Banks.' Though never having been in love, she didn't feel she was in love with Artie, but she was in love with his family! After much tossing and turning and emotionally exhausted, Gustavia fell into a deep sleep.

The next morning, Gustavia awoke early, refreshed. She showered and dressed quickly.

Breakfast with Artie, his parents and younger sister was delightful. She felt totally at home with them. Mrs. Banks was a wonderful cook. And Mr. Banks had a great wit, making her and everyone around the table laugh. She thanked them profusely for their hospitality.

Mid-morning, Artie took her for a drive through the canyons. She had seen nothing quite like it in Europe. After a quick lunch, he drove her to the airport. It had all gone by far too quickly.

As she prepared to leave for her gate, Artie told her she would be hearing from him, that he wasn't giving up until she made up her mind.

She smiled at his persistence. "All right. Thank you for inviting me out. I needed this time with your family. You see, I only had my mother, so to have the privilege of seeing a family like yours has been invaluable to me. Tell your parents thanks again for me." She walked briskly to the security line, turned and waved at him just before entering.

Once on the plane, and settled into her seat, she sighed. As soon as they were in the air, she leaned back, relaxed and let her mind wander aimlessly, not wanting to think about the weekend nor what was ahead of her.

Thirty minutes later, she awoke, surprised that she had fallen asleep. Still groggy, the first thought that came into her mind was of Paul, the Paul she met two-and-a-half months ago, whose presence cheered her up and made her time with Ada bearable, who took her on delightful walks and drives, who took her to dinner and listened with his heart, whose smiling eyes overtly appreciated her and her oddball ways, who had become the friend he promised to be, and who had forced Ada and Edgar to give up what had been illegally taken from her. She found herself missing him! For the first time, she realized that she had subconsciously fought a growing attraction to him, hoping to find Freddie first and resolve the promise made to him.

She considered Artie and his special family and felt confused. *What will Paul think about me flying out to meet Artie's family?* The thought worried her. She pulled herself up short. She was grateful to Paul beyond words. But since she hadn't made any commitment to him, she should be able to visit, without compunction, whomever she wished! Nevertheless, she thought, *I would prefer that he doesn't find out about this trip. I don't feel like being interrogated again!*

❧CHAPTER 23❧

Driving from the airport to Belford, Gustavia was beset by myriad emotions leaving her one moment breathless, the next, her heart thumping against her ribs. *In case Paul learns about it, how am I going to explain my desire to meet Artie's family?* But why, for goodness sake, was she so fearful anyway? Hadn't she decided her gratitude to him needn't make her obligated to account to him? Artie, not knowing about her friendship with Paul, had mentioned she shouldn't feel obligated to Freddie either. She wasn't so sure about the latter. After all, she had made him a promise. But why was she going over and over this?

She knew. Try as she would, she cared terribly what Paul thought and how this trip was going to affect him. He had been wonderful to her since she had been at Ada's and had done so much for her.

Reaching the lumber mill at 6:00 P.M., she parked and ran in, anxious to retrieve the diaries and get home just in case Paul should show up that night. She reassured herself. *I have no reason to be nervous. He said he would be gone for a couple of days.* "In all probability, he won't be over to Ada's until tomorrow morning," she whispered to herself.

Edgar looked up and smiled as she entered his office. "You're back." He unlocked a drawer and pulled out the diaries. "Here you are, Gustavia, I kept them safe as you asked."

"Thank you, Edgar. Uh, Paul hasn't returned from Boston has he?"

"It turned out I didn't have to go to Boston," came a voice a few feet away.

Gustavia gasped. "Paul! I didn't see you."

"I guess it was because my back was to you. I was using Edgar's copy machine."

"Oh," she said in a small voice.

"Where have you been?" he asked. "Ada said she didn't know where you went, only that you left with a suitcase."

"Uh . . . are you through here?" she asked nervously.

"For tonight. How about going with me for a hamburger?"

～

Charlie's Choices, the hamburger place, was casual and cozy. Selecting a booth in the corner, they seated themselves across from each other. Immediately a waitress placed menus before them and Gustavia fidgeted as she tried to decide on one of the many different kinds of hamburgers they offered.

After the waitress had taken their orders, Gustavia, trying to put off the questions she knew Paul was going to ask her, queried him. "Why didn't you have to go to Boston?"

"After several phone calls, I was able to solve the problem without going. I came over today because I had something I needed to cover with Edgar."

"Oh."

He noted that her right hand was picking at a nail of her left. Something he had never seen her do before. "You seem nervous about something, Gusty. What is it?" When she seemed hesitant to answer, he asked, "Where did you go?"

"Well . . . you seemed so distant when you left Saturday, and you left so abruptly, I felt lonely. I needed to get away for the two days you'd be gone. It was difficult being at Ada's after everything that has happened," she answered honestly.

"I'm sorry you felt I was distant. You misread me. I can understand why you didn't want to stay at Ada's. So . . . where did you go?"

Gustavia panicked for a moment, took a deep breath and said a little prayer. "I went to Salt Lake City."

His eyes turned wary. "Why?"

"Well . . . uh, after we parted Saturday, I got a call from Artie Banks." She became silent, thinking how to tell him the rest.

Frowning, he nudged her. "And?"

"He asked me if I could come out and meet his family some time in the future."

Paul waited uneasily. Once more he had to pull it out of her. "Go on."

"I told him no because it would give him false hopes, but he wouldn't let it go. He promised me that I needn't feel obligated to him or his family in any way. In fact, he said that no matter how I felt about him, his parents wanted to meet me."

Paul's jaw rippled. "And—what did you think of his family?"

"They're wonderful people."

The waitress brought their hamburgers and malts. Gustavia tried to look engrossed in her food.

"Didn't you tell me that you're drawn to something in Artie's face or . . . uh something?"

"Yes. But . . ."

"Eat your hamburger," he said grimly, taking a bite himself. After a swallow of malt he said, "It sounds like you'd like to be part of the Banks family."

"For mercy sakes. I didn't say that."

"You didn't have to. I saw it in your eyes."

"Well, anyone would want to be part of a nice, loving family." She took a big bite, and fumed as she chewed. Taking another big bite, she deliberately took her time chewing and swallowing. Finally she said, "You think I'd marry him for his family?"

"No, but it sounds to me like you're beginning to care for Artie himself."

"I do, but . . ."

"I rest my case."

"Don't play the attorney with me, Paul Camden!"

Paul ate in silence, thinking. *Here I promise Gusty I wouldn't expect any-thing from her except friendship, then this Artie Banks comes along and wants her to meet his family! He's probably already told her he loves her!*

They were almost through when Paul stated adamantly, "This *friend-ship* thing between you and me is over, Gusty."

She practically choked on her last bite. "Wh-what?"

"You heard me. I don't even need to ask. I know that this Artie char-acter has professed feelings for you beyond friendship."

She was silent.

He smiled. "I thought so. Well—I'm not going to stand back and watch. I'm going to give Artie Banks some tough competition."

"H-he doesn't even know about you. He only knows about Freddie."

"Hm, why didn't you tell him about me?"

"Why should I? You promised me that you would keep our relation-ship on a friendship basis."

"Promise? I only said I would until the circumstances changed." His blue eyes flashed with unsettling eagerness. "They've changed all right and I feel justified in reneging."

Gustavia frowned. "You're complicating things, Paul. I feel Freddie is looking for me as I have him. I don't want to hurt you. I don't want to hurt Artie and I certainly don't want to hurt Freddie."

With the usual half smile on his lips, Paul's smiling eyes gazed at her. "Let me tell you the facts, my beautiful Gusty. That old adage: 'All's fair in love and war,' is true. When a man goes after a woman, he takes a chance on getting his heart broken. And that's just the way it is. You can't protect everyone."

"I . . . I don't know what to expect from you, Paul."

He grinned. "Wait and find out."

"I'm warning you, Freddie is still in the picture."

"How can I forget him? You mention him often enough. Let's get out of here."

Looking a little wary at her once reliable 'friend,' she scooted out of the booth.

He laughed, went over and paid the bill.

They were silent on the way to Ada's. Parking, he led her to her favorite place, the garden bench.

He took a big breath of the fragrance all around them. "Smells great here."

Still not knowing what to expect from Paul, Gustavia sat, stiffly apprehensive.

He gazed at her and smiled. "Relax, Gusty. I'm not the big bad wolf."

She laughed. "That's reassuring."

He laughed and pulled her next to him, cradling her in his arm. "I feel better already. How about you?"

She lay her head on his shoulder and sighed. "A lot better. I don't like you to be distant with me."

He kissed the top of her head. "I'm sorry, Gusty. I'm afraid I was and am a little jealous of Artie. He's a nice guy."

She looked up at him and smiled. "Thank you for admitting it." She kissed him on the cheek. "That's another thank you for making it possible for me to get 'the box' way ahead of Edgar's schedule and subsequently, the diaries."

"What about another kiss for the other part of your inheritance—you know, for making you wealthy?"

Tickled, she laughed, then quickly kissed him on the cheek once more.

He took her face in his hands, his eyes entreating hers. "That's not exactly the kind of kiss I had in mind, but it will do—for the present."

๛CHAPTER 24๛

The moment Gustavia opened her eyes Tuesday morning, her thoughts were on Paul. It was the day he usually came over, but everything had changed. Most importantly, their relationship had changed—and she had no idea how she was going to handle it. Since Paul had quit, he and Ada would no longer be working together. Instead, he and Edgar would be working on the problems created by the illegal activities of the past. But while this was going on what was she supposed to do? She certainly would be of no help. She had a difficult time even managing her own finances. If it hadn't been for her mother's insistence that she learn about such things and what to do in various situations, she would have been in terrible straits when her mother passed away.

And how was she going to bear living here in Ada's house until everything was settled? Dealing with her coldness was difficult enough, now she would have to live with her hate. She needed Paul.

Peeking into the dining room, Gustavia saw that Ada was already there, glowering over the newspaper. "Good morning, Ada," she said deciding to leave off the respectful title of 'cousin' from now on. Ada didn't acknowledge her greeting.

When Carol brought in the food, Gustavia smiled, happy to see a cheerful face. "Good morning, Carol."

"Good morning, Gustavia," she answered, smiling.

"Mmm, those omelettes look good." At least her appetite had returned.

Ada kept her eyes glued on the paper as she ate and Gustavia ate with a relish. "You know how to hire good help, Ada. Carol is an excellent cook," Gustavia stated between bites. She hadn't expected a response, and got none. After she was through, she sipped her tea and stared at her cousin, hoping she would look up. When she didn't, Gustavia asked the question anyway. "Ada, why do you hate me? Isn't it I who should hate you?"

Ada's gaze settled on her like a cold mist. "We have nothing to say to each other, Gustavia."

"Why? Why shouldn't we talk this all out?"

"What is there to talk about?"

"It's rather obvious, isn't it? You could say, 'I'm sorry, Gustavia.'"

"For what! My mother was responsible for all the difficulty we're in now."

"Edgar apologized for perpetuating it."

"Edgar's a weak man."

"I think it's just the opposite, Ada. It took a great deal of courage on his part."

"Courage? Hmph! Only when he was caught."

Gustavia silently agreed, but her heart went out to Edgar. His sincere remorse had touched her. Thoughtful for a moment, she asked, "What was your mother like, Ada? I would like to know my aunt Melissa."

The question took Ada by surprise, and momentarily she let her guard down. The expression of pain in her eyes was unmistakable. Her chin quivered slightly before she could resume the remote, unapproachable role at which she was so adept. "I don't feel like discussing my mother with you." Her gaze returned to the paper.

It was at that moment Gustavia made a decision. Excusing herself from the table, she left the room.

Entering the library hastily, she went over to the computer where she had left the material she had been working on. Relieved, everything was just as she had left it. Ada hadn't removed it as she had feared. She began where she left off, hopeful that she now could finish the biography. Surely Ada wouldn't dare be as critical of her work as she had been. *What am I thinking? I'll just finish the rest of it and hand it to her. If she isn't pleased with it, at least I will have done what I agreed to do.* As she began, she felt her attitude toward Ada's life and accomplishments changing. Was it the pain she had seen in her cousin's eyes that made her feel more charitable toward her?

Edgar entered, carrying two large briefcases. "Oh, good morning, Gustavia."

She smiled. "Good morning, Edgar."

He remained standing, puzzled. "Are you still working on Ada's biography?"

"Yes."

"Why?"

"Because I said I would."

His deep-set eyes moistened. "That's rather decent of you, Gustavia, considering the circumstances. Thank you," he said quietly. "Thank you."

Paul entered, briefcase in hand. "Good morning, Gusty, Edgar."

Edgar responded, and Gustavia, after greeting him, returned to work.

Paul set his briefcase down near Ada's desk, pulled up another small chair and placed it beside Ada's, which Edgar would now occupy. He glanced back at Gustavia, curious.

Moving to stand behind her, he asked. "Gusty, are you working on Ada's biography?"

"What does it look like?"

"Are you being snippy with me, Gusty?"

She swivelled her chair around and looked up at him. "After your pronouncement last night, everything has changed and I feel snippy."

His smiling eyes turned warm. His hand caressed her cheek. "It's very kind of you to finish Ada's biography."

Flustered, she quickly turned back to the computer, His hand had sent shivers of delight through her. Pretending to study Ada's records, she tried to gain control enough to concentrate on the less-than-exciting task in front of her.

The day dragged for Gustavia. The biography was going slower than she had hoped. Paul's presence was distracting and her thoughts kept straying to him.

Ada had not shown her face and Gustavia wondered what she could possibly be doing with herself since business was her whole existence.

At 6:00, Edgar and Paul quit for the day. Edgar smiled at Gustavia as he said good night. He had changed from a somewhat somber, withdrawn man to a friendly, more outgoing one. Grateful to see the real Edgar emerge from his self-imposed shell of guilt, she returned his greeting with warmth.

"Good night, Gusty," Paul said, closing his briefcase. "See you tomorrow."

"Good night," she answered quietly. Her hope that he would stop and talk with her was in vain. He didn't even look back.

Paul and Edgar resumed their work Wednesday morning. Now that they had finished sorting through all the documents, Ada had to be summoned to sit in for the rest of the time. Her body language was a picture of rigid opposition. Leaning back in the chair as far as she possibly could, arms folded tightly against her ribs, her chin protruding up at a defiant angle, she resentfully answered their questions, not offering any more help than she was forced to.

At one point, Ada finally noticed Gustavia typing at the computer. She sprang from her seat and stomped over to her. "What are you doing, Gustavia?"

"I'm doing what you asked me to do; I'm writing your biography."

Her voice rose peevishly. "You have no right to do that!"

"You've already given me the right," Gustavia replied calmly. "Because Paul discovered what he did, and because you weren't intending to give me my grandmother's diaries, doesn't mean I no longer have the obligation to finish what I said I would do."

Ada blinked several times, the struggle going on inside her obvious. The desire to make the world know that she existed, that her existence had been valuable in some way, fought with her continuing resentment toward Gustavia. "You . . . you are no longer obligated, Gustavia."

"I realize that, Ada, but I want to finish it. May I?"

Ada was at a loss how to answer. To conceal her relief, her pride compelled her to deliver an imperious reply. "Well—do what you want, Gustavia." She returned to her seat with an air of indifference.

Gustavia bristled, then recognizing Ada's attitude for what it was, dismissed it and returned to work.

Not one of the four stopped for tea. They only broke for lunch. Edgar had arranged with Carol to prepare food for all of them, but Ada continued to eat in her room whenever Paul was present.

At lunch, Gustavia felt like a lump sitting at the table with Paul and Edgar. They ignored her and continued to discuss business, the intricacies of which she didn't understand, and in which she couldn't participate.

Returning to the library, Paul and Edgar began to work. Gustavia sat down at the computer. Almost immediately she began feeling restless. *This would be a good time*, she thought, *to begin reading my grandmother's diaries!* Quickly, she saved the material on the hard drive, then on a floppy. Scooting her chair back, she stood up, shoved it under the desk and started to walk out.

"Where are you going, Gusty?" Paul asked.

"Oh, you remembered I was here?" she retorted.

Ignoring her sarcastic reply, he repeated the question.

"I'm going to my room."

"All right. Just don't leave the house. We're going to need your signature on some documents before long."

"Can't I sign them tomorrow?" she asked, still piqued at being ignored again today.

"No, you can't. I have to get this wrapped up. I'm sorry to give you such short notice, Gusty, but I wasn't sure until I finished with Edgar a few minutes ago, that if we can get reservations, we need to get on a plane for England tomorrow morning early."

"Tomorrow! But I had other plans this afternoon, and packing wasn't one of them."

Paul stood up, puzzled, but impatient with the unaccustomed recalcitrance from her. "If you want me to remain your lawyer, Gusty, you'll go upstairs and start packing your suitcase."

Gustavia knew she was acting childish, nevertheless, she gave a stubborn flip of her head and walked out.

Upstairs, she pulled out a suitcase and flung it on her bed, not in the least inclined to begin packing. She stood there thinking. *No, I promised myself I was going to begin reading the diaries. I'll pack later!*

Pulling out the first volume, she curled up on the window seat. Her hand trembling, she turned to the first page.

☙CHAPTER 25☙

HULL SEAMEN'S AND GENERAL ORPHAN ASYLUM, HULL, ENGLAND, JUNE 1910:

"Fanny Sullivan!" Mrs. Prickett cried in exasperation. Marmaduke Prickett, affectionately known by all her co-workers as Marmie, was a strong-willed woman of fifty, with a face to match. Her prominent jaw, worthy nose and high cheekbones gave her face a look of strength. Her standard uniform was a white bonnet over her brass-blonde hair, a white bodice, and a violet blue skirt that matched her attentive blue eyes. Ordinarily, Mrs. Prickett was a patient woman, but her patience was being sorely tried. The new child, Fanny Sullivan, had gone into hysterics. and it had taken far too long to calm her. "Will you please take those fancy clothes off and put on the uniform."

Fanny sat on the dorm bed, her arms folded tightly across her chest, her eyes shooting fire. "No! I'm not an orphan! I have a sister named Melissa who'll take care of me."

"You must stop saying that. I'll tell you once more, you were brought here by friends of your sister telling us that both your parents were dead and that your sister couldn't take care of you because of her ill health. Since it was approved by the Board of Management, I'm sure they felt it wasn't possible for her to take you in."

"But I'm old enough to help Melissa. I can learn to cook and clean and—"

"I said, change into that uniform or I'll call the headmaster, Mr. Wimble."

"Go ahead—call him!"

Mrs. Prickett studied the small ten-year-old girl. Her thick, naturally curly, reddish blonde hair, tied back at the nape of her neck with a green ribbon, would soon have to be cut to ear length like all the other girls. She had large eyes the color of mid-day sky, light and bright. A sprinkle of freckles dotted her nose and cheeks. "A stubborn lass, that's what you are," Mrs. Prickett muttered as she turned and walked down the aisle between two rows of beds.

After Mrs. Prickett disappeared, the fear and confusion that had held back Fanny's tears suddenly burst into angry, hurt sobs. "Melissa, why did you send me here?" she cried. Her heart was already breaking over her papa drowning on one of his fishing boats, and so soon after her sweet mother had died! Now, it felt as though she had lost her sister too!

Heavy purposeful steps on the white-scrubbed floor boards echoed through the large room. They were coming toward her, but she couldn't stop the flood of tears that had been released.

Arthur Wimble, a tall, slightly stooped man with wisps of light brown hair encircling his bald head, wore dignity as if it were part of him, fitting him like the black suit, high white collar and black tie he wore. His even brows, long nose and thin lips made up an ordinary looking face until one gazed into his deep-set hazel eyes, which revealed such tenderness, one expected them to water at the slightest injustice.

He gazed down under hooded lids at the sobbing child, feeling uneasy as he always did over female tears, whether they be young or old. "Miss Sullivan, will you please get hold of yourself." After waiting a reasonable length of time and observing no change whatsoever, he repeated the request once more, louder and more firmly.

The sobs subsided to soft sounds coming from her heaving chest.

"Miss Sullivan, we at the orphanage are always sad when a child has to be admitted. We only work here. We don't have the authority to change the situation. Our job is to care for that child as best we can, and that's what Mrs. Prickett is trying to do, care for you and help you get integrated into our system of doing things. I would appreciate it if you would cooperate with her."

The small face looked up, blue eyes defiant. "I don't belong here!"

"Many of our children here feel the same way, but as I said, Miss Sullivan, even as headmaster, I cannot change the decision." He paused, then added in a kinder tone of voice, "As much I would like to."

Fanny noted the change of tone and nodded.

"Maybe soon your sister will be healthier and will come for you. We must all have hope for better things, or life can be very dreary indeed. I'll send Mrs. Prickett back in to assist you."

Fanny nodded and watched him walk briskly out of the room. Though the tears had stopped, her heart was still breaking. *Soon, it will break right in two, I'm sure of it. Then I'll be dead, and Melissa will be sorry!*

She picked up the uniform and examined it. It was light brown with no waist. The sleeves came a little below the elbow. A white apron that came to the neck, over the shoulders and down three-quarters of the length of the dress, went over it.

Mrs. Prickett appeared. "That's a good lass."

"It's ugly!"

"That's only the second best uniform. You have a Sunday one that's nicer. There are two hooks on which to hang them when you're not wearing them," she said, pointing to the hooks between the beds. "Place your shoes neatly under the dresses as you prepare for bed, so no one stumbles if they have to use the water closet in the middle of the night."

Glumly, Fanny unbuttoned her favorite green dress with its lace collar. "What shall I do with my nice dress, Mrs. Prickett?"

"Put everything you have on in your suitcase, then shove it under the bed. All the children here have to wear the same type of clothing. Also under the bed you'll find a box that contains a second set of your everyday uniform. There are two pairs of underwear, two white knee-length stockings, two white pocket handkerchiefs, one red flannel petticoat, and two nightgowns. At present, we're trying to find a Sunday best uniform your size. You're a small one, Miss Fanny."

In spite of her heavy heart, Fanny found herself drawn to the kind Mrs. Prickett. "Thank you," she murmured, trying to smile.

Mrs. Prickett led Fanny into the dining room for supper where the children were already seated. The boys sat at three large tables at one end of the room and the girls at tables at the opposite end. All eyes were upon the new arrival as Mrs. Prickett took her to the place she had prepared for her. She introduced Fanny and told everyone to introduce themselves to her after grace.

Fanny ordinarily wasn't shy around strangers, but she wasn't inclined to get acquainted with this group. She didn't belong with them—and she certainly wasn't going to stay long enough to form any friendships!

The girls' supervisor, Miss Locke, signaled with a grave and courteous nod for the boys' duty master to start singing grace. Afterward, one of the girls next to Fanny explained that Miss Locke was their sewing mistress. Fanny didn't respond to the information.

Not rebuffed by Fanny, the girl informed her, "My name's Sophie Hunter, and I'm nine. How old are you?"

"Ten."

"I know how you feel, Fanny. You don't think you belong here, do you?"

"How did you know?"

"Because that's the way I felt when I first came because I have a mother and five brothers and sisters at home."

Fanny's eyes widened in disbelief. "Wh-why are you here then?"

"Mum is a widow. My father fell under a steamer keel in the Albert dock He broke his spine."

"I'm sorry, but why aren't you with your mum?"

"She's very poor and has to go out to work. My other brothers and sisters are older and care for themselves and even earn a little money. Mum couldn't afford to keep us. My little brother is here too. He's seven."

Horrified that Sophie's family had to be separated, she asked. "Do you ever get to see your family?"

"On special occasions Alfie and I get to go home for a couple of days."

"I'm glad for that, Sophie."

"Thank you."

At this point, the other girls at the table took turns introducing themselves to Fanny, who by that time had warmed up considerably.

Four older girls, who had been assigned the task, placed a bun in front of each child.

Fanny studied it, frowning. "Is this all we get to eat?"

"We had Irish stew for dinner, and with tea this afternoon we had bread and butter and cake, so we don't need anything more than a bun. That's what they think anyway."

Fanny wasn't the least bit hungry. She kept having to swallow the lump in her throat which threatened more tears.

Sophie, who had been hungrily eating her bun, stared at Fanny's. "Don't you want your bun?"

Fanny shook her head.

"Can I have it then?"

Fanny nodded and pushed it over to her, determined not to embarrass herself by breaking down and blubbering in front of everyone at the table.

After supper, Mrs. Prickett asked her if she would like to go outside and play games with the children before bedtime. She shook her head, so Mrs. Prickett escorted her back to the dormitory. "Tomorrow, we'll get you started on a routine of chores like the other children. The busier you are, the better. And after chores, the children can play games outside, read or whatever they please. Do you have any questions?"

She shook her head. Mrs. Prickett smiled kindly. "You'll make friends here, and it won't be so bad after a time."

Fanny nodded and Mrs. Prickett left the room.

Lying down on the lumpy straw-filled mattress, Fanny put her hands behind her head and stared at the ceiling, going over in her mind how she had ended up here. It all had occurred so strangely, so quickly after her father's funeral she hadn't realized what was actually happening to her.

Standing beside Melissa and her new husband, Sir John Redmore, at her father's graveside, she had sobbed her heart out. Melissa, tears running down her own cheeks, had put her arm around her and together they grieved over their loss.

After the service, Melissa and Sir John took her back to the only home she had ever known, the large four story, three-bay house on Corve street in Ludlow, telling her to pack a suitcase, that she couldn't stay there in the house alone. Feeling as though she were walking around in a bad dream, she did what her sister told her, certain that they were going to take her back to London with them. Her heart ached at the thought of leaving home and going to such a big, strange city.

When she was through packing, she closed her suitcase and went downstairs to tell Melissa she was ready. Instead of Melissa and her husband, she found an older couple.

"Where's my sister?" she had asked.

"You sister wasn't feeling well. My husband and I are to accompany you to your destination," answered the woman.

"But why can't I go with them?" she asked, feeling confused and frightened.

"They've already gone."

"Gone? Why didn't they tell me? Why . . ."

"You'll understand why later, Miss Sullivan," the man answered firmly.

Her voice had risen. "Where are they? I know they wouldn't go without me!"

"They're gone," replied the man gruffly. "They left instructions for us." He took hold of her arm. "Now don't give us any trouble, you hear?"

She glared at him. "My suitcase is upstairs."

"I'll go get it, and you two go get in the carriage."

She and the woman waited in the carriage. Fanny watched the man come out with her suitcase. He locked the door securely before he joined them. The driver of the carriage took them to the Ludlow-Hereford railway station to wait for a train. It wasn't long before it arrived and they were settled in a compartment. She sat across from the unfriendly couple but stared out the window to avoid looking at them.

Soon they reached Birmingham where they had to change trains. When they reached Sheffield, they had to change trains again. At last they arrived at the railway station in Hull. Fanny, certain that they were on their way to London to meet up with her sister, was surprised when the man said, "This is our stop."

Speculating that they were going to change trains again, she was shocked to see the man hail a carriage.

"Where are we going?"

"You'll see," the woman said.

Fearfully, Fanny watched out the window. *Maybe Melissa is meeting me in this city*, she thought. She took a few deep breaths and felt calmer, certain that this was the case.

When the carriage stopped at a large nice-looking building, she wasn't concerned, feeling that this was where Melissa was waiting for her.

Suitcase in one hand, the other hand gripping her arm painfully, the man almost dragged her inside the building.

"Ow!" she exclaimed indignantly. "I can walk in without your help!"

While the man still held Fanny, his companion rang the bell for him. A kind-faced woman answered.

"I have a Miss Fanny Sullivan here. I believe you're expecting her?"

"Yes. Please come in," she said, smiling at Fanny.

"Here are the signed papers, and here is the note," the woman said, pulling them out of a large handbag.

The woman looked over the papers and thanked them. They nodded and exited quickly.

"It's nice to meet you, Fanny. My name is Mrs. Prickett." Placing the papers on a hall table but keeping the note, Mrs. Prickett picked up her suitcase. "Come and I'll show you where you'll be sleeping."

"Sleeping? Where's my sister?"

"Why, I don't know, dear. I have a note here. Let me show you where you'll be sleeping, and I'll read it to you."

Feeling more apprehensive by the minute, Fanny followed her to a long room that had four single beds on each side. Mrs. Prickett led her to one on the far end. "What is this . . . this room?"

"This is a dormitory, dear. You'll be sleeping with seven other girls around your age."

"Wh-hat is this place?" she asked fearfully.

A bit startled, Mrs Prickett asked, "Don't you know?"

Fanny shook her head, her large blue eyes troubled.

Troubled herself, Mrs. Prickett said, "Sit down, dear, and I'll tell you."

Fanny sat down. Mrs. Prickett sat beside her, opened the note and read it. "This note says that your sister isn't well and can't take care of you."

Fanny shook her head, bewildered. "But I just saw my sister at my father's funeral early this morning. She was unhappy over my father dying, but she wasn't sick!"

Mrs. Prickett frowned, her lips set in an angry line at the cavalier way this child had been treated. Getting hold of herself, she said gently, "Fanny dear, this is an orphanage. Your sister has placed you here because of her ill health."

Fanny shot to her feet. "An orphanage! I don't belong in an orphanage! My sister can take me in. I know it."

Mrs. Prickett stood up and had put her arms around Fanny, trying to calm her rising hysterics. Another woman apparently heard the ruckus and came in to help Mrs. Prickett, blocking the space between the beds so Fanny couldn't get out.

Still lying on the bed, Fanny's agitation returned as she remembered how she had jumped over the other bed and run down the aisle. The younger woman caught her and held her fast. Tears trickled down Fanny's cheeks as she thought of how she had screamed over and over. "I don't belong here! There's been a mistake. My sister wouldn't do this!"

It had taken both the women to get her back to her bed. They stayed with her until the hysterics had subsided, but the terror at being abandoned remained.

It was then she had secretly made a decision to escape and find a way to get to London to her sister. She had obeyed Mrs. Prickett, put on the uniform and gone in for supper.

Now, looking around, she saw that she was still the only one in the dorm room. *Since no one has come back from playing outside, maybe now's the time,* she thought. Quickly pulling out her suitcase from under the bed, she searched for her purse. She had saved up quite a few pence. She hoped it was enough to pay for the train ticket to London. Quickly taking off her uniform and the disgusting petticoat and underwear, she put on her own clothes. She grabbed her light coat, her small purse and her suitcase and shoved all the orphanage clothes under the bed.

Stealthily, she walked down the wooden floor to a hallway. Looking around carefully she saw no one. She ran to the foyer, unlocked the door and stepped out, closing it quietly behind her. She noticed it was beginning to get dark, which was all the better. She ran as fast as she could in the direction the carriage had come from, having no idea how to get to the railway station. *Somehow I'll find it!* she thought.

Meanwhile, Mrs. Prickett was having a conference with the headmaster over Fanny Sullivan. "Mr. Wimble, Fanny's father died unexpectedly by drowning. It takes time for the Board of Management to decide what child needs to be taken into the orphanage. How could Fanny's sister and husband have applied before the father had even died?"

Mr. Wimble rubbed his chin as he studied the papers. "It says here, Mrs. Prickett, that the father's health had been waning since the death of his wife and the only sibling Fanny had was an older sister who had ill health. They asked the board to consider taking Fanny in the event of her father's death."

"But," Mrs. Prickett protested, "the father lived in Ludlow. The rule is a family has to be living in the Hull/Grimsby area before they can admit a family member into the orphanage."

Mr. Wimble glanced down at the papers before him. "It says here that the father owned a fishing fleet in Grimsby and had stayed there at times so it qualifies them."

"If they sold the fishing fleet, Fanny would inherit some money and . . ."

"It says here that the fishing fleet had not been profitable."

"Still, Mr. Wimble, as Fanny said so herself. She's old enough to help her sister."

Mr. Wimble thoughtfully nodded. "It would seem so, Mrs. Prickett, it would seem so. I think I'll write to the sister in London. I have her address here."

"Thank you, Mr. Wimble. In the meantime, we'll try to acclimate the child to the orphanage in case her sister will not take her."

Gustavia closed the diary, stunned. Tears trickled down her cheeks. Fanny had been put into an orphanage! "So that's what happened to her," she said aloud. She jumped to her feet and moved about the room in agitation. "It's unbelievable. How could Melissa have been so cruel?"

She looked at her watch. She had to shower and get packed. She decided to take only modern-day clothes for practicality. Reluctantly, she placed the diary with the other volumes, determining that, as much as she wanted to continue, she would have to leave them with Edgar again for safe keeping.

❧CHAPTER 26❦

The long flight to Heathrow airport in London went by quickly for Gustavia and Paul. Though Gustavia knew Paul had been busy taking care of her inheritance problems, she still felt neglected, foolishly so, she knew. Consequently, she treasured this uninterrupted time to talk with him. She was anxious to share her tragic discovery of the night before.

"You'll never believe what I read last night in Fanny's diary."

"You mean you stayed up and read her diary last night?"

"Only a little of it." She lowered her voice, her dark eyes shafts of anger. "I found out what happened to Fanny!"

Paul, his mouth slightly ajar at her emotion, asked, "What?"

"Right after her father's funeral, Melissa had a man and a woman take her to an orphanage in Hull and just dump her there without any explanation to her beforehand."

"An orphanage!" He passed a hand across his forehead. "What a terrible shock that must have been to the young child. What happened after that?"

"I don't know. She had just run away from the orphanage when I had to stop reading and pack. I'm anxious to read the next part." Gustavia brightened. "I see now why I couldn't find her name on the family history Web site. She was born in Ludlow—where we're going."

Paul nodded, but made no comment.

Renting a car at Heathrow, Paul took the motorway that would be the quickest route to Ludlow.

Rolling hills and trees and sheep grazing in green fields appeared as they neared their destination. Reaching the beautiful little city of Church Stratten, Paul drove up a winding road to an imposing hotel on a hill which he had seen on his other trips. The name, Long Mynd, evoked past centuries in this area where Wales and England converged.

Gustavia was delighted with the room Paul had reserved for her. The bed was a charming four poster with sheer curtains on each corner and a lace bedspread. It had a wonderful view of the countryside. Leaving their luggage in their rooms, they drove back down the winding road reaching Ludlow in twenty-five minutes.

Ludlow was everything Gustavia had expected. It was a picturesque, charming, historic town. "Can we see the town this afternoon and do our business tomorrow?"

He hesitated. "I've wanted to look around while on my trips here before, but felt I couldn't take the time. Oh, what the heck, it may be a long time before we get back again. I'm sure Edgar wouldn't mind in the least."

Parking the car, they got out and strolled the streets. They stopped and bought some fish and chips wrapped in paper, then went on their way. Crossing a narrow street sandwiched between two buildings, they saw an interesting looking church called St. Laurence Parish Church, with beautiful stained glass windows. Gustavia stopped and gazed at it.

Paul put his arm around her and tilted her face to his, his eyes warm and intimate. "Someday, Gusty, I hope we'll have time to investigate all we want." He watched her flustered reaction and knew she was still holding back for Freddie. He kissed her brow. "I'm afraid it will have to be a cursory inspection today. But there's one place where I must take you. I haven't had time to see it myself. Someone told me the location."

"Where?" she asked a little breathlessly.

"You'll find out," he whispered mysteriously. "Let's meander down several of the interesting streets first."

He led her down Corve Street. "I like this street because of the view of the stately tower of Ludlow Parish Church."

"What a charming old street." She gazed at the three and four story row houses on both sides of the street, connected by their common walls. "I like that pleasant three-bay Georgian house right there," she said pointing. She stopped suddenly. "Paul! I just remembered. Fanny lived on Corve street in a three bay house. Maybe that's the very one!"

They approached and stood looking at the house. Gustavia's eyes brimmed with tears."

Paul gently put his arm around her and drew her to him. She leaned her head against his chest, too full of emotion to speak.

After a few minutes, they began walking. As they moved down Bull Ring Street Paul told her a little of what he knew about the town. "Ludlow is built on the bank of the River Teme. Ruins of a castle still remain over there," he said pointing, "on the steepest slope of the bank. I'd like to take you to see it sometime. Along the rest of the bank, there are still some trees and foliage, but now it's mainly pasture land."

Taking her hand firmly in his, Paul led her down Old Street. Sauntering along, they came to a lane next to a house. Turning onto it, he led her down the path into a cemetery. His eyes were filled with excitement. "This is the place I wanted to bring you to, Gusty."

Gustavia gasped at the sight. Hidden among an overgrowth of weeds and foliage, and shaded by several large old trees were many shapes and sizes of old head stones. "Oh, Paul, this is utterly beautiful. It must be an old-old cemetery."

"It is. From what I understand," he said slyly, "your ancestors are buried here."

Her eyes widened in disbelief. "Who?"

He smiled, eager to surprise her. "John and Sarah Sullivan."

She drew in a quick breath. "Oh! Where? Show me!"

"I don't know where. Let's look for them."

Excited, they waded through the overgrowth reading all the decipherable names on every headstone. Through the leafy limbs the warm sunshine dappled the stones and vines with light, giving it the aura of a magic garden—something from a fairytale, something so mysterious and charming that it made one hope that no human hand would ever change it.

At last, entangled in a most delightful flowering plant, they discovered an elegant old stone. "Here's one!" cried Gustavia. "It's Sarah Sullivan!"

"Paul pulled out a pen and paper from his pocket. "Let's write down the dates of her birth and death."

"Oh yes! Thank you."

Putting the pen and paper back a moment, he helped Gustavia pull a cluster of weeds away from the stone next to hers. "And here's John Sullivan's head stone." Paul said. "Not quite as elegant, but nice." He recorded the birth and death dates.

Gustavia gazed at both stones, a far away look on her face. "I have the most unusual feeling."

"Oh? What is it?"

"I . . . I don't know how to describe it except that it's a very poignant emotion."

Paul took this opportunity to put his arm around her shoulders. "I wish I could share it with you. I do feel a peacefulness. I always feel that way in a cemetery, and especially in this one."

"I wish we could stay here for hours," she murmured.

They gazed at the two stones, the silent, mysterious aura of John and Sarah's lives seemed to surround them. The mystery of all the lives put to rest here in nature's garden seemed to whisper through the leaves on the trees, rustling gently with the breeze.

Paul reached out, gently moving away some other weeds from the head stones so they could be in full view and Gustavia helped him. Almost immediately Gustavia cried out, "Ouch! My hands and arms are stinging."

"Mine are too," Paul exclaimed. He looked closer at the weeds they had just touched. "Oh for crying out loud, those are patches of stinging nettle. Let's get out of here."

Laughing, they rubbed their small welts as they waded through the vinery toward the entrance as fast as they could.

"That was a rude ending to my surprise for you."

Gustavia laughed. "Nevertheless I enjoyed every minute of it. If it hadn't been for the stinging nettle you might not have gotten me out of there."

It took three days to get the legal entanglement of Gustavia's inheritance righted.

The first step was to file the Quit Claim Deed which Ada and Edgar had signed. In this document Edgar and Ada deeded over to Gustavia all claims and title to the quarry. At Gustavia's insistence everything was handled very carefully so that Ada and Edgar would not be implicated in the inheritance fraud their parents had committed.

Since Paul had informed Gustavia she had to be in attendance most of the time to sign legal documents when needed, she went to a book store and purchased a book on the history of Ludlow to read while waiting.

To Gustavia's delight, a trip to the stone quarry with the barrister was necessary. They drove north of Ludlow, past Clee Hill to the quarry that had belonged to John and Sarah Sullivan.

The barrister remarked to Gustavia, "It's a good thing you're an English woman, Miss Browne. Quarrymen hand down the employment from father to son and form a guild among themselves. The intrusion of strangers or 'kimberlins,' as they're termed, are warmly resented."

Paul stopped the car in front of some stone cliffs, cut away with exposed grey, jagged roots of rock, now covered here and there with grass and wild flowers.

"How lovely!" cried Gustavia.

"This is the older section of your quarry, Gusty. There are more hills, and also areas which are mined in an open-pit fashion. Your quarry has a plentiful supply of stone."

"What kind of stone comes out of the quarry?" she asked.

"Fine-grained stone—cream and buff in color, hard white flagstone and grey building stones from the hills. Most of the pit-mined stone is limestone."

"This is fascinating. I had never stopped to think where building stones come from. And I can hardly believe I own all this."

"It is rather unbelievable," Paul said, smiling at her. Starting the car, he drove them to the other parts of the quarry.

While Paul and the barrister, with the help of a recently completed survey, made sure the map of the quarry and legal description matched that of the quarry itself, Gustavia watched with fascination the industrious amount of activity going on.

Finally, everything was in order and it was time for them to pack up and leave the lovely old city of Ludlow, leave the graves of her great-grandparents, tended only by nature itself. Silently, Gustavia said goodbye to them, promising to return.

Leaving Heathrow airport, the plane climbed to its cruising altitude and leveled out. When the seatbelt sign went off. Gustavia leaned close to Paul and sighed. "I wonder if you can really understand how much this trip has meant to me. Thank you, more than I can say." She leaned over and kissed him on the cheek, her lips lingering momentarily.

Impulsively his hand grasped her shoulder and his face moved toward hers. The intensity of his gaze brought color to her face, her cheeks burning. Instinctively she pulled away.

Paul smiled and sighed. "Is that still all I get. A kiss on the cheek?

Disquieted, she said smiling, "Maybe it would be easier if we could go back to being just friends."

Her smile helped ease Paul's disappointment.

❧CHAPTER 27❧

Monday morning, after returning from England, Gustavia entered the dining room and found Ada already eating breakfast. "Good morning Ada." There was no response. This made Gustavia want to lash out at her, to hurt her as the cruel Melissa had hurt her little sister. But she held her tongue. She had to keep reminding herself that Ada had had nothing to do with it.

Sitting at her usual place, she filled her plate. "I had a wonderful experience while I was in Ludlow, Ada. Paul took me to a beautiful old cemetery and showed me the graves of our grandparents, John and Sarah Sullivan."

"I've seen them," she replied curtly, not looking up.

"He also took me to Corve street where little Fanny had lived for only ten years of her life and then . . ." She stopped herself.

"That's not news to me, Gustavia."

"I suppose it isn't," Gustavia said quietly. Ada's attitude didn't make it easy to go into the library and work on her biography. Paul was going to be in Augusta until Thursday and she felt at loose ends. In fact, she definitely wasn't ready to start on the biography again—Fanny's diaries were calling to her.

Finishing her breakfast in silence, she excused herself and went upstairs.

Curled up on the window seat, she opened the diary.

HULL SEAMENS' AND GENERAL ORPHAN ASYLUM, HULL, ENGLAND, JUNE 1910:

"Where's Fanny Sullivan, Mrs. Prickett?" Sophie asked as she followed the rest of the girls into the dorm room.

Mrs. Prickett glanced at her empty bed. "Girls! Did any of you see Fanny Sullivan out on the playground?"

The round of "no's" and shaking heads alarmed Mrs. Prickett. Quickly, she went to Fanny's bed and pulled out her box. With it came the brown uniform. Her breath short, she looked again and found her suitcase gone!

Jumping to her feet, she ordered everyone to bed and left the room as quickly as her legs would carry her without unduly alarming the girls.

Finding Mr. Wimble ushering a rowdy bunch of boys through the hall to their rooms, Mrs. Prickett rushed up to him. "Mr. Wimble," she whispered, "I'm afraid we have an emergency."

"Oh?" Turning his attention back to the boys, he said, "On with all of you!" he ordered sternly.

Unused to that tone of voice from Mr. Wimble, the boys calmed down and walked quickly and orderly to their rooms.

"What is it, Mrs. Prickett?"

"I think Fanny Sullivan has run away."

His brows rose in consternation. "Are you certain?"

"Fairly so. She left the uniform under the bed and the suitcase she came with is gone. If I had my guess, her mind is set on getting to her sister in London."

"I'll ring up the constable and inform him straightaway, then the Mrs. and I will get into the carriage and go looking for her ourselves. You stay here in case the constable finds her before we do."

The constable sent out bobbies on their bicycles scouring the neighborhoods, fanning out in all directions from the orphanage as well as checking the railway station.

In the meantime, to calm her anxiety, Mrs. Prickett went about her usual routine overseeing the girls' young supervisors, then personally making certain that all the girls were obeying them and preparing for bed. In each room, from the younger to the older girls, she reminded them that they were not to visit after lights out, suggesting that it would be well to say their prayers. And she herself said a prayer in her heart for the safety of the lost little girl.

Three hours later, a weary and worried headmaster and headmistress, Arthur and May Wimble, returned empty handed. But to everyone's relief, it was only moments later that two bobbies showed up with one tired and frightened little girl.

Mr. Wimble sternly ordered Fanny into his office, requesting that his wife May and Mrs. Prickett accompany him. Seated behind his desk, Mr. Wimble glared at Fanny. She glared back.

"You gave us quite a scare, Miss Sullivan. We usually punish children severely who try to run away." He paused to watch her reaction, but saw only defiance. "However, Mrs. Wimble and I have decided that your case is a little unusual—so we're going to let it go this time. But I'm warning you if you ever try running away again, you will find yourself in a serious predicament. Do you understand?"

Fanny, tight-lipped, her hands clasped in her lap, refused to reply.

May Wimble, a slight woman with large, kind, brown eyes which matched her light brown hair pulled up into a bouffant style, addressed her. "Fanny, Mrs. Prickett here brought something to Mr. Wimble's attention that we ourselves have wondered about. We have decided to bring these questions to the attention of the Board of Management immediately. We're also going to write to your sister in London and suggest that you are old enough to help her in her ill health."

The defiance in Fanny's face crumbled and her chest jerked with dry left-over sobs.

"Nothing was said that indicated your sister and her husband were struggling financially, so that's one of the questions we'll ask the Board," added Mr. Wimble. "If they can afford to have you, and since you are most certainly old enough to be of help to her, it may be possible to place you in her care. As I told you before, as headmaster I have no control other than to place all this before the Board. Please, Miss Fanny, do not get your hopes up. If your situation can't be changed, you must be brave and adjust to it. Is that clear?"

She nodded. "Th-thank you, Mr. Wimble, Mrs. Wimble. I'm sorry I caused you to worry."

"Well now," Mrs. Prickett piped up cheerfully, "I think it's time that you join the other girls in sleepy land. Your little legs must be very tired."

Fanny took her proffered hand. "Thank you," she said, swallowing back buckets of tears, "I am tired."

The next day, Fanny awakened to a loud bell. It took her a moment to remember where she was. She wasn't home with her father. She was in an orphanage! The pain seemed too much to bear. *First Mum gone, then Dad!* The only sliver of light in her life was the hope Mr. Wimble talked about, hope that she could go live with her sister.

She looked about her and saw the girls getting dressed quickly, so she did too. Mrs. Prickett stood sentinel, forestalling questions she knew would be fired at Fanny Sullivan.

At breakfast, Fanny stared at the fare—bread and drippings, sausage and tea. She picked at it, but wasn't hungry in the least. Sophie was full of questions about her runaway last night. Several of the other girls close around also wanted to hear all about it.

Fanny didn't want to talk about it, but felt beholden to say something. "I was wrong to try to run away."

The questions kept coming, but all she could do was shake her head and mutter, "I don't want to talk about it."

After breakfast, everyone started doing their various chores. Some of the girls were assigned to work in the laundry, others helped Miss Locke with the mending, and the rest helped with the cleaning. The boys were required to do some of the same tasks—cleaning and working in the laundry helping the laundress. Others assisted the handyman or helped with the gardening and yard work.

The chores were assigned by the week, then they traded off so the children could learn proficiency in every area. Fanny's chore for the week was helping the cook, Mrs. Mabel Cracken, prepare dinner. Several older girls were helping also. Her job was to peel potatoes, something she had never done before. As far as Fanny could remember, her parents had a housekeeper and cook who did everything. All she had to do was make her bed and clean her room.

Mrs. Cracken frightened Fanny. She was a stout woman who permanently wore a fierce frown.

"What do you mean, you don't know how to peel potatoes?" Mrs. Cracken asked sharply.

"I just don't, that's all," she fired back before she thought.

"Oh, a smart-mouth huh? You won't get dinner today if you mouth off once more. Now here's how it's done." Fanny watched carefully. "Here's the knife. It's sharp. If you cut yourself it will be because of your carelessness."

It was slow, laborious work and several times Mrs. Cracken scolded her for making the peels too thick, for being too slow and finally for not having a good attitude. When tea time came, Mrs. Cracken told her she hadn't earned it and to keep on working. Fanny was beginning to feel weak from not eating and by 11:30 she was also feeling dizzy. She slumped to the floor.

"Mrs. Cracken!" screamed one of the girls. "The new girl's fainted."

"She's just putting on," the cook said, stomping over to her, shaking her. "Stand up!" she ordered. Fanny tried, but her legs felt too wobbly. Mrs. Cracken panicked. "Go get Mrs. Prickett," she snapped at one of the girls.

Presently, Mrs. Prickett's kind face bent over her. "What's the matter, dear?"

"I don't know. I just felt a little dizzy and my legs wouldn't hold me."

"I've noticed you haven't been eating, Fanny. I think all you need is a good solid meal."

"But I'm sick of the smell of cooking fish, and all the other smells in the kitchen. I'm not hungry."

"Nevertheless, my girl, you're going to eat." She lifted Fanny to her feet and helped her walk into the dining room to a chair at one of the tables. "No one is here yet, but you stay put and I'll bring you dinner."

Mrs. Prickett came back with a tray of food. She lifted a plate of steamed cod, mashed potatoes and greens and placed it before her, then added a bowl of milk pudding.

Fanny pulled a face. "I can't eat, Mrs. Prickett, honest."

Sitting beside Fanny, Mrs. Prickett picked up a fork, pushed a mouthful of mashed potatoes onto the back of it with a butter knife and put it to Fanny's lips. "Open your mouth, dearie, you need your strength."

Reluctantly, she did as she was told. Mrs. Prickett kept right on, bite by bite. "I've lost a loved one, dearie, and it does take away your appetite, but here you don't have the luxury to rest until it comes back." Fanny was at last able to get it all down. The milk pudding tasted the best.

"I think I'm feeling better already, Mrs. Prickett. Thank you." Just then someone rang a bell and the children started coming in and taking their places.

"Come with me, little one," Mrs. Prickett said, holding out her hand. Leading Fanny into the library, she found one of the few soft seats and told her to sit down. Finding a book, she brought it over to her. "I know your mind isn't on reading, but I think this book will pique your interest and for a short time take you out of your world of grief."

Tears glistened in Fanny's eyes. "Thank you, Mrs. Prickett."

❧CHAPTER 28❦

HULL SEAMEN'S AND GENERAL ORPHAN ASYLUM, HULL, ENGLAND, JUNE 1910:

Miss Locke, the seamstress, was by nature more patient than Mrs. Cracken. She was also as thin as Mrs. Cracken was stout. Her fingers moved quickly, and professionally while making uniforms for the new children and altering those which had been outgrown. Though only in her thirties, she looked older because of her pinched features, and overly serious expression. Her unbecoming hairstyle was that of an older woman. It was a nondescript color of dull blonde, pulled up off her neck into a bun on the top of her head.

Many of the newer girls had never used a needle and thread so Miss Locke, with the help of a few older girls, had to teach them the basics of sewing.

Fanny's week in the kitchen was over and her assignment this week was to help Miss Locke with the mending. She liked this chore. She found it much easier than peeling potatoes and washing heavy pots. Her mum had taught her to embroider when she was seven so it wasn't long before Miss Locke complimented her on how quickly she learned to mend.

While her fingers worked, her mind did also. All she could think of was the letter from her sister that was sure to be coming soon. Mr. Wimble had informed her that he had written the letter as promised. Already, she had asked him twice if a letter had come. He patiently explained. "Miss Fanny, do not ask me once more. It has barely had time to reach London. We can't expect to hear for at least another week or so."

Fanny's appetite hadn't improved, but she forced herself to eat so she would be strong when her sister came to get her. She liked tea time the best because they were served something sweet; bread and butter and jam, or cakes. Everyone complained that the portions of food weren't large enough, but they were still too large for her.

Fanny hated bath time the most. Yesterday she had experienced her first bath. Because of the shortage of tubs, two girls had to bathe together. Everything was done in unison by numbers. At 'one' you scrubbed your partner's back, at 'two' you turned around and scrubbed yourself. The same system was used for the morning wash, 'one' hands, 'two' face, 'three' towel dry. She put up with all the strangeness of the activities and routines because she was certain she would not be remaining here much longer.

Someone rang the bell for dinner. Everyone filed out in an orderly manner. She took her place beside Sophie, the only one she had allowed to become her friend. She was content to not form any other friendships. However, during the last two meals, Helen, an eleven-year-old, large for her age, who sat across from her, had begun saying unkind things. Fanny had ignored her, trying to bite her 'wayward' tongue as her mum had often referred to the distressing habit of speaking her mind, no matter what it was.

Today, Helen grimaced as Fanny sat down. "Oh look, everybody, here's Mrs. Prickett's pet." The nearest girls tittered.

Fanny's face flushed with anger, but before she could retort, the servers were placing the food before them and the moment passed. Fanny pulled a face at the plate of boiled mutton, chipped potatoes and greens. The only thing that looked good was the stewed fruit and custard.

"You pullin' a face over Mrs. Cracken's cooking?" Helen asked Fanny. "We all like her cooking, so if you don't want it, hand it over."

It was too much for Fanny. "I'm pulling a face because I have to look at your disagreeable puss across the table."

"Is that so?" she said, swiping Fanny's custard.

"Give that back to me right now," Fanny demanded.

"Come and get it, Prickett's pet."

Fanny stood up, reached over and grabbed Helen's plate of food."

Helen screamed. "Help! Fanny Sullivan took my food!"

Miss Locke hurried over. "Fanny, give that plate back to Helen right this minute."

"Tell her to give me back my custard, then."

"Give it back, Helen," Miss Locke ordered. "If this happens again I'll go get Mrs. Prickett and . . ."

Helen glowered at Fanny. She sullenly complied, shoving the bowl across the table so that some of the custard spilled on Fanny's fingers as she caught it.

Afternoon play outside was no fun for Fanny. Refusing to get acquainted with other girls, she could only watch them. She found her eyes straying to the boys playing cricket. That looked like a lot more fun.

Walking over to them, she asked one of the boys if she could play. He looked at her like she was crazy and moved away.

A taller boy intercepted her. "Be off with you! You ain't welcome here," he said with disgust.

Fanny looked up defiantly into the dark morose eyes of the boy. He had a shock of dark, unruly hair and a brooding mouth. "There's no rule I can't play cricket with you!"

"Oh yes there is. I made up the rule just now. I'm the captain of this team."

Fanny glared at the boy and walked off, squelched, her back rigid with defiance. She sat down on the lawn cross-legged and watched them instead. Before long the boys were playing a different game called 'Slug the Monkey" which got rough and a fight ensued, the boy who had declared himself captain was in the middle of it. The supervisor soon stopped the ruckus, reprimanding them harshly.

After supper that night, Fanny asked Mrs. Prickett if she could stay in and write in her diary. She was given permission, but first had to endure another lecture about running away.

"There's no need for me to run away, Mrs. Prickett. You'll soon get a letter from my sister and I'm sure she's ready to let me come and live with her."

Mrs. Prickett only nodded, dreading Fanny's possible disappointment and pain.

Sitting alone in the dormitory room on her bed, Fanny let the tears fall. The loss of her father was a physical pain inside her chest that threatened to overwhelm her. She felt it would never go away. And this strange place made her feel so homesick, she thought she might die before Melissa's letter arrived.

After a while, she pulled the diary and her small purse out of the suitcase. Opening her purse, she pulled out a small, flat leather holder and took out the picture her dad had given her after her mum had died. It was a picture of her at nine, standing beside her beautiful mother. The pain in her chest tripled as she studied her sweet mum's face. Another torrent of tears followed.

When the tears could be controlled, she replaced the picture in the leather holder and returned it to the purse. Picking up the diary, she remembered the day her mum had given it to her. It was just before she died. She asked her to write down her feelings, times she felt sad, times she felt happy and to record her life the best she could. She had started soon after arriving at the orphanage. Doing so let out some of the pain she was feeling.

When everyone came in to go to bed, Fanny quickly put the diary and purse away. After the lights were out, she softly cried herself to sleep, as she had every night since arriving.

≈

A WEEK-AND-A-HALF LATER:

Fanny and some of the other girls were down on their hands and knees scrubbing the dorm room floor when Mr. Wimble came in.

"Fanny, come with me into my office."

She jumped up, wiped her hands on her apron and looked up eagerly into his face. "The letter from Melissa has come!" Her enthusiasm waned when she saw the solemn expression on his face.

"Follow me."

In his office, he instructed Fanny to sit down. Mrs. Prickett was there, also looking solemn. Fanny's heart plummeted.

"Fanny, two days ago the letter we wrote to your sister came back, address unknown." He picked it up and showed it to her.

"Wh–why? Why did it come back?"

"Your sister doesn't live at that address anymore. We've investigated the best we could. We've tried to find another address for Sir John Redmore in London, but with no success. Also, we checked in Ludlow and it doesn't seem they have moved there either." He shook his head in resignation. "We have no idea where to look. You'll have to stay here until you hear from her or until we learn where she's moved."

"Why did she move and not tell me?" she asked, not wanting to believe what was told her.

"We don't know, dear," Mrs. Prickett answered.

"But she'll write and tell me. I know it!" Fanny cried.

"Fanny," Mr. Wimble began, "Mrs. Wimble, Mrs. Prickett and I feel that it is in your best interest to not expect a letter from your sister."

"Why?" she screamed.

"Please, Fanny, no yelling. Let Mrs. Prickett ask you some questions and maybe your answers will help you understand our position, or on the other hand, make us less concerned."

Fanny's chest heaved with anxiety.

"Fanny dear," Mrs. Prickett said softly, "breath deeply and calm down. Think carefully before you answer the questions. "How much older is Melissa?"

"Ten years. Why does that matter!"

"Fanny!" Mr. Wimble cautioned. "If you raise your voice once more, we'll talk another time."

"I . . . I'm sorry."

"Were you close?" continued Mrs. Prickett.

"What do you mean?"

"Did you have fun with your sister, talk together?"

Fanny's brows twisted as she tried to remember. "No. She was too much older."

"Was she kind to you?"

Fanny's brows drew together and she looked down at her lap. "Not very," she said, looking up, "she's only my half-sister. She had a different mother. Her mother's name was Jane Hornby. She died when Melissa was my age, ten." Fanny tried to swallow the lump that threatened to choke her words.

"She used to tell me that when her mother was living, she got all her parents' attention and they gave her everything she wanted. She told me that Dad should never have married again, because when I was born, she didn't get any attention at all. But that wasn't true, Mrs. Prickett. Mum was so kind to her. Dad told me so when I was older. Both Dad and Mum loved Melissa, just like they loved me." The lump in her throat dissolved into tears. "Mum and Dad didn't play favorites like she said, honest."

Mrs. Prickett and Mr. Wimble exchanged glances.

"We believe you, Fanny. Think about the answers you've given me and answer this carefully. Do you think your sister will want you to come and live with her?"

Fanny's breathing accelerated. Mrs. Prickett went over to her and put an arm around her small shoulders. "Just relax, dear and think about it slowly and carefully."

"But she's married. That means she's grown up. She won't feel like she used to."

Both Mr. Wimble and Mrs. Prickett remained silent, allowing Fanny time to think.

It was a long time before Fanny could say any more. At last she looked up at Mr. Wimble, swallowed hard and said, "She should have told me she had ill health and couldn't take care of me. I . . ." She shook her head. "I don't believe she has bad health! She looked healthy to me. If she did, why didn't she tell me instead of telling that mean man and woman to bring me here?"

It was a question that Fanny didn't need answered. She now knew the answer.

✂CHAPTER 29✂

Gustavia put the diary down on the window seat and dissolved into tears. It was as plain to her as it was to Fanny that Melissa intended to leave her in the orphanage indefinitely! How could Melissa be so cold-hearted? If that kind of a woman raised Ada, no wonder her cousin was devoid of affection.

Suddenly her anger turned toward Ada. "How dare she blame Fanny for anything after the way her mother had treated Fanny!" she cried aloud. *And how can she in turn treat me the way she does,* she thought, *all the while knowing how her mother had treated Fanny and stolen her inheritance? The inheritance, which would have been my father's eventually.* A terrible thought entered her head. *My father wouldn't have had to work on the fishing trawler. He wouldn't have died!*

This was too much to think about. Still, her chest heaved with broken-hearted sobs. Slowly, her hands clenched into fists, helpless fists, the tears turning into anger as she stormed around the room. Her first impulse was to go downstairs and give Ada a tongue lashing she would never forget, though she knew that venting her anger on Ada would accomplish nothing. Nevertheless, the need to confront Ada was overpowering. Before she allowed herself to do this, she had to calm down—take a walk.

Running downstairs and out the front door, the smell of rain-fresh foliage greeted her. The temperature was a wonderful 78 degrees, a perfect time to enjoy the outdoors. She wished Paul were here so they could go for a walk along the Kennebec. She needed the comfort of his presence while she examined and evaluated how wrong decisions can affect lives, not just in the present, but through generations!

She ran up the hill to the lane where they usually veered off, then turned and walked briskly back down, sufficiently calmed enough to confront Ada. Entering the door, she looked at her watch and found it was past tea-time. She found Ada in the library at her desk.

"Ada, I'd like to talk to you for a few minutes."

"I'm very busy, Gustavia."

"I know. You always are," Gustavia said, pulling her desk chair over near Ada.

Ada swivelled around, impatience on her face. "All right. What is it?"

"I'm sure you've read Fanny Sullivan's diaries."

Her eyes shifted away from Gustavia's gaze. "I . . . uh, glanced through them."

"You wouldn't have kept several back from me if you hadn't read them. I'm curious, Ada, how do you feel about the terrible injustice your mother did to her little sister, my grandmother?"

"That was just one side of the story. My mother had her side," Ada retorted defensively.

Tears glistened in Gustavia's eyes. "Ada, I've been in tears since I began reading them. My heart is breaking for the little girl, Fanny, who was abandoned and put into an orphanage in such a cruel way. What kind of a mother did you have anyway?"

Ada turned her head away from Gustavia and looked down, her mouth trembling slightly, one hand gripping the other. For a moment, Gustavia thought she was going to break down, but true to form, Ada regained control. She looked up, her chin high, and answered. "My mother was a leader in Grimsby social circles. She and my father were stalwart members of the community."

"I didn't ask that. I asked what kind of a mother was she to you?"

Ada tensed. "That's none of your business, Gustavia."

Gustavia hadn't expected a forthright answer. She went on. "Why do you treat me the way you do, Ada? Why are you so cold, so unfeeling about the theft of my father's inheritance? You treat me as if it were the other way around, as if I had done you a terrible injustice."

Gustavia waited only seconds before she stood up to leave. She hadn't expected Ada to give her a satisfactory answer to these questions either—she simply had to unburden herself.

"I have an errand to run, Ada. Have a good day." She quickly left the library, went outside, got into her car and drove over to Edgar's for some real answers. She hoped he wasn't too busy to talk with her.

His face lit up as she stepped into his office. "Gustavia! This is a treat. What brings you here?"

His kindness was almost her undoing. She sat down in a chair near his desk and tried to control the emotional overload inside her. "I . . . I've been reading Fanny Sullivan's diaries."

Edgar gazed at her. "What have you learned so far?"

Gustavia told him what his mother did to Fanny.

He was silent, his gray wispy brows furrowing, his head bobbing back and forth in shock.

Gustavia waited.

At last he let out a weary breath. "From the documents in the box, I knew Fanny was in the orphanage. Though I wondered why mother had allowed such a thing, I refused to let myself believe that she could have put her there. I'm terribly sorry, Gustavia."

She acknowledge his deep-felt apology with only a nod.

A heavy sigh escaped his lips. "Would you like some tea?"

"No thank you."

"Please excuse me, but I feel the need of some."

Gustavia waited while he went into the next room. It wasn't long before he returned with a cup of steaming hot tea. Sipping carefully, he set it down.

"Mother ran the businesses, with Ada's and my help, till the end. She was healthy and going strong when she died of a stroke. Apparently, she hadn't expected to die for a long time because she hadn't destroyed her father's old will in that box I gave you. There is information in there you needed to have—the information I promised you, but I knew it would raise more questions. Fanny's diaries may answer them. I hope, anyway."

"I hope so too. May I ask you a question that has been at the back of my mind since Mum's funeral?"

He took several sips of his tea. "I'd be glad to if I can."

"You aren't a cold man, Edgar, but you were also cold to me at the funeral. Why?"

"I'm slow at getting acquainted, Gustavia. I didn't know you well enough at first to care for you personally. Also, I was feeling terrible guilty about what we had discovered. I wanted to keep track of you so I could tell you of your inheritance and make it all up to you someday." He rubbed his brow with a bony, arthritic hand. "But I let six years slip by. Then I intended to give you the box with all of its contents, but I found I didn't have the courage to leave in the wills. It took Paul's discovery to make me come forth. I'm sorry." He raised his remorse-filled eyes to meet hers.

Gustavia nodded. "Thank you, Edgar." She was just about to ask him how his mother had treated Ada—and him—but something in Edgar's face told her that this wasn't the time.

She stood up. "I must be off." Stepping over to him, she leaned down and hugged him. "Thank you, dear cousin, for wanting to make it right, but especially for making Ada give me the diaries." She turned and walked out of his office, leaving a tearful old man.

❧CHAPTER 30❧

HULL SEAMEN'S AND GENERAL ORPHAN ASYLUM, HULL, ENGLAND, JUNE 1910:

After the meeting with Mr. and Mrs. Wimble and Mrs. Prickett, Fanny sat for some time in a daze, at last able to acknowledge the truth of Melissa's betrayal. Finally, Mrs. Prickett took Fanny by the hand, her heart breaking for the child. "What would you like to do right now, dear?"

"Since everyone is still doing chores, could I go outside and find a place to be alone for just a little while?"

Mrs. Prickett wondered if perhaps the child didn't fully comprehend, that the awful truth hadn't really sunk in yet. Often, as children do, they accept slights and injustices without question, forgiving and forgetting as Fanny had with her sister until forced to think about it. "Of course you can," she replied finally.

"Thank you, Mrs. Prickett."

Fanny found a place behind a bush and sat down, trying to accept the fact that Melissa would never come and get her. She had never felt like Melissa was a sister, but thought it was because she was so many years older. Then in Mr. Wimble's office when Mrs. Prickett was asking her questions, she remembered some things she hadn't really thought about. Now, she began remembering some more.

When Melissa was in her last year of high school and Fanny was eight, Melissa had said to her, "You're Dad's favorite."

"I am not!" she had retorted.

"He's always hugging you, not me."

"But Dad doesn't think to hug either one of us, so I hug him anyway. You could do that too, Melissa."

No matter what, Fanny couldn't convince Melissa to make the effort. She always hung back resentfully, waiting for him to go to her. Then the episode of the necklace made it worse. Melissa had seen a large pearl stick-pin in her dad's drawer that he didn't use any more. Unknown to Fanny, Melissa had mentioned to him a couple of times that she would like a necklace made out of it.

The Christmas that Fanny was nine and Melissa nineteen, her dad handed them each a gift to open. What Melissa opened she couldn't remember, but hers was a beautiful pearl necklace made from the old stickpin. While exclaiming over the gift, she had unconsciously sensed her sister's heavy silence. It wasn't until she and her sister were alone that Melissa tore into her.

"See! You are Dad's favorite! I asked him over and over if he would make me a necklace out of it. Instead he made it for you!"

"I didn't know that, Melissa." She took it off and handed it to her. "You can have it."

"No! I don't want it now."

"But you know how Dad is. He's kind of absentminded. Maybe all he remembered was one of us asking him about making the necklace, but forgot which one it was and guessed it was me." Fanny sincerely believed this. She knew her dad wouldn't have a favorite, and her mum, who was Melissa's stepmother, was so kind to Melissa.

Melissa kept taunting her about the necklace until one day Fanny threw the abhorrent thing away, and told her step-sister what she had done.

The painful truth finally sank in. Melissa hated her. *She isn't going to come and get me! I am an orphan! I really do belong here.* At last, the terrible choking feeling in her throat released a flood of tears. All the pain and hurt she had been holding in kept the tears flowing until her pocket handkerchief was soaked and her eyes were swollen.

Some time later, Mrs. Prickett found her. By then, Fanny's tears had stopped. Only the lingering staccato gasps of breath remained. Sitting, Mrs. Prickett put an arm around her, holding her tightly until they too had stopped. Exhausted, Fanny sat quietly within the motherly and compassionate arms.

Once again, Mrs. Prickett led her into the vacant library and brought her a cup of tea and a cake and stayed with her until she finished this small bit of sustenance before she spoke.

"Fanny, you're a very bright girl, a very strong girl. You're going to make it through the next few years and come out of the orphanage a very special young woman, but only if you pray and rely on the good Lord. You do pray, don't you?"

Fanny nodded.

"Good. Continue to pray night and morning, and in between in your heart. The Lord will not forsake you, remember that."

Fanny nodded, her face expressionless.

☙

Since Fanny was definitely going to remain, Mrs. Prickett took her to Mrs. Locke who was also adept at cutting the girls' hair and keeping them trimmed to the manageable length below the ear.

Fanny, who would have otherwise been horrified to have her long curly locks cut off, watched stoically as the long tresses fell to the floor.

For some time after that, it was all downhill for Fanny. Her natural fiery red-headed personality would ignite into anger with very little provocation. On the playground Helen began to tease her. Fanny hit her in the stomach. Helen let out a squawk and ran inside to tattle. Mr. Wimble and Mrs. Prickett decided to look the other way this time.

At times, Fanny left the girls' side of the yard and insisted on getting in the boys' way during cricket. One day they'd had enough. The dark-eyed, morose boy took it upon himself to be the one to oust her. As he caught hold of her arm, Fanny kicked him in the shin. He hollered, grabbed his knee and cussed. She stood by, grinning in delight.

Infuriated, he grabbed her by the hair and pulled her off the field. The rest of the boys yelled and clapped with approval. Pulling her to the back steps, the boy sat her down holding tightly to her hair.

Her dignity hadn't allowed her to make a sound until now. "Ow! Let me go!" she yelled.

"Not until you say you'll never bother us boys again."

"No!"

"Okay," he said giving it another yank.

"Ouch! You big bully! I'll get you for this!"

He gave it another yank.

"Stop it!" she screamed.

"Promise, I said."

"No!"

She received another yank, but she endured it quietly.

"Promise?"

"No!"

By this time the boy lost heart, but kept hold of her hair. "What's your name, brat?"

"Fanny Sullivan. What's yours?"

"Josiah Browne. Most people call me Jo."

"All right, Josiah, let me go."

"Promise?"

"No."

"All right. We'll just sit here until you do."

"I guess you'll have to sit here all night with me then."

"Fine with me if you can stand it, I can."

"You're the brat, Josiah Browne! You go around never smiling, looking as dark as a rat hole."

"There ain't nothin' to smile about."

"There isn't."

"That's what I said."

"No. You said 'ain't' and it's 'isn't'."

"Well, if you ain't a snooty little up-town brat with your fancy language."

"Let go of my hair, I say."

"Promise?"

"No."

"All right, brat."

The supper bell rang and Josiah kept hold of her hair, deciding he wasn't going to get supper.

Fanny eyed him with determination. "I'm hungry. Let go."

"I'm starvin'. I never get enough to eat, but I'm gonna stay here until you promise—if it means goin' without supper."

Fanny glared at him, then her eyes slid over his scrawny frame and bony arms. "You look like you don't get enough to eat. You're skinny as a broom."

"So?"

"So, nothing."

The boy, sticking to it, said once more, "Promise?"

"I promise, if you'll let me share my food with you."

Josiah was so surprised, he nearly let go that very minute.

"What did you say?"

Fanny repeated it.

"Why?"

"Because that's the deal."

Josiah felt an unaccustomed lump rise in his throat. "All right," he said hoarsely.

"Let's shake on it," she said.

He let go of her hair and shook her hand.

June moved into the middle of July with Fanny becoming more and more irascible. Mr. Wimble and Mrs. Prickett watched and waited. They knew the child was full of anger and hurt so they didn't punish her as much as they ordinarily would have, but they were getting near the end of their patience. A day didn't go by without Fanny getting into a physical fight with a girl or a boy.

As a rule, May Wimble and Mrs. Prickett left the monitoring of the meals to the supervisors, who were older, responsible children of the orphanage, but they had taken to helping out since a lot of squabbles erupted at Fanny's table, inciting too much excitement at the other tables.

For some time now, at breakfast and dinner, they had watched Fanny push half her food to one side of her plate, get up and go over to Josiah Browne, the most choleric boy in the orphanage, and slide it onto his plate. When it first happened, the boy remarked with a grimace, "Well if the brat ain't keepin' her word."

The other boys at the table were agog with surprise, but as it continued, it eventually turned into envy. Mrs. Prickett had allowed it for the sake of both children, the one giving and the one taking, but knew it would soon have to be stopped.

At breakfast one morning after grace, Fanny picked up her plate of bread, drippings and sausages, and went over to the boys' table where Josiah was sitting. He smiled smugly at the other boys and held up his plate while she slid half of hers onto it.

The boy next to Josiah taunted loudly, "The brat is sweet on Jo Browne!"

"I'm not either!" she yelled back.

All the boys around the table began jeering. "The brat is sweet on Jo Browne!"

Before May and Mrs. Prickett could forestall it, Fanny poured her half of bread and drippings and sausages on top of the head of the boy who started the problem. He hollered like a stuck pig. Josiah nearly fell off his chair laughing, all of which provoked a fit of loud hilarity around the table.

May took the plate from Fanny's hand and Mrs. Prickett led her out of the room post haste, leaving May to see about the cleanup.

Mr. Wimble, who was enjoying a peaceful breakfast in his office, was greeted by an angry Mrs. Prickett and a defiant Fanny. Though momentarily startled, he had been expecting May's and Mrs. Prickett's leniency in the dining room to eventually cause a problem.

"All right, Miss Fanny, what did you finally do to make Mrs. Prickett this angry?"

Fanny was all too eager to tell the story in colorful exaggeration, slanting it smartly toward her own innocence.

Glancing at Mrs. Prickett's face, Mr. Wimble read between the lines. "Please be seated Mrs. Prickett—you too, Fanny." Taking a big swig of his tea, he shoved his breakfast plate back. Clasping his hands on the desk he leaned toward Fanny, irritated that his breakfast had been interrupted, and totally out of patience with the child's ongoing antics and fighting. "Fanny, you are not to share your food anymore with Josiah Browne."

"But I gave him my word!" she exclaimed.

"Keep your voice down," he said, holding back his anger. "And why did you do that? Did he coerce you into giving it to him?"

"No. I offered to do it if he'd quit pulling my hair."

"And why was he pulling your hair?"

"Because he's a bully."

Mr. Wimble breathed deeply. "Answer me, Miss Fanny," his patience getting thinner by the minute.

The expression in Mr. Wimble's usually gentle eyes prompted Fanny to confess forthwith. "Oh, all right. The girls' games aren't as fun as playing cricket with the boys, so I went over and tried to play with them. Josiah asked me to leave and I wouldn't. He tried to drag me out of the way so I kicked him in the shin. But he is a bully—he grabbed me by the hair and took me over to the steps and he wouldn't let go until I promised not to bother the boys again." Having offered this explanation, she clamped her mouth shut, determined not to say another word.

"Go on, Fanny," Mrs. Prickett insisted.

Fanny's lips tightened, remaining silent.

Mrs. Pricket had sudden inspiration. "Mr. Wimble, maybe it would be a good idea if we took away Josiah's meals for three days."

Very aware of Mrs. Prickett's overly kind heart, Mr. Wimble's brows rose, shocked at her suggestion, but before he could react, Fanny came alive with vociferous indignation.

"You can't do that! He's too skinny. He's always hungry, he said. Why can't the orphanage give the boys bigger portions!"

Mr. Wimble was taken by surprise at the outburst, but Mrs. Prickett smiled at him knowingly, nodding her head slightly. He caught the message. His heart softened and his eyes almost watered.

"Fanny," he began gently. "We already give bigger portions to the boys than the girls. I wish we could give them enough to satisfy their growing appetites, but the orphanage doesn't have the funds to buy enough food to do that."

"I'm not very hungry most of the time so why can't I share with Josiah?"

"The reason the boys at Josiah's table teased you, Fanny," Mrs. Prickett said, "is because none them get quite enough to eat either and they were envious that Josiah was getting extra."

"They were?"

"Yes. So you see why it has to stop, don't you?"

Fanny's lips trembled and tears glistened in her blue eyes. She nodded.

"Now that that's settled, Fanny," Mr. Wimble stated with as much sternness as he could muster, "I have to tell you that you're going to have to be punished for pouring that valuable food over the boy's head. Also, Mrs. Wimble, Mrs. Prickett and I are sad that you're rewarding our kindness with all your trouble-making."

Fanny thought about this a moment. "I don't mean to get so mad. Mum used to tell me I had an unruly temper and that I must try to control it. I didn't really understand what she meant, but I do now. I'm sorry. I'll try to do better."

"Thank you, Fanny," Mr. Wimble said, "we'll appreciate your efforts in that regard. However, you'll still have to be punished."

Fanny nodded, her eyes downcast.

Six days later, it was a subdued Fanny who walked to church with the girls in an orderly fashion, while the boys lagged as far back as they dared. She had been consigned to working in the kitchen all day for four days under Mrs. Cracken's evil eye, and helping the laundryman for two more without any play. She even missed the trip up Mucky Peg Lane to the new Pearson Park.

During breakfast and dinner, Mrs. Prickett had stood guard at Fanny's table, trusting her only at supper.

Fanny hated her Sunday-best uniform. It was a navy serge dress with long sleeves with a white collar, and anchor on each side. Cumbersome oversized navy bloomers were worn underneath.

The boys' best suits were made of blue cloth with brass anchor buttons and a white anchor on each corner of the jacket collar. Their everyday outfit consisted of a blue coat and waistcoat with corduroy 'trowsers.'

Both boys and girls were forced to wear navy blue stockings and the same heavy leather, hob-nailed boots with their Sunday clothes. Fanny found them disgusting.

After church while walking back to the orphanage, Josiah Browne managed to sneak up by her. "You sure ruined everything, brat, getting angry like that. Now I don't get enough food."

She whirled, turning smoldering eyes toward him. He stopped, taken back at her reaction. "I don't care, Josiah Browne. I'm not going to be accused of being sweet on the likes of you."

His face looked as if she had slapped him.

"What're you looking like that for?" she asked, suddenly worried about hurting his feelings.

"Oh, nothin'."

"Oh yeah? I dare you to tell me."

"You just feel like everybody else feels—that I'll end up like me dad, a drunken bum. Had a nice business goin' he did. He was a shoemaker. One day when he was drunk, he tried to cross Elm Tree Avenue level crossing and got hisself killed. Left Mum without any money, then she ups and dies with consumption or somethin,' so here I am."

"How long have you been here?"

"Two years."

"That's awful. I guess we're both going to live in the orphanage forever."

"No! I'm not. Boys get to leave when they turn fourteen. That's when I'm going to leave—if I don't run away before then."

"Don't run away. They'll just find you. Besides, you get into almost as many fights as I do, so they'll punish you like they did me."

"I'm used to being punished. I don't care a whit."

"I'm sorry I can't give you half my food anymore."

"Ah, that's okay. The fellas around the table are just as hungry as I am. Kind of hated to have more'n them anyway."

"Hey, brat!" called a boy behind them. "You still sweet on Jo?"

Fanny turned around, her hands on her hips, pinning him with her eyes. "I just might be at that!" she answered loudly, then turned and continued walking beside Josiah.

Josiah, who didn't smile often, smiled broadly. His shoulders straightened a little higher. After all, as bratty as Fanny Sullivan was, she was the prettiest little thing he had ever seen.

❧CHAPTER 31❧

BELFORD, MAINE, JUNE 2001:

Wednesday morning, Gustavia forced herself to return to work on Ada's biography. Anxious to get back to the intriguing story of Fanny and Josiah, she wondered how much longer she could summon willpower to continue. As she got back into it, however, an interesting phenomenon occurred. She was able to look at it all from a different perspective. This was the secular history of a woman raised by a cruel, cold-hearted mother. Because of this knowledge, she began reading between the lines—correctly or incorrectly—enabling her to write it up in a better manner and style than she had before. *Odd*, she thought, *that I'm able to do this after learn - ing what I have!*

The phone rang. Ada wasn't at her desk, so Gustavia answered.

"Hi, Gusty,"

"Paul! I'm so glad you called. I've been reading Fanny's journal and it's been so heart-wrenching."

"Oh? You'll have to tell me about it. Actually, I'd like to read it myself sometime soon. I've had so much to catch up on and so many cases piling up, I haven't even had a minute to call you. How about we go get another one of those good hamburgers tonight?"

"I'd love to."

"All right. I'll pick you up at 5:30."

As soon as she hung up, she went into the kitchen and told Carol not to plan on her for dinner. Her spirits higher, she returned to the computer.

Ada walked in. "I presume that wasn't a business call for me."

"No. I wish I had my own phone, Ada."

"You won't be here that long, Gustavia."

I certainly hope not, she thought. Out loud she said, "Just as long as it takes to finish your biography and settle the legal issues."

"At the rate you're working on my history, it might take a year," Ada stated sarcastically.

Gustavia bit her tongue. *The audacity of the woman!*

❧

Lunch was a welcome break. She took it outside and sat on the garden bench to eat. She missed Paul working with Ada. If he were, he could be sitting with her right this moment. Now, he worked mainly with Edgar, who had re-hired him in spite of Ada's objections.

The birds were chirping and singing in the various trees. It was a regular surround-sound chorus. Lovely as it was, she would enjoy it much more if someone were there to share it with her.

Reluctantly, she went back into the library and sat down at the computer. However, with her new insight into Ada, the task was amazingly less tedious. She quit at 4:30 to go upstairs and get ready for her date with Paul.

She was in the mood to wear a period dress, especially after reading the diaries, but squelched the urge and put on a strawberry linen jacket with a floral mesh tee under it with pants to match. It was more practical for the warm evening.

Brushing her hair, she pulled it back with a clip and let it hang down her back. Daubing on her favorite perfume, she went downstairs to the garden to wait for Paul.

Paul drove up just as the local florist shop van was driving away. He frowned and wondered who would be sending flowers to Ada. "Only at her funeral," he muttered, a half smile on his lips. Opening the gate, he started for the front steps when a, "Hi" came from the garden.

He stared at the stunning sight—a picture to be framed—Gustavia in red, holding a bouquet of red roses. He sauntered toward her smiling. "You've never worn red. You look beautiful."

"Thank you," she said, sounding a little strained.

It finally sank in—the florist, the bouquet. They were for Gustavia! Of course. What a dunce he was. "Who sent the flowers, Gusty?"

"Uh, Artie."

Paul was silent. He had never been one to send flowers. It almost never entered his head to do so. It seemed such a waste; they wilted so quickly.

"That was nice of him," he managed to say.

"Yes. It was quite a surprise. I never expected it." She put the roses to her face and smelled the fragrance. "I love flowers."

Paul felt like the odd man out, wishing he had thought to send her flowers. "Shall we go?"

"Oh, yes. Let me just run in and put these in a vase of water. Wait for me here."

"Gladly. I don't relish running into Ada."

He sat down on the bench, feeling disgruntled that Artie had come into the picture again. A white card lay on a patio stone. He picked it up and without thinking he read it:

> Gustavia, I'm in Boston on business for my
> father. May I take you to dinner tomorrow
> night around 6:00?
>
> Love, Artie.

Paul muttered something under his breath. He was planning to meet Edgar tomorrow afternoon and took it for granted that Gustavia would be available that night. Quickly releasing the card, watching it flutter to the ground, letting it appear as though he had never read it, he planned to beat Artie to the punch and ask her to dinner himself.

He waited for her at the gate. She came out the door and ran to him. Her glowing smile, and the excitement in her eyes sent his heart on a one-hundred-yard dash.

"I'm glad you came over, Paul. I've missed you."

"I've missed you, too. How about dinner tomorrow night?"

The smile left and she stammered, "Uh, I, uh, am afraid Artie has already asked me. I'm sorry. A card came with the roses."

"Oh?" A long pause followed. "Did you accept?"

"Well, no. How could I? He's not here."

"So tell him you have a date with me."

"But I didn't have one before he asked me, before the roses and card came. You're taking a lot for granted, Paul."

"Holy mackerel! Am I going to have to ask you weeks in advance?"

Gustavia laughed. "Apparently the women you've dated were always at your beck and call. It doesn't sound like you've ever had much competition. It appears you're a novice at dealing with it."

Grabbing her hand, he led her quickly to the car. "I couldn't care less about competition with any man—except one who comes on to you."

Gustavia laughed. "That sounds like a non sequitur if I've ever heard one."

Oblivious to Gustavia's quip, he growled, "Frankly, I wish Artie would get lost."

He started the car and drove toward Charlie's Choices.

"I think you and Artie have forgotten I'm betrothed. It seems neither of you are taking it seriously."

"How can we take it seriously when we don't know how you feel about him." He waited for her to answer. "Well, how do you feel about him?"

"I love him as the best friend I ever had."

"Is that all?"

"I pretended I didn't like him telling me he loved me, but I really did."

"Hmm, a ten-year-old told you that he loved you?" he interrogated.

Her voice rose protectively. "Yes!"

"Did you think you loved him—more than a friend?"

"Paul! Why all these questions? How can I answer that. I was just a child."

"If he came along right now, do you think you'd love him enough to marry him?"

"I don't know," she answered, exasperated, realizing they had arrived at the hamburger place and Paul had parked.

Paul smiled, crooked his fingers under her chin, leaned over and kissed her cheek so close to her lips, it left her breathless. *If Freddie doesn't show up in my life soon, I don't know what I'm going to do!* She was struggling with her attraction to Paul—then there was that delightfully charming Artie with his special something. In all her years of dating, she had never been in this kind of situation! As a matter of fact she had never before found even one man to whom she was attracted. And now there were two of them!

❧CHAPTER 32❧

Thursday afternoon at 4:30 Gustavia gratefully left the computer to go upstairs and get ready for her date with Artie. The thoughts of Paul and Artie both being in town the very same evening made it more difficult to concentrate on Ada's project.

After showering, she put on a white camisole. Over it, she put on something she hadn't worn for some time. It was an Ana cardigan, hand crocheted in linen yarns of oyster with oyster linen pants to match. Around her neck, she wore a thin gold chain with one large imitation pearl in the center.

She was anxious to see Artie again, but nervous. Here she was, trying to look her best as she had for Paul last night. Why? "Vanity I suppose," she said to her image in the mirror.

Just as she was coming down the stairs to wait for Artie, the doorbell rang. She opened it and instead of Artie, it was Paul! "Wh-what are you doing here?"

"Well, that's a nice greeting."

"But, uh, Artie will be here any moment."

Paul looked her up and down. "You look great, Gusty."

"Thank you. But what are you doing here?"

"Edgar sent me over to ask Ada something. Do you mind if I come in?"

"Yes I do mind," she said stepping aside, "but apparently I can't do anything about it."

"Nope," he said, grinning as he entered.

At that very moment, Artie was coming through the gate, dressed in a light blue sports jacket, white shirt and tie with light tan pants. He smiled at her standing in the doorway waiting for him. "Hi, beautiful maiden. You look nice."

"Thank you, Artie. It's good to see you."

Gustavia was about to step out and shut the door, but Paul held it open.

"Hello, Artie," Paul said.

Surprised, Artie paused. "It's Paul, right?"

"Right. You're a long ways from Salt Lake."

"I am. Business in Boston. Thought I'd take the opportunity to come and see Gustavia."

"So I see," Paul said, unsmiling.

Artie glanced at Gustavia who looked very uneasy. "Shall we go, Gustavia?"

"Yes."

"Nice to see you again, Paul."

Paul nodded and closed the door without speaking.

In the car, Artie turned on the motor and drove off. "We're going to the Senator Inn in Augusta. Have you ever been there?"

Gustavia nodded.

Artie's brows furrowed in thought. "It's good to see you again, Gusty, but I sense some tension between you and your cousin's attorney. Am I right?"

"Well, not exactly."

"What then? You were acting nervous there on the doorstep when Paul and I greeted each other."

Gustavia didn't know how to answer. She knew Paul had come right then on purpose, and she was feeling rather put out at him for placing her in that awkward position!

"Are you dating Paul, Gusty?"

"Artie, I'm with you. I don't care to discuss Paul."

"I think that means 'yes.'" He ran a hand through his hair. "That shouldn't surprise me. Anyone would want to date you, but how serious is he?"

"Artie! I wouldn't have accepted a date if I didn't want to be with you. That's all you need to know."

Artie let out a heavy sigh and shook his head. "And I thought way up here in Belford, I wouldn't have competition. Oh well," he turned to her and grinned, "I'm glad to hear you want to be with me. That gives me some encouragement. What have you been doing since I last saw you?"

"I'm still working on my cousin's biography."

"Then what are your plans?"

"I don't know actually. I came from England to the U. S. because Boston University offered me the position of an assistant professor in costume history and design." She then told him of the events that had brought her here to Belford.

"That's a strange story. So when you get your cousin's biography done, you'll leave?"

Gustavia pondered the question. "At the moment, I can't plan that far ahead."

Seated in the Senator Inn eating lobster reminded her of the time Paul had brought her here. Still put out with him, she shoved the thought away and noticed how nice Artie looked in his blue sports jacket.

"How are all your family, Artie?"

"They're fine. They all fell in love with you, Gusty. They want me to bring you back with me. How about it?" he asked, his blue eyes twinkling with entreaty.

Gustavia smiled. "I wish I could." She sighed. "The love and affection your family have for each other was wonderful to watch. Actually, I fell in love with all of them."

"Well, at least I have that going for me. Mmm . . . this lobster's great."

"What business is your father in that took you to Boston?"

"My father is a financial consultant and investment advisor."

"What does that mean?"

"In simple terms it means he manages other people's money and invests it for them."

"Oh? Do you work for him?"

"Yes. That's why I'm in Boston. I'm looking at a company whose stock he's considering as an investment for some of his clients."

"Interesting. But way over my head. I'd be terrible at business."

"But you have other talents that can support you apparently."

The evening went by delightfully. She felt comfortable around Artie and he didn't make any demands on her.

When they finally drove up to Ada's house, Artie said, "I don't know how much longer I'm going to be in Boston. I may finish tomorrow, but I'm not sure. May I take you out again tomorrow night if the business keeps me here longer?"

"Yes. I'd like that."

"I'll call you tomorrow and let you know."

He led her to the door and took her hands in his, and smiled. "Thank you for spending time with me."

"Thank you, Artie. I enjoyed it very much."

Changing into her nightgown, Gustavia washed her face and brushed her teeth. She wondered if she could sleep. She felt keyed up, and unsettled in her mind. Nevertheless, she knelt and prayed for help, then got into bed.

She lay there thinking and talking to herself. "I can't go on like this. I can't go on expecting Freddie to come into my life miraculously. It's utterly impractical. I'm acting like an idealistic ninny hanging onto my hopes. I've got to let it go!" Tears flowed onto the pillow. If only she knew what had happened to him it would be easier.

Before she realized it, she had drifted off to sleep. The sound began so softly that she was hardly aware of it. As the volume increased she realized it was music coming from somewhere. The notes took on a familiar pattern. She knew that tune. She knew that sound. It was coming from a harmonica! Freddie! It was Freddie, but where was he?

Her eyes fluttered open just as the last note faded away. She threw off the covers and stood up, still groggy from sleep. She looked around trying to orient herself. Was it a dream? She moved to the turret window and looked out into the lamplit street. No one was there. A soft moan escaped her lips and tears sprang to her eyes. "I can't go on like this."

She took a blanket from the bed and sitting on the window seat, pulled it around her. What was happening to her? She awoke, still in the window seat as the morning light flooded the room.

❧CHAPTER 33❧

Friday morning she put on a white puff-sleeved blouse, circa 1905, and modern-day black pants. She entered the dining room barefooted and tired.

Ada looked up surprised. "You lack a little luster, Gustavia. That's what happens when you stay out late."

"I didn't stay out late," she said flatly, "I didn't sleep well." After a few bites she stopped. "Ada, did you hear anything last night. Any, uh, noise or music?"

Ada looked up, surprised. "Noise, music? If there were I would know. I'm a very light sleeper."

Deflated, Gustavia returned to her meal. Breakfast consisted of sliced fresh peaches, eggs and bacon and whole grain bread. It tasted good to Gustavia. She ate in silence, and for once was grateful for Ada's. When she was through, she felt somewhat revived. Excusing herself, she left for the library.

The day matched her mood; dark and dismal. It began to rain. "A perfect day to read the diaries," she muttered, not moving from the computer. Trying not to think about anything but the work before her, she listened to the comforting sounds of rain, lightening and thunder.

By noon, the rain was over. The bright sun emerged, drying up vestigial droplets of moisture on the trees, flowers and grass. She ate lunch out in the garden again and basked in the sunshine and the fresh, rain-drenched air.

All afternoon, she expected to hear from Artie or Paul, but it wasn't until 5:00 that the phone rang.

Ada answered it. "It's for you, Gustavia."

"Hi!" came Artie's cheerful voice. "I'm sorry for not calling sooner, but some interesting things have been happening here and I didn't have an opportunity to call until now."

"That's all right, Artie. You have to take care of business."

"I'm sorry to say I have to stay in Boston tonight and work. I'll be flying back to Salt Lake day after tomorrow, so are you free to go to dinner with me tomorrow night?"

"Yes. I'm free. I'd like to, but give me your hotel number in case I need to call you."

"All right!" he exclaimed, sounding relieved. He gave her the hotel name and number. "I'll pick you up around six again."

After the call she tried to settle down, but felt restless. She wanted to go browse through some antique shops, go for a hike through the woods, anything but remain in this room, in this house!

Listlessly she climbed the stairs. Positioning herself in the window seat, she picked up Fanny's diary, then put it down. "What's the matter with me?" Placing a pillow under her head, she dozed off. Twenty minutes later, she awoke feeling less languid. She looked at her watch and saw that she was ten minutes late for dinner, not that that worried her any longer.

When Gustavia entered the dining room, Ada looked up, annoyed, but said nothing. Nor did Gustavia. At least she still had an appetite. She enjoyed the tasty dinner Carol had prepared.

Since Artie wouldn't be coming and she hadn't heard anything from Paul, she grimly decided to work on the biography and get as much done as she could tonight. What she really wanted to do was read the diaries straight through without stopping. She needed to take her mind off her own life!

When it was almost dark, Gustavia closed down the computer, got up from the desk, picked out a book to read and went upstairs.

Propping up the pillows of the bed, the book in her hand, she leaned back thinking and enjoying the cross breeze between the open turret window and the small window on the other side of the bed.

She had made a painful decision the night before—to give up her long time hope of finding Freddie—only to dream of hearing his harmonica! She thought of Paul. She thought of Artie. *I can't go on with my life until I give up on Freddie once and for all! Oh Mum, if only you were here and I could ask your advice. I'm so confused.*

A sound wafted in through the breeze ever so softly, then subtly getting louder. It was music! *Where is it coming from? Could Ada be playing music in the parlor?* She knew that would be highly unlikely since she had never heard music in this house. She listened intently. It was beautiful, hauntingly so—like a harmonica. "It *is* a harmonica!" she burst out.

She sat there frozen for a moment. She wasn't asleep. She wasn't dreaming this time. At last able to ease herself off the bed, she moved slowly toward the turret window. Reaching it, she knelt on the window seat and gazed down. A man stood beneath the window, music pouring from the instrument in his mouth—from a harmonica! She held her breath, trying to put a name to the man. Could it be? . . . Unable to finish the thought, she squinted, trying to see his face, but couldn't. The lamplight behind him shadowed his features. He waved at her!

"I love you, Gustavia Browne!" he yelled.

Her heart was pounding. She could scarcely breathe. Staring down at his dark figure, she was unable to speak. He waved and again played another beautiful song—a beautiful and tender song of lost love—stirring unspeakable emotions inside her. When the piece ended, he stopped and once more yelled, "I love you, Gustavia Browne!"

Dare I believe? "I hate *you*, Freddie Finch!" she shouted back.

The man laughed with joy. "I *love* you, Gustavia Browne!"

Gustavia laughed, tears rolling down her cheeks. "I hate *you*, Freddie Finch!" She moved off the window seat and raced out of the room, down the stairs and out the front door to her long lost Freddie. She ran headlong into his arms. "Oh Freddie! Freddie! Where did you come from? I've been looking for you for so long!"

"I've been looking for *you* for so long, my Gusty," he whispered in her ear.

She looked up at him through blurry eyes, trying to distinguish his face. *No! It can't be!* Turning him around to the light, she gasped, "Paul!"

"Yes, Gusty, it's me, Freddie Finch, now Paul Frederick Camden."

"You can't be Freddie! You don't look like him. You're the middle child of a large family! And . . . and the people who adopted Freddie weren't named Camden." She backed away from him. "Don't be cruel, Paul. Why are you doing this to me?" she cried.

In a calm and gentle tone, he stated, "Yes, I was adopted by a Robert and Sharon Banks. It's a long story, Gusty. I have so much to tell you, and to explain."

Gustavia looked around nervously, her breath still coming out in shuddering gasps. "I thought that Ada would have heard the music and been out here by now."

"I asked Edgar to call her up to his house on pressing business so she wouldn't be here when I presented you with your long lost friend."

"Oh. This is . . . is too much to take in. I . . . is there some place we can go talk?"

"How about a walk along the Kennebec in the moonlight. We can sit on the bank and talk. It looks like you're dressed for it," he said, smiling as he looked her up and down . . . except for the bare feet."

Her emotions still close to the surface, she gazed up at the boy—now the man—for whom she had been searching for so many years. *How can this be the face of Freddie Finch of long ago? Is he really Freddie?* She couldn't internalize it. "Oh, yes," she murmured, dazed, "my bare feet. I'll be right back."

❧

The walk to the river was a silent one. At the turn-off, Paul took her hand to protect her from tripping on the undergrowth of the dark path, but when they reached the opening she pulled it away. "If you're really Freddie, why did you wait so long to tell me?"

"As I said, I have much to explain and I will—as much as I can anyway."

"Until then, I don't know who you are," she retorted.

Reaching the river, they sat down on the bank. The reflection of the moon on the Kennebec was a shimmering ball of light. Gustavia's eyes gazed at it, mesmerized, but her mind was far from it. She had waited years for the moment she and Freddie would meet again! And now she was having a difficult time believing it, and even . . . accepting it. This wasn't how she had played and replayed it over in her mind!

She turned to him. He was staring into the water, silent, his arms resting on his knees. "If you're Freddie, Paul, it was cruel of you to keep it from me for so long. I've been fighting my growing attraction to you because I was waiting for Freddie! And now I don't know what I feel, what to believe even." She stabbed at her eyes, wiping away the tears that had begun to blur her vision.

"I'm sorry I couldn't tell you sooner, Gusty. I didn't dare tell you until I had faced Ada and Edgar with the inheritance fraud. I didn't want to put you in the middle like that. If by chance you let it slip before I found out all the facts, Ada would have fired me. Then I couldn't have done anything for you."

"Oh." *Of course*, she thought. "When did you know or learn I was coming to Ada's?"

"It all seems like a twist of fate, but that's not true. I believe it was God who led me to seek out the Redmore's account." He paused, thinking. "When we were children, you and you mother talked about your grandmother and grandfather Josiah and Fanny Sullivan Browne. I couldn't believe it when, in Ludlow, I found those names in Ada's and Edgar's parents' will. I was thrilled. At least I had found your ancestors. Then when Ada told me her niece, Gustavia Browne, had moved to Boston and was going to come to Belford and do her biography, I thought I hadn't heard her correctly. I kept asking her to repeat it until she was quite annoyed. I almost jumped for joy right there in front of her. I about gave it away."

Tears rolled down Gustavia's face, torn by conflicting emotions. She stood up, walked away a few feet and pulled out a tissue.

Paul shot to his feet, took hold of her shoulders and turned her around to face him.

He gazed at her. The moon shone down on her hair, turning it blacker, the highlights brighter. It hung loose over the white blouse. She gazed back at him, her eyes black, unfathomable pools.

"You're Freddie? You're really Freddie?"

"I'm Freddie, Gusty. I meant what I said to you as boy when I got through serenading you. I meant what I shouted tonight under the turret window. I love you. I've always loved you and since getting reacquainted with you, I love you even more, my darling."

Gustavia threw her arms about his neck, kissed him on the cheek and held him tightly. "Oh Freddie . . . how I've missed you. What happened to you after we were separated? Mum and I were so worried. I have a million questions."

His arms wrapped around her, he replied, "I want to tell you everything—I *need* to. Not telling you that I was your long lost Freddie has been the most difficult thing I've ever done in my life. I've had to watch everything I said, hold back everything I felt."

She pulled back a little and gazed at his face. "I don't know what I expected you to look like. I guess more like Artie Banks. Some people don't change very much when they grow up. You have."

"You haven't changed, Gustavia. I would have recognized you anywhere, anytime. I first saw you about a block from the business district staring across the street. You were wearing that old-fashioned wine-colored dress holding an umbrella above your head. You looked as though you belonged in another time—some bygone era. You were too far away for me to recognize you, but I was so intrigued, I followed when you started for town. When I turned the corner, I could have reached out and touched you, but I still couldn't see your face. I stayed close behind, watching you, and waiting on the sidewalk for you as you went in and out of shops. At last I finally saw your face. My heart almost stopped when I saw it was *you*. It was all I could do to keep from grabbing you and yelling, 'I've found you at last, Gusty. After all these years I've found you!'"

Gustavia leaned her face against his chest and wept. After a while, when the tears had abated, she murmured "I wish you had. No wonder I've had my mind on 'Freddie' so much since I've been at Ada's. You've been right here *with* me, once more being a friend—a true friend, helping me cope while writing Ada's biography—all the while trying to keep it a secret for my sake. Thank you." She hugged him fiercely.

"Oh. Last night I dreamed . . . or heard you playing the harmonica . . . but you weren't there." She looked up at him. "Was it a dream?"

Paul looked sheepish. "I'm sorry, Gusty. You didn't dream it. I was there, out on the sidewalk. I couldn't stand the thought of you being with

Artie, so I impulsively started to play, then chickened out and walked away. I knew it wasn't the right time." His heart full, he bent down to kiss her, but she pulled away.

"No, Paul . . . Freddie. What do I call you?" she asked distressed.

"Both adoptive parents thought they should call me Freddie because that was what I was used to, and because they said it fit my personality. They've called me Freddie all my life and still do. My clients, as well as some friends, call me Paul."

"I don't know how I can call you Freddie. You . . . you look too mature. The name Paul fits you better now."

"Call me Paul then. I'm used to that coming from you." He took her face in his hands. "Gusty, I've longed for the day when I could hold you, kiss you. Why did you pull away from me?"

"Because I'm feeling confused. I've felt there was something mysterious about you. I understand why you couldn't tell me who you were until you confronted Ada, but why didn't you tell me *afterward*? You've had ample time. It wasn't fair to me. I've been on an emotional roller coaster feeling attracted to you, trying to wait for Freddie—then I meet Artie, which complicated it further."

"Now that you know who I am, how do you feel about Artie?" he asked stiffly.

"Don't change the subject, Paul. You even took me to Ludlow and still didn't tell me you were Freddie. Why, Paul?"

He sat on the bank and she sat beside him. Trying to sort out his thoughts and emotions, he threw a rock into the river, making ripples, his jaw rippling with it. How could he tell her that he had intended to do just that right after he broke the news to Ada, but—Artie Banks coming to see her two days before, and staying until that very day, had upset his well-laid plans! And when she told him there was something special about Artie, how could he tell her? She would feel obligated to keep her promise made to him long ago—in spite of how she felt. With Artie in the picture, he felt he could only tell her if she were to fall for the man he was now.

But as time passed and Artie continued to be a factor, he could see that she was stressing over both of them, all the while still worrying about being true to Freddie. He had to relieve part of that stress by revealing his identity. He wasn't sure if it would help him win her or be the cause of losing her. He took the chance—and now it didn't look good.

"Are you going to tell me why you didn't tell me sooner?"

"No. I can't. Not now anyway."

"I'm feeling a little distrustful because you haven't been up front with me, Paul."

He stood up. "Let's go back," he said, his voice cold.

She got to her feet. Despite the chill in his voice, Paul took her hand to guide her along the bank and through the woods. This time she didn't pull it away. His hand felt strong and safe—despite her doubts.

At Ada's front door, Paul said. "Where do we go from here, Gusty?"

"I don't know. I need to hear all about your life after we were parted. It's terribly important to me, but I'm on emotional overload right now. You held back your identity far longer than necessary and it . . . it feels to me like . . . deception."

It was like a knife to his heart. He swallowed hard. "I guess it might feel that way. Please trust me, Gusty, I had a good reason. "

"A good reason?" She shook her head in denial. "I think we need some time apart to think things over. Until you can tell me why you you've held back something so important to me, we have no future. Nevertheless, in a few days I do need to hear what happened to you, why your name is Camden instead of Banks and a hundred other things."

"All right." He took her in his arms and kissed her temple. "I love you Gusty. I always have." His voice broke. "I always will." He let her go, turned and walked briskly down the walk to the gate and out.

Gustavia couldn't move for a moment. His words of love reached deep into her soul, and it had felt so good to be in his arms! She didn't want him to leave. But his duplicity left her confused and unhappy.

Up in her room, she let the tears come—tears of relief that she and Freddie had been brought back together, tears of confusion, and tears of loneliness.

❧CHAPTER 34❧

Gustavia woke with a start. Was it all a dream? Did Freddie really show up under my window last night? Yes! It was true. After so many years of praying and looking for him it had really happened!

Yet the yearning was still there. Freddie—Paul was holding something back. Why? Why hadn't he been forthright with her sooner? Why was he refusing to tell her? Until he did, how could they be the friends they once were? She was the one who said they needed time apart, but the thoughts of not seeing him for a while only brought more distress.

Quickly dressing, she threw on jeans and a T shirt and went for a brisk walk in the early morning air. When she arrived back at Ada's and saw that it was a little after 7:00, she remembered the date with Artie. She needed his company, his cheerfulness, but she knew she wouldn't be in any state to go out with him tonight.

This was the second time she had to break a date with him! Nevertheless, she went into the library, picked up the phone, dialed the hotel and asked for his room.

He answered quickly.

"Artie. This is Gusty. Did I wake you?"

"Hi. No, I have an early morning meeting. I was just going down for breakfast. You barely caught me. What's up?"

"Something quite amazing has happened. I have found my friend, Freddie, or to be exact, the most unusual circumstances have brought us together."

The silence that followed told her how shocked he was at the news. "I'm happy for you, Gusty, but a little wary at how it's going to affect us. Who . . . when? . . ."

"Paul Camden is Freddie Finch."

"Paul Camden! How . . . could that be? I thought he was adopted by someone by the name of Banks."

"I was so stunned last night when he revealed it to me, I wasn't able to learn all the details."

"Paul seems like a nice guy, but are you sure he's Freddie?"

"I know he's Freddie. He let me know in a way that only Freddie would know."

"Why has he kept it from you all this time?"

"He had a good reason for not telling me for part of the time."

"Only part of the time?"

"That's what's troubling me, Artie. I'm in no condition to go out tonight. I've even refused to see Paul for a while. I need time to think."

"I'd like to see you anyway. You don't have to talk, smile or anything, unless you find one of my jokes funny."

Gusty smiled. "Oh, Artie, your upbeat personality would be good for me, but I wouldn't be good for you."

"Just being with you would be good for me, Gusty."

"I'm sorry, Artie. I just can't."

Another long silence followed. "Well then, will you think about coming out to visit for a week?"

"Yes. I will. Thank you for being so nice about tonight."

Hanging up, she felt a wave of depression wash over her. To take her mind off Artie and Paul, she determined that right after breakfast she would return to the diaries.

HULL SEAMENS' AND GENERAL ORPHAN ASYLUM, HULL, ENGLAND, SEPTEMBER 15, 1910:

Summer, or what passed for summer, bustled into fall with no major mishaps for Fanny. Only a few times did she find herself doing those distasteful chores reserved only for the most disruptive and disobedient—cleaning the lavatories, scrubbing the greasy kitchen floor, helping the housemaids gather up bedding to be washed from those who wet the bed, or getting up earlier to clean the kitchen flues so they could be lighted.

A new band master, Mr. George Pitt, had arrived the middle of August, posted the band rules and started up the band again, encouraging any child who was interested to join. Benefactors of the orphanage saw to it that there were enough instruments because in the past whenever the band played for the public, increased donations were made to the orphanage, helping defray expenses for the institution.

Always wanting to play a flute, Fanny got to do so and encouraged Josiah to join the band with her.

"I ain't no musician."

"How do you know until you try? How about playing a drum? You must like noise, you make enough of it."

"You ain't so dumb. I might like that."

In the end, however, Josiah surprised himself by choosing the cornet.

Band practice was right after tea in the afternoon, and an hour after supper. Great and terrific was the noise and din made by the booming of the big drum, the rattle of the side drums and the clash of the cymbals, accompanied by all the other unmusical sounds produced by bandsmen in the making.

To the credit of the respected bandmaster, Mr. Pitt, six weeks later the band made its debut playing as they marched down to the Victoria Pier and back. They had already learned four pieces and were asked to play for cricket matches and special holidays. But to Fanny's dismay, Mr. Pitt organized a boys brass band for special occasions and it seemed to be more popular than the general band.

Birthdays were celebrated in multiples, standing as a group while the other children clapped and sang to them. Then the birthday children were each given an extra big portion of dessert at dinner. Josiah had turned 12 in August and Fanny turned 11 in September.

School began at the orphanage and Fanny delighted in it. Mr. and Mrs. Wimble had only been headmaster and headmistress since last March, succeeding the previous ones who had retired. The quality and depth of instruction of the new school year was due to Mr. Wimble, a fine scholar himself, and a good, sound disciplinarian. Reading, writing, poetry, literature, impressive mathematical standards, nature study, geography, history and religious knowledge were all part of the curriculum.

The brighter students were often used to instruct small groups of pupils. It wasn't long before Fanny was helping with reading and literature. Josiah was proving to be almost a genius in mathematics and was helping other children. Much to his delight, Fanny was one them. There he could show off for her and his confidence grew.

In the winter months when it was raining, instead of the children going outside for the twenty minutes of play after morning tea break, Mr. Wimble would read a story to all of them. Some days when it wasn't even bad weather, Fanny would sneak into the library and read. Also she liked to be alone once in a while so she could let the ever-present tears fall, not over Melissa's unkindness, but from the terrible homesickness and loneliness for her Mum and Dad. The tears didn't last long. Something would always remind her that many children in the orphanage hadn't had loving parents as she'd had.

She was wiping the tears away when Josiah walked in one day.

"How come you ain't out playin,' Fanny?"

"I used to live in Ludlow where it isn't quite so cold. I shiver too much sometimes when I go outside here in the winter."

"Ah, you're just turnin' into a book reader. I never see you without one, it seems."

"Reading takes me away from the orphanage into other worlds and makes me forget how homesick I am."

"Would you help me read better, Fanny?"

"Can't you read?"

"Yeah, but I stumble over big words."

"I'll help you if you'll try to use better grammar."

"I've tried a little and it's hard to change the way you've talked all your life."

"I know, but you're so smart, Josiah, and using wrong words makes you sound dumb, and one day maybe you could go to a university, like my dad."

"You think so?"

"Of course. You're so smart in mathematics you could be a teacher or something. My mum and dad always talked to Melissa and me about how important it was for a boy to get educated. My sister, Melissa married an educated man. He was even knighted by the queen. His name is Sir John Redmore."

"Keen! Me dad . . ."

"*My* dad," she corrected.

"My dad didn't finish high school. Neither did me mum . . . my mum. They probably didn't think to talk to me about schooling. They were so poor, I guess they thought it wouldn't be no use talkin' about it."

It wasn't long after the visit with Fanny in the library that Mr. Wimble called Josiah into his office and talked to him about the same things, except in much greater detail. With great enthusiasm, Mr. Wimble explained the power and independence education gives a young man.

Immediately, Josiah reported to Fanny the details of the meeting and how special it made him feel. Under Mr. Wimble's tutelage he progressed in leaps and bounds. And under Fanny's tutelage in grammar and speaking, he began to sound educated to his own ears.

BELFORD, MAINE, JUNE, 2001:

As she read, Gustavia marveled at the ability of this abandoned little girl to accurately record the events and emotions in such detail. Her heart felt more at ease as she read further. Fanny became more adjusted to the orphanage, and her relationship with Josiah turned into friendship.

Page after page revealed something happening all the time. Boys running away, new children admitted, the girls taking turns going on delightful shopping trips with Mrs. Wimble, fights between the girls, fights between the boys. Such events rarely concerned Fanny or Josiah, much to Gustavia's relief. The boys' band became more and more popular, bringing in a few extra funds, giving Josiah many outings.

Gustavia smiled when she read of an experience Josiah and a couple of other boys had. They were due to practice marching with the band at the same time they were supposed to be washhouse boys. Mrs. Sellars, the laundress, refused to permit any of the boys taking off work to march with the band. To ensure this she locked them in. Mrs. Sellars, thinking the boys were securely fastened in the washhouse, was mortified to see out the window, the boys dressed up and marching. Josiah saw her looking out, caught her eye and grinned at her. She in turn shook her fist at him, but in the end was so pleased with their performance, that by the time she again saw the boys, her anger had died away and their offence forgiven.

Though Fanny and Sophie continued to be good friends, Fanny developed other friendships by taking parts in plays and pantomimes, which were later put on in front of the whole school. Other times, band concerts were presented.

Gustavia noted that Fanny had quit writing in her diary on a regular basis. Only when she was especially unhappy or a crisis occurred did she make an entry. One such occurrence in 1913 when Fanny was thirteen, elicited more tears as Gustavia read the account.

HULL SEAMENS' AND GENERAL ORPHAN ASYLUM, HULL, ENGLAND, APRIL, 1913:

The bell rang for tea and as Fanny was moving toward the dining room, Mrs. Prickett intercepted her. "Fanny dear," she whispered, "why don't you and I have tea in the library today."

Fanny's eyes lit up. It had been awhile since she had been able to talk with Mrs. Prickett alone. "Oh, that would be the jolliest. Let's."

Mrs. Prickett carried the tray of bread and butter, jam and tea while Fanny bounced along beside her. When they had seated themselves, they visited while they ate and sipped their tea.

Mrs. Prickett tipped her cup for the last swallow of tea, smiling tenderly at Fanny as she put the cup down. "I'm so proud of the way you've adjusted to being here, Fanny."

"You are?" she asked surprised. "But I've still gotten into trouble once in a while."

Mrs. Prickett smiled. "Of course you have. You have a spunky nature, but I think you've controlled it quite well, considering. There isn't a child anywhere who is perfectly behaved all the time. You just keep trying and you'll get better and better at controlling yourself."

"I'll keep trying, Mrs. Prickett, I will."

"Good. I regret having to tell you this, Fanny, but I have to quit working here at the orphanage."

"Quit?" The word didn't have meaning for Fanny. Mrs. Prickett was an important part of her life. One didn't quit something like that!

"Yes, dear. You see, I have grandchildren now, and my husband wants me to quit work so I can have more time to enjoy them."

"B-but I need you, Mrs. Prickett, I . . ."

"Fanny, my grandchildren need me too. I wish I could do everything, but I can't. I'll miss all the children here—but I'll miss you the most, love."

Fanny felt like her world was falling apart again. Once more, she was losing someone she loved.

Mrs. Prickett gazed at Fanny's stricken face and reached for her. Fanny went into her arms sobbing. Mrs. Prickett shed tears along with her, frightened how Fanny would fare without her.

"We have to have faith, dear, faith that all will turn out well for both of us. You're praying aren't you?" Fanny nodded. "Then you'll be all right, I promise."

"I don't think I'll ever be all right without you, Mrs. Prickett."

"Yes you will, love. You'll be fourteen in just over four more months. It won't be long before you can leave here and make a life of your own. You're already a pupil teacher now. You can become a schoolteacher someday and help many children."

"You think so?" she asked, reaching for her pocket handkerchief and wiping her nose.

"I know so. You can make a good living. One day you'll get married and have children of your own."

"When can I leave here, Mrs. Prickett?"

"Some boys are permitted to leave at fourteen, others at fifteen or sixteen. But the girls aren't allowed to leave before sixteen years of age. And this brings me to something I want to talk to you about, Fanny. I want you to promise something."

"I'll promise you anything, Mrs. Prickett."

"I don't want you to promise me anything. I want you to promise yourself. Keeping promises to yourself is more important, Fanny dear. I want you to promise yourself that you will remain a good girl until the day you get married."

Fanny's brows twisted questioningly. Mrs. Prickett frowned in concern, hoping Fanny understood. She had caught girls whispering among themselves about titillating subjects, but she had never seen Fanny among them. Most of the young girls in the orphanage would be sheltered if it weren't for the new girls, with their worldly knowledge, being admitted on a regular basis, all too eager to share information with their new-found friends at the orphanage. Then she realized why Fanny reacted as she had. *Of course*, she thought. *Much of the time Fanny kept apart from most of the girls, associating mainly with innocent little Sophie.* Mrs. Prickett felt very uncomfortable. If she weren't leaving, she would wait until the child was older, but she had to forewarn her now. She had already talked with each of the older girls. She didn't know the new assistant matron who was taking her place and she didn't want to leave the girls in her hands.

"When you leave the orphanage, Fanny," she began "there are wicked men who may wish to take advantage of you. You're growing up to be quite a beautiful young lass."

"I am?" she asked surprised.

"Yes you are and the good Lord has commanded us to be unsullied before marriage."

Fanny's freckled nose wrinkled in thought for a moment, then she said, "Oh. I'll be a good girl, Mrs. Prickett. I promise."

Mrs. Prickett was relieved that Fanny seemed to understand.

"I heard some girls talking about Helen and a boy kissing in the hall. Is kissing bad?"

"Oh dear. I didn't know about that. And I'm sure Mr. Wimble doesn't either."

"I don't mean to be a snitch, Mrs. Prickett. I didn't see them."

"Never mind about that. Now to your question on kissing. Fanny, kissing in and of itself isn't wrong. It doesn't make you impure. But sometimes, boys or men will try to go farther than kissing.

A round-eyed Fanny nodded, understanding as much as she was capable, but grief over Mrs. Prickett leaving superceded any more thought on the embarrassing subject Mrs Prickett had talked about. Fanny threw her arms around her and sobbed.

"You'll be all right, dear. You're going to be all right. You're a strong girl."

When her tears subsided, Fanny looked up into Mrs. Prickett's kind face. "I promise I'll be a good girl, Mrs. Prickett."

"That does my heart good, love."

A week later at breakfast, Mrs. Prickett introduced the new assistant matron, Ellen Peel, a woman in her late forties dressed all in black. She looked much older because of her prematurely gray hair and thick spectacles. She was as thin as a young spear of asparagus and just as straight. Her thin lips were pursed tightly together in a forbidding manner.

All the girls gave her uneasy stares, politely nodding at the introduction, then as instructed took turns standing and introducing themselves to her.

"Thank you girls," Mrs. Prickett said, smiling warmly. "I'm sure Mrs. Peel would like to say a few words."

Mrs. Peel nodded primly and cleared her throat. "It will take me some time to learn your names, but I expect you to respond when I speak whether I say your name or not. I anticipate getting along well with all of you. All I expect is obedience and respect. Thank you."

Without any more painful goodbyes, Mrs. Prickett quietly left the orphanage. After breakfast everyone disappeared from the dining hall to attend to their various chores. All except Fanny who went to search for Mrs. Prickett. Unable to find her, she asked one of the pupil supervisors

"She has already gone. You'd better get to work, Fanny."

It wasn't long before the new assistant matron was called on to solve a problem.

Helen blustered up to her, red in the face with indignance. "Mrs. Peel, Fanny Sullivan is supposed to help me in the laundry room and she's skipped out!"

A little surprised that a crisis had developed so soon, Mrs. Peel studied the girl through the thick spectacles. "Where is Fanny Sullivan?"

"I don't know. She might have run away. She did that once," Helen was happy to inform her.

"Oh my. I must go speak with Mrs. Wimble," she replied nervously.

Finding Mrs. Wimble, Ellen Peel blurted out, "Fanny Sullivan might have run away."

May tipped her head to one side quizzically. "I just saw Fanny in the dining hall. Who told you this?"

"A girl named Helen."

"Helen has a way of exaggerating when it comes to Fanny. Let's you and I go look for her."

They couldn't find Fanny anywhere in the building. They stepped out into the large backyard and looked around. "Hmm, I'm sure she's around somewhere," Mrs. Wimble said smiling. "She promised us she wouldn't run away again. I'm sorry that straightaway you have a small crisis to deal with, Mrs. Peel. Let me think. To shorten our search, let me get someone who might know where she is. You wait here."

Presently, Mrs. Peel saw Mrs. Wimble come out the door with a tall dark-haired young man with eyes dark as bitter chocolate.

"I'd like you to meet Josiah Browne, Mrs. Peel. He's a friend of Fanny's. He thinks he might know where she is."

They followed Josiah out on the lawn toward a cluster of bushes. Looking behind them, he shook his head. Running over to another large bush, he motioned them over.

"What are you doing here, Fanny?" Josiah asked, already knowing.

"It's none of your business, Josiah Browne!"

"But it's ours, Fanny," Mrs. Wimble said, walking up with Mrs. Peel. "Thank you, Josiah. You may go finish your chores."

Fanny glared at him. "Snitch!"

"Brat," he replied, grinning as he ambled off.

"What are you doing here, Fanny?"

"I wanted to be by myself."

"I'm sorry, but you can't do that during chores. I know you're sad about Mrs. Prickett leaving. We all are, but we have to go on as we were."

Fanny got up and ran into the building.

"Does she do this kind of thing very often?" Mrs. Peel asked, concerned.

"No. She was brought here under unusually cruel circumstances, but she's been doing rather well in spite of it. She was very attached to Mrs. Prickett so it would be wise to let it go this time. If she does it again, she'll have to be disciplined."

⁊

The whole atmosphere changed when Mrs. Prickett left. But Fanny and the other girls were relieved that Mrs. Peel wasn't as strict and mean as first impressions indicated. However, she didn't allow herself to get emotionally involved with the girls, so the only mother figure they had was the busy Mrs. Wimble who didn't take time for one-on-one talks with the girls as Mrs. Prickett had.

Fanny tried to fill the void Mrs. Prickett left by reading every chance she got.

During a time when everyone was supposed to be outside, Josiah found her in the library again. "Hey, brat."

"Hey, snitch."

"You know I had to help them find you. Did you want them to call the bobbies again?"

"No. What're you in here for? I want to read."

"I just came in to tell you that I'm thinking of leaving the orphanage."

Fanny looked up from her book, startled. "Why? You're only fourteen."

"I told you before, the board lets boys leave from fourteen to sixteen, depending on their ability to take care of themselves."

"But Mr. Wimble said you were his best student in mathematics. Don't you need to study under him longer?"

"I think I do actually, but I'm tired of being regimented."

"Have you talked with Mr. Wimble?"

"No."

"Before you decide, will you talk to him?" she asked, hoping fervently that Mr. Wimble would talk him out of it.

"What do you care whether I leave or not?"

"I'd miss you if you left. Too many people in my life have left me."

"You'd miss me?"

"I said that didn't I?"

Josiah looked at Fanny for some time, an odd light in his eyes. "All right. I'll go straightaway and talk with Mr. Wimble."

Josiah found the headmaster in his office and knocked on the half-open door.

"Josiah. Come in. What can I do for you?"

"I understand that a boy can leave the orphanage at fourteen if he's ready."

"Yes. Please have a seat, Josiah."

"Am I ready?" he asked sitting down and leaning toward Mr. Wimble eagerly.

"Partially. You're a bright boy and could apprentice as a bookkeeper—even at your young age. But if you'll stay here until your sixteen, you'll be much better prepared. In fact, Josiah, you're so bright I've talked with the Board about paying you something for being a pupil teacher. The salary will be small, and we can't hand it to you. It would be put in a bank for you to withdraw when you leave. This is highly unusual for the Board to agree to this, but I've shown them what you've done."

Josiah could hardly believe his ears. "I had no idea I was smart enough to be paid for helping other students."

"You wouldn't just be helping. You would have several classes, just like the other teachers. The only thing is, you'd have to study history and English on the side."

"I'm rather blown off the rail, Mr. Wimble."

Mr. Wimble smiled. "How about it? Do you accept the teaching job?"

"I'd consider it a privilege, sir. Thank you!"

Leaving Mr. Wimble's office, Josiah caught Fanny just as she was leaving the library and told her the good news.

She gave him an exuberant hug. "That's extraordinary, Josiah! Simply extraordinary. I'm so glad you're not leaving."

"Me too," he said, not daring to tell her how much he would miss her if he did.

❧CHAPTER 35↶

HULL SEAMANS' GENERAL ORPHAN ASYLUM, HULL, ENGLAND, AUGUST 1914:

Mr. and Mrs. Wimble asked the children to stay a short while after they had eaten their supper. This wasn't unusual. When the Headmaster had special instructions to give them, he often called a meeting in the dining hall right after supper.

"Children, Mrs. Wimble and I have enjoyed our time with you here, but with many regrets we must inform you that we're retiring in a week."

This announcement was greeted with shocked exclamations and groans. The Headmaster and Mistress were both touched by their reactions, and also saddened.

"We're sorry we have to leave all of you. We've become much too attached to those of you who have been here for the duration of our term. And all of you new ones, we have already begun to care for you also. This is very difficult for Mrs. Wimble and me, but some health challenges have beset both of us, so we think it's time for us to retire."

Josiah could hardly believe his great teacher was leaving. Distraught, he wondered how long he could stay without him.

"A Mr. and Mrs. Henry Crumby will be taking over in a week as Headmaster and Mistress. I'm sorry I don't know very much about them, but the Board tries to get capable people to run the orphanage. Tomorrow, they arrive. They will spend the week with us learning the procedures. You are now excused."

Instead of the children dispersing immediately, most of them gathered around Mr. and Mrs. Wimble, some in tears, some stoically asking them questions, other begging them to stay on.

Josiah left the dining hall immediately, unable to handle it emotionally. He went outside and headed toward the bushes that Fanny usually hid behind. Unknown to him, Fanny was following a discreet distance behind. Only when he sat down did she make herself known by sitting down beside him.

Surprised, he said, "Hey, brat, I want to be alone."

"That's all right. I won't say a word. Pretend I'm not here."

He couldn't let her know about the lump in his throat and see the tears that threatened to follow, so he swallowed it back the best he could. He had turned sixteen, and Fanny would turn fifteen in September, and their relationship had begun to change. He longed to put his arm around her and kiss her. He could tell that she was looking at him differently, too. But what was he going to do about it?

"I'm so sad for you, Josiah. I know how close you are to Mr. Wimble."

"I thought you weren't going to say a word, Fanny."

"Oh. I'm sorry."

"That's okay."

They sat there silent for some moments. Josiah couldn't resist. He impulsively put his arms around her. "Thank you for caring. I love you, Fanny."

"I love you too, Josiah."

"You do?" he asked incredulous. Then he frowned skeptically. "You love me like a friend or a beau?"

"A beau? How can you ask that, Josiah?" she retorted, her face flushing with embarrassment.

"Because I love you like a beau loves a sweetheart."

"B-but how can you, you're so young?"

"I've had to grow up fast, Fanny. I'm a teacher now. I can go out and apprentice and soon make my own way."

"I like you, Josiah. You're the smartest and handsomest boy I've ever known."

He laughed. "You haven't known very many."

She laughed too. "I've known enough."

"When I leave, I want you to come with me, Fanny."

Shocked, she asked, "Wh-what do you mean?"

"I want to marry you."

Fanny's heart started beating fast, as if she had been running. "Josiah Browne," she began, taking a deep breath trying to get her heart back to normal. "I certainly didn't expect this kind of talk when I followed you here."

"I didn't expect to say it either. But I've been feeling this way for a long time."

Not knowing how to react, she said, "I've got to go, Josiah."

Before she could make a move, he pulled her over and kissed her on the lips.

"Josiah!" she exclaimed, jumping up.

His heart pounding, he quickly replied. "I've also been wanting to do that for a long time, Fanny. Don't tell me you didn't like it, too."

Fanny gazed at him, assaulted by conflicting emotions. Whirling around, she ran across the lawn toward the building. Then, fearing she had hurt his feelings, she turned and ran back. However, she remained hidden on the other side of the bush, still too confused to talk to him.

Behind the bush, Josiah was feeling as though Fanny had deserted him, just like his parents, just like Mr. Wimble. Fanny heard him break down and cry. Tears blurring her own eyes, she stealthily tiptoed away, then ran into the building.

The next day at breakfast, Mr. and Mrs. Wimble introduced the new headmaster and mistress, Henry and Dora Crumby. In turn, Mr. Wimble had each child stand up and introduce themselves.

Josiah warily studied Mr. Crumby. He was a short, stout man with dark brows and dark hair. He had a square jaw and an unyielding expression. Holding in his chin, his back straight as if he were standing at strict attention, he stared at the uneasy group. Josiah feared the worst. Mrs. Crumby looked timid and weak. She was a mousy-looking little woman with her brownish-blonde hair, pale brown eyes and a light brown dress. She kept her hands clasped and her head down when Mr. Crumby began to speak as though she didn't dare look any of the children in the eye. *Or even*, Josiah thought, *as though she were trying to make herself invisible.*

Mr. Crumby's speech was as stern and unbending as his appearance. He explained that he had been a colonel in the army, and he intended to run the orphanage in as orderly and disciplined a manner as possible. "However, the schooling will be as our scholarly Mr. Wimble has set it up. The Board is very pleased with the education of the children who leave this institution. Mrs. Crumby and I will be in charge starting tomorrow, though Mr. and Mrs. Wimble will continue as instructors for the rest of the week. Thank you."

Mr. Wimble clapped, nodding for the children to follow. An unenthusiastic round of applause echoed through the hall.

As Josiah headed toward the back door to help the gardener, Mr. Wimble caught up to him.

"Josiah, I would like to talk with you in my office."

Josiah's face lit up. "Yes sir!"

Seated across from each other, Mr. Wimble smiled at Josiah. "Since you've just turned sixteen, Josiah, you may leave anytime this year. I've arranged with the bank that when you leave you can withdraw the small savings that you've earned teaching." He handed Josiah an official paper with his signature on it authorizing him to withdraw his funds at any time. "Give this to the banker, and he'll give you all or part of it as you wish."

"Thank you, sir!" Josiah exclaimed exuberantly, his eyes bright. "I also want to thank you for everything you've done for me here. You've been the father I never had, Mr. Wimble."

"Your welcome, Josiah. I assure you, the reward has been mine. I'm always exhilarated when the rare young man comes along who is as brilliant as you. And this brings me to the good news I have for you."

Josiah leaned forward eagerly.

"I have contacted a businessman in London, a friend of mine, and he has agreed to let you apprentice with him as a bookkeeper whenever you decide to leave. Here is his card. It gives his name and business address. I've also included his home address. If you decide to accept his offer, write to him in advance, so he can arrange a place for you to stay."

Josiah took the card with the name of one Simon Sisbee, Banking and Investments. He stared at it, not believing his eyes. He looked up into the kind face of Mr. Wimble, his eyes misting with gratitude. "I can't thank you enough, Mr. Wimble. Knowing you these few years has influenced my life more than I can say."

Mr. Wimble stood up, came around to Josiah, and shook his hand, then heartily embraced the tall young man, who returned the embrace with great affection.

Josiah left Mr. Wimble's office, his shoulders straighter, his head higher, as confidence rushed through him. He was ready to leave the orphanage! Quickly returning to his dorm, he pulled out a small box, deposited the precious documents inside, and shoved it back under the bed.

Out in the garden, Josiah's mind worked as furiously as his body. *What about Fanny? Will she go with me? I can't leave her here under the heavy hand of Mr. Crumby!* Not being able to tell Fanny of his good news immediately was almost painful. She was the only one he could tell. He had to be exceptionally careful with this information. He didn't know the Crumbys yet, but he had a feeling he couldn't trust them.

Immediately after dinner, Josiah went over to Fanny. "Could you come outside with me?"

Fanny hesitated, not sure if she wanted to go behind a bush with Josiah again. "It has been raining, and it's bitter cold outside."

"All right, let's go into the library. No one is in there now. I have some good news to tell you, but we have to be very secretive about it. You mustn't tell anyone."

"Oh, I won't, Josiah," she said, her face alight with excitement.

Sitting in a small alcove surrounded by shelves of books, Fanny said, "Tell me! Tell me."

"What will you give me if I tell you?" he asked slyly.

Fanny noticed that he had that look in his eye, the same as he had before he kissed her out behind the bush. "Josiah Browne, I am not going to let you kiss me again."

"You didn't let me. I stole it."

"That's right, you did," she said, displaying a miffed expression that shortly disappeared. A shy one replaced it. "You know, Josiah, that was my first kiss."

"I figured it was." He gazed into her large, bright blue eyes; then his eyes slid up to her untamed mop of curly reddish hair, and down to her pert little nose with its freckles, and the full pouty lips below. "I didn't want anyone else beating me to it."

Fanny smiled. "I'm glad it was you who gave me my first kiss instead of someone else."

"You are?" Hope rose in his breast. "Fanny," he began in a lowered voice, his dark eyes sparkling, "Mr. Wimble called me into his office this morning . . . ." When Josiah finished telling Fanny, her eagerness was gone; instead, she looked close to tears.

"What is it? I thought you'd be happy for me."

"Oh, I am, Josiah. And I'm so proud of you, but the thought of you leaving is almost more that I can bear."

His heart leapt with joy. "Then come with me!"

"Come with you?" She looked horrified. "Wh–why . . . I mean, what for? I'm only fifteen or will be next month."

"I know you're young, but what is there here for you?"

"More schooling and teaching, then I'll be old enough to leave next year."

"Fanny," he whispered. "I want you to run away with me."

This suggestion almost took Fanny's breath away. "I . . . I don't think I dare."

"Do you *want* to come with me."

"I want you to stay here until I'm old enough."

"Then you're saying you want to come away with me later?"

"I, uh . . . think so. It's rather hard to think of life without you in it."

Afraid to push Fanny, he nevertheless took the risk. "Then would you consider marrying me?"

"M–marry you? Oh, Josiah," she breathed out. "I'm too young to marry."

"I know. I don't even know if we could get a license, but we could try."

"But I don't feel ready to be married."

"Maybe we won't have any choice about it either way. Forget about not feeling ready. Do you want to marry me?"

"I . . . I think so. I haven't had any experience with boys. How do I know what I want?"

"If I give you a little more time here, will you think about it seriously?"

"Y-es," she said, hesitantly.

"Promise?"

Studying Josiah's intense brown eyes, his handsome face, Fanny's heart fluttered in a way it never had before. "I promise."

"Can I kiss you?"

She nodded shyly.

He pulled her up, slid his arms around her slender body, bent down and kissed her sweetly and tenderly.

❧CHAPTER 36❦

HULL SEAMANS' AND GENERAL ORPHAN ASYLUM, HULL, ENGLAND, SEPTEMBER 1914:

A pall settled over the orphanage the moment the Wimbles left and the Crumbys began their term as Headmaster and Headmistress. The first thing Mr. Crumby did was meet with all the children in the dining room after breakfast and lay down some strict rules.

"I've been here only a week and have seen much laxity. I've noticed how slowly most of you work. This will not be allowed any longer. You will speed up and accomplish much more. You will be expected to work harder at your studies. If I see anyone fighting, no matter who started it, both parties will be paddled by me. When it's outside time, all of you, and" he reiterated, looking directly at Fanny, "I mean all of you, will be expect-ed to go out. No one will be allowed to stay in the library. If it's raining, you may play quiet games in the dining hall."

Josiah caught Fanny's eye, and he could see her dismay.

"Young lady," he said, pointing to a girl who had been whispering to her neighbor, "Come here." Surprised and frightened, she got up and stood before Mr. Crumby. He gripped her shoulder hard. "This young lady was whispering to someone while I was speaking. "I will not allow that. Mrs. Crumby, do your duty."

Mrs. Crumby stepped over to the girl. "Hold out your hand," she demanded in a voice that was surprisingly shrill and sharp for one who looked so diffident.

The girl did so. Immediately Mrs. Crumby pulled a willow from one of her pockets and switched her hand. The girl winced with pain. Striking her hand twice more, Mrs. Crumby stated icily, "You may return to your seat." The girl, fighting back tears, went quickly back to her seat.

Well, thought Josiah, *I misjudged the woman. She isn't timid in the slight - est!* He was more concerned than ever over leaving Fanny here when he left. That is, if she didn't decide to go with him.

Within the week Mr. Crumby had dismissed a boy. Josiah could remember only one time Mr. Wimble had expelled anyone. He was always able to turn them around.

Three weeks later, two boys, who claimed they had been paddled more brutally than was necessary for their small crimes, ran away. The bobbies never found them.

The nurse's office was busier with ill children than Josiah had ever seen it. Fanny had developed a bad cough and fever, much to Mrs. Crumby's irritation, and had to be put to bed for three days, along with several other children. Josiah fretted and worried over the possibility it might turn into something serious.

By December, a terrible scandal erupted. Helen, who was sixteen, ran away with a boy who was only fifteen. Rumor was that they had been kissing and canoodling every chance they got. Once Mr. Crumby had learned of these disgraceful shenanigans, he detained the children the next morning after breakfast.

"The large number of you here at the orphanage," he began, "present a problem. As you know, we've recently had a regrettable occurrence—a sixteen-year-old girl and a fifteen-year-old boy have run off together." He shook his head grimly. "This is most scandalous indeed. It puts a black mark upon this institution. Mrs. Crumby and I have decided that from now on the boys will not be allowed to mingle with the girls, whether it be playing games inside on rainy days or in the school room. The only time intermingling will be allowed is during band practice and performances. Boys and girls will be separated in all work and all other activities. Is that clear?"

Stunned silence filled the vacuum. Of the fraternization to which Mr. Crumby alluded, Fanny's was the most obvious. Josiah gritted his teeth, his determination to leave growing stronger by the moment.

"Today, go to work, school, play as usual. We'll post all your assignments and new arrangements here in the dining room tomorrow morning before breakfast. You are now excused." Everyone got up mechanically, as if in partial shock, and began to walk out of the dining hall.

"Move!" bellowed Mr. Crumby, startling the children, who then almost ran out of the room.

Josiah managed to step in beside Fanny as they walked down the hall, hardly daring to glance in her direction for fear of getting her into trouble. "Don't worry, Fanny, we'll find ways to talk."

"I hope so, Josiah," she said, breathless with anxiety.

JANUARY, 1915:

It was a bitter cold day when Josiah knocked on Mr. Crumby's office door. It opened slightly when he did so. He had been putting off this visit to let Fanny grow up a little. She was still too frightened to run away with him, but Mr. and Mrs. Crumby's cruelty was getting worse, not better, so he decided to tell Mr. Crumby that he would be leaving and that he needed to find a replacement for him in the schoolroom

"Yes?" Mr. Crumby's deep impatient voice answered.

Josiah pushed open the door. "Mr. Crumby, may I speak with you for a moment?"

"You may, but be quick. I'm very busy."

"As you're aware, sir, I turned sixteen in August and could have left here. I stayed on to get a little more experience, but I feel it's time I leave now and get on my own."

Mr. Crumby's eyes narrowed as he scrutinized the young man before him. "You know we're shorthanded for pupil teachers don't you?"

"I do, Mr. Crumby. That's also why I stayed on longer," he lied.

"That's admirable, but it doesn't change the fact that you'll be leaving us shorthanded."

"I wish it could be otherwise, Mr. Crumby, but I must leave."

Mr. Crumby leaned back in his seat, clasped his fingers together and stared at him coldly. "I'm sorry, Josiah, but I'm not giving you permission to leave."

"You have no right to do that."

"I do have the right. You're excused. I have things to do."

Josiah glared at him. His jaw rippling in anger, he pivoted on his heel and left. He had been wise not to trust the headmaster. He had been afraid that if he wrote to Mr. Sisbee in London, Mr. Crumby might possibly intercept the letter. His mind raced. *I know, I'll ask Mrs. Sellars the laundress if she could have Mr. Sisbee write him at her personal address.* Mrs. Sellars liked him and disliked the Crumbys.

He and Fanny had been communicating by note, and several times behind the bush for a few moments, the bone chilling cold causing them to shiver as they talked.

JANUARY, THREE WEEKS LATER:

Mrs. Sellars secretly handed a letter from Mr. Simon Sisbee to Josiah one day in the laundry.

"Thank you, Mrs. Sellars," he whispered as he tucked it into his pant pocket. "I'm much obliged."

"Your welcome, Josiah. I was glad to help out."

The moment Josiah got a chance, he opened the letter. As he had hoped, Mr. Sisbee was eager to have him come and apprentice. All he had to do was let him know when to expect him. Bursting with excitement, he wanted to find Fanny and tell her. Instead, in the school room, he dashed off a note telling her of the letter and his plan to escape.

Fanny was almost afraid someone might hear her heart, it pounded so loudly in her ears as she read Josiah's note. The thought of Josiah leaving and never seeing him again was unbearable enough, but to be left here and watch the Crumby's cruelty to the children made it more unbearable. She had to go with Josiah! Then she wondered how she was going to conceal her diaries. *Of course, the horrible oversized bloomers. Anything would fit nicely in them!* she thought ruefully. She could even stash an extra set of under-clothes in them.

In a few days, she received another note from Josiah explaining in detail the escape plan. He'd had Mrs. Sellars ring the railway line and find out the schedules for London. The day of the escape was planned for February 1st, the afternoon the whole band was to play for the public at the Jarrett Street Music Hall. Hopefully neither of them would be missed as they slipped away while the others entered the building. They were to edge over to the large elm tree, hide behind it until all were in, then run around the corner on Trippet St. There, a hansom cab would be waiting for them, called by their friend, Mrs. Sellars.

Josiah didn't want to spend any of his small savings on a hansom, but he had no choice. The cab would take them to the bank where he would withdraw his savings and from there to the railway station. The train for London would be leaving soon after. Everything had to be timed perfect-ly, and he prayed that he could withdraw his funds quickly in order to reach the railway station in time.

Finally, February 1st arrived, and a bitter cold day it was. Nevertheless, each child was expected to play most of the way as they marched toward Jarrett Street. Fanny's hands were so cold and shaky, she could hardly hold her flute much less play it. Josiah, on the other hand, was just the opposite. The adrenalin flowing through him gave him energy, heightening his determination and excitement at starting a new life with his love. He played his cornet with confidence, his marching steps sure and steady.

❧CHAPTER 37❧

BELFORD, MAINE, JUNE 2001:

Hoping that Fanny's and Josiah's escape from the orphanage was successful, Gustavia turned the page. To her utter shock it was blank! Flipping from blank page to blank page until the end she was stunned. "No! This can't be the end!" She rubbed her temples, thinking. *Surely there has to be more. Is this the scandal that Ada had talked about? Them running off together? No, it couldn't be! Josiah was planning to marry Fanny.*

Like a cancerous cell, suspicion began to grow. If Ada had hidden some of the diaries, she might have hidden another one. *But if there was another one, why didn't Fanny finish writing in this one? Why did the date on the front say it ended in 1933?* A large center portion was gone it seemed. Quickly she paged back to the last entry, then turned the page and looked carefully at the inside spine. It looked like it had been cut. It was almost imperceptible. She pulled on the page she had just turned. It came loose. Pages had been cut out! All the rest of the written pages of the last diary were gone! Fear gripped her heart. It didn't make sense that Fanny, herself, had done it. It had to be Ada. "She can't have destroyed them!"

She didn't trust herself to approach Ada right now. She had to talk to Edgar! She looked at her watch and realized she had forgotten lunch. It was 1:00 when she drove into Edgar's parking lot. Turning off the motor, she literally ran inside.

Edgar looked up, surprised. He was about to greet her when he noticed the expression on her face. "What is it, Gustavia."

"Do you have some time to talk with me?"

"I always have time to talk with you," he said, smiling affectionately.

"I need you to be forthright with me. It's very important, Edgar."

"I'll do my best to do so. What is it?"

"How did your mother treat Ada?"

Edgar blinked a couple of times, dumbfounded. "I certainly didn't expect that question."

"It's important that you tell me, Edgar, because at the moment, I'm trying to hold in my anger toward Ada for something she may have done."

Edgar's shoulders slumped. His hope that his lovable young cousin could soften Ada's heart was sorely being tried. "All right," he began hesitantly, "I'll tell you. Ada always told me I was Mother's favorite. It used to upset me as a boy. But as I got older I realized she was right. Not only that, my mother was . . . uh, somewhat cruel to Ada. She ridiculed her, criticized her—in fact mother was rather a cold person. Even to me."

This was almost exactly what Gustavia had expected to hear. "Was your father aware of this?"

"Yes. But he didn't want to deal with it. Mother was a much stronger person than he. If my parents' marriage is any example, it appears the selfish one in the marriage always wins out—unless the unselfish one can help the other. Father apparently wasn't strong enough to do this or chose not to try. He buried himself in work, turning a blind eye to it all."

"This is why you wanted me to do Ada's biography."

"Yes. She deserves something good in her life."

Gustavia's heart softened. Edgar's life had been a lonely and sad one, but his concern was only for his sister. She blinked back tears. "Thank you, Edgar." She pressed her cheek to his and gave him a squeeze. "Thank you for being forthright with me." She let out a tremulous breath. "I don't want to bring more worry to you, but I'm terrified that Ada has destroyed most of Fanny's last diary. Pages have been cut out."

Edgar's brows furrowed, his deep set eyes full of concern. He rubbed his mouth and stared at the floor, thinking. Raising his eyes to Gustavia. "I pray she hasn't because . . . His voice trailed off.

Before Gustavia could stop him, Edgar dialed Paul's office. "Paul, Edgar here . . . Well, I'm concerned about something. Ada may have cut some pages out of the diaries. I hope she hasn't destroyed them. Is it possible for you to call Ada this morning? . . . Good! If she has, you're the only one who can find out, as we discussed before. Also, if you haven't already, it would be wise for you to go over the contents of the box I gave Gustavia . . . You can? Thank you, Paul."

"What was that all about, Edgar?"

It's nothing you need concern yourself with, Gustavia. Paul will take care of it."

Gustavia wasn't ready to see Paul yet! But of course she couldn't tell Edgar. He was trying to help her.

"I'm going over there now and talk to Ada. Maybe I won't need Paul's help."

"If you need me, call."

"I will. Thank you, Edgar."

ॐ

In the parlor Ada sat rigidly in the high-backed chair, her hands twitching slightly. The expression in Gustavia's face was something she hadn't seen before, and it unsettled her.

"Ada, I have come to the end of Fanny's diary."

"Oh?" Her brows rose imperiously. "Now you know what scandal I'm talking about."

"No, I don't."

"What do you mean you don't? Josiah and Fanny ran off together and they were much too young to marry, so of course, one can fill in the blanks."

"I can't. Fill me in, Ada."

Slightly flustered, Ada breathed deeply to regain composure. "I'd rather not be so crass as to explain it. You're not that innocent, Gustavia."

"I'm afraid I am. I have no idea what you're talking about."

Frustrated, Ada spoke impatiently. "It went all through the orphanage that Fanny Sullivan and Josiah Browne ran away together and cohabited. Now is that clear enough?"

"How did you know this, Ada?"

"That information is in that box."

"You cut out the rest of the diary, Ada. Where is it?"

A faint flicker of fear in Ada's eyes came and went. "If anything was cut out, it must have been by Fanny herself."

Gustavia grimly persisted. "What have you done with the pages, Ada?"

"I . . . I don't know what you're talking about."

"If you've destroyed them I'll . . ." The thought of this brought so much fury, Gustavia couldn't finish. "Where are they? I've already told Edgar about this. He said to call him if I needed him to come over."

"He can't make me say anything different, Gustavia."

The phone rang.

Gustavia got up and walked rapidly into the library. Ada followed her. By the time Ada walked in, Gustavia was talking with someone.

"Here, he wants to talk with you."

Cooly, Ada took the phone and said hello. "Paul! I thought it was Edgar. . . I will not speak with you. . . I . . .what?. . . What document?. . . You wouldn't dare!" Her face blanched. "How could Edgar think of doing such a . . . He did? . . . Yes. . . No, I haven't . . . All right!" She slammed the phone into its cradle.

Ada was shaking with anger and with something Gustavia had never seen in her before—defeat.

"I'll be right back," Ada muttered through clenched teeth.

Gustavia seated herself in one of the leather chairs and waited anxiously. *What had Paul said to her?* she wondered.

The ten minutes Ada was gone seemed more like thirty. Ada stepped over to her and thrust a thick manila envelope into her hands.

Gustavia was so relieved, tears blurred her eyes. "Thank you for not destroying them, Ada."

"Don't thank me. Thank Edgar. He threatened to sever all ties to me if I did anything to any part of the diaries, or if I already had."

"Ada," Gustavia said softly, "please sit down a moment."

Unable to accept the kindness in Gustavia's voice, she asked, "Why? You got what you wanted."

"No. I haven't."

"You now have every page of the diaries, Gustavia."

"Thank you. But that isn't the only thing I want."

"I have nothing else of yours," she said through tight lips.

"Yes you have. You have my sympathy."

"What?"

"Since you read the diaries, you know how your mother treated her little half-sister. I'm wondering if your mother treated you just as cruelly as she did Fanny. If she did, I'm sorry. You didn't deserve that. No one does."

Shocked at Gustavia's disclosure, Ada stumbled over her words. "H-how dare you make . . . make that assumption, Gustavia."

"It was easy. You and your mother are too much alike."

"I am nothing like my mother!" she replied vehemently.

"Tell me how you're different?"

"I most certainly will not. It's none of your business."

"Yes it is—because you're treating me exactly like you were treated."

"That's not true!" Her voice had become shrill. "I don't ridicule you and tell you how homely you are . . ." She caught herself. Covering her face with her hands, her shoulders shook convulsively, yet no tears came.

Gustavia got up, went over to her and touched her shoulder. Ada callously shoved it away. Gustavia took Ada's bony cold hands in hers. Ada tried to extract them, but Gustavia was stronger.

"Ada, we need each other, you and I. We're all the family we have left."

Ada's convulsive shaking had subsided, but the hostility hadn't. "It's not much of a family. We're only half-cousins."

"I know, but I would like us to become close, Ada. Please." Tears surfaced in Gustavia's eyes. "It has become important to me."

Ada looked almost frightened as she viewed the tears, heard the pleading. "I . . . I don't . . . I can't believe I could be important to you."

"I can understand why you would feel that way, but it's true."

Ada's chin trembled, her hands shook beneath Gustavia's. Her chest began to heave and at last, years of holding herself rigidly from any relationship began to weaken. Gustavia released Ada's hands so she could have the dignity of covering her face as she tried to hide the healing tears that followed.

After some time, Gustavia thrust some tissues into her hands which Ada used to wipe her nose and eyes.

"Are you satisfied now, Gustavia, now that I've humiliated myself before you?"

"You haven't humiliated yourself. You can't do that with someone who cares." Ada found no words to respond to that.

Gustavia took a deep breath. "Can you forgive Edgar? Can you forgive Paul?" And at last, the difficult question. "Can you forgive your mother?" She felt like a hypocrite, wondering if she could have forgiven Ada if she had destroyed those precious last pages of her grandmother's diary.

"I don't want to carry on this conversation any longer."

Gustavia knew she had expected too much too soon. But there was no way she and Ada could make amends unless Ada could forgive Edgar and Paul. She moved toward the door. "All right, Ada."

Just as Gustavia entered the hall, the doorbell rang. Her heart responded first, knowing it was Paul. She moved quickly to the front door and opened it.

She and Paul gazed at each other for a moment, the strain still between them.

"I've come over to—"

"I know, but Ada hasn't done what we feared. She has given them to me."

"Good! But I do want to go over the contents of the box Edgar gave you. Or have you looked through it?"

"Only a little. I needed my attorney to go through it with me." She smiled.

"Have you had lunch, Gusty?"

"No. Have you?"

How about getting the box and let's go down to the Soup and Salad here in Belford. I hear it's quite good."

She hesitated, troubled by mixed emotions. She wished she could tell him how happy she was to see him, but his refusal to tell her what she needed to know made it impossible.

He raised his eyebrows at her hesitation. "You don't feel free to open it here, do you?"

"No. Wait in the garden, and I'll go get it. Since it isn't large, we can easily manage it at the restaurant."

❧

Parking at the restaurant, Paul turned to Gustavia. "When you first answered the door, you looked quite upset."

"I had been trying to accomplish something with Ada."

"Tell me about it."

Here he was being her friend when she needed to talk. In spite of her feelings, she told him what Edgar had said about his mother's treatment of Ada, then of her conversation with her.

"Ada is a fortunate woman to have you in her life."

"But she won't let me into her life."

"Not now. Maybe later."

"Oh, I don't know, Paul. On the surface, at least, it all feels rather hopeless. I don't know if I can break through Ada's hard shell. Her self-protective covering will probably have to break from the inside out—you know, like a chick inside an egg."

Paul's eyes roved over Gustavia's face—her eyes, soft with compassion, her hair piled willy-nilly up off her neck, her fine features set into a creamy complexion, all combined to make her face look like an exquisite piece of porcelain. It was all he could do to keep from taking her in his arms. "Shall we go in?"

The box tucked under his arm, he led Gustavia into the buffet.

Settling themselves in a booth near a window, they eased into comfortable conversation as they always had.

When they were through eating, Paul said with great curiosity, "Now, let's look into that box."

After perusing several papers, he said, "Fanny's sister, Melissa, hired a detective to keep track of her."

Gustavia, who had been sorting the material by dates and handing them to Paul, looked up with raised brows. "That in itself explains a lot of things I didn't understand."

"These papers are official correspondence between Melissa and the detective. She kept copies of her own letters and kept the detective's reports to her."

"But why would Melissa want to keep track of Fanny?"

"The only reason I can see is that she didn't want Fanny to discover her whereabouts. If Fanny did, she could possibly learn that Melissa had stolen her inheritance and perhaps bring the law into it."

"Oh, yes, of course."

Fingering through some more papers, Paul said, "Here is where Ada got the information she mentioned today. Apparently the detective checked with his private source at the orphanage on a regular basis to make sure Fanny hadn't been adopted or run away. When he last checked, fifteen-year-old Fanny had run away with a sixteen-year-old boy named Josiah Browne. Hmm, your grandfather." Gustavia nodded. "Interesting. I'm anxious to read the diaries. It says here the detective's source told the detective that Mr. Crumby had related to the whole staff the lurid tale of them running away together, making it sound quite indecent."

"Right after that Ada cut out the pages. I'm very curious as to why. Maybe she wanted me to think the worst of Fanny, so she and her mother would look better."

"Possibly." Paul quickly gave each of the remaining papers a casual glance. "Somehow the detective found Fanny in London. They continued using the detective up to the time of Fanny's and Josiah's deaths. Ah . . . ha, here's a report that says after their deaths the detective and his assistant went into their flat in London and confiscated all of Fanny's diaries and any other records which could lead the law to Melissa."

"So that's how Melissa got the diaries. I supposed Melissa learned of my father's death the same way."

He looked through some more pages. "Yes, but by that time they had hired a different detective, obviously to create a break in the continuity— the before and after, so to speak. Edgar put his records in here showing that he had hired a third detective to keep track of you and your mother, a move strongly opposed by Ada."

"Where are the wills?"

"Edgar gave those to me immediately, so we could reinstate you as an heir."

"Oh, of course. At last, most of my questions have been answered. The only remaining questions I have may be answered in the diary pages Ada gave me this afternoon."

When Paul drove up to Ada's, he rolled down the windows and turned off the key.

"Thank you for going through the contents of the box with me. How can I ever repay you for everything you've done for me?"

His eyes burned into hers. "I can think of something right this moment."

Gustavia looked down, her cheeks burning.

"How was your date with Artie last night?"

"You want me to answer your questions, but you won't tell me why you didn't reveal your identity right after you confronted Ada.

Ignoring her statement, he asked, "Are you going out with him tonight?"

"You answer my question first."

"When the time is right, Gusty, you'll know the answer to your question."

"I'm not going out with Artie tonight. He flew back this morning. Even with the difficulties between us right now, Paul, I need to know what happened to you when we left for Cornwall."

"Well then, how about tonight?"

❧ CHAPTER 38 ❧

Paul led Gustavia up to the second level of the old red brick building which housed his apartment in Augusta. He had suggested they go there where they could have some privacy when he told her about his life and where they could throw something together for dinner later.

Gustavia was delighted—though her mind was still not completely at ease. When she thought of Paul as her friend, Freddie, she loved him and wanted to smother him with affection, but when she thought of him as Paul the attorney who had hidden his identity far longer than was fair to her, she was troubled and confused. Yet unable to meld the man, Paul, with the boy, Freddie, she, nevertheless, was relieved that finally, after all these years, she would learn what happened to her Freddie!

She had worn one of her 1890s designs, a deep green dress made of a cooler summer material. When she had come downstairs in it, Paul had smiled, the familiar twinkle back in his eyes, lifting her heart.

"Well, here's my place of abode, such as it is," Paul said, closing the door behind them. Gustavia surveyed it. The room was small but well-decorated. One thick-armed couch and chair to match we re covered in a sturdy tweed-like material in muted tones of red, blue, green, and orange. Several solid-colored pillows of the same colors were thrown on the couch. A magazine table, a lamp table, and a bookcase were made of heavy knotty pine. "Nice," she murmured.

"Thanks. The kitchen is through that door. It's small but just right for me. Would you like something cold to drink?"

Before Gustavia could answer, the doorbell rang. Paul frowned. "I brought you here so we wouldn't be disturbed." Reluctantly, he stepped to the door and opened it. He gaped in surprise. "Dad, Mother!"

"Hello, son," his dad said as they stepped in. "We're glad you're home. We took a chance."

"I can hardly believe it," he said, hugging his mother and then his dad. "What in the world are you doing way out here?"

"We have some old friends who live in Boston," his mother answered. "They invited us to visit them and see the sights. We took them up on it because we could visit you also."

Gustavia, shocked at the sudden appearance of Paul's parents, had quickly stepped back and to the side, not wanting to interfere with their greetings. Mrs. Camden was the first to notice her.

"Oh! You have company."

Paul stepped over to Gustavia and took her hand. "Mother and Dad, I want you to meet Miss Gustavia Browne. Gustavia this is my mother, Karla Camden and my father Bruce Camden."

It seemed to Gustavia that Paul was not at ease. She certainly wasn't. Mr. and Mrs. Camden stared at her and her attire. It was clear to Gustavia that Mrs. Camden especially disapproved of what she saw, though her breeding and social grace kept her feelings from being overt. Gustavia, to bridge the uncomfortable silence, reached out her hand to Mrs. Camden. "I'm glad to meet you both."

"Thank you," Mrs. Camden replied. "Uh, are you in the theater? Your costume is lovely."

Gustavia glanced at Paul who gave her no help whatsoever. "No, I'm not in the theater. I'm a clothes designer. I'm intrigued with clothing from different periods, so I design and make them, then I wear them once in a while."

"Why?" Mrs. Camden asked in a tone that stopped just short of an open challenge.

"I don't know really," she answered lamely.

"Gustavia Browne. Where have we heard that name?" Mr. Camden asked.

Why is Paul so ill at ease? Gustavia wondered. When she first learned who Paul was, she had felt it important to meet these people, but now she found herself wishing she were anywhere but here.

"Dad and Mother, please be seated. Gustavia, sit here in the chair and I'll go get a kitchen chair for me."

When they were all seated, Paul asked, "Would any of you like something cold to drink?"

"Where have we heard this young lady's name, Freddie?" his father asked again, clearly unaware that his son had asked a question.

"Remember the little friend I wanted you to find when I came to live with you?"

"This is she?" his mother asked, incredulous.

"Yes, Mother, she is."

"But I thought we agreed not to look . . ."

"You and Dad agreed that it was best not to search for her, but I didn't."

"You never said so, son," his father stated.

"When we moved to San Diego, it upset Mother to tell our new acquaintances that I was adopted, so I kept it to myself. You both might as well know now—I've searched for her much of my adult life. I even took a trip to England to look for information that would lead me to her."

Gustavia's heart swelled with tenderness toward Paul at this admission. But it didn't calm her fast-beating heart. She wished she could disappear! Then just as quickly, she realized she needed to know what kind of people had raised Freddie. Were they kind and loving parents or somewhat cold and rigid as they seemed to be at the moment?

Neither of the Camdens could readily respond to Paul's confession. Finally, Mr. Camden broke the silence. "Since it apparently has meant so much to you to find her, we're happy that you did."

"Mr. and Mrs. Camden," Gustavia said, "I too have been looking for Freddie. I've missed him all these years, and I'm happy to meet the people who adopted him, loved him, and raised him. But I know now I couldn't have found him because the orphanage told Mum and me that he'd been adopted by a Robert and Sharon Banks."

All the while Mrs. Camden had remained silent. With the mention of Robert and Sharon Banks, an expression akin to hostility crossed her face. It was gone almost as soon as it had appeared.

Paul quickly added, "I haven't had time to explain anything to Gustavia, Mother. It has been such a short time ago that we found each other."

"I see." Her pause was purposeful. "Your father and I were hoping to take you out to dinner tonight, Freddie."

Gustavia stood up. "Mr. and Mrs. Camden, I don't want to interfere with your visit with Freddie. I'll call a taxi."

"We wouldn't hear of it, young lady," Mr. Camden said. "You must come to dinner with us."

"Thank you, Dad," Paul said.

Paul's thank you sounded as stiff as Mrs. Camden's back looked, Gustavia thought miserably. It was obvious to her that Paul had been caught completely off-guard by his parents' unexpected visit. She felt sad for him that he had to prepare them ahead of time before they could accept her. *Maybe his mother would never accept me under any circumstance,* she thought. How she wished she hadn't worn this dress tonight! It was obvious that the way she was dressed had added to the already existing problem—the taint, in Mrs. Camden's mind, that came with adopted children.

❧

The meal at the Senator Inn was awkward at first, but Gustavia began asking the Camdens about their other children, something she hadn't been as curious about until she had learned of Paul's identity.

She learned that Paul's brother was named after his father, Richard Bruce Camden. They called him Rick. His oldest sister was Shari and the youngest, just older than Paul, was Shelly. Mr. Camden proudly announced that they had six grandchildren.

Studying the Camdens as they visited with their son, Gustavia decided that Judge Bruce Camden looked like a judge. He was the picture of dignity. His tall stature, the gray at his temples, and his quick intelligent blue eyes set in a long square-jawed face would look natural in a judge's robe.

Karla Camden would have been a plain woman but her stylish short brown hair and expensive up-to-date clothes gave her the confidence and distinction of a more attractive woman. Her best features were classic cheek bones, and green eyes which turned wary when gazing in Gustavia's direction. Gustavia hoped that, given enough time, they could get to know each other.

Paul bragged on Gustavia and her achievements and explained that she gave up a teaching position with Boston University to write her cousin's biography and that her cousin happened to be his client. All this was presented briefly because his mother's reaction was that of only polite interest. Afterward, he had tried to bring Gustavia into the conversation several times, but Karla always diverted it to news about the family, the judge's career and memories that only included the three of them.

At last, Paul said, "Well, I think I had better run Gustavia home."

"We'll ride with you, Freddie," his mother said, "then you'll have company on the way home."

"Thanks, Mother, but I'll be fine."

"But we've come all this way to see you. We'll need this evening because we only have tomorrow to visit with you. We're leaving Monday. I'm sure Gustavia wouldn't mind, would you?"

"It's really up to Freddie, Mrs. Camden."

The conversation on the way to Belford showed no improvement and Gustavia was actually glad to be back at Ada's. After thanking the Camdens for dinner, she walked with Paul to the door.

He picked up her hand and pressed it to his lips. Gustavia was aware that Paul had placed himself in a position that screened this action from his parents.

"I'm sorry the way my mother acted tonight. I'm sorry we didn't get to have our talk. You see . . ."

"You don't have to explain to me, Paul."

"All right. I'll call you."

Gustavia watched him run down the walk and get into the car and drive off. She felt empty. Paul had not been himself, not even on the doorstep. So many years apart from each other—each living such different lives—made her feel that she and Freddie might be strangers forever. It was unrealistic to think they could pick up where they had left off, and yet—that's exactly what she wanted.

❧CHAPTER 39❧

Monday evening, Paul got home late, feeling more tired than usual. The interruption of his and Gustavia's evening Saturday had been very disconcerting and at times the visit Sunday with his parents had been a tense experience. He was sincerely glad to see them as they were him. He knew he was fortunate to have them as a family, except when it came to Gustavia.

In addition, some legal problems in a case he was working on would keep him tied up for several days, leaving no time to see Gustavia.

He had grabbed a hamburger on the way home because his cupboard was bare. As he took off his tie and suit, he thought of the way his mother had treated Gustavia. More than once, he had recalled what Gustavia had said about Artie's family. How could she help but compare his parents to Artie's? The old insecurity that he had often felt in the orphanage rose up in his throat.

Already, he was competing with Artie personally. That was difficult enough. But he had no control over the family issue!

In addition, two people had been on Paul's mind. One he could understand, the other he was a little puzzled about. He hadn't called his brother Rick to tell him he had found Gustavia. The other person was Sharon Banks, that special woman who first adopted him. He couldn't figure out why she kept coming to mind of late.

He sat down at the kitchen table and dialed Rick's home. After several rings his brother answered.

"Hi, Rick.

"Freddie! It's about time. I was all set to call you. What's up?"

"Mother and Dad were just here, and I had a good visit with them."

"They said they were going to be seeing you."

"They met someone that is special to me. Remember the young girl, the friend I always wanted to find after I was adopted?"

"Yes. Gusty Browne."

"I found her!"

There was a momentary silence on the phone. "You did? How? When?"

"It's all rather amazing—coincidences that couldn't be coincidences. More like answers to prayer."

"Tell me about it. Let me get Melanie on the other phone. She would love to hear this."

"Hi, Freddie," Melanie said. "It's about time we heard from you. I hear you have something amazing to tell us."

"I have, Mel." Paul told them as briefly as the complicated story would allow.

"Wow! That's some story," Rick said.

"And so romantic," Melanie chimed in. "When do we get to meet her?"

"Before I could reveal myself, another guy came on the scene and is giving me some competition. If it all works out, I'm bringing her out to California."

"We'll be pulling for you, brother."

"Thanks. There's something I've been wanting to ask you, Rick . . ."

"Excuse me, Freddie," Melanie broke in, "I've got to get off and take care of a problem with the children. We hope to see you soon."

"Thanks. I hope so too." When she hung up the phone, Paul continued. "I don't know why, but Mother's sister, Sharon, who adopted me first, has been on my mind lately. It seems a little odd to me since I didn't know her very long. As I remember, Mother and Sharon weren't close. Is that right?"

"They were at one time, but when Aunt Sharon joined the Mormon Church, it put a big rift in their relationship."

Paul wondered why this shocked him. *The unbelievable coincidence of Sharon also being Artie's aunt, of all things, of course it was likely she was a Mormon. The Mormon Church again! Artie's church. Artie with that special some - thing,* he thought. "Do you know why Mother was so against the Mormon Church?"

"Why are you asking this, Freddie? You thinking of joining too?" he teased.

Paul laughed contemptuously, "Hardly. I know nothing about it. I'm just curious is all. Can you answer my question?"

"Let me think. For one thing, Mother has it in her head that the Mormon Church is some kind of cult. I remember them arguing heatedly one day after Aunt Sharon joined. I can't quite swallow the cult thing myself. I know some members of that church, and they're very nice people."

"I don't know what to think about all that, Rick. All I know is I remember Sharon's sweet face, and I've often wished I could have gotten to know her."

"I always loved Aunt Sharon, but I didn't like Uncle Robert very well."

"I didn't either. He wasn't good to me. Well, Rick, it's been great talking with you. Tickle the kids for their Uncle Freddie."

"I will. Thanks for calling, brother. I appreciate it a lot."

Paul felt better just talking to Rick. However, it didn't last long. The dear woman who had been responsible for taking him out of the orphanage was a Mormon! He shook his head as though to clear away the fog. *The fact that my mind has been on her and the fact that she was a Mormon certainly couldn't have any connection whatsoever.*

Sunday, Gustavia hoped Paul would at least call since they had parted under such tense circumstances. Restlessness soon sent her hiking. Upon returning she asked Ada if Paul had called. Ada seemed delighted to tell her he hadn't.

Monday, she drove to Augusta to sightsee and browse through antique shops. Back at Ada's, she asked her again if Paul had called. The answer was the same. Languidly, she climbed the steps, took a shower and went to bed.

Lying there thinking, she couldn't help but compare Artie's wonderful warm family, who had taken her in immediately, with Paul's. She hoped that the Camdens had been more loving to Paul as they raised him than it appeared they had on short acquaintance.

She finally slept, only to awaken shortly after, her thoughts on her grandmother's diary, wondering why she had put off reading it for two days. *Am I fearful of finding out that John and Sarah's daughter, Fanny, really did bring some terrible shame upon the family?* The intensely tender emotion she felt in the presence of her great-grandparents' graves came back to her and all she could do was hope for their sake she would find it wasn't true.

Again she dozed, or had she? It was suddenly 4:00 A.M. She woke feeling so stunned, so incredulous, she couldn't move. She glanced around her to make sure everything was real.

Thirty minutes later, she was able to move. She reached for her small Bible from the night stand, slipped out of bed and went over to the window seat. She stared out at the darkness trying to internalize the dream she'd had—the dream that didn't seem like a dream. It felt too real!

Flipping the light switch that turned on the inset light of the turret, she sat down, opened the book and stared at the words. Unable to focus her mind on their meaning, she slipped to her knees and prayed for help, for understanding.

Some time later, a hint of light filtered through the windows. When full sunlight washed the room with brightness, she awakened, surprised to find herself curled up on the floor, her head and arm resting on the window seat, the small Bible in her hand.

She stood up, stretching out the kinks. *The dream!* "The dream that kept me awake! What did it mean?" she asked aloud as if something in the room could answer.

Once more, she felt all the emotions that went with the dream as well as the aftermath. One emotion stood out, a feeling of urgency—an urgency for what? The answer came to her clearly, as though it had been spoken in words: *Finish Fanny Sullivan's diary.* Why? was her immediate response. But why was she even questioning it? Her desire to finish the diary had increased three-fold!

She looked at the time. It was 5:30, two-and-a-half hours before breakfast. She would read until then and again after breakfast.

❧CHAPTER 40❧

ENGLAND, FEBRUARY 1915:

Fanny sat across from Josiah in the compartment of the train, wide-eyed with disbelief. They had actually escaped! The train was moving at an increasing rate of speed down the tracks. The cadence of the rapidly turning wheels was a comforting shoosh-shoosh, taking them further and further away from the cruel Crumbys.

"You really are a genius, Josiah. All your plans went as smoothly as a swallow of Mrs. Cracken's treacle covered pudding."

Josiah basked in Fanny's admiration. Nevertheless, he attempted to understate his part in the escape. "Ah, some of it was just good luck. I was able to get my funds out of the bank with no problem, the cab was waiting, and it got us to the railway station just in time to meet the train, you know."

"I know no such thing, Josiah." She stared out the window at the scenery slipping by so fast the fascinating images of towns and country barely had time to register. "I've never been on a train," she murmured.

"I haven't either. I feel rather posh sitting here in our very own compartment."

Fanny giggled. "We're quite a couple of swells aren't we?"

Josiah laughed. "We are at that."

"Are you hungry Josiah?"

"Drat! I didn't think of food."

"I did," she said slyly. "Turn around and I'll get it."

"Why do I have to turn around?"

"Because," she began, her face turning pink. "I have it hidden in the legs of my . . . my bloomers, along with several other things."

Josiah blinked in surprise. "You have?"

"Yes. Now turn around."

Glad to get rid of the encumbering load, Fanny pulled out her diaries, and the food wrapped up in a clean petticoat, but left the rest of the underclothes tucked securely down inside. "You can turn around now."

He stared at the diaries, the two big pieces of bread and two buns placed beside her on a neatly spread out petticoat. He grinned. "No wonder you seemed a little clumsy."

"I have clean underclothes in there still."

Josiah doubled over with laughter. It was so joyously infectious, Fanny laughed with him.

"Well, I'd say you are a little genius, too, Fanny."

"Thank you. Help yourself."

"Thanks! I'm starved. I was so nervous today I couldn't eat all of my dinner."

"Me neither."

Josiah ate the bread and began on the bun. When he was almost through with the bun, Fanny offered hers to him.

"No thanks."

"I'm not that hungry, Josiah."

"Sure you are."

"No. Really."

"All right, I'll take half." He broke it in two. As he suspected, she was still hungry because she ate every morsel of her half. His heart swelled with love for her, grateful she was here with him.

The excitement of their new experience waned slightly, forcing Fanny to face the reality of their situation. "Josiah, since we can't live together, where are we going to live?"

"Why can't we live together until your old enough to marry me?"

"Josiah! I promised Mrs. Prickett I would be a good girl."

Josiah's face turned a deeper color. "Ah, Fanny, I didn't mean live together in that way. I meant we could live in the same flat. My ol' man may have been a drunkard, but there was something he said to me once that stayed in my brain like a hunk of glue. He said: 'I may be a drunken sot, Josiah, but I'm true to yer mum. She wuz pure as a new born lamb, she wuz, when I first met 'er, and I's made certain she stayed thet way till the very day I married 'er. An I've been faithful and true to er, I'll 'ave you know.' There's not much I can be proud of, Fanny, but I'm proud of my ol' man's morals. I had a lot of friends whose dads weren't faithful to their mums."

"That's something to be very proud of, Josiah."

Exhausted, it wasn't long before Fanny and Josiah lay down on their respective seats and fell asleep. They woke with a start when the porter went down the aisle knocking on each door yelling "King's Cross, King's Cross Station. London!"

Fanny sat up, sucked in her breath, suddenly afraid. "Did you tell Mr. Sisbee you were bringing me?"

"No, but it will be all right, Fanny. I promise you. He's a nice man. Mr. Wimble said so."

Fanny's heart raced. She shakily wrapped her diaries in the petticoat and held them tightly under her arm.

Josiah, who had nothing but the coat on his back, stood up when the train stopped, took hold of Fanny's arm and opened the compartment door that would lead them to a strange city, a strange man, and an unknown future.

They looked around as they descended the steps of the train. The terminus was overwhelming compared with the one they had left in Hull. It was big and crowded with people hurrying in all directions. The noise was deafening with the hiss of escaping steam, clanging doors, pounding feet on the platform, wheels of luggage trolleys, people shouting greetings and farewells, a place of excitement that neither had ever seen before.

Josiah had no idea what Mr. Sisbee looked like except that he told him he would be wearing a black homburg hat, a black overcoat and, oh yes, he remembered now, spectacles.

There seemed to be a lot of black hats and black overcoats moving about. Josiah had tried to describe himself—but Mr. Sisbee wouldn't expect him to be with anyone, he suddenly realized. "Wait here, Fanny while I look for him."

After walking a few yards away from Fanny, he looked for spectacles on a man. It wasn't long before he saw a short rotund man with a black coat and hat and spectacles looking around.

Walking over to him, Josiah said, "Sir, could you be Mr. Simon Sisbee?"

"I am. You're Josiah Browne?"

"Yes sir, I am."

"Glad to meet you, my boy," Mr. Sisbee said, holding out his hand.

"Glad to meet you, Mr. Sisbee," Josiah said, accepting his firm handshake.

"Where's your luggage, lad?"

"I have none. It's a rather complicated story, sir."

"Oh?" A long pause ensued, making Josiah uncomfortable. "Well . . . in that case it appears we have to take you to a clothier before you start work."

"Uh, there's one more thing, sir. I have a young lass with me."

"What? A young lass? Didn't you just come from the orphanage?"

"I did, sir, but . . ." Josiah had no other choice but to blurt it out. "Sir, the orphanage has a new headmaster, and he isn't the kind man Mr. Wimble was. The conditions there had become rather unbearable, so I helped a friend of mine to escape the orphanage with me."

"This puts a whole different face on the situation, my boy."

Josiah intently studied Mr. Sisbee's face. The only thing he could discern in the dim light of the terminus was kindness. "I assure you, sir, she'll not be your responsibility."

"Where is the lass?"

"I'll go get her." He went back to where he had left Fanny. "Come on, Mr. Sisbee wants to meet you." Hesitantly, she went with him.

"Mr. Sisbee I'd like you to meet Fanny Sullivan. Fanny this is Mr. Sisbee."

"It's nice to meet you, sir," she mumbled.

"How old are you Miss Sullivan?"

"Fifteen."

He rubbed his chin, studying the young girl before him. "Hmm. Well, we can't solve our dilemma standing out here in the cold. The Mrs. is home preparing a big meal for our supper tonight, thinking she would be feeding a hungry young man. She'll be surprised to find she'll be feeding two hungry young people."

"I have some schillings left, sir. There's no need to feed us."

"My wife, Anna, would indeed be put out with me if I didn't bring you both home."

"That's very kind of you, sir," Josiah said.

"I have a carriage waiting for us," he said, motioning them to follow.

As they left the bustling railway station, Josiah and Fanny stared out the window to see as much of the big city of London as they could. It was dark out, but an occasional street lamp illuminated streets, buildings, narrow canyons of row houses, and finally what looked like an upperclass neighborhood on Regent Street.

When the carriage stopped, Mr. Sisbee said, "Here we are." They all exited the carriage and the driver drove around back to the stables.

As they entered Mr. Sisbee's home to present Mrs. Sisbee with an unexpected visitor, Josiah kept hold of Fanny's hand to comfort her.

Mr. Sisbee took off his hat and coat and hung it up on a hall tree, then suggested they do the same. In the light, Fanny and Josiah could see Mr. Sisbee more clearly. His blue eyes were set in a broad face which sported a notable nose, wide mouth, and firm chin. If one were to ask, they would likely say his most noteworthy feature was the twinkle in his eyes.

A slight, energetic woman with a full bouffant of blonde hair bustled in and stopped short when she saw the strange young girl. Fanny's eyes were agog at the beautiful dress the woman wore. It was a pale olive green with fitted undersleeves. The three-quarter-length pleated oversleeves with a frilled edge, giving them a pleated cape effect, were caught into a wide cummerbund. The bodice was trimmed with braid and small rosettes. The hem of the flared skirt was banded with scallops of ribbon and braid and tipped with rosettes.

Anna Sisbee, aware of the young girl's perusal of her dress, noted the coarse woven uniform she was wearing. Mrs. Sisbee smiled, her green eyes warm. "Well, young lady, this is a surprise. I thought we were only going to be favored with a young man. I'm Mrs. Sisbee and you're . . .?"

"Fanny Sullivan, ma'am, a friend of Josiah's."

"I'm happy to meet you." Turning, she gazed up at the tall handsome youth before her. "So you're Josiah Browne."

"Yes ma'am. It's nice of you to be accepting of my friend, Fanny. You see, I had to bring her. The circumstances at the orphanage since Mr. Wimble left have gone downhill considerably."

"Oh? That's regrettable. We must try and do something about that, mustn't we, Mr. Sisbee?" Not waiting for his answer, she continued. "We were certain you would be hungry when you arrived, so we have prepared dinner for you rather than our usual skimpy supper. Follow me."

She led them through the oak paneled hall to the dining room. It was brightly lit by a shimmering crystal chandelier above a long elegant table. Mrs. Sisbee ordered the maid to add another setting of china for their extra guest. Both Josiah and Fanny were in awe at the sight before them.

After they were seated and Mr. Sisbee had offered grace, they were treated to roast beef and Yorkshire pudding, brussels sprouts steamed in butter, and sliced tomatoes. Though it brought back memories to Fanny of her home in Ludlow, Josiah couldn't remember having eaten such wonderful food.

After a delicious custard eaten from crystal-stemmed dessert dishes, Mr. Sisbee suggested they retire to the sitting room.

"Why Mr. Sisbee!" Mrs. Sisbee exclaimed, "Miss Fanny Sullivan has the same reddish blonde hair you do."

"So she does, but I'm certain it's a much prettier color than mine—and considerably thicker I assure you."

"You see," Mrs. Sisbee said, "we have only two children, both girls, and neither inherited Mr. Sisbee's nice color of hair."

"How old are your daughters, Mrs. Sisbee," Josiah asked politely.

"Oh, they're both married with two children each, so far."

After some more polite exchanges, Mr. Sisbee got down to business. "I think we had better figure out how we can be of help to you, Fanny."

"I've given it a lot of thought, Mr. Sisbee," Fanny said. "I know I must work, but since I'm only fifteen I'm at a disadvantage. I was a pupil-teacher at the orphanage. I may be too young to be a governess, but maybe I could be a tutor."

"She's accomplished in English, grammar and literature," Josiah related proudly. "I know, she tutored me."

"Is that right?" Mrs. Sisbee said. "I have a younger sister who married a wealthy man. They have three children who need tutoring. They have a nanny who is attempting to teach them, but she isn't capable in those areas. I don't know if my sister would be interested in hiring you for a short time on approval, but I'll ask. If she does, part of your pay would be board and room, which would be a good thing for one as young as you. It's a dangerous world out there, my dear."

"That sounds wonderful, Mrs. Sisbee. I would so appreciate you asking her."

"She lives in the Mayfair district on Park Lane in a magnificent house close to Hyde park and not too far from Piccadilly Circus. Oh my, how I do run on. You probably have never been to London."

"I was in London with my parents when only two years old," Fanny informed her, "so I don't remember it at all."

Mr. Sisbee, wanting to get down to the business at hand, forestalled Mrs. Sisbee's penchant for asking many questions that would lead them far astray. "Josiah, my boy, you will be apprenticing as bookkeeper under a Mr. Langley Moore. He's my head bookkeeper and a brilliant one. From what Mr. Wimble said, you will learn fast. As for your lodgings, we're still working on that. Until you and Fanny are situated, you will both be staying here with us."

Josiah felt as though a heavy burden had been lifted from his shoulders. He knew he couldn't adequately express his gratitude, but he gave it a try. "We appreciate yours and Mrs. Sisbee's kindness. Thank you."

"Yes, thank you," echoed Fanny, happy she wouldn't be separated from Josiah—just yet.

❧CHAPTER 41❧

LONDON, TWO WEEKS LATER:

Josiah felt as though he were out of prison. To be on his own—to be able to come and go as he wished—was exhilarating. He felt a sense of importance as he walked into Mr. Sisbee's prosperous establishment on Moorgate Street each morning. He found out with excitement that just around the corner was the entrance to the Bank of England, the great institution which, Mr. Sisbee said, was affectionately referred to as 'The Old Lady of Threadneedle Street.'

The first day he entered the bank to start his apprenticeship, Mr. Sisbee sat him down in his nicely furnished office. "I'm glad to have you here, my boy. Before I introduce you to Mr. Moore, I need to tell you what we do here."

He cleared his throat and began. "My small investment bank buys bonds and stocks and resells them at a small markup to individual investors. We buy these from the Bank of England, corporations wishing to sell stock to the public, or through other much larger investment houses such as Lloyds.

"Since our markup is very small, we must exercise extreme caution in the various securities which we buy. You come highly recommended by Mr. Wimble and I place a great deal of confidence in his judgement. Apply yourself, Josiah. Observe everything that happens and," handing him two volumes said, "read these books. They will help you understand how individual fortunes, and a country's wealth can be built. There need be no limit to what you can learn, provided you're willing to put in the work it requires. Now, my boy, let's go meet the man you're going to apprentice under."

Josiah's head was swimming with everything Mr. Sisbee had told him. Though it all sounded fascinating, he didn't understand most of it. He knew he would learn it eventually. It would just take time. He vowed to begin reading the books that very night.

Before Josiah started work, Mr. Sisbee had taken him to a tailor and paid to have him fitted for two suits, one for work and one for church. In addition, Mr. Sisbee had also purchased, from a clothier, a set of everday clothes—a warm coat, scarf and gloves, then suggested that he and Fanny throw away all clothing and shoes from the orphanage, which they were very glad to do.

His apprenticeship was stimulating, for not only was he learning bookkeeping, but he was beginning to understand what Mr. Sisbee had talked to him about on that first day—finance and investment banking— from the patient Mr. Moore.

Only two things were dampening his spirits. The most important was that he hadn't seen Fanny for ten days. The second was his concern over the children left in the care of the Crumbys. Mrs. Sisbee had mentioned that maybe something could be done about it. He hadn't wanted to bother Mr. or Mrs. Sisbee about these two things until he had adjusted himself to work and his lodgings, and until Fanny had settled into her position as tutor for Mrs. Sisbee's sister's children.

The Sisbee's had found him lodgings less than three blocks from the bank with a family by the name of Dees on Aldermanbury St. He was paying for both board and room. The food was somewhat bland and didn't have as much variety as Mrs. Cracken's cooking, nor was it as tasty as Mrs. Sisbee's. And of course, there wasn't enough of it. But then he was used to his huge appetite not being satisfied. He had a furnished room on the   second floor of the home. It had a bed, a two drawer chest doubling as a wash stand, an armoire and a coal burning fireplace. It was much nicer than what he had lived in as a child. He felt very fortunate. And having Fanny living safely with Mrs. Sisbee's sister gave him great comfort.

His room and board cost him 10 schillings a week and he only made 18 schillings as an apprentice. If he wanted to save for the future, he couldn't spend too much on extras. Somehow, he and Fanny would find things to do together that didn't cost money.

He had already written to Mr. Wimble and told him how well Mr. Sisbee was treating him and thanked him once more. Also, he told him about the bad situation at the orphanage and asked him if there was anything he could do about it. He explained how he'd had to escape in order to leave, taking Fanny Sullivan with him.

Mary Hartnell, Anna Sisbee's sister and her brother-in-law, Edward, came over right away when Anna told them about the cultured young Fanny as a possible tutor for their three little daughters. Thoroughly impressed with Fanny, they immediately offered her the job, with room and board included.

Fanny was thrilled and accepted the job eagerly. Upon leaving the Sisbee's the next morning, Mrs. Hartnell, as kind and generous as her sister, had taken her to some of the finest retail shops and purchased proper clothing for her. When she looked into the mirror, a stranger stared back at her. She looked every bit as fine a lady as her mother had! Remembering how she loved wearing the beautiful clothes her mother bought for her, she whirled around in happiness and thanked her kind employer. She could hardly wait for Josiah to see her!

The Hartnell's house was a mansion, and at first she often lost her way when trying to find the various rooms. The bedroom she occupied had taken her breath away, it was so beautiful. It was on the second floor near the children so that if the nanny had to take time off, she would be there to care for them.

She loved the three little girls. Amy, eleven, was the oldest; Jane, ten; and Alice, seven. They were obedient children and learned quickly. They had school five days a week. The evenings and weekends were usually hers to do with as she wanted. She took walks around the neighborhood admiring the beautiful homes and ventured into other parts of the surrounding area.

She was terribly lonesome for Josiah and was anxious to meet him somewhere, maybe Piccadilly Circus that Mrs. Sisbee had mentioned. She was disappointed to learn that circus only meant a traffic circle and open square, a theater and amusement center with shops of all kinds. Anyway it sounded intriguing. Josiah had promised he would ring her up and make a date, but she hadn't heard from him.

The only thing that put a blot on her good fortune was the sad fact that her friends back at the orphanage were still suffering under the Crumby's cruel management. Sweet Sophie was still there. She heard Mrs. Sisbee mention doing something to help out. She prayed every night that things could somehow change for the better.

Friday afternoon, Mr. Moore told Josiah he could take Saturday afternoon off. Hoping Fanny had an afternoon off too, he asked permission to use the telephone. First however, he asked Mr. Moore where he could take a young lady who lived in the Mayfair district, somewhere, he asked sheepishly, that wouldn't cost anything. Mr. Moore suggested, since Mayfair was close to Piccadilly Street, they might meander down the sidewalk of that street to Piccadilly Circus. Mr. Moore drew a rough map for him showing how to get to the Hartnell residence. Josiah stuffed it into his pocket and went to the telephone.

Mrs. Hartnell answered and graciously agreed to send for Fanny.

A breathless hello came over the line.

"Fanny, this is Josiah."

"Josiah! I'm so glad you rang me up. I've been anxious to hear from you."

"If you're not working tomorrow afternoon, could I come by and take you out right after dinner?"

"Oh yes! Where are we going?"

"I thought it might be interesting to walk along Piccadilly Street to Piccadilly Circus."

"Oh, Josiah, that's just what I've been wanting to do."

"I'm glad, Fanny. I have to walk, so I don't know exactly when I'll arrive."

"I'll be waiting."

Josiah hung up the telephone, thrilled at hearing Fanny's voice and her eagerness to go with him. He decided he had better take some money to buy a bun or sweet roll for her since he wanted to be with her till almost supper time.

Saturday after dinner, Fanny eagerly changed from her everyday dress to one of the two nice dresses Mrs. Hartnell had purchased for her. It was a light green wool dress with full sleeves edged with two tiers of cream-colored lace frills, which matched the inset of the bodice. Mrs. Hartnell said it looked stunning with her red hair. She never dreamed she would have a nice dress like this so soon after leaving the orphanage. It made her look so grownup because it had a waist and a full long skirt. Her curly hair, however, was a problem. She was letting it grow out, and it wasn't yet long enough to make it stylish.

She grabbed her purse and dark green wool cloak and ran downstairs to watch for Josiah. As she stepped off the last stair, she heard the brass knocker. She ran to the door and opened it.

"Josiah! How did you ever get here so quickly?"

"Mr. Moore, with whom I apprentice, gave me a ride in a hansom he ordered for himself."

"How nice of him. Come in." Josiah stepped in. "Why, Josiah, you look so grownup. You're wearing a suit and tie. Take off your coat and let me look at you."

He did as he was told and Fanny's heart skipped a beat. She was very aware of Josiah's good looks, but he was even more good-looking in his suit. "You're so handsome, Josiah."

For the first time, he felt shy around Fanny. He had been gazing at her from the moment she opened the door. The only thing he had seen her in was the orphanage uniform. The clothes she had on enhanced her beauty, taking his breath away. "Ah, Fanny, it's you who looks grownup. You look beautiful."

Josiah had never told her she was beautiful, and she had never thought herself as such. All she had seen in the mirror was her unattractive haircut and her unbecoming uniform. A tingle of excitement went through her. *Beautiful? Josiah thinks I'm beautiful!*

She smiled shyly. "Thank you, Josiah."

His eyes reflected the admiration he felt. "Shall we go?"

Still smiling, she gave him her cloak. "Yes."

As he put it over her shoulder, Mary Hartnell came in.

"Hello, Josiah. You look nice in your new suit."

Josiah noted, as he had when he first saw her, that Mrs. Hartnell had the same kind expression as her sister, but was much different in looks. She was tall and slim with light brown hair and hazel eyes. "Thank you, Mrs. Hartnell. The Sisbees have been very kind to me, just as you have been to Fanny. I'm grateful to you for giving Fanny such a nice position."

"We're fortunate to have her, Josiah. The children love her and are learning much more than they were before. Now be off you two, and have a good time. But I'll have to say you may turn a few heads. You're a most attractive young couple."

"We are?" Fanny asked, her blue eyes sparkling with delight and with a new awareness that now she and Josiah were a 'couple.' "Thank you, Mrs. Hartnell. I'm certain it's the clothing we're wearing that make us so." Proudly, she took the crook of Josiah's arm and said, "Let's go, Josiah."

Once outside, Josiah put his arm around Fanny's shoulders and gave her a hug. "I've missed you so much, Fanny."

"I've missed you, too. I thought you'd never ring me up."

"This is some grand neighborhood. I've never seen the likes of it. And the house you live in almost looks like a palace."

"It does. And I have the loveliest room. I wish you could see it. Where do you live, Josiah?"

He described it as best he could and added. "It's very comfortable, and it's less than three blocks from Mr. Sisbee's bank."

They walked down the stone-laid sidewalk along Park Lane. Turning onto Piccadilly Street, they passed fashionable residences and shops on their way to Piccadilly Circus. When they reached the famous site, they stood for a moment taking it all in.

Josiah turned to Fanny. "Did you ever think when we were in the orphanage that we would ever be in a place like this, in London? I never could have dreamed that such a place existed."

Fanny clung to Josiah's arm. "It's all because of you, Josiah, that I'm here now having this wonderful time. Thank you."

He covered her gloved hand with his for a moment, his dark eyes soft. "I should thank you, Fanny. You coming with me was a favor to me. I love you." He quickly changed the subject, so she didn't feel obligated to reply. "Let's get on with our adventure." They resumed walking. "Look at this grand bookstore," he said pointing to a shop called Hatchard's."

"Oh! Let's go in and look around."

They entered and immediately took off their gloves so they could browse through the books. The clerks smiled and nodded their heads at the well-dressed young couple. This was not lost on Josiah. This was what he wanted for Fanny, nice clothes and a nice home, and to be accepted in society.

After an hour, Josiah suggested they leave and continue their investigation of Piccadilly Circus. One of the clerks approached them as they were about to leave. "May I help you two find something?"

"Thank you, no," Fanny said smiling. "You see, we're new to the area, and we were just looking. Maybe later."

Josiah smiled as they left. "What a smooth lass you are, Fanny."

"Thank you. It's easy to be smooth in my new clothes. I feel like a high-class lady."

Josiah smiled. "Me too."

Fanny laughed. "You feel like a high-class lady?"

They both laughed heartily.

They passed a shop called Lilywhite's Sports Wear and walked on. As they meandered, they came to a magnificent building called London Pavilion Music Hall.

"Oh, Josiah, look, they're advertising an American singer, Sophie Tucker!" She was about to say how much she'd like to hear her, but she held back knowing Josiah would feel bad because he couldn't afford to take her. Instead she said, "I'm earning 6 schillings a week, Josiah, and I'm saving it. Maybe we could use some of it to go to a performance sometime."

"You can use your earnings as you wish, Fanny, but I, uh, I'm saving mine for when we can get married."

Fanny stopped dead-still and stared at him for a moment, her blue eyes suddenly full of angry sparks. "You're taking a lot for granted, Josiah Browne. You talk about us getting married as if I had agreed upon it. I haven't even been courted by any other boys. In fact, this is my very first experience. Besides, isn't it proper for the man to propose and the woman to accept before they can plan on marriage?"

This completely took Josiah by surprise, realizing he had taken too much for granted. The silence grew heavy. The thought of not having Fanny as a wife someday was more than he could cope with, and his words came out sharply. "All right. Forget about what I said."

"I will!"

They walked on, both feeling miserable. At last, Josiah said, "I'll come back to the Music Hall Monday, and I'll buy us tickets to hear Sophie Tucker."

"Why?" she retorted.

His jaw rippled with irritation. "Because you want to hear her sing, Fanny."

"Why really Josiah?"

His voice rose. "Because I don't need to save my money if you don't want to marry me!"

"That's what I thought!" she exclaimed with equal volume. "You're making assumptions again, Josiah Browne."

"What other assumption can I make? Would you like to go out with other boys?"

Fanny thought about it. She hadn't known any other boys except at the orphanage. There were several nice boys who paid attention to her, but she hadn't been attracted to them. From the very first time she saw Josiah, he had intrigued her and continued to do so the more she got to know him. The more she thought about it, the more she realized she wanted Josiah in her life. *As a friend or a beau?* she wondered. Then she answered herself, *A beau definitely! But marriage?* How could she know?

"I haven't met any boys I would like to go out with, but you."

Hope returned to Josiah. He led her over to a small alcove against a building, away from the milling crowd. "I mean it, Fanny. I love you, and I want to marry you. I know I'll never change my mind. Do you think that in the future you could possibly feel the same way?"

Fanny could feel her heart pulsating in her throat as she looked up into Josiah's handsome face, his smoldering dark eyes. It was exciting to be told she was beautiful and to be almost proposed to. Maybe that was all it was.

"I know you're young, Fanny, and maybe you can't answer now, but I can't bear to live life without you."

Their eyes locked, and Josiah noticed the tears forming in Fanny's eyes, looking like two bright blue lakes. He held his breath, fearful. The tears could mean anything—pity or—.

"I can't say what the future will be, but I can't imagine life without you, Josiah."

Josiah let out a slow breath of relief. "You can't? That's good enough for me."

With Fanny's arm in his, they walked on together, each grateful for the understanding between them.

Finally, Josiah said quietly. "To celebrate our first date, I'd like to take you to hear Sophie Tucker."

"No," she replied smiling. "Let's celebrate by finding a shop where we can sit down and eat the treat I brought you."

The lump that formed in Josiah's throat was almost too big to manage. Once again, she was thinking of him always being hungry.

"Look, Josiah," she said, staring through a window. Here's a store that has small tables and chairs." They looked up to see what it was called and saw a sign that said Fortnum and Mason.

"It doesn't seem like a restaurant, but let's."

They entered, seated themselves and looked around.

"This looks like a fancy food market, Fanny."

They glanced around to see what people were eating. It was tea and chocolates! Only that. The other amazing thing was the staff serving the customers wore tail coats!

One of the fancy-dressed clerks approached them. "Would you like some tea and chocolates?"

Josiah, afraid of what it would cost, replied, "We're new to London, uh . . ."

"Oh? Welcome to Piccadilly Circus, sir. Fortnum and Mason is known for its free service of tea and chocolate to its prospective customers. Would you like some?"

"Why yes, we would, thank you," Josiah said with relief that they were free and with confidence that the 'sir' had given him.

When the clerk left, Fanny giggled. "Well, if you aren't the swell, Josiah. You're smoother than I."

"He chuckled. "Thanks. I've been watching all the wealthy gentlemen that come in and out of the bank, as well as Mr. Sisbee. I've already learned a lot."

"What have you learned?"

The clerk brought them the tea and chocolates and said, "Since you're new here, we would like you to know that one of the things we special-ize in is providing picnic hampers stocked with elegant provisions for events such as the Ascot races."

"Thank you. That's a good thing to know," Josiah responded, acting as if he knew what the Ascot Races were.

Fanny and Josiah chuckled when the clerk left, then savored the delicious refreshments, feeling right at home with the well-dressed people at other tables.

"We'll save my treat until we finish this," Fanny whispered. "So tell me what you're learning at the bank."

Excitedly, Josiah launched into finance, bookkeeping and investments and found Fanny an avid listener.

Some time later after they had finished their tea and chocolates, Fanny pulled a long-strapped purse from the folds of her cloak.

Josiah's brows rose. "Nice. I didn't see that."

"It's because it was hanging from my shoulder," she said as she pulled out a neatly wrapped package. From it she extracted two cinnamon buns, and two hunks of cheese.

"Wow, that looks good! What you don't carry around with you Fanny," he said, chuckling, remembering the load in her bloomers.

Fanny smiled and handed Josiah the largest bun and the largest piece of cheese. "Thanks," he said grinning and taking a big bite of the bun.

A clerk stopped, and stared at their fare.

Fanny gave him a glowing smile. "We're new to London, and we knew nothing about Fortnum and Mason and their nice treats, so we brought our own."

The clerk nodded his head and smiled. "That's perfectly fine with us, miss."

"Thank you," she smiled.

Josiah grinned at how well she handled the awkward situation, then took a bite of cheese. Fanny watched him in delight. When they were through eating, they put their wraps and gloves on and went out into the cold weather of late afternoon.

"I think I had better take you home, Fanny. I have to find my way back to my lodgings, and I'm afraid until I've done it a few times I might get lost in the dark."

On the way to the Hartnell's, Fanny filled Josiah in about the children she was tutoring and how much she liked them and how smart they were.

"I'm glad you're enjoying it there. We're both fortunate beyond my wildest imagination. Tell me what Mr. Hartnell is like."

Fanny thought a moment. "It's hard to describe him. He's difficult to know. He holds himself aloof from me, and even from his wife and children much of the time. He seems to always be thinking of something besides what is right around him. He's tall and nice looking, even though he's almost bald."

"But he's nice to you?" Josiah asked, concerned.

"He's nice enough. His aloofness doesn't bother me. I do think it bothers his wife now and then though."

"That's a shame. I don't want to get like that, Fanny. If I do, let me know."

Arriving at the Hartnell's doorstep, Josiah gazed into Fanny's beautiful blue eyes. He bent down and pressed his lips to her forehead, then kissed her lips. "I love you, Fanny."

The kiss sent a tingle all the way down to Fanny's toes. "I don't know if I love you, Josiah, but it rather feels like it," she said shyly, a tender smile on her lips. She reached for the brass knocker. "Good night."

"Goodnight, Fanny. I'll ring you again soon." He drew in a deep contented breath and smiled. Turning, he took a joyful leap off the porch and walked down the path to find his way home.

❧CHAPTER 42❧

BELFORD, MAINE, JUNE 2001:

Gustavia sighed with relief as she placed the loose pages inside the diary and closed it. Fanny and Josiah had escaped the orphanage without mishap, and had entered into such fortunate circumstances! She remembered what her mother had told her about Fanny and Josiah's later circumstances and their deaths. *How could it all have degenerated to that? What could have gone wrong?* She shook her head as though to clear it.

She stood up and stretched, deciding to go for a quick walk in the sunshine before she continued. As she was running downstairs, she heard Ada yelling for her from the library. When she entered, she heard Ada say, "No, she certainly isn't busy. She hasn't touched the computer once this morning."

Ada handed her the phone. "Make it quick. I have a business call to make."

"Hello?"

"Hi, Gusty. It's Artie. I think your cousin thought it was someone else."

She laughed. "She did. How are you Artie?"

"I'll know better after you answer my question. I'm calling to see if you're ready to come out and visit for a week."

Gustavia moved into the hall. "Artie, we're going to have to put everything on hold. You see, things aren't settled between my friend Freddie—Paul Camden—and me yet."

"I don't mind telling you I'm disappointed. Would you call and tell me when it's settled one way or another?"

"I will, Artie, I promise. Thank you for calling." As she hung up the phone, it rang again. "Hello," she answered.

"Hello, Gusty."

"Hello, Paul."

"I thought I was going to be tied up for several more days, but as it turns out, everything fell into place and I was able to close the case this morning. I'd like to spend the afternoon and evening with you if you can."

"I was planning to read the diaries all day today," she stated more abruptly than she intended.

Paul's voice took on an edge. "I thought you wanted to hear about my life after we were separated."

"I do, but I thought you might call after your parents left, so I figured . . ."

"I've been swamped with a difficult case, Gusty."

Her thoughts seemed to flit from one thing to another. She wanted to tell him about the dream, hoping he could help her figure out its meaning, but for some reason she felt that this was not the right time. They seemed to be sparring with each other.

Taking her silence as no, he said, "I get the message."

"No you don't, Paul. You have no idea what I was thinking."

"Okay, what were you thinking?"

"What time will you pick me up?" she asked instead of replying. "And where are we going?"

"Well . . . do you want to try my apartment again?"

"Yes, if you're certain you're parents have gone back home," she replied facetiously, an attempt to lighten the mood.

"I'm sorry for the way Mother acted, Gusty. I'll explain a little more when I see you. I'll pick you up after lunch around 1:00. Is that all right?"

"It's perfect. I'll see you then."

She handed the phone back to Ada.

Excited, she ran upstairs, took a shower, put on casual beige pants and a red T shirt, since he said she looked good in that color, and left her hair loose. As she got ready, she was amazed that there was no feeling of guilt at putting off her reading. Her heart and that of her Mum's had anguished too long over what happened to Freddie! It was about time she learned.

Driving to Augusta, Paul told her that one of the reasons his mother wasn't as warm to her as she should have been was because she had picked out a girl for him in California. "A young woman with an illustrious and wealthy family. I'm afraid you have neither, Gusty," he said, his eyes smiling. "However, she might change her mind if she knew you were independently wealthy," he added grinning.

"Did you date her?"

"Who? Oh, yes. I tried to like her because Mother wanted me to, but I wasn't attracted to her at all. For some reason, Mother thinks I just haven't given it enough time."

"Did you have a good visit with them after you brought me home?"

"Yes. They've been good parents, especially considering the circumstances surrounding their adoption of me. I would like to take you to California sometime and let my family get to know you."

Gustavia was silent. She didn't look forward to that at all.

Paul seemed to read her thoughts. "Since you keep trying to win over such a cold, unresponsive person as Ada, it will be a piece of cake winning over my family."

"You think so?" she asked doubtfully.

"I know so."

They had just seated themselves on the couch to have that long awaited talk when the doorbell rang.

"Mercy! Do you suppose your parents are back?"

"No. But whoever it is, I'm going to make short work of them."

Paul opened the door. "Oh, hi, Phyllis."

"Hi. I just dropped up to see if you'd like to join me for dinner. I've made your favorite dish . . . oh, I see you have company," she said, trying to hide her disappointment.

"Come on in and . . ."

"No thanks. I'll uh, see you around."

"Okay, Phyl, and thanks for the nice offer."

Paul resumed his position on the couch beside Gustavia, smiled and shrugged his shoulders. "I think she was embarrassed."

"Have you been dating her?"

"Yes, that is, until you arrived on the scene."

Gustavia felt a stab of jealousy. "Are you sure? There were weekends I didn't see you, and I wondered what you did with your time."

"Well, uh, Phyl lives in this apartment building, and she and I run into each other often. There were times she'd arrange things I couldn't get out of tactfully."

Gustavia frowned. "I don't think I like you living here."

Paul looked askance at her. "Surely, you're not jealous?"

Thoughtful for a moment, she replied hesitantly. "I've never felt jealous, but I . . . think I might be . . . a little."

Paul laughed. "Good! Now you have an inkling what I've been through since Artie Banks showed up and invaded my territory."

"You sound like our scarred-up old tomcat, Pug, who marked his territory and dared any other cat to invade it."

"Old Pug and I would have been friends." He chuckled. "When did you have a cat, Gusty?"

"After we moved to Cornwall permanently. He adopted us, much to Mr. Fretwell's annoyance, but Mum persuaded him to let us feed him as long as we didn't let him in the house."

"That was nice for you, Gusty."

Gustavia curled her legs up and faced Paul. "It was. Now go on, Paul, before the doorbell rings again."

His arm up over the couch, his eyes glazed over as his thoughts returned to Hessle on that cold wintry day. "Oh, Gusty, it nearly tore my heart out when you and your mother left for Cornwall with Mr. Fretwell. I don't know how I knew, but I had a terrible sinking feeling I would never see you again. I was almost right—I never saw your mother again." He looked down and blinked back the tears stinging his eyes.

"Day after day," he continued, "I'd hop up over the wall and walk around the yard and house, hoping you might be back."

Gustavia felt a stab of pain in her chest. She reached up and took hold of his hand.

"One evening when I was playing my harmonica at the Music Hall on Jarrett Street, this nice couple came up to me and complimented me profusely. Then they asked me a lot of questions. Their names of course, were Robert and Sharon Banks. I didn't think anything more about it, but a couple of days later, Mr. Torr called me into his office and told me that a couple wanted to adopt me. I could hardly believe it at first, then I got excited. I had quit hoping for adoption. It didn't take me long, however, to decide I didn't want it, realizing that it would mean they'd take me away, and I wouldn't see you or your mother again." He gripped her hand for a moment.

"When Robert and Sharon Banks came to talk with me, I told them I didn't want to be adopted and why. Sharon promised me that I could communicate with you often and that they would bring me back from London and say goodbye to you and your mother. Even that didn't convince me. After they left, Mr. Torr and I had a long talk and he convinced me that it was best. Reluctantly, I agreed. Apparently, the Management Board was so eager for me to have a family, they hurried things through."

"When you left with them, how did you feel?"

"I had to fight back tears constantly. Hesslewood had been the only home I had ever known. I was attached to Mrs. Mullin, Mr. Torr, and others, as well as a few friends. But mostly, they were taking me away from you."

Tears pooled in Gustavia's eyes. "Mum and I were afraid you would feel that way and we fretted terribly. Mum especially understood how it might be for you. Go on."

"Sharon and Robert were in their early thirties, I believe, so Sharon told me to call her by her first name until I felt I could call her mother. But from the moment all the legalities were taken care of and we were on our way to London, Robert changed from nice to morose. It wasn't long before I realized he only went along with the adoption to please her. This made me even more homesick, or perhaps it was the sudden isolation from all that was familiar.

"Robert had been working in London for a company in the States and his assignment was about over. He quickly began working on getting a passport for me. They had been living in a one bedroom apartment, so my bed was on the couch in the living room, which made me feel more isolated and displaced than ever.

"We had only been in London two days when Sharon took sick. She was very kind to me even when she was ill and told me not to worry that she would keep her promises to me. Apparently Sharon was not able to have children because of her health. On the third day, she became even more ill. As soon as my passport was in order, Robert packed up their things, hardly speaking to me. In private, he told me I was nothing but a nuisance. I begged him to send me back to Hesslewood, but he said it would upset Sharon."

"Oh Paul, this is worse than Mum and I thought."

"On the fourth day, we were on the plane flying to America. In the rush of the adoption, I didn't think to get Mr. Fretwell's address or Hesslewood's. I mentioned this to Sharon and she said she'd see to it that I got them. When we arrived, Sharon's parents met us at the plane. They were shocked to see me, and when they learned that their daughter and son-in-law had adopted me in spite of Sharon's frail health, they weren't too pleased and weren't warm to me at all. Hey, Gusty, it's all over. Don't cry."

"Do you have any tissues?"

"I'll get them." He got up, went into the bathroom, and came back with a box.

"Thanks." She pulled out a couple, wiped her eyes, and blew her nose.

"I love you, Gusty." He smiled. "Thank you for caring what happened to me." He continued, "Sharon had to be put into the hospital immediately. And all the promises she made me went with her because Robert wouldn't have anything to do with me. Sharon had only one sibling, and that was Karla Camden."

Gustavia gasped in surprise. "So that's how it happened."

"Yes. Sharon knew she was dying, and since she knew Robert wouldn't take care of me, she asked her sister to adopt me. I learned later from Robert that I wasn't wanted by the Camdens either, and that Sharon had to beg her. Against her will, Karla broke down and promised to adopt me because of her grief over the impending death of her sister. Apparently, Karla wasn't close to her sister and resented her for reasons I've just recently learned. Their parents had, by this time, taken a liking to me. When Sharon died, they insisted that Karla follow through on her promise to Sharon. So it was under duress that the Camden family took me in."

"Your story just seems to get worse," Gustavia cried. "If Mum and I had only known this and known where you were, we would have begged Mr. Fretwell to let us go get you."

"I know you would have. I finally began writing letters to Charles Fretwell in care of Hesslewood. They each came back, 'address unknown.' I don't know why I didn't think of his shop in Hull. I thought of it only when I was older."

"You have letters to me also?"

He nodded, smiling. "I'm looking forward to us reading our letters together."

"Oh yes! Me too. Tell me the rest."

"I'm going to make it short. Needless to say, the older Camden girls weren't happy at all at my coming. Rick, on the other hand, was delighted to have a brother—for a while anyway. Karla was very cool with me. The Judge was warmer. The adoption went through, and I became a Camden. We were living in Los Angeles at the time. It took me a long time to call Karla mother, but she insisted on it after a while for appearances sake. Why it embarrassed her that I was adopted, I didn't know. When I got older I asked her why. All she would say is: 'One can never tell what kind of bloodline an adopted child comes from. The Camden name is well respected.'"

"When did it get better? I hope it wasn't too long."

"One of my sisters, Shari, told me that I wormed my way into all their hearts because of my cheerful and happy personality. When Rick didn't do well in school and I did so much better, he became jealous. I started helping him with his school work, and when he started to improve, that's when Mother warmed up to me. My scholastic record apparently put her in a good light. After that, Rick and I became close friends, and we still are. We talk on the phone about once a month. My sisters care for me, and I care for them, but we're not as close. My grandparents on both sides were good to me.

"So, my kind-hearted Gusty, my life became better and I felt loved to some degree by both parents. I'm sure you could tell that they care for me."

"Yes. I'm glad it turned out fairly well for you. Tell me a little about Sharon. What was she like?"

"I've been thinking about her lately for some reason. Even though I knew her for such a short period, she had an effect on my life. There was something special about her."

"If she's the same person as Artie Bank's Aunt Sharon, she was probably a member of the Mormon Church."

"She was."

Gustavia raised her brows in surprise. "How do you know this?"

"I called Rick after my parents left and asked what the rift between our mother Karla and her sister Sharon was. He said that it was because Sharon had joined the Mormon Church and Karla felt and apparently still feels that it's a cult of some kind."

"Oh, mercy. That isn't true."

"Rick doesn't think so either. He knows some Mormons. You know," he began, a far away expression in his eyes, "I just remembered something. After I was adopted by the Camdens, I often thought of Sharon and day-dreamed what it would have been like if she had lived and been my mother. Though I knew her for such a short time, I actually missed her.

"I knew there was something different about her. When you mentioned something unusual in Artie's face, I didn't connect it to Sharon—until the other day. I remembered thinking she had sparklers in her eyes. You know one of the fireworks, called sparklers, that you light and hold while it shoots out hundreds of sparkling lights?" Gustavia nodded. "I didn't know how to explain it to myself other than that. Robert didn't have them at all. In fact, now that I think of it, his eyes looked as though he didn't live there. Does that make sense?"

Gustavia nodded. "Maybe that's because he left the Mormon Church."

"But why would belonging to the Mormon Church have anything to do with what I saw in Sharon's eyes?"

"I don't know."

"There are a lot of good people who aren't Mormon, such as the Camdens," he stated defensively.

"Of course there are. I didn't mean to imply otherwise."

It felt like heaven to Paul having Gustavia all to himself in his small kitchen. They had pizza and root beer delivered, so they didn't have to go out. They had the rest of the evening to spend together. It could go either way, but he was hoping that Gustavia would say the right thing, so he could tell her why he hadn't been forthright with her as soon as he had planned.

They laughed and talked and felt comfortable with each other, just as they had the moment they got back together after all their years of separation.

Back on the couch, they visited. Most of the story had been told, but there was so much they still hadn't had time to talk about now that Gusty knew his true identity. Paul hoped they had a lifetime in which to do it.

Gustavia became silent. She seemed to be studying his face intently. Her lips began slowly turning up into the child-like joyous smile that had taken his breath away that first day in the library.

His face broke into a wide smile, returning hers.

"You do look like Freddie after all!" she exclaimed. "Why haven't I noticed it before? Your smile is just like that boyish smile that charmed Mum and me so many years ago."

"I'm certainly relieved to hear that. Excuse me a moment." He got up and left the room. Shortly, he returned with something in his hand. "Here's the small Bible your mother gave me."

Gustavia's heart did a painful flip flop. "Oh! Oh, Freddie, you've kept it all these years. I have mine too." Her dark lashes held in hovering droplets of tears. "This makes me feel so lonesome for Mum."

"It does me, too. I loved her. I was more upset than I can tell you when you told me she had died. For years I've longed to see her." His voice broke. "She was like a mother to me. I don't know how I would have turned out if you and she hadn't come into my life when you did."

"That's why you reacted the way you did when I told you she had died. I saw it, though you explained it away." Gustavia took the Bible from his hand and studied it. Carefully, she opened its pages. "This looks like it has been read often."

"I promised your mother I would read it. And it has helped me throughout my life."

"I'm so happy to hear that," she said, thinking of the lonely little boy who had been whisked away by strangers, only to be placed in the care of other strangers. Impulsively, she threw her arms around his neck, hugging him tightly. Then, without releasing her hold, she told him how she and her mother had searched for him through the years. Removing her arms, she gazed into his eyes as she related their last heartbreaking visit to Hesslewood. Suddenly overwhelmed with gratitude that she had found him, she took his face in her hands and covered it with kisses.

"Thank you," he said hoarsely. It was all he could do to resist kissing her with the passion he had suppressed from the first moment he saw her, but he wasn't sure if what she felt for him was only that of a rare and beautiful friendship. Looking deeply into her eyes, he tried to read her feelings.

"You promised to marry me, Gusty, but you were only nine years old. My love for you goes far beyond the boyish infatuation I had for you then, and far beyond our friendship of the last two-and-a-half months. I want to marry you. But I only want you for my wife if and when you can love me as I love you."

Moved, she gazed at him, unable to voice what she was feeling. She didn't know how to unravel her love of Freddie, the little boy of long ago, from her attachment to the grown man she had come to know as Paul Camden. Also there was the unsettling emotion of distrust. Why had he been secretive longer than necessary about something so important to both of them?

"Paul, I . . . have come to care for you," is all she could say.

"That's an ambiguous answer. You've come to care for me when you knew me only as Paul?"

"Yes."

"What do you mean by 'care for'?"

"I don't really know. I feel rather confused right now. I . . . I can't seem to meld Paul and Freddie into one person yet."

"And you won't be able to until you know how you feel about Artie Banks."

"I've told you how I feel about him."

"You wouldn't have flown to Salt Lake to meet his family if you weren't beginning to care for him enough to consider the possibility of marriage. As of now, Gusty, you're released from your promise. "We're no longer . . . what was the word you used? Oh yes." He smiled. "Betrothed. You're no longer betrothed."

"Oh!" She stood up and walked away from him, wanting to stamp her foot like an angry child might. "But I don't consider myself un-betrothed."

"Well," he replied, "I'm afraid that's your problem."

"And it's yours, Paul Frederick Finch Camden! It's definitely yours too. Please take me home."

Stopping in front of Ada's, Gustavia made no move to get out. They both remained silent as they had during the drive, each feeling it was up to the other to take the next step.

Gustavia finally broke the silence. "I wonder if you love me as you say you do. You're acting so noble about it all. No one is that perfect—not even you."

Paul stared through the window, his jaw working. He turned to her. "I'm far from noble, Gusty. It's taking all the strength I can muster to keep from taking you in my arms and kissing those lips of yours until all thoughts of Artie Banks leave your mind."

Gustavia's heart hammered as she thought of him kissing her. "You wanted to kiss me when we were young, remember?"

He nodded, his eyes burning into hers, accelerating her galloping heart . "I'm giving you permission to . . . to kiss me now," she said in a whisper.

Tempted almost beyond his ability, Paul looked away unable to respond to her tantalizing offer. He was silent for such a long time, Gustavia began to feel embarrassed at her boldness.

Paul ran a hand through his hair a couple of times, rubbed his forehead, then at last turned to her. "I'm serious, Gusty. Under the present circumstances, we can only remain friends until, or if, those circumstances change."

Gustavia stared at him, frustrated beyond words. Opening the door, she got out, slammed the door, opened the gate and slammed it shut as loudly as she could.

Paul watched her go in, not attempting to stop her. It took all the fortitude he could summon to keep from calling her back—but he had to give her the freedom, the space to learn how she really felt about him, how she felt about Artie. One thing was certain, Artie could give her the family he couldn't.

His hands gripping the top of the steering wheel, he leaned his head against them, anguish overwhelming him.

❧CHAPTER 43 ❦

Gustavia had gone down to breakfast Wednesday morning feeling miserable and exhausted. She couldn't even muster up a 'good morning' to Ada. Unhappy over the misunderstanding with Paul the night before, she had lain awake for hours until fatigue overcame her, and she fell asleep.

Feeling a little more energy after eating, she forced her thoughts away from Paul and curled up on the window seat. Opening the diary, she picked up the loose sheets wondering why she was feeling so deeply about grandparents she had never known? In the past, she had told herself it was probably because she had always longed for grandparents, aunts, uncles, and cousins, the kind she had vicariously experienced in books and stories. Now it seemed more than that, something more profound somehow.

Finding where she left off, she lifted the page. "No!" she exclaimed aloud. There was only one paragraph on the page. Turning to the next, she found that Fanny had written only two paragraphs, leaving the rest of the page blank, probably intending to finish writing more when she had time, but never had. Terribly disappointed, Gustavia quickly read those two pages. Several pages that followed contained only a line or occasional paragraph, condensing days and weeks into a few lines.

Each entry was about something she and Josiah had done together: They had gone to Trafalgar Square to feed the pigeons, then on to see Big Ben. At other times, they had gone to see a cricket match, the British Museum, Westminster Abbey, the Mayfair Shepherd Market and Kensington gardens in Hyde Park.

Gustavia was relieved to read one of Fanny's happy reports. Mr. Wimble had written to Josiah telling him that Mr. Sisbee had promised the Board of Management of the orphanage that he would donate a generous sum of money if they would dismiss the Crumbys and get a kinder Headmaster and Mistress to run the institution. Mr. Wimble told him that the Board had investigated the situation and indeed found it deplorable and had dismissed them. Both Fanny and Josiah visited Mr. and Mrs. Sisbee and thanked them profusely.

One glowing entry, which was a little longer, related how the Sisbees' had taken her and Josiah to see a Gilbert and Sullivan musical in the very theater in which Sophie Tucker had performed. She had described how beautiful and ornate the inside of the theater was and how elegant she and Josiah felt attending it along with all the beautifully dressed people around them. It was then that Josiah told her that he had gotten a raise and that Mr. Sisbee was very pleased with his work. Indicating the theater with a sweep of his hand, he told her that this kind of life was what he wanted to give her.

It wasn't until just after Josiah turned eighteen and a few weeks before Fanny turned seventeen, approximately one-and-a-half years later, that she wrote a longer entry.

LONDON, AUGUST, 1916:

Fanny and Josiah walked hand in hand in the beautiful Kensington Gardens, each absorbed in their own thoughts. It was a delightful afternoon, warm and sunny.

From the moment Josiah had picked Fanny up he noticed that she was a little pale. He had tried to draw her out, but with little success. Thinking at first that she was tired, he told her a couple of experiences he had at work. She listened with interest, but offered nothing about herself or the children, which was totally out of character. He was almost afraid to ask what was troubling her for fear she might be waning in her affection for him. Nothing, however, in her past behavior had indicated this. Actually, it was just the opposite. Nevertheless he worried. A starling piped dismally on a nearby tree branch, matching his mood.

Finally she spoke. "Josiah?"

He looked into her troubled face and his heart plummeted. "Yes, Fanny?"

"I . . .uh, need to tell you something, but I hesitate for fear I'm imagining it."

His anxiety eased somewhat, feeling it wasn't about their relationship after all. Still, he was concerned. "Let's sit here on the lawn and talk. Don't ever hesitate to tell me anything, Fanny. You're not one to imagine things."

She looked down, running her fingers through the blades of grass. "Do you remember me telling you that Mr. Hartnell was aloof with me and at times even with his wife and children?"

"Yes, I do."

She looked up, her brows twisted in misery. "Well . . . uh, about a month ago, Mr. Hartnell began acting more friendly to me. I was surprised at first, but then I decided that it was because he had begun to feel more at ease with me now. I didn't think anymore about it, just accepting it for the next few weeks until I noticed he wasn't any warmer with his wife and children. But, I told myself, maybe that was just the way he was when people were around. Then—"

Josiah waited and watched her lips try to move. "Go on, please, Fanny."

"All last week after he came home from work, he always seemed to be where I was. He smiled and talked to me, asking me questions about how I liked tutoring and so forth. His conversation and questions were harmless enough, but then . . . he put his hand on my shoulder one evening. The next evening, he put his arm around my shoulders and gave me a squeeze. I looked up at him shocked, and oh, Josiah, the glint in his eyes gave me the creeps."

Josiah clenched his fists. "Why that no good trout! You aren't imagining it!"

"Please, Josiah, we have to talk about this calmly."

Holding his anger in check, he asked, "What did you do?"

"I pulled away from him and quickly busied myself with one of the girls. Then Mrs. Hartnell came in. She was surprised to see him there, but he quickly picked up his youngest and proceeded to talk with her. Mrs. Hartnell seemed overjoyed that he was paying attention to the children. I left. I've been dodging him ever since."

Josiah took Fanny's hand and kissed it. "I'm so sorry this has happened. We have to do something!" The muscles in his jaw rippled. "I'm going to tell Mrs. Hartnell."

"Please don't do anything rash, Josiah. I don't want her to know. It would hurt her unmercifully. And think what it would do to Mrs. Sisbee to learn of this?"

Tears of frustration filled Josiah's eyes. Alarmed, Fanny asked, "What is it, Josiah?"

"I . . . I've had such plans for you, and now . . ." He swallowed his disappointment. "What I'm trying to say, Fanny, is that I wanted to be financially well-off before I asked you to marry me. In six months, Mr. Sisbee says I might be ready to take over some more of the work and get a better salary. Then in another year, if I continue to progress, I can become a full member of the staff. He said that this was unusual for one so young, but that I have an exceptional mind and ability for investment banking."

"Oh, Josiah," she breathed, "I'm so proud of you."

He was thrilled over her admiration. However, the fear over the present situation prevented him from dwelling on it. He wasn't prepared for what he had to do next!

Fanny waited, knowing Josiah had more to say, but all he was doing was shaking his head, his eyes troubled. "What is it? You have something else to tell me?"

"Fanny, my Fanny, I wanted this to be a special moment. I wanted it to be in a romantic place, and I wanted to be rich, but . . ." With sudden intensity, he took both her hands in his. "Will you marry me, Fanny? I love you so much, I think my heart might burst wide open."

She hadn't expected this. All she could do was stare at him wide-eyed.

"I can see no other way out of this situation, Fanny, without hurting some very nice people. If you weren't there in the evenings when Mr. Hartnell comes home, you'd be safe."

"But Josiah, I had plans myself. I was hoping for a teaching position at a private school in a year."

"You still can."

Tears surfaced in Fanny's eyes. "Josiah, you're so wonderful my heart is almost bursting wide open too. This last month, I realized how badly I needed you." She looked down shyly. "And I've discovered that what I've been feeling for you is love. I love you, Josiah. Yes, I will marry you."

In spite of the frustration he felt over having to hasten what should have been thought out carefully, his heart leapt with joy. He pulled her to him and held her tightly. "I can't believe God has blessed me so. He allowed me to be put into an orphanage, but gave me a prize for it. *You* are my prize, Fanny. If I hadn't been there, I wouldn't have found you."

Fanny smiled, her eyes sparkling with happiness at Josiah's disclosure. "And—wouldn't Melissa be surprised if she knew that she had given me a prize by sending me to the orphanage."

Surprised, Josiah pulled away and looked into her face. She had told him that her parents had died and he thought he had winkled all of the other secrets out of this private little girl. "What? Who is Melissa?"

"My sister, who is ten years older than I am, and who was married by the time our father died."

"Why . . . why couldn't you live with *her*?"

"That's what I had to figure out. With the help of Mr. Wimble and Mrs Prickett, I finally did."

Josiah took Fanny's hand in his. "Tell me about it?"

"I have long put it behind me because it was so painful, but I'll tell you."

Josiah held himself together while she told the heartrending story. When she was finished, he spoke slowly. "And I thought I had it hard. How could anyone be that cruel?" He abruptly turned away from her, his shoulders shaking.

"Josiah, oh, Josiah, it's all right. I have you," she said, putting her arms around his back, holding him until the storm had abated.

He turned around, his tear-rimmed eyes gazing into her face. "And to think I was so mean to you during that time you were suffering so. I grabbed your hair and called you a brat."

Fanny laughed. "I was a brat."

He laughed too. "Yeah, you were, but . . ."

"But think how romantic it all was, the way we met, our whole relationship. You kidnapping me out of the orphanage and all?"

He thought about it a moment. "I haven't thought about it that way. Then you don't mind my proposing so . . . so soon, so suddenly?"

"No. It just tells how much you love me."

Overjoyed, he felt like doing somersaults. Instead, he leaned over and kissed her like he never had before and it sent his senses reeling.

And Fanny, having never been kissed like that, melted in his arms.

❧CHAPTER 44❧

LONDON, AUGUST, 1916:

"Mr. Sisbee, do you have time to talk with me?" Josiah asked.

Looking up from his desk, he smiled. "Of course, Josiah. Have a seat."

"As you know, Fanny and I have known each other for about six years and we've been good friends most of that time."

"That's what I understand."

"Well, sir, I'm in love with Fanny and she with me. We'd like to get married."

Mr. Sisbee blinked in surprise. "You intend this to be in the future I hope. You're both very young."

"I know, sir, but Fanny'll turn seventeen in three weeks. That's when we want to get married."

"In three weeks!" He shook his head dismally. "I'm disappointed, my boy. You're doing so well, but not quite well enough to support a wife."

"I know, sir, but we've waited so long to be together."

"Mrs. Sisbee and I will be most happy to help you with your wedding plans, but only when you're older."

"You don't need to help us, sir. You've already done so much for us."

"What if I tell you that I won't let you continue to apprentice with Mr. Moore if you get married now?"

Josiah's heart almost stopped. "Are you serious, sir?"

"I am, my boy, very serious."

Running a hand through his hair, Josiah's mind raced. How much could he tell Mr. Sisbee? "I assure you, Mr. Sisbee, this wasn't my plan. I was intending to wait until I was much better off financially."

Mr. Sisbee frowned in concern. "Then . . . why did you change your plans?"

"Because we *have* to get married. We can't wait more than three weeks."

Mr. Sisbee's eyes widened in shock. "Don't tell me you got Fanny in trouble."

"What do you mean, sir? Oh—" Josiah paled. "Oh no, sir! It's not that at all. She's a good girl and I intend that she stay that way."

"Are you telling me the truth, son?"

"I am, sir," he stated with conviction.

"Then tell me. Why the rush? You owe me that much."

"Fanny doesn't want me to tell you or anyone else why, but . . ."

Mr. Sisbee's concern grew. "I demand you tell me, Josiah."

"If I tell you, sir, promise me you won't tell Mrs. Sisbee."

"I can't do that, Josiah. Mrs. Sisbee and I hold no secrets from each other."

His heart heavy, he knew he had to tell him, no matter the consequences. "When I tell you, sir, you may not want to tell your wife."

Mr. Sisbee let out an impatient breath. "Get on with it, boy."

"May I close your office door, sir?"

"You may."

Josiah reseated himself, took a deep breath and hesitantly related the circumstances that brought him to the decision of marriage. He watched Mr. Sisbee's face turn grim and angry. He waited uneasily. What if he didn't believe Fanny?

At last, Mr. Sisbee spoke. "I have no reason to doubt Fanny. I might have thought she read more into it than there was, but I'm sorry to say I've seen Edward at parties when he wasn't aware anyone was watching. I'm afraid he has an eye for the ladies. I haven't even mentioned this to Mrs. Sisbee. You're right, Josiah, I don't want to tell her, but I don't know how I can get her support otherwise." He was silent for a moment, then nodded his head. "I'm afraid it's time for her to start looking out for her sister. It's a shame. Mary is a grand lady. The only woman grander is my wife, but then, you see I'm not very objective."

"I'm sorry to have added more to your worries."

"Let's keep this between you and me, and Fanny of course. If you get married, will Fanny quit working for the Hartnells?"

"No sir. Not for a while. It's in the evening when Mr. Hartnell is there that she doesn't feel safe." Suddenly, Josiah's shoulders sagged. By telling someone else about his and Fanny's plan, the impact of the responsibility he was taking on began to settle heavily upon him. "This isn't what either of us wanted right now, Mr. Sisbee. You see, I recently learned that Fanny has been wanting to prepare herself to apply for a teaching position at a private school. But—I don't know what else we can do at this time."

"Considering the circumstances, I think you and Fanny are doing the only thing you can do. You have my support."

Josiah stood up and held out his hand and shook Mr. Sisbee's with great affection. "How can I ever repay you for your kindness, Mr. Sisbee?"

LONDON, SEPTEMBER, 1916:

On the day of Fanny's birthday, she and Josiah were married in the St. Andrews Parish Church. Dressed in a simple white dress Mary Hartnell had purchased for her, Fanny was glowing and beautiful. The Hartnells and the Sisbees were present, along with some of the employees of Mr. Sisbee's bank, who knew Josiah.

The bride and groom had been given a wedding gift from both families—a two-day honeymoon at the Ritz Hotel. After many congratulations, the couple eagerly left in a hansom for the hotel. Josiah turned to his bride, his eyes burning with anticipation for their future. "At last, I can have your company day and night, my beautiful bride."

"And I yours, Josiah. Now we don't have to wait a whole week to see each other."

They marveled together that they were actually husband and wife, something they hadn't expected to be for several years, and in this frame of mind they arrived at the Ritz. Entering the magnificent lobby, they looked around in awe, feeling totally out of place. Only by the grace of their good friends could they actually spend the first two days of their married life in such a fancy hotel!

Josiah straightened his shoulders, certain that this was the kind of life he wanted, the kind of life he wanted to give Fanny. With their bags under one arm, he took her hand and led her to the desk clerk. He swallowed hard, mustering up the confidence he thought a man of means should have. "I believe you have a reservation for a Mr. and Mrs. Josiah Browne." He heard Fanny gasp and turned to her questioningly.

"My name's Fanny Browne," she stated in amazement.

Josiah grinned from ear to ear. "Yes, it is. Not quite as nice-sounding as Fanny Sullivan, but I find myself liking it much better."

She giggled nervously, "Me too."

"Yes sir," the clerk said, finding their names, "we do. It's the honeymoon suite on the third floor. Here is your key. Do you need some help with your bags, Mr. Browne?"

"No thank you."

"Well then, sir, you might want to take the lift right over there," he said pointing.

"Thank you," Josiah said, putting the key in his pocket. He and Fanny went to the lift and stepped through the open doors. A uniformed lift operator, stationed inside, greeted them cordially, closed the doors and pulled the lever.

Both Fanny and Josiah, having never seen a lift, let alone ridden in one, were all agog over the experience. It groaned and rattled on the way up, startling Fanny.

"Oh dear, is this safe?"

The operator smiled. "It's noisy, madam, but it's as reliable as Big Ben."

The lift groaned to a stop on the third floor. "Thank you," Josiah said to the operator, as they stepped out. Looking both ways, Josiah led Fanny to the room number shown on the key.

He unlocked the door, turned the knob and held it open for Fanny. They looked around the lovely room and Josiah said, "I've never seen a room like this. I can't imagine staying in one for two days."

"I've been more fortunate than you, Josiah. I've been staying in a lovely room for a year-and-a half"

He set the bags down and gazed at her. "Not with me you haven't, Mrs. Browne."

"Mrs. Browne," she repeated. "Imagine!" She threw her arms around his neck, and kissed him. It was such a pleasurable experience, she kissed him again—igniting a flood of yearning and love.

It didn't take long for Fanny and Josiah to move their few belongings to the flat Josiah had found on Primrose Street, close to where Fanny could take the tramway to the Hartnell's residence. It was further from Mr. Sisbee's bank, but he could take the tram part way and walk from there. It was a meagerly furnished flat with a sitting room, a bedroom and a small kitchen. The furnishings consisted of an old sofa and chair and bookcase in the sitting room. The bedroom had an armoire, a bed and a chest of drawers. It was the cleanest and cheeriest of those Josiah had looked at, and they could make it on both their wages, plus save a little.

Josiah's heart was heavy when they first entered the flat, knowing what a nice place Fanny had been living in, but Fanny's buoyant spirit brought sunshine into the cheerless surroundings.

"Oh! This is much nicer than I expected it to be, Josiah. Our first home!" Immediately, she went into the kitchen and opened the cupboards and drawers. "I forgot to tell you," she reported, excitedly, "Mrs. Hartnell has been going through her cupboards, and through her attic for cooking utensils and dishes they don't use any more. I have them in that box you brought in for me."

He hadn't even thought of pots and pans and dishes! Once more, he felt grateful for such good friends. "That was jolly good of her."

The first thing they did after putting away their things, was go to the market and buy some food. Fanny found herself excited at the prospect of making a home for Josiah.

When Fanny cooked their first meal, Josiah was astonished. "How did you learn to cook?"

She smiled slyly. "I watched Mrs. Cracken cook and decided I would remember how she made some of the things we liked. Even though she was mean, she was a good cook. Also, after my tutoring sessions, I've been going into the kitchen and learning from Mrs. Hartnell's cook. I have a lot of recipes."

Josiah's heart swelled with contentment. He had Fanny, the only person who, though only a child, cared whether he was skinny and hungry—even while he had a handful of her hair! The person who made life worth living from that moment on. The person who by her caring gradually took away his bitterness. The person who made him want to improve himself in every way, who brightened his life in an institution where he once felt hopeless. His childhood sweetheart.

It was a time of contentment for Fanny, also. She had Josiah by her side, loving her and protecting her. Years ago when he dragged her by the hair and deposited her on the steps, she sensed a gigantic heart in the dark-eyed, sullen boy. She hadn't recognized it at first, but his ability to love was immense and she had felt it all through their years together in the orphanage. Having read the few romantic fairy tales available at the orphanage, Fanny thought of Josiah as her valiant prince. The prince who had rescued her twice.

As the weeks went on, Fanny learned the quickest way to the Hartnell residence, and was no longer nervous about Mr. Hartnell making advances toward her. Every day when she and Josiah parted, they had the tranquility of knowing they would be together at the end of the day—that nothing could ever keep them apart.

It was a time when the sun shone brightly on Josiah and Fanny. As husband and wife their vision of the future was clear and certain.

❧CHAPTER 45❧

BELFORD MAINE, JUNE 2001:

Gustavia found that once again Fanny's entries in her diary were sporadic, a line here, a paragraph there, much of it stating just facts.

LONDON, ENGLAND:

February 1917: Mr. Sisbee gave Josiah a raise.

June 1917: Having children was something Fanny and Josiah looked forward to, but in their youthful outlook, expected to start sometime in the future, nevertheless, when in June Fanny realized she was pregnant, she and Josiah were ecstatic.

Only three months pregnant by the end of August, Fanny miscarried. It was a traumatic experience for her and Josiah, but the doctor told them that it wasn't unusual for a woman to miscarry at least once.

March 1918: Good news. Mr. Sisbee informed Josiah that he felt he was fully trained and ready to become a regular employee. This came at the right time, for that same month Fanny found out she was expecting again.

April 1918: Fanny had found a position as a probationary school teacher at St. Anthony's, a small private school, and wondered how long she could continue. She still tutored the Hartnell children when she could. By the middle of April when she was two months along, she had another miscarriage. Totally distraught, Fanny couldn't eat or sleep. Since Josiah had never seen Fanny like this, he asked for a few days off to care for her.

August 1918: Fanny experienced another devastating miscarriage. It was at this time, Fanny felt the need of a Bible and purchased one. She had never had one, but her dear mother had read to her out of it and she remembered the sweet feeling she had as she listened to the words her mother believed. And now she felt if she and Josiah read it together, they would heal faster.

Fanny was still teaching at the school, but in less than a year, she would be fully accredited and become a fell-fledged member of the staff. She loved teaching, but she wanted her own children and continued to hope.

December 1920: With their savings and combined incomes Josiah and Fanny purchased a two-story, two bay row house with a backyard. For awhile, Fanny's whole attention focused on furnishing and making the home theirs. When spring came, they planted two trees, a lawn, flowers and a small vegetable garden in the backyard. A calm assurance came over her that she and Josiah would have children, and the yard was for them.

October 1928: Fanny recorded briefly in her diary the birth of a baby girl when she was eight months along. The baby seemed healthy, but she lived only two hours. They named her Sarah after her mother.

February 1930: Fanny gave birth to a baby boy. They named him Thomas Sullivan Browne. She and Josiah were thrilled that he was full term and healthy. Though they hadn't gotten over the death of baby Sarah, Fanny declared she had no words to express the happiness the birth of their son had brought into their lives. She was certain that a miracle had occurred.

BELFORD, MAINE:

The diary was filled with everything about little Thomas. Gustavia avidly read every word about her father. Her first thought was, *If only Mum could have read this. What a tragedy that my father didn't have the diaries! He would have learned what outstanding people his parents were and how much they loved him.* Gustavia felt a deep sense of loss.

LONDON, ENGLAND, JULY 1931:

England was feeling the effects of Black Friday, October, 1929 when the stock market crashed in America, sending shock waves throughout the world. The depression had become worldwide and Mr. Sisbee's investment bank was feeling the effects. Josiah had been promised a raise, but due to economic circumstances Mr. Sisbee was unable to provide it.

Every evening Josiah looked forward to seeing his little son. Thomas was walking now. He was a happy, smart baby and a handsome little fellow. Fanny told Josiah she was happy that Thomas had his dark hair and eyes.

It was wonderful for Josiah to see Fanny happy at last. When they lost little Sarah, she hadn't been the same—neither had he, but in spite of the economic downturn, he was feeling fortunate to have a wife and child, and an income to support them. Unemployment in Britain was increasing.

⁊

Fanny and her friend, Evelyn, were sitting in Fanny's backyard watching Thomas get excited over attempting to play ball, in his clumsy toddler fashion, with Evelyn's six-year-old son. Evelyn's little girls, two and three, sat on the lawn trying to give tea to their dolls. She and her husband Charlton were neighbors, two houses down. Fanny and Josiah were drawn to them immediately. They had quite a few friends, but felt closer to Evelyn and Charlton. Josiah and Charlton had much in common, enjoying discussions on politics, world affairs and sports.

Evelyn was tall and slim with cocoa brown eyes and hair to match. Always smiling and cheerful, she matched Fanny's own disposition. When they lost little Sarah, Fanny thought she could never smile again. Josiah hadn't been able to help her because of his own grief. It was Evelyn with her tender empathy and constant cheerfulness who had helped both of them. Out of all the neighbors, it was Evelyn and Charlton who had been so excited for them when Thomas was born. They felt as close to them as they did to Mary Hartnell and the Sisbees.

Today, Evelyn was acting a little differently—just as cheerful, but more contemplative.

"All right, Evelyn, what is going on with you? Are you expecting or something?"

Evelyn laughed. It was a musical laugh that reflected her personality. "I can understand why you might think one has to be expecting to be excited."

Fanny laughed with her. "Of course. What else is there to be excited about?"

Evelyn sobered. "Oh, Fanny, there is so much more. Have you ever thought about where little Sarah is?"

"I'm sure she's in heaven."

"Will you see her . . . have her . . . in the next life?"

Pain flickered across Fanny's face. "I don't know. I want to believe I will. From what Josiah and I read in the Bible, I believe there's a life after this one. It seems right to me that if God is a kind and loving God, He'll let us know each other, perhaps be together always."

"You're right, but we have to obey the commandments and keep our covenants with Him in order to have that blessing."

"What do you mean?"

"Years ago when Charlton was a young boy, some missionaries knocked on his parents' door. They were elders from The Church of Jesus Christ of Latter-day Saints."

"I've never heard of that church."

"The nickname of the Church is the Mormon Church. Is that more familiar?"

"Yes. I've heard of it. I don't know where." She thought a moment, then a look of concern came across her face. "When I was over at Mary Hartnell's place, she was telling me that some friends of theirs joined the Mormon Church and that she was . . ." Fanny stopped and bit her lip.

"Go on, Fanny, you can't tell me anything I haven't heard."

"She said she was concerned because she'd heard that the Mormon Church had false prophets. Some of their friends told the Hartnells what terrible things the Mormons do in their temples."

"What did she say they did?"

Fanny frowned, thinking. "You know, I've simply put it out of my mind. It sounded so farfetched. I couldn't imagine anyone doing those things."

"Fanny, Charlton's parents and their children joined that church many years ago. I was investigating the Church when I met him. I joined before we were married."

"Oh?" Fanny's brows rose. "Maybe that's why you and Charlton seem . . . uh, different—kind and thoughtful."

"I hope that's how you see us. Before I joined, I had gone to two different denominations and to many different parishes and never found the truths that I found in the Mormon Church."

Fanny was completely dumbfounded to hear all this from the lips of her friend. She could think of only one thing to say. "Evelyn, if you and Charlton belong to that church, it can't be as bad as they say. Oh . . . a . . . I," she stammered, "I didn't mean it the way it sounded."

A grateful smile crossed Evelyn's face. "You're a true friend, Fanny. We've been afraid to tell you and Josiah for fear you might react like other friends we've told, who, though they know us, believe the Church members are harem keepers, delusional and so forth. Thank you. There are two reasons I finally got the courage to tell you. Charlton and I feel that out of all our friends, you and Josiah would be more likely to listen to the missionaries and find out for yourselves about the Church. Secondly, the Church teaches us we can be married for eternity. The Church calls it sealing. You and Josiah can be sealed for eternity and have your children sealed to you. This way you would know for a certainty that you could have little Sarah in the next life."

Something inside Fanny quickened, "Have you and Charlton been . . . sealed?"

"Yes. We had to wait a year to make certain we remained true and were worthy. We had to go all the way to Salt Lake City in America. That's where the headquarters of the Church is, and that's where the temple is. It's in a temple that the sealing must be performed."

"But why do we have to be sealed in a Mormon temple to have Sarah?"

"Why did Christ say we have to be baptized? He was baptized by immersion, not sprinkling. Should we follow His example?"

Fanny could only nod. She and Josiah had wondered why Thomas, as an innocent baby, had to be baptized. The idea that a little child was born in sin seemed repugnant to her. They also had questioned the sprinkling since Christ himself was immersed in the water. Feeling confused, she and Josiah hadn't attended church regularly.

Uneasy over Fanny's silence, Evelyn said, "I can't explain it very well, Fanny. Would you and Josiah at least hear the missionaries and decide for yourselves?" When Fanny didn't respond, she added, "You have everything to gain and nothing to lose."

"This is all such a surprise, Evelyn, I don't know. I'll have to discuss it with Josiah."

When they had put Thomas to bed, Fanny led Josiah to the couch. "I have something to tell you."

He smiled at the expression on her face. "Uh-oh, I see it's something rather serious."

She returned his smile and squeezed his hand. "I love you, Josiah."

He pulled her to him and held her a moment. "And you my sweetheart, are the light of my life. Now tell me."

Fanny related the strange conversation she and Evelyn had earlier.

Josiah listened attentively, his face reflecting the same surprise she had felt. "Well, it seems our friends have been searching for truth, and they think they've found it, but—" He shook his head skeptically, "as far as this sealing thing goes, it sounds a bit off to me."

"Evelyn asked if you and I would listen to the missionaries and decide for ourselves."

"Why?"

"Because of Sarah."

When Josiah allowed himself to dwell on it, it was still painful to think of his lost baby daughter. He spoke slowly as if he were weighing each word. "It sounds good to know for certain that we could have her in the next life . . . if there is one."

"There has to be one, Josiah. Nothing makes sense if there isn't. Why would Jesus tell us to lay up treasures in heaven if there wasn't a heaven?"

Josiah's eyes watered. "I miss our baby Sarah, and I didn't even have time to get to know her. I . . . I think maybe . . . we ought to listen. It won't hurt to listen."

Fanny threw her arms about his neck. "Oh, thank you, Josiah. That's exactly the way I feel after thinking about it. I'll run over to Evelyn's and tell her. I'll be right back."

The first meeting with the Mormon missionaries was held in Fanny's and Josiah's home the next night with Evelyn and Charlton present. Josiah and Fanny noticed the eagerness on their friends' faces. A touching prayer was given by Charlton, and the meeting began.

The missionaries, who called each other Elder, were from America; Elder Mason was from a place called Mesa, Arizona. Elder Gibson was from Salt Lake City, Utah.

Fanny and Josiah were surprised at the youth of these two. Fanny's first thought was, *what could these two know about something as difficult to under - stand as the scriptures? Wasn't this the province of older, more educated men who had spent a lifetime of study?*

Even so, it was obvious that these two were humble young men who felt deeply about what they were teaching. Fanny and Josiah were impressed.

The elders—it seemed so odd to call such young men 'Elder'—taught them a lesson about the Godhead, quoting scripture after scripture.

At first, the concept was so unlike their lifelong beliefs of the trinity that it seemed difficult to grasp. Yet, the explanation and the scriptural passages were so logical they found themselves wondering why they hadn't understood it before.

The elders talked about feeling the Spirit and explained what it was. Fanny and Josiah knew they felt it throughout the meeting. When the elders asked if they had any questions, both had immediately asked about sealing Sarah to them and about the next life. The elders explained it so simply and beautifully that it soothed Fanny's and Josiah's hearts, giving them hope.

They decided to have the missionaries meet with them every night until they had finished with the teachings. Afterward, Charlton, his eyes moist, grabbed Josiah's hand in his and shook it affectionately. "We're happy you're going to hear the rest."

Evelyn, with tears in her eyes, hugged Fanny. "Thank you for . . . for being so humble and willing to listen."

"Thank you, Evelyn, for telling us about it."

During each meeting, Fanny and Josiah became more excited about what they were hearing and learning. They hadn't realized they were searching, but as the missionaries unfolded the truths of the Gospel of Jesus Christ, and as they began reading out of the book the elders had given them, *The Book of Mormon*, they consented to attend church on Sunday.

Charlton prepared them. "The members meet on Sunday in a rented town hall in Battersea. The congregation sits on folding chairs on a hardwood floor and there's a lot of racket from shuffling chairs. It will be a far different experience than you've had meeting in the nice parishes. The members socialize rather noisily before and after meetings—sometimes during. It could be a little more reverent. At times we have other discouraging experiences—times when some members find it easier to stay home when they feel opposition to the Church is a little too intense."

Josiah laughed. "It would seem you're discouraging us from coming, Charlton."

Charlton smiled. "It would seem so. But we've had investigators come and never return because of the noise. We don't want that to happen with you. The good part is, if one goes with a humble spirit, one will feel the Spirit. The Church is true regardless of its imperfect flock."

"Now we're very curious, Charlton," Fanny said, smiling.

Two weeks later Fanny and Josiah were baptized into The Church of Jesus Christ of Latter-day Saints. They grew in their testimonies and served in every way possible. Faith that they would have Sarah again and that they would be a family for eternity filled their hearts with peace. They began saving for the time they could attend the temple in Salt Lake City and be sealed as a family.

☙CHAPTER 46❧

BELFORD, MAINE, JUNE 2001:

Shocked, Gustavia put down the diary. Her grandmother and grandfather had joined the Mormon Church! Artie Bank's church!

Her mind was whirling with thoughts and emotions. *Sealing.* Like Fanny and Josiah, she had never heard of it! How strange to meet Artie Banks and then learn about her grandparents! She remembered, once more, *The Book of Mormon* she had so carelessly put into her drawer. *What does it all mean?*

She wished she could talk with Paul! Yet, why was she wishing this after the way they had parted? It was then she realized that she kept forgetting his 'deception,' as she first called it. It simply kept fading from her mind. Why? It was still an issue—yet at the moment other things seemed more important.

Why was he being so stubborn? When she was a child, hadn't she been able to manipulate Freddie any way she wanted to?

The things she and Freddie did together raced through her mind. Reading and dancing to Freddie's harmonica were her favorites. Playing house didn't even count because it was so minimal. Freddie liked to play soccer, spy, chase, catch and other games like these—and these, she realized, were the things they did most of the time! Since she hadn't dared suggest they play dolls and dress-up, she played these by herself.

Why hadn't she dared?

Perplexed by these recollections, she asked herself for the first time why he had been her favorite friend? A smile stole across her face as she recalled how hard he worked at making her laugh. Because she was such an appreciative audience, his crazy antics often had them laughing till their sides hurt.

In spite of the good times she had with her friend, Enid, in Cornwall, she still missed Freddie. The adult she was now felt Freddie's boyish kindness and constant cheerfulness had to some extent been a reflection of her own happy nature, encouraging her to cultivate it further. It was clear to her now why Freddie had been her favorite friend. She sighed, finding herself missing him terribly.

A startling question jarred her sensibilities, sending her to her feet. She paced around the room. *Have I been falling in love with Paul all along? If so— why only now am I realizing it?* She knew she had subconsciously fought what she thought was only attraction to him, hoping to find Freddie and resolve the promise she had made to him. But *he* was *Freddie!* And they had *found* each other! And he had released her from her promise. *Is this why I'm at last realizing that I love him?*

Unexpectedly, in her mind and heart, the boy and the man—Freddie and Paul—melded together into one wonderful man. The kind of a man she and Mum always thought Freddie would become!

Impulsively, she ran to the library and asked Ada for Paul's work number.

"Why?"

Gustavia was tired of Ada's recalcitrance. "Because I want it, that's why."

Ada wrote a number on a piece of paper and coolly handed it to her.

Gustavia grabbed it from her hand, picked up the phone and took it into the parlor. A receptionist answered, "Pinkham, Myer and Shanks."

"Hello, could I speak to Mr. Paul Camden, please?"

"I'm sorry, but he's with a client. May I give him a message?"

"Tell him to call Gustavia Browne."

"Would you please spell that first name?"

After she did so, Gustavia said, "Tell him it's very important."

They disconnected and Gustavia returned the phone to the library. She paced around the room.

"Please sit down, Gustavia. You're making me nervous."

Plunking herself down in her computer chair, Gustavia wondered how she could concentrate on anything until she could talk with Paul— see Paul. She forced herself to start working on Ada's biography, hoping to be in the room when Paul called.

Two grueling hours later, the phone rang. Ada answered it and promptly handed it to Gustavia without so much as a courteous response.

"Hello, Paul?"

"What's so important?" he asked without ceremony.

"I have to see you as soon as possible."

"Why?"

"Because it's very important."

There was a long pause before he replied. "I'll look at my schedule and see if I can move anything around. Just a minute."

Gustavia waited, her heart already out of control.

"I can be there around 4:00 this afternoon. What's the plan?"

"We need to talk and you're invited to dinner here tonight."

Ada turned around and glared at her, but Gustavia ignored it.

"Are you sure it's all right with Ada?"

Gustavia laughed. "Of course it isn't, but nevertheless you're invited."

He chuckled. "All right. I'll see you."

As soon as Gustavia had put the phone down, Ada opened her mouth, but Gustavia stopped her. "Don't say a word, Ada. Remember you owe me my inheritance? Consider a meal for Paul part of the payback."

"Well, I'm not eating in his presence. I'll take mine in the bedroom."

Gustavia couldn't have been more pleased.

Seated on the bench shaded by the dogwood tree, Gustavia, dressed in a pale yellow, filmy 1920 creation she had designed, waited anxiously for Paul's arrival. The birds were twittering in the trees, a humming bird hovered over a chrysanthemum nearby, and a variety of fragrances filled the garden. Everything in nature harmonized with her happiness, expanding it till she almost burst with anticipation of Paul's arrival.

She caught her breath as he drove up and parked in front. He hadn't even taken time to go home and change. He was still in his suit. The moment he closed the gate, she said, "Hi."

Surprised, he turned, his eyes traveling over her. "You look like a beautiful butterfly from Ada's garden, Gusty."

"Thank you."

Only stepping in a few feet, he asked in a cool voice, "All right, what's so important that I had to juggle everything to get here?"

"Come and sit down beside me and I'll tell you."

"Not on your life. Tell me from there."

"No."

"All right. See you sometime." He turned and stepped to the gate.

"I knew it!" Gustavia exclaimed, standing up, her hands on her hips.

"What?" he asked before he opened it.

"That you've grown up to be the most unreasonably stubborn man I have ever known!" Before Paul could think of a response, she added. "I knew you must have been a very strong little boy to be happy under the conditions in which you had to live all your young life, but I didn't realize what a strong-willed and stubborn boy you were. You *always* got your way and you're still getting your way!"

Paul thrust his head toward her. "What? What in the heck are you talking about, Gusty?

"When we were children we always did what you wanted to do. We hardly ever did what I wanted to do."

He moved slowly over to her, scratching his head. "Why in the blazes are you bringing all that up?"

"Because it's true!"

"That's not the way I remember it. We read the books you wanted to read. I played the harmonica so you could dance till your heart's content and—" He stopped in mid-sentence, surprised that he had allowed himself to be drawn into this absurd argument.

Gustavia's voice rose. "But most of the time what did we play? Soccer, spy, ball—"

Paul grabbed her hand, pulled her unceremoniously toward the steps, up the steps and into the parlor, shutting the door. "If you insist on continuing this absurd game, we don't have to shout it to all the neighbors. Now, as you were saying."

Still worked up, her voice was decibels higher than normal. "Three-fourths of the time, we did what you wanted to do, Freddie Finch! I longed to play house for just a little while, but in about two minutes you were bored and quit. Then, of course, we did what *you* wanted to do—play some boy game!"

"You enjoyed all those games, Gusty, and you know it."

"But I would have liked to play dolls or something like that once in a while."

"Dolls? You never once mentioned that to me, Gusty."

"I didn't dare."

It was Paul's voice that rose. "Didn't dare? Where did that come from? Was I some kind of an ogre or something that you didn't *dare* mention you wanted to play dolls?"

"Well," she said, picking at her nail, "you might as well have been an ogre, you were so hardheaded! I even wondered this morning why I considered you my best friend."

He glared at her. "And—what answer did you come up with?"

Tears hovered at the corners of her eyes. "I . . . I remembered how hard you worked at making me laugh."

Baffled, Paul shook his head and moved toward her. "That's why?"

"And," she began in a small voice, "you always were so kind, always so cheerful, constantly making me happy and . . ." The tears spilled over onto her cheeks.

Paul wrapped her in his arms and groaned. "Oh, Gusty, Gusty, what am I going to do about you?"

"You can continue to make me happy like . . . like you used to," she murmured.

"And how can I do that'" he asked hoarsely.

"By letting me tell you something."

Paul loosened his grip on her and gazed into her face, puzzled. "Is that all?"

"For the moment, anyway," she said, noticing that endearing half-smile had appeared on his lips. "Out in the garden you were going to leave, remember?"

"All right, I was going to leave; now I'm not, so tell me something."

"I wish I were up at the turret window and you were below playing your harmonica like you did, and I wouldn't feel so shy about telling you."

His eyes suddenly warm and eager, he let go of her. "Hold that thought. You go on up to the turret, and I'll go out into the car and get my harmonica."

They each dashed out of the parlor, Gustavia upstairs, Paul outside.

Gustavia sat on the window seat in front of the open window and waited. Soon Paul was standing below playing a beautiful love song. When it ended, he yelled, "I love you, Gustavia Browne."

Blinking back tears, she shouted in return, "I love you, Freddie Finch."

Paul was incredulous, almost dizzy with happiness. "You do? You really do?"

"I really do."

"What about Artie Banks?" he yelled.

Frustrated, she yelled back. "I don't love him. I wanted to tell you out in the garden, but you were so obstinate, so . . ." Seeing him dash toward the front door, she ran downstairs and they met in the parlor.

Paul shut the door, and before she could say another word, he took her face into his hands and smothered it with kisses. Taking a breath, he gazed down at her, his eyes radiating love, his voice husky with emotion. "Thank you, Gusty, thank you—for loving me." Slowly, he bent down, his lips touching hers—those delectable lips that had been driving him wild from the moment he had seen her.

Gustavia, intoxicated by the kiss, threw her arms about his neck, returning it passionately. Paul's arms locked her in an embrace that held her fast—their mutual bliss carrying them away in a sudden storm of emotion neither could have experienced with anyone else.

When it ended they clung together, almost afraid to let go after so many years apart. They kissed again and again, then Paul said, "I have something of the utmost importance to say to you. As of here and now—" he paused smiling, "I promise to 'play house' with you for the rest of our lives." He then proceeded to detail all the things he would do as the man of their imaginary family.

Gustavia's bursts of laughter persisted until they were both laughing. Catching her breath, Gustavia said, "It's about time Freddie Finch."

A knock on the parlor door startled them. Paul opened it to see a disgruntled Ada standing before him.

"What is going on? First I hear yelling, running, then music and more running and doors slamming."

Gustavia laughed. "Sorry, Ada, but Paul and I have been betrothed since we were children, and he just asked me to marry him."

Ada's eyes became slits of suspicion. "You . . . you mean behind my back you've been engaged all along?"

Paul grinned. "No, Ada, just betrothed." He then turned to Gustavia. "I don't think I got your answer, Gusty. Will you marry me?"

"Yes!" she cried, throwing her arms around his neck and kissing him.

Paul's smile covered every inch of his face. "At last, Gusty! At last, not only are we betrothed, but we're actually engaged." He pulled his eyes away from his beautiful Gustavia to Ada. "Did that answer your question?"

"In a most indelicate and inappropriate way, yes."

Sitting across the table from each other eating dinner in Ada's dining room, Paul's and Gustavia's happiness was so apparent, Carol had remarked about it. They told her their good news and got a hearty congratulation and a glance at Gustavia's left hand. Paul quickly explained the event had only just happened.

"What about an engagement ring?" Paul asked when Carol left.

Her face turned serious. "That brings me to the other thing I wanted to talk with you about. I need you to read Fanny's diaries and I need you to read them as quickly as you can."

"Now? Right away?"

"Yes. I don't know why I feel such an urgency, Paul. For one thing, I need to tell you about an amazing dream I had. It was so real it didn't seem like a dream. It's still so clear in my mind I can remember every detail of it. The trouble is, I don't understand what it meant. But I want us both to read the diaries before I tell you. Maybe it's because I'm hoping to find a clue in the pages of the last diary—the loose pages that Ada cut out. Fortunately, Fanny has numbered each page."

"Hmm. You've piqued my curiosity. But what about setting a wedding date?"

"Oh Paul, I so want to do that, but—"

"Okay." He smiled. "We'll wait for a while. Bring me the diaries. I'll take them home and begin reading them immediately."

Before Paul left, they went out to the garden bench. Paul took her in his arms and kissed her, gazed into her face and kissed her again. "Oh Gusty, what you do to me," he said, his voice ragged.

"And what you do to me," she said, caressing his face tenderly. Nestling into the crook of his arm, she said, "I'm almost through with Ada's biography. With that done and the diaries read, we can plan our wedding," she sighed.

He kissed her forehead. "I'm glad to hear that."

Suddenly, Gustavia pulled away from him. "Just a minute, Paul Camden. I just remembered you have something to tell me."

"I do?"

"You most certainly do. Why did you continue to keep your identity a secret from me? You said when I'd made up my mind about Artie—and I guess that means about you as well—that you'd tell me. So . . . get on with it!"

He nodded and smiled, glad for the opportunity to set things straight. "Well, I was going to introduce myself with the harmonica that night after we talked with Ada, but two days before that Artie Banks showed up, and you had a date with him the night after I confronted Ada. Even though you broke it, it was obvious you liked him."

"Not in that way, I . . ."

"I know that now, but I didn't know it then. You're such an honorable and loyal person, Gusty. If you did start to care for him you wouldn't have let yourself do anything about it. You would have kept your promise to me—or you would have tried.

"Artie continued to stay in the picture; we both began competing for your affection, and all the while you were still trying to stay true to the elusive Freddie. I could see the stress it was causing you. It was then I decided to reveal my identity to reduce the suitors from three to two."

Gustavia was heart-stricken. "And I told you I thought it was deception—and you were just putting me first—being unselfish and . . . and noble. I'm sorry. I'm so sorry."

Paul kissed one eye then the other, stopping the threatening tears, then held her close. "Thank you. If I were in your shoes I would have felt the same way. There's no need for apology."

"If only Mum were here now and could see what a wonderful man our Freddie has become."

"If I've turned out to be a decent human being, Gusty, it's because you and your mother made me feel valued—special."

When at last they reluctantly decided it was time to say goodnight, Paul said, "I'm going home to call all my family and tell them the good news."

"I hope your mother will think it's good news."

"She will, eventually. I promise you that."

At the gate Paul set down his briefcase containing the diaries, except the last one with the loose pages. He took her into his arms again and kissed her goodnight. Though it was distressing to leave each other's presence, they were at peace for the first time since they had parted as children.

❧CHAPTER 47❧

LONDON, ENGLAND JULY, 1932:

At long last—the year was over. Little Thomas had turned two and Fanny and Josiah had been interviewed by the branch president and found worthy to have a temple recommend. They had been saving, even skimping on many things, and now they had almost saved enough money to go to Salt Lake City and be sealed as a family. Josiah was nervous about asking Mr. Sisbee for time off. Because of the depression, he'd had to cut back on his help. He and Fanny had discussed it over and over, but found no answer other than to prepare Mr. Sisbee that in three months Josiah would need four weeks off.

He and Fanny were concerned about the anti-Mormon sentiment that raged in London now and then. They knew that Mary Hartnell was against the Church because of what her friends had said about it, but did Mr. and Mrs. Sisbee feel the same way?

They decided the best thing to do was not tell Mr. Sisbee why they wanted time off. But, as nice as Mr. Sisbee was, Josiah knew he was determined to know everything about his employees, so it was with trepidation that Josiah approached Mr. Sisbee's office that morning. He knocked on the half-open door.

"Come in, Josiah," Mr. Sisbee said smiling. "Sit down, my boy. What can I do for you?"

Josiah cleared his throat. "Sir, as you know, Fanny has gone through three miscarriages and lost one baby. We've been saving and doing without so we could have a vacation. Would it be possible in about three months from now to take off work for four weeks?"

Mr. Sisbee leaned back in his chair and mulled it over. "I appreciate you giving me that much time ahead, but it's hard to say yes for sure. Anything could happen between now and then. At the last minute, I might have to say we need you."

Josiah knew he was caught. Mr. Sisbee had made it impossible to keep their trip a secret. "Mr. Sisbee, we need to make boat reservations ahead of time. Whenever I make the reservations, we have to go."

Mr. Sisbee leaned toward him, his eyes wide above the spectacles. "Boat reservations? Isn't that a rather expensive trip?"

"Yes sir, it is."

"Where are you going?"

"To the United States."

Mr. Sisbee's jaw dropped. "Why?"

"It's for family, sir."

"Of course it's for your family. Why not go on a vacation somewhere in Europe? Economic times are not good, my boy."

Josiah said a quick prayer in his heart. "I don't know quite how to tell you this, but straight out. We're going to Salt Lake City where there is a Mormon temple. Fanny and I are going to be sealed in the temple, then seal our little Sarah and Thomas to us."

Mr. Sisbee blinked a couple times in shock. His face grew dark. "Don't tell me you and Fanny have been duped into joining that Mormon group?"

"We haven't been duped, sir. We thoroughly investigated the Mormon Church and its teachings and found truths we've been searching for all our lives."

"Truths? What truths?"

"Truths about the church Christ established when he was on this earth."

"Do you know what those people do in those temples, Josiah?"

"Yes sir. They make covenants with God and our savior, Jesus Christ. Worthy members of the Church may enter and make these covenants, then they may have the privilege of getting married for time and eternity, which means the family is sealed on earth and in heaven so that they can continue to be a family in the hereafter. If we're sealed as a family, we'll be able to have our baby daughter, Sarah, in the next life."

Mr. Sisbee's eyes were hard, his brows furrowed. "So that's how they got to you. They played on your grief over Sarah."

"That's what got our attention, sir. But, as I said, we prayed and studied and listened to the Gospel of Jesus Christ with open hearts. When we pray for help, Mr. Sisbee, God guides us. He doesn't allow us to be deceived."

Mr. Sisbee's face turned grim. Josiah's heart sank, for it appeared that his employer hadn't heard a word he had said.

"They caught you when you were vulnerable," Mr. Sisbee said through tight lips. "You and Fanny are only in your thirties and have been somewhat sheltered from the wicked ways of the world. No. I'm not giving you time off to go partake of that delusion, that place that only gives you false hopes."

Josiah rubbed his brow, his desperation growing. What was he to do? He gave it one last try. "Please, Mr. Sisbee, allow us to believe as we want to. It hasn't affected my work adversely. Actually, my mind has been clearer. I've been happier than I've ever been in my life, and I think my work has reflected it."

"You have done well in your work, Josiah, but I don't think it has anything to do with that group you've joined. I would say—it was in spite of it."

Josiah remained silent. There was nothing more he could say. His beloved benefactor had closed his heart.

"I'm going to have to go home and talk with Mrs. Sisbee about you and Fanny getting involved with that heretic group. I'm certain she'll be as concerned as I am. You're excused to go back to work, Josiah."

"Yes sir."

That night with a heavy heart, Josiah told Fanny about his talk with Mr. Sisbee. She broke down in tears. He held her in his arms. It was painful for both of them that the man of whom they had grown so fond was closed-minded and unbending.

Without conviction, Josiah tried to comfort Fanny. "Maybe Mrs. Sisbee's kind heart will soften her husband's."

Two days later, Mr. Sisbee called Josiah into his office. "Sit down, my boy, I need to talk with you."

Josiah studied Mr. Sisbee's face, looking for some kind of softening, but saw none.

"Josiah, Mrs. Sisbee and I have had a couple of serious talks and have thought it over carefully. The decision we came to was made for yours and Fanny's good. You have to believe that. We have become quite attached to you both."

To forestall what was coming, Josiah spoke quickly. "Fanny and I love you and Mrs. Sisbee like second parents. You both have been unbelievably good to us."

"I'm glad you feel that way, son, because we've decided to ask you to give up your association with the Mormon Church."

Josiah was aghast. He hadn't expected anything like this. All he expected was a firm "no" to his request to take time off. "Uh, Mr. Sisbee, how can you ask that? It's our life. The Church means everything to us."

"I see. They've hooked you worse than I thought. What is your answer?"

"It's no, Mr. Sisbee. We can't give it up."

"Maybe you need to go home and discuss it with Fanny."

"No. I don't need to discuss it with her. She'll feel just as I do."

"Think about it, my boy. Think about it seriously, then come back to me."

"No, Mr. Sisbee, I don't need to think about it," Josiah stated firmly. "We don't want to give up The Church of Jesus Christ of Latter-day Saints, nor will we. We have a testimony that it is the only true church on the face of the earth."

Mr. Sisbee looked down to hide his disappointment, then looked up. "That's a bold statement."

Josiah watched his beloved employer struggle with his emotions.

His voice hoarse, Mr. Sisbee's words came out in a rush. "If you and Fanny don't give up your association with the Mormon Church, I'm afraid—I'll have to let you go."

Josiah was stunned. "Why, Mr. Sisbee? What difference does it make which church we belong to? It doesn't affect my work."

"If people find out that I'm employing someone who belongs to that Mormon group, it will reflect upon my establishment. Since we talked two days ago I've gone to our priest and, because we care so much for you and Fanny, I even went to the Archbishop. Josiah, you have no idea what goes on in that Mormon temple. It's blasphemy!"

"But Mr. Sisbee, the things they say are nothing but lies. Please, if you and Mrs. Sisbee will look into it, you'll find out that the things they say are not true. If you won't allow the missionaries to tell you about it, let Fanny and me answer your questions."

"Mrs. Sisbee and I both are devoted to the Church of England. We don't have any questions. We have read enough about the Mormon Church to feel very concerned for you. We're doing this for your own good."

"If someone wanted to know the facts about the Church of England, wouldn't it make sense to go to that church to find out the facts rather than read something by people who are against the church?"

Ignoring his question, Mr. Sisbee leaned toward him and stared directly into Josiah's eyes, weighing each word carefully, "Josiah—are you willing to lose your job because you won't give up the Mormon Church?"

"I'm not willing, sir, but if I have to make a choice between The Church of Jesus Christ and my job, I choose the Church."

"Are you certain, Josiah? I won't give you a letter of recommendation—and jobs are very scarce. Unemployment is higher this year."

Josiah's heart was breaking. It seemed incomprehensible that he had to leave his dear friend, Mr. Sisbee, that he had to give up the pleasant atmosphere here in the bank and give up all he had worked so hard to achieve.

"I'm certain, Mr. Sisbee."

Mr. Sisbee seemed to wilt before his eyes. His shoulders sagged. "I'm sorry, Josiah. More sorry than you know. I've had great hopes for you. Clean out your desk, then pick up the wages you've earned so far this month."

Josiah stood up and gazed into the face that had become so dear to him. "I . . . I can't begin express to you how much I regret not being able to work with you anymore, Mr. Sisbee. You've taught me more than I thought I'd be fortunate enough to learn. You've given me opportunities I never thought I'd have. Leaving here is the most difficult thing I've ever done. Fanny and I love you and Mrs. Sisbee. Your kindness to us has been overwhelming, and we're grateful beyond words." Josiah swallowed back the lump in his throat and blinked a couple of times. "I can't begin to thank you for all you've done for me, sir." Josiah got up and slowly left Mr. Sisbee's office for the last time, feeling the numbness of despair.

❧CHAPTER 48❧

BELFORD, MAINE, JUNE 2001:

Gustavia put the pages down, and dissolved into quiet tears. The terrible sacrifice Josiah and Fanny had made for their church was unbelievable and tragic! *Why was it necessary to make that sacrifice?* she asked herself. *Why?* Her emotions were so mixed, she hardly knew what she was feeling.

She heard Ada's shrill voice call for her. She ran to the door and downstairs. "What, Ada."

"The phone for you again," she said impatiently, handing it to her.

"Thank you, Ada." Running upstairs with it, she sat on the window seat and said hello.

"Gusty, I'm at the office and I only have a small break. I just called to tell you I love you, and incidently, to congratulate you on using such good judgement in your choice of a fiancé."

Gustavia laughed. "I love you too. I woke up this morning feeling deliriously happy."

"I didn't wake up. I stayed up most of the night reading those diaries. It nearly tore my heart out to read about the way Fanny was put into the orphanage. I couldn't put it down."

"Thank you for reading them with me," she said softly. "If anyone can understand what Fanny and Josiah went through, you can." A sudden thought struck her. "I just remembered something Mum told me! Hesslewood Orphanage used to be in Hull and was called 'Hull Seamans' and General Orphan Asylum.' Don't you think it's rather a strange coincidence that Fanny and Josiah were in the same orphanage as you, but at a different time, in a different location and called by a different name?"

"It is strange. I don't know what to think, Gusty. I know that sometimes things happen for a reason, and sometimes we learn what they are—like me meeting you because I was in the orphanage, or like your mother finding the job with Mr. Fretwell and on and on. God often works in coincidences it seems." He paused. "Well, I must go, my beautiful one. I'll call tomorrow."

❧

LONDON, ENGLAND, JULY 1932:

Through the window, Fanny was surprised to see Josiah walking towards the house with a satchel in his hand. It was early afternoon, and she had just put Thomas down for a nap. It was too early for him to be coming home . . . unless . . . . Fear seized her when he entered the house. His face was ashen.

She took the satchel from him and set it on the floor. Taking his hand, she led him to the couch. "What has happened, Josiah?"

"Mr. Sisbee let me go."

She caught her breath. "What? That can't be, Josiah. He told me he didn't know what he would do without you, that you were worth three employees."

"Nevertheless, I no longer work for Mr. Sisbee."

"No! You can't mean it, Josiah. Tell me everything."

Josiah did so, telling her in as complete a detail as he could, knowing how much she needed to hear it. When he finished, all Fanny could do was shake her head in disbelief.

Finally, she said, "It doesn't seem possible that people as wonderful as Mr. and Mrs. Sisbee could be so hostile toward something they know nothing about. Oh, Josiah, I simply can't grasp it. This . . . this means they won't want to associate with us any more."

"That's right. It feels like we're losing family again, Fanny."

"It does. And I know Mary will feel the same way. Oh, how can we bear it?" Sobs of anguish poured out, and Josiah took her in his arms and they cried together.

A short time later, Fanny began to face the reality of their situation. "Does this mean we can't take our trip to the United States?"

"If I could have worked only three more months, Fanny, we would've had enough."

"Can we get a cheaper ticket?"

"I've checked on every boat line. This was the cheapest fare I could find."

"Oh! And you don't have a job to bring in more. What are we going to do, Josiah?"

"I'm going to look for a job."

"When you find one, we can continue to save for our trip."

"Sweetheart, I may not find work for a long time. Unemployment is growing worse every day. We have to prepare ourselves to live on our savings until I find a job."

"No! No, Josiah."

He took her in his arms once more. "I know the Lord will bless us.

We must have faith that we'll find a way to get to the temple. The Lord wants us to have the temple blessings more than we do."

"We can sell our home and rent a flat, Josiah."

"You're willing to do that?"

"I am."

Josiah let out a desperate breath. "Fanny, oh Fanny, before we were married, I had such great plans for us. I was going to give you the lifestyle that would allow you to attend the theater, have lovely clothes, and live in a beautiful house and . . ."

"We *are* rich, Josiah. We have the gospel. We don't need that kind of lifestyle."

"I know, but I still would . . ."

Fanny put her fingers over his lips. "I have you and Thomas, and someday we'll have Sarah."

They stayed in each others arms for a long time, silently contemplating the future without their dear friends the Sisbees, and Mary Hartnell and her wonderful children.

After supper, with Thomas holding onto his father's hand, Josiah and Fanny went over to Evelyn and Charlton's to tell them what had happened that day. They listened attentively, shedding tears with their friends.

"I can fully empathize," Evelyn said. "My parents and siblings won't have anything to do with me since I've joined the Church."

Fanny gasped. "Oh no! You have it much worse than we do, Evelyn."

"No, I don't. At least I had a family, a mother and a father, growing up. Neither of you did, and the Sisbees have been rather like parents to you. Besides that, Charlton's parents and family joined the Church years ago, so we have a lot of support from them. Also, Charlton has a fairly secure job as a school teacher—so far, that is."

"That's right," Charlton agreed. "And, if there's any way I can help you find employment, Josiah, let me know. I'll ask around and be on watch for a job opening."

"Thank you. Tomorrow I'm going to start looking. I'm afraid it will be a vain search for a while. I'll need your prayers."

A week later, Josiah dragged himself home at 5:00 P.M., exhausted. He was fighting back discouragement. So far all the positions in which he could use any of his skills were scarce and already filled. If he couldn't find one in his area of expertise, he would have to settle for something less. The trouble was, there were men in long lines waiting for even menial labor jobs.

In another two weeks, they would have to start living on the savings they were planning on using to go to America. Somehow, he had to find employment somewhere, but more than likely it wouldn't pay him enough for them to keep their home, and this was devastating to Josiah. Nevertheless, he and Fanny had discussed it and had decided that they were willing to do anything they had to do to get to the temple.

Two weeks passed with no luck. Josiah began dressing in work clothes, and went looking for any kind of a job. He and Fanny fasted and prayed. Soon after, one late afternoon, Josiah was walking by a meat processing plant where half-beeves were hanging from low ceiling hooks. He heard a commotion and stopped. The owner was arguing with an employee. Both were angry. The employer was accusing the employee of stealing some beef. The other one was in hot denial. Before long, the employer fired the man on the spot.

Josiah waited until the hapless man left, then went in and offered his services to the owner of the market. The owner looked him up and down. Apparently pleased at what he saw, he immediately hired Josiah and told him to report to work the next morning. The wages were low, but it would feed his family. He thanked the Lord for leading him to the right place at the right time.

He knew the time had come to let go of their home and move into a two-bedroom flat somewhere. Yet his heart felt leaden at the thought of taking his beloved wife and child out of the home they had put so much work into, the home they loved.

≈CHAPTER 49≈

LONDON, ENGLAND, SEPTEMBER 1932:
Josiah and Fanny moved out of their home to a West-side flat on a street called Petticoat Lane. They had now been living in the flat for one month, and Fanny had cleaned it up and managed to make it into a homey little place.

They soon got acquainted with their next door neighbors, William and Ellen Beddow. Josiah and Fanny liked them immediately. They were warm, friendly people in their early forties. The Beddows had never been able to have children and immediately fell in love with little Thomas.

Fanny and Josiah found much in common with William and Ellen. Will, as he was called, had also lost his higher-paying job. He and Ellen had to give up their home and move into something less expensive as Fanny and Josiah had. Unlike most of the other people on the street, the Beddows were high-class people who neither drank nor smoked. Again the Lord had blessed them. In fact, Josiah and Fanny hoped in the future they could introduce them to the gospel.

LONDON, APRIL 1933:
It had been almost seven full months since Josiah had started working at the meat plant. It was tedious, hard work, and during the cold winter, his hands had become red and raw. Never had it entered his mind that he would be doing this kind of work one day. But through it all, he felt fortunate. Many men were still out of work. He and Fanny had had to pitch in and help other members of their branch who were without jobs.

They were still saving a small amount each month toward their temple fund, but because they'd had to use most of it to live on, and because they'd had to help others in the branch, they were at least nine months away from having enough. A peace had settled over their hearts. They knew without a doubt that they would eventually have the opportunity to be sealed as a family.

Their friends, Charlton and Evelyn, were starting to have more serious opposition from Evelyn's family concerning the Church. They wouldn't leave them alone. It seemed that of late anti-Mormon sentiment had been on the rise. Josiah tossed it off as coming from the depression. Men's hearts were uneasy and many felt an unrest, making their tempers flare at almost anything.

The last three Sundays, a small mob of sorts had gathered outside the building in which their branch was meeting. They yelled obscenities and threatened the congregation during most of the meeting. The first two times the bobbies dispersed the rabble-rousers. For some reason, Evelyn felt it was instigated by her family—not her own parents, but by an uncle with whom she had never felt comfortable.

Something changed on the last Sunday, however, something that had caused everyone in the branch great uneasiness. The noise became so unbearable outside the door that the branch president and one of his counselors went outside to try to appease the angry group. At that moment, the bobbies arrived and not only did they arrest two of the leaders of the mob, but the branch president and his counselor also. Upon their release, they were warned that if it happened again, all four would be put in jail on a charge of disturbing the peace.

SATURDAY EVENING:

After putting Thomas to bed, Fanny told Josiah she wanted to talk with him. They seated themselves at the kitchen table.

"What is it, Fanny?"

"Ellen Beddows asked me an unexpected question this afternoon. I don't mind saying it rather shocked me. She asked if we had assigned guardians for Thomas if anything ever happened to us."

Apparently it shocked Josiah too. He blinked and was silent a moment. "That is rather extraordinary, I would say."

"I thought so too until she explained further. She said she and Will had talked about it at some length. It came to their minds, that because neither of us have relatives, Thomas would in all probability be put into an orphanage if anything happened to us."

"Good gracious, Fanny! I never thought of that. That would be terrible."

"I know," Fanny said, shuddering at the thought. "Ellen told me that she and Will would love to be Thomas' guardians if we didn't have anyone else. I thanked her and went home trying to think who we would like as guardians. Of course, I immediately thought of Evelyn and Charlton. But since they now have four children, I don't want to put them on the spot in case they feel they couldn't afford to care for and raise Thomas."

"But they would be the most desirable. Thomas would be raised in the Church."

"I know. I suppose we can change the guardianship if the Beddows don't join the Church. I'm feeling hopeful that they might. They've asked us questions about the Church, as you know, even though they don't as yet want the missionaries."

Josiah rubbed his forehead in thought. "Let's go ahead and tell them, for now, we would be most grateful to have them as guardians of Thomas—unless in the future we can find someone who will raise Thomas in the Church. Maybe that will spur them on to listen to the missionaries."

"That's a wonderful way to put it. Let's go over there and draw up an agreement right now. We might as well get it done."

"And I'll let them hold a copy of the will I had written up while working at Mr. Sisbee's. This stipulates that if anything happened to us, all our savings and belongings go to Thomas for his education."

The Beddows were elated and flattered. Josiah and Fanny thanked them for their kindness, for their love for Thomas. They drew up the guardianship paper and all signed it.

Afterwards, Josiah frowned, shook his head slightly as if to shake off a troubling thought. He turned to Fanny and suggested that if the Beddows were willing, that maybe they ought to leave Thomas with the Beddows tomorrow while they went to church. Fanny hesitantly agreed and the Beddows accepted eagerly.

Back at home Josiah and Fanny sat down on the couch and discussed what they had done. "I'm a little worried that you felt the need to leave Thomas with the Beddows while we go to church, Josiah."

Josiah put his arm around her. "My common sense tells me that since a couple of the rabble rousers were arrested last week, the pack won't be back, but . . ."

"But what?" she asked when he paused.

"I don't know why, but I felt we should leave him with the Beddows this one time, just to make sure. Anyway, in case there is more trouble we don't want to risk Thomas being hurt."

Fanny nodded her agreement, yet she felt some misgivings. "It will be the first time we've been separated from our little Thomas, Josiah, but now I too am feeling a little uneasy about taking him tomorrow."

"You are?"

Fanny nodded.

"Well, then I guess we're being guided to leave him home this once."

"What do you suppose it means, Josiah?"

"I don't know. This I do know: whatever happens tomorrow, we'll rest a little easier knowing he's home safe with the Beddows."

"What about us and all the other branch members? Do you think there's a chance some of us will be arrested tomorrow?"

"I don't think so. If the pack shows up, I think everyone will stay inside this time no matter how loud they get. This group of foul-mouthed ruffians will probably disperse and won't bother the branch anymore. One thing I'm certain of is the Church is going to grow here in England and become more well-known and respected."

Fanny leaned her head upon Josiah's shoulder. "You do? If that happens, maybe someday the Church will build a temple here in England."

"That's very possible. There's so much work to do."

Fanny sighed, feeling great contentment next to her husband, knowing their baby boy was safely sleeping in the next room, and knowing without a doubt that the Lord's loving hand had been guiding them all their lives and would continue to do so. A tear of gratitude trickled down her cheek.

❧

BELFORD, MAINE:

Gustavia stared at this last page. There was no more! This was the last entry Fanny would ever write. She felt bereaved, cheated! Her thoughts were in turmoil. *What happened to Josiah and Fanny?* She knew they had died—been killed, but how, where? Gustavia covered her face in frustration. *How can we possibly find out?*

It was at that moment, like an electric shock, that Gustavia realized that Fanny and Josiah had been unable to fulfill their dreams of getting sealed as a family! And they both believed without any doubt that they would. *So much for their faith!* Gustavia thought bitterly.

She got up and gazed out into the garden, wishing Paul were here with her. Turning from the window, she paced the floor. I *need to talk to a Mormon, maybe one can help me understand.* But Artie Banks was the only Mormon she knew. On impulse, she told herself aloud, "I can call him!" Going down to the library, she looked up his phone number in her planner. She knew he would be at work, but maybe she could get his work number. Ada wasn't in the room, so she remained there to call.

Artie's mother answered and sounded happy to hear from her. Gustavia asked about the family, then asked if she could possibly talk to Artie at work. Mrs. Banks graciously gave his work number to her.

Dialing the number, she asked to speak with Artie Banks. Soon a vibrant hello came over the line.

"Artie, this is Gustavia ."

"Gustavia! What a surprise. What's up?" he asked eagerly.

"I need to tell you something and ask you some questions. Do you have a moment?"

There was an interval of silence on the phone. "Do I detect something in your voice that hints that things don't bode well for you and me?"

"I told you I would call you when something was settled between Paul and me. Well, it happened rather soon after I talked with you. I want you to know, Artie, that because you are such an exceptional and charming man, I was confused for awhile. But, I realized that I do love Paul. We got engaged last night."

Another silence stretched out. "Well," he began trying to sound cheerful, "It must be right. You both have a long and unusual history. I wish you happiness."

"Thank you, Artie. I so appreciate meeting you and getting to know your family. You've had more of an effect on me than you know."

"That's nice to hear. You had some questions?"

Gustavia told him of reading her grandmother's journal and of learning that they joined the Mormon Church.

"Wonderful!"

She related as briefly as she could their great faith and desire to be sealed as a family only to be killed before they could. "The question I have is why would God deny them that when they'd had so much faith?"

"Wow! What a story. The answer is very simple, Gustavia. Contact someone in The Church of Jesus Christ of Latter-day Saints there in Belford and ask for the missionaries to come and teach you. If you can't find members in Belford, call Augusta."

"The missionaries taught my grandparents. But what good did it do them? All that resulted was Grandfather losing his good job, both losing their dear friends and eventually getting killed."

Artie's voice was gentle. "There's no need for such bitterness, Gustavia. Their dream of being sealed in the temple can be realized. But it depends on you."

"Me! How in the world can I do anything?"

"You'll have to find that out for yourself by asking for the missionaries as your grandparents did."

This time the silence was on Gustavia's end. At last she said, "All right, Artie. I have no idea what good it will do, but thank you for listening to me."

"You're so welcome. Please call me and tell me the end result, will you?"

"If there are results, I will."

Gustavia disconnected and sat there in a quandary. She didn't know anymore than she did before she called him. Asking for Mormon missionaries was the last thing she wanted to do after what had happened to her grandparents! Disconsolately, she pulled out the Belford phone book, looking under churches, but was unable to find it. She looked in the Augusta phone book and there it was, staring back at her. The Church of Jesus Christ of Latter-day Saints. She dialed the number. A voice answered.

"Hello, my name is Gustavia Browne. To whom am I speaking?"

"I'm Silvia Martin. My husband and I are helping to clean the building."

"Are you members of that church?"

"Yes, we are."

"Uh, I'm not a member of your church, but I need to have the missionaries come and talk with me."

"Really?" The woman, Silvia, sounded both surprised and excited. "May I have your phone number, and I'll reach them as soon as I can and ask them to call you?"

Gustavia recited the number and thanked her. She hung up the phone, feeling lost with no more to read—without knowing what had really happened to her grandparents. The Beddows told her father all they knew—that they were killed by some ruffians who got away. The law knew no more than that since they got there right after it happened, and after the killers ran away.

From what she had read, Gustavia felt certain that the next day, Sunday, when they planned on leaving Thomas in the care of the Beddows while they went to church, was the very day they were killed. *Would her father have been killed if his parents hadn't felt so strongly about not taking him with them?*

Gustavia covered her face trying to remember if her mother had told her anything else. Yes! She had put it out of her mind because it hadn't seemed important. Since reading the diaries, she knew it was important.

The Beddows had mentioned a couple, a man and a woman coming to their door who claimed to be friends of Josiah and Fanny wanting to know about little Thomas. When the Beddows told them that Josiah and Fanny had made them his guardians, they offered to help in any way they could and left their names and address. More than likely, those friends were Charlton and Evelyn! But what did the Beddows do with that information? As far as she knew her father didn't have it. The Beddows knew which church Josiah and Fanny belonged to. *Why didn't they tell her father? Or did they? If only Mum were alive, I could ask her!*

She went back upstairs and picked up the last diary and turned to the place where the pages had been cut out in order to place the loose pages back where they belonged. Before she did so, she stared at the last several empty pages left intact which hadn't been cut out. Forlornly, she turned one, then another to the end. Why, she didn't know. She stared distractedly at the inside of the back cover, then started to close it when she noticed something she hadn't before. The inside of the cover bulged a little. Her first thought was that the back cover was warped. Looking at the back of it, she found it perfectly straight. Studying the inside of it again, she felt a bulge. There was something there! Her heart pounding, she carefully examined i t . Near the spine she saw what looked like a pocket. It *was* a pocket! Gently, she slipped a couple of fingers inside and pulled out a picture.

It was a picture of her father with a man and woman. It definitely wasn't the Beddows! She had seen several pictures of them with her father. All those pictures belonged to her now, and to this day she pulled them out every once in a while and looked at them. This picture had been taken by a professional photographer whose name was in small print on the bottom: Chislett Photography, Oxford St. Holding her breath, Gustavia turned the picture over. She uttered a cry of joy. It was a picture of Josiah and Fanny with their little Thomas, taken in 1933!

How wonderful to see the faces of the two she had come to know so well! Josiah *was* handsome! *And Fanny was—what was it about Fanny?* Her heart started beating so wildly she could scarcely breath. Something prompted her to put her fingers gently back down into the pocket and, as she hoped, found one more picture! Pulling it out, she gazed at it and gasped. Unable to believe what she saw, she asked aloud, "How . . . how can this be?" Everything momentarily seemed to be suspended in time— her breathing, her heart. When at last she could get her breath she stood up almost shakily, went downstairs and called Paul at work, surprised that this time she was put through without question.

"Hello," came his welcome voice.

"Paul, I need you to come as soon as you can get off work."

"Is something wrong?" he asked concerned.

"No. But I have something incredible to tell you and show you and . . ." her voice trailed off.

"I'll get there as quickly as I can arrange it."

❧CHAPTER 50❦

Waiting restlessly for Paul to arrive, Gustavia walked up and down the sidewalk, totally unaware of her surroundings.

At last Paul's car arrived and parked. He got out. She ran to him and threw her arms around his neck. "I'm so glad you're here. I need you."

He held her in his arms, savoring the feel of her for a moment, then gazed at her with concern. "Are you all right?"

"Yes," she said almost in a whisper. "Let's go into the parlor."

Inside, Paul took off his suit coat, loosened his tie and sat on the couch, patting a place beside him.

Gustavia gave him a small uneasy smile and nodded. "Give me a moment," she said, pacing to and fro. "I've thought and thought how to tell you so you'll understand. Though how can I expect you to when I'm not sure I can myself?"

"What in the world are you talking about, Gusty? We communicate better than most couples. We've had more years together to know each other, so sit down here beside me this minute."

Gustavia exhaled and smiled at the man she loved with all her heart. "All right." She picked up the last diary from a table nearby and sat down beside him. "I've finished."

"Good!" he replied. "I'll be glad to get this behind us. It's been occupying your thoughts nonstop. And I'll finish it tonight."

She muttered an appreciative, but distracted, "Thank you," while rubbing her fingers over the diary. Noticing as she had before, the cover of this one was different. It appeared that Fanny had made a special cover for it. Of course, the pocket was put there by Fanny's own fingers! She had returned the pictures to the pocket, so she could show Paul what she had discovered. Handing him the diary she asked, "Do you see anything different, Paul?"

He studied it a moment, turned it over a couple of times then opened it to the first page and examined the inside cover. "It's obvious that your grandmother has made a cover for this diary." He flipped the pages over and examined the inside of the back cover. "The inside of this back cover is not as smooth as the front."

"Is that all you see?"

"I don't know. What you want me to see, Gusty?"

"Keep looking."

Paul rubbed his hand over it. "It is bulging a little. Hey! It looks as though there might be slit or opening close to the spine. It's a pouch of some kind."

"Yes, it is." Gustavia slipped her fingers inside, pulled out the first picture and showed it to Paul.

"That's your father," Paul said. "I remember you showing me over and over the pictures your mother had of him." Gustavia nodded. "But I don't recognize the couple." He flipped the picture over and read. Excited, he turned it back over and studied it. "So this is Josiah and Fanny. A handsome couple. What a find, Gustavia!" he stated enthusiastically. Seeing the expression on her face, he stopped short. "What is it, Gusty? I would think you'll be ecstatic at finding this."

"I am."

"You're looking and acting strangely for someone who's supposed to be excited."

Before he could say another word, Gustavia reached into the pocket again, pulled out the second picture and handed it to him. Surprised, Paul studied it carefully. It was a picture of a tall dark-haired woman with a young girl. He turned it over. On the back in nice penmanship was written: 'Sarah Sullivan with daughter Fanny 9 years old.'

"Well I'll be darned! Another find," he said beaming. His smile left when he looked at Fanny. He was unable to fathom her expression. "What . . . what is it, Gusty?"

"I . . . I don't know what to make of it, Paul, but . . . I saw Sarah Sullivan and the adult Fanny nine days before I saw these pictures."

Paul's jaw dropped. "I don't understand." He held up the pictures. "You saw them before you saw these?" She nodded. "But how is that possible? You uh, you've seen a couple of women who looked like them, so they seem familiar?"

"Remember the dream I wanted to tell you about? As I told you, it was so real, it's hard to believe it was only a dream. The powerful feeling that came with it and the dream itself made such an impact on me, I couldn't go back to sleep. I just lay there thinking about it and wondering what it meant. I finally got up, knelt down by the window seat and prayed about it, asking God what it meant, for the feeling I had was something I'd never experienced."

"Really?" Paul deliberated a moment. "Tell me about the dream."

"In my dream two grown women appeared to me. One was tall with dark hair and eyes, dressed in an 1890s dress similar to my wine colored one. The other woman had strawberry blonde hair, blue eyes and freckles sprinkled across her nose and cheeks. She wore a 1920s dress. It was Sarah and Fanny Sullivan, Paul!"

"Are you sure?" he asked, incredulous.

"I'm as positive as I am that you're sitting right here."

Paul shrugged his shoulders. "Is that all there was to the dream?"

"No. Both were holding one hand out to me. The younger one, Fanny, spoke. She said, 'Help us, Gustavia, help us.' Then they left, or I woke up or . . . something."

"Are you sure that was what was said?"

"I heard her voice as clearly as I hear yours. I didn't mistake what she said."

Paul rubbed his chin, his brows furrowed. "I don't know what to make of it. Did you know who they were?"

"No. I had no idea. But I did know without a doubt that they were relatives. I knew they were relatives, Paul! How I knew that I have no idea. I guess that's why I felt I needed to finish the diaries in case I could find out who they were. Of course I didn't until I stumbled onto the pictures."

"And when you discovered the pictures . . ."

"It stunned me to pull out the pictures and learn that it was Sarah and Fanny I saw in my dream."

He burst out in frustration. "Why didn't you tell me about the dream right away, Gusty?"

"Since I knew the women were relatives, I wanted you to read the diaries first so that maybe together we could come up with an explanation of sorts. From the descriptions in the diaries, I began to wonder if the two women I saw were Sarah and Fanny, but I couldn't comprehend such a thing and kept putting it out of my mind, certain my imagination was carrying me away. It seemed much too farfetched."

"No wonder you seemed obsessed with the diaries, Gusty."

"It wasn't that I was obsessed, Paul. It was more that I felt an urgency to read them."

"Well, I guess I had better get down to the business of finishing these last pages myself. Since I don't have work at the office that can't wait, I told everyone that I wouldn't be back until Monday. So—if you'll excuse me, I'm going to get these read right now."

"Thank you, love. I'll go tell Carol to expect you for dinner again. I'll go work on Ada's biography while you're reading."

❧

Paul found himself living Josiah's and Fanny's life with them as he read, but something troubled him. It seemed everywhere he turned, the Mormon Church was in his face. First, Gustavia flew up to the headquarters of the Mormon Church, Salt Lake City, to find out information about her ancestors, and immediately Artie Banks, a Mormon, hit on her and even flew out to see her! He knew he was being unreasonable, but whenever he thought of Artie Banks, he felt unsure of himself. He and Gustavia were engaged! So what was the matter with him?

Next, he found out from his brother that his beloved Sharon Banks was a member of the Mormon Church! And now—here on the last pages of the diaries, he found that Gustavia's grandparents *joined* the church and sacrificed *everything* for it!

Paul, trying to thrust all the negative thoughts from his mind, resumed reading. Fanny's penmanship was very legible and being an exceptionally fast reader, he finished before long. The end left him feeling up in the air—unsatisfied, as it must have Gustavia. What happened to them? Did their deaths have anything to do with the Mormon Church?

He thought that when they were through reading the diaries they could get on with their lives. But now what? He got up and paced the floor, wishing he could forget the diaries—and the dream!

Gustavia came in and saw him pacing. "Paul?"

"Oh, hi," he said, putting on a smile.

"You're through."

"Yes."

"And?"

"I hadn't expected to become so drawn into your grandparents' lives, but I'm feeling unsettled, confused and frustrated. How about you? All of the above?"

"Yes."

He wrapped his arms around her. "What's next? What are we expected to do?"

"That's an interesting question. What is expected of us? After reading the diaries, do you have any clue as to what my dream meant?"

"None whatsoever."

"Me neither." She was nervous about telling him of her call to Artie Banks and then to a Mormon church building. "Maybe . . . we uh, should talk with some Mormons and perhaps . . ."

"No," he retorted adamantly.

Concerned at the tone of his voice, she looked up into his face. "Why?"

"I don't want to, that's all."

Her heart sank. Maybe she shouldn't have been so rash. Nevertheless, she had to tell him what she had done. "Paul," she began in a small voice, "I was rather impulsive today, I uh . . ."

"What did you do?" he asked warily.

"I felt that, in order to understand Fanny and Josiah a little better, I had to call a Mormon. The only one I know is Artie Banks." She saw his face close. "Please, Paul, don't look like that."

He dropped his arms from around her. "How could you do that without talking with me first?"

Gustavia's brows rose in surprise. "You mean I can't call a friend without talking with you first?"

"You know that isn't what I mean."

"No, I don't. What do you mean?"

"That I don't want you to call Artie Banks—ever."

"I can't believe you're still jealous of him, Paul? It's you I love. It's you I'm engaged to."

Paul couldn't explain to her the dark feeling that had come over him. He didn't understand it himself.

"Paul, I need to tell you something."

"What?"

"Please, Paul, let's sit down and be calm," she said, sitting on the couch. Finally, he sat down beside her.

"I didn't tell Artie about my dream," she said softly, "but I did tell him a little about Fanny and Josiah and how their dream of being sealed had been thwarted by their deaths."

"And—what answer did he give you?" he asked, his tone darkly skeptical.

"He said that their dreams of being sealed could still be realized, but it depended on me."

"You! What in the heck did he mean by that?"

"I don't know, Paul," she replied, trying to keep her voice from reflecting her rising irritation. "He said to do as Fanny and Josiah had. Ask for some missionaries to come over and tell us about the Church. So I looked in the phone book and found the phone number of a Mormon church and called. I reached a woman who was cleaning the building."

"And?" he asked testily.

Gustavia stood up, her lips tightening in defiance. "There's no need for you to act like this, Paul."

"Tell me what she said."

"She said she'd have someone call us. That's all."

"You can listen to the missionaries, Gustavia, but I'm not."

"But we have to listen to them together, Paul!" she cried out in desperation.

"Why?"

"I can't do anything without you."

"You can, and you did. Go ahead with it."

Ada appeared at the door with the phone in her hand. "I'm weary of answering the phone for you, Gustavia. Something has to be done about it." She handed her the receiver.

"Hello."

"Am I speaking to Gustavia Browne?"

"Yes."

"I'm Elder Ream. I'm a missionary from The Church of Jesus Christ of Latter-day Saints. Sister Martin called me and my companion and told us to call you."

He sounded young to Gustavia. Then she remembered the young 'Elders' who had taught Josiah and Fanny. "Thank you for calling. I needed to talk with some missionaries from your church."

"We'd love to come to your place and talk with you tonight."

How was she going to handle this? "This isn't my home, so I can't have you come here. Is there somewhere else we could meet?"

"We can arrange to meet in a member's home. I'll call you right back."

"Thank you." She saw Paul staring out the window. "Paul?" He remained as he was. "That was one of the missionaries. He's going to arrange a meeting tonight at another member's home. Will you come with me?"

He turned and went over to her. "No. I'm going now." He started to leave and stopped. "Could I take the last diary with me? I want to reread something."

"Yes," she said, looking puzzled.

He picked it up and walked out, leaving her in shock. She had never seen him like this. *What's behind it, what's causing it? Oh, Mum, I need you. I need to talk with you about Freddie!* She sank to the floor, holding her knees, rocking back and forth in anguish. "Dear God help me. Help me!"

Driving home, Paul felt totally miserable about treating Gustavia as he had. What was the matter with him? This was more than unreasonable! He felt out of control. All his life he had been able to keep his insecurities in check. As a child in the orphanage, he held his loneliness, his feelings of abandonment to himself. He only let it out at night when the lights were off and everyone was in bed. He remembered feeling as though he were the only one in the whole orphanage who had not been wanted at all. Both parents had given him up when he was only a baby!

When he was older he had asked Mr. Torr why he hadn't been adopted as a baby. He had learned one day that people only wanted to adopt babies, not older children like himself. Mr. Torr answered with a shake of the head. "I wish I knew, master Finch. I wasn't here when you were left, but there was a note that said: 'This baby is not for adoption. The parents are coming back for him.' I don't know why they never came back for you, Freddie, but I'm sure it was for a very good reason." For a while he had felt better knowing that his parents had intended to come back for him, but it eventually wore off and all the old insecurities returned. He felt worthless most of the time, but his happy-go-lucky-nature masked it well.

Several times he had sneaked out of bed at night and gone outside into the back yard behind a bush as far away as possible and cried, the heartache and hurt at last ending in exhaustion.

Paul's eyes blurred. He wondered why all this was coming back to him tonight? Maybe it was because he had lived through the orphanage days with Fanny and Josiah and it brought back his own experiences.

He needed to apologize to Gustavia for his actions, but for some reason he was feeling that he couldn't match Artie and his 'special something'—that Artie was the better man. What was he thinking? Gustavia was engaged to him! No matter what he told himself, the old demons were still getting the best of him. He couldn't get control of himself.

He arrived home, fixed himself a peanut butter sandwich, and turned on the television. The phone rang. He went into the kitchen and answered.

"Paul, this is Gusty. Elder Ream called and told me that the meeting would be held in the Martin home. Mrs. Martin was the lady I talked with at the church. The meeting will start at 8:00. Will you come?"

"No."

A strained silence followed. "Do you have a pencil and paper handy?"

"Yes."

"I'm going to give you the address and phone number in case you change your mind. They live in Augusta."

Paul wrote it down. "Thanks, but I have some thinking to do."

"All right. I love you, Paul." She hung up.

Paul went back into the front room feeling miserable. He felt weighed down by self-doubt. He remembered his brother Rick saying, 'I've never known anyone so secure.' *I guess I fooled him as well as everyone else.*

He swallowed his sandwich and drank a glass of milk, not enjoying it at all. He needed desperately to talk with someone, but there was no one with whom he could share his feelings. Not even Gustavia—especially not her! Alice Browne's face came into his mind for some reason. He could almost hear her telling him to say his prayers as she had many times.

He knelt beside the couch not knowing what to say. "Dear God, What is the matter with me? Please help me." That was all he could muster. He got up and paced back and forth. Presently, he noticed the diary on the couch where he had left it.

He sat down and picked it up, trying to remember what he wanted to reread. He aimlessly flipped it to the back cover and studied the pocket Fanny had made. He carefully pulled out the pictures and studied them. As he slid them back, he became aware of something else. It looked like *anoth - er* pocket behind that one! The edge of it was closer to the spine. Or was it a pocket? He tried to loosen it but it was stuck in several places as if some of the paste Fanny had used got spread accidently. Prying it ever so carefully, Paul was able to loosen it.

His heartbeat accelerated. It was difficult reaching inside without tearing it. Apparently it fit Fanny's fingers just fine, but his were larger. He took the pictures out of the first pocket and felt carefully to see if he could feel anything. It felt like there might be another picture. *Gustavia will be thrilled!* Tear or not, he eased his fingers in and pulled out a picture. It was a family. A father, a mother and four children. *Who could they be?* He wondered.

He turned the picture over and started to read the names. He read the first one and stopped. So did his breathing, and so, it felt, did his heart. The name he read was: Charlton Frederick Finch. "Finch!" he cried aloud. Could it be a relative? He shook his head. No. It would be too much of a coincidence!

As his breathing returned to normal, he read on: Evelyn Finch. *These people are Fanny's and Josiah's friends, Evelyn and Charlton! The ones who intro - duced them to the Mormon church!* He read on: Their oldest boy was named, Paul Frederick Finch! The same as his own! His breathing again became labored. *Could it be . . . ?* Quickly, he read the other names, Clara Finch, Sally Finch, and Charlton Finch after his father. By this time, he was sweating profusely. His emotions, like a horse on a madly spinning carousel, were up and down. Was this an answer to the short prayer he had offered?

He returned to his knees, tears stinging his eyes. Whoever *these* Finches were, they were good people, friends who helped Josiah and Fanny during their hard times, and . . . they were members of the Mormon Church! "Dear God, help me to find out who these people are—if they're my relatives." He remained on his knees for some moments, hoping to get an answer. The only thing that came to him was he needed to get to the meeting Gusty was attending. Grateful that she had called and given him the address, he got up, grabbed his coat and tie and ran from the apartment.

❧CHAPTER 51❧

Gustavia looked around the Martin's nice living room. It was tastefully decorated and comfortable. Bob Martin was a well-built man of short stature, gray at the temples, but with a full head of otherwise wavy brown hair. His blue eyes, set into a broad face, easily twinkled with humor. He had made her laugh a couple of times, easing her tension. She felt totally comfortable here among these people she had never met.

Silvia Martin was an attractive woman. She also had blue eyes with many laugh lines and a wide warm smile. Her short brown hair had no gray in it, yet all their children were grown and away from home. They were both warm and vibrant people and made her feel completely at ease.

The young man she had talked with on the phone, Elder Ream, was a stocky young man with short and very straight hair that stubbornly stuck out in a couple of places. He was oozing with enthusiasm, and his grin spread across his face almost constantly. A young man with him, whom he referred to as his companion, was Elder Larsen. He was tall, thin, and red-headed and the more reticent of the two. But he had a wide, ready smile and blue eyes that had the same light in them as Elder Ream's. Gustavia was impressed that two such young men could be so happy about disrupting their lives to do missionary work.

They all visited a while, asking if Gustavia was from England because of her accent and other things about her life. It was then Elder Ream asked what had prompted her to ask for missionaries. Gustavia told her story as briefly as possible. The four found it gripping.

Elder Ream cleared his throat. "Since we feel that we're all brothers and sisters. Do you mind if we call you sister?" With Gustavia's affirmative answer he began. "Well, Sister Browne, before we start, we need to have a prayer to know what to start teaching you. After hearing why you called us, I know what I would like to teach you, but we need to pray for the Spirit to guide us."

"What do you mean by the Spirit? I read about that in my grandmother's diary, but I'm not sure I fully understand it."

Before Elder Ream could answer, the doorbell rang.

"Excuse me," Bob Martin, said, as he got up and went to the door. He opened it to a stranger, a nice-looking young man who looked very anxious. "Hello, may I help you?"

"I'm looking for my fiancée, Gustavia Browne."

"She's here. Come on in," he replied exuberantly.

"Thank you."

As Paul entered the room Gustavia blinked in surprise. "Paul!" She ran to him, throwing her arms about his neck. "I'm so happy you're here." She studied his face and found that he looked shaken. "What is it. Paul?" she asked, a little frightened.

"I . . . found out something rather astounding," he whispered. "I can't tell you now, but I also learned I was supposed to come to this meeting."

Gustavia, eyes wide with astonishment, whispered, "I wish you could tell me right now." She took his hand and smiled. "Come in and meet all these nice people."

Paul was amazed at how overjoyed everyone seemed at his arrival, and almost immediately his uneasiness left as he shook hands with Mr. and Mrs. Martin and the two young men who called themselves 'Elders' just as the missionaries had when teaching Josiah and Fanny.

He sat beside Gustavia on the couch. Taking her hand, he clutched it like a lifeline, feeling grateful to be by her side, hoping with all his heart that he would never allow another painful rift to come between them.

The four asked Paul a few questions about himself as they had Gustavia. Then Elder Ream began again, suggesting they pray for the Spirit to be with them as they all learned together. Before he did so, he answered Gustavia's question about the Spirit, explaining what it was, its role and how to know when one was feeling it. When he was through, he said, "We can't teach unless the Spirit is with us, and unless it's also with you."

Elder Ream bowed his head and all followed. Paul was touched by the simple, heartfelt prayer and found himself praying with him in his heart.

Elder Ream remained silent a moment, then quietly handed Gustavia and Paul each a *Book of Mormon* and a Bible which were ready for them on the coffee table.

"We used to give specific lessons in a set order," Elder Ream said quietly, "but recently, we've been instructed by the prophets to teach by the Spirit and go where that leads us." He paused, meditating a moment. "Brother Camden and Sister Browne, we're all children of God. We refer to Him more often as our Heavenly Father. He knows each of you well. He loves you individually and personally as He does all His children. We are worth much in His eyes, so much so, he was willing to sacrifice His beloved Son, His only Begotten son, Jesus Christ, by having Him come to earth, take our sins upon His shoulders, and die for us on the cross so that we could all come back to Him. "

Elder Ream then looked deep into Paul's eyes. "Do you know about the Atonement of Christ, Brother Camden?"

"Yes, I do. Gustavia's mother gave us each a small Bible when we were children and instructed us to read it every day."

"I'm happy to hear that. Then you know," he said, looking only at Paul, "that during that night in the Garden of Gethsemane, Christ took upon Himself all our sins, no matter how abhorrent they were?"

Paul paused. "I thought that this happened when He was on the cross."

"Many churches teach that," said Elder Ream, "however, a careful reading of the scriptures will show us that His greatest suffering occurred in the Garden of Gethsemane."

Paul nodded. "That seems to make sense."

"Did you know that he suffered everything you have suffered?"

Paul wasn't sure and didn't respond.

"When you were a young boy, He knew what you suffered and was with you. He understood."

Paul was startled. He glanced over at Gustavia, and she shrugged her shoulders indicating she was as puzzled as he was. He returned his gaze to the young man, astonished, his heart burning within him.

"Brother Camden, The Savior took upon Himself all our burdens of loneliness and pain. He took upon Himself all our feelings of worthlessness and insecurity. He carried these upon His shoulders that night."

Paul was speechless. While Elder Ream was saying those simple but eloquent words, it felt as though the Savior Himself had reached in and plucked out those very feelings that had lain so heavy upon his heart tonight—leaving in their place peace and warmth. Emotion constricted his throat, and try as he might to swallow it away, a few tears came to his eyes.

Hesitantly, Paul asked, "Why . . . did you say that to me, Elder Ream?"

"I don't know. I just felt impressed to do so."

Paul, deeply moved, looked down. Regaining control, he said, "Thank you. You have no idea how much I needed to hear that. Could we continue learning more about the Atonement?"

"We certainly can," Elder Ream stated warmly. "Elder Larsen can lead us to some scriptures."

❧

Gustavia and Paul drove their separate cars, anxious to get over to his apartment as they had planned. Once inside the apartment, they held each other tightly, both certain that the Spirit Elder Ream talked about was still with them. For a few moments they remained silent.

Taking Gustavia by the hand, Paul led her to the couch.

She gazed into his face questioningly. "Now, tell me, what made you come to the meeting?"

He opened his mouth, paused and shook his head, not knowing what to tell her first. Then the feeling came over him that he should share all the debilitating emotions he had felt as a child in the orphanage, how they had remained hidden deep inside him, and how they had risen tonight when he thought of Artie Banks. He hadn't wanted her to know the extent of his weaknesses. He wanted to be strong in her eyes, but how else could he explain how the Spirit had guided Elder Ream?

He gazed at Gustavia whose large tender eyes were upon him, her ears eager to hear anything he had to say, her heart accepting. "I haven't wanted to share this with you, Gusty. I didn't want you to know my weaknesses. But I'm afraid I've been humbled tonight. I need to tell you so you'll understand why Elder Ream said what he did to me." He cleared his throat and began to open up the most vulnerable part of himself, a part he had never shared with anyone.

When he was through, Gustavia had a greater understanding of what he had suffered as a little boy. She reached for him, laying her head upon his shoulder. In almost a whisper, she said, "Mum and I used to wonder how you could be so cheerful, knowing you had been in the orphanage since you were a baby. Of course you would feel as you did." It wasn't until then that Gustavia realized the significance of it all. "The Spirit guided Elder Ream to help you!" she exclaimed.

"Yes," he said quietly.

She hugged him. "God *does* love us, Paul. We *are* His children as the elders said."

"Apparently so. We knew this as we read our small Bibles, but somehow it didn't sink in like it did tonight."

"I know," she murmured.

"And now—I have something quite miraculous to show you."

"I can't imagine what it could be," she said, shaking her head. "I'm already feeling astounded over everything we've heard tonight."

"Well, prepare yourself," he said smiling. He reached for the diary he had placed on the end table. He grinned at her puzzled expression.

Opening it to the back inside back cover, he said, "Look carefully and see if you see something."

She grinned. "What are trying to pull, Paul Camden? I already did this to you."

He smiled. "What do you see?"

"I see the pocket."

"Pull out the pictures."

She did as he asked. "All right. So?"

"Look carefully."

"I am. I don't see anything different. What are you trying to show me?"

"Feel it."

She rubbed her hand over it several times. "It feels like something else is in there," she stated excitedly. "But I felt inside the pocket carefully. There aren't anymore pictures in there."

Paul's eagerness was contagious. "Look closer."

"I don't see . . . wait a minute. It looks like something near the spine. She eased her fingers inside. "It's another pocket! You found this while I was gone?"

"Yes. It's part of the reason I came to the meeting."

Gustavia reached in and felt another picture. Her heart raced with excitement as she pulled it out and looked at it. "It's a picture of a family. Who are they?"

Paul's heart was also racing. "Turn it over and read the names."

Gustavia did so. "It's Josiah's and Fanny's friends, Charlton and—"

She stopped and looked over at Paul, her eyes as wide as dollars. "Th-their last name is *Finch*! Paul! Could they be . . ."

"Read all the names."

She slowly read the name of the first child out loud, "Paul Frederick Finch." She jumped up. "Paul Frederick Finch!" She danced around in excitement. "Oh Paul, could he be your father?"

He stood and took her hands in his. "That's what I wondered. I had just gotten up off my knees when I felt as though I should look at the diary again. I thumbed through it aimlessly until I came to the inside back cover. At that point I was feeling bitter about things that didn't make sense. It seemed that everywhere I turned the Mormon Church was in my face. And when I saw the last name of those good people who were so kind to Josiah and Fanny, suddenly the negative feelings I've had about the Mormon Church were gone. It was at that moment I felt I needed to be at the meeting with you."

"I can scarcely take it all in!" Gustavia cried, looking up into his face, tears streaming down her cheeks.

"It seems as though God *has* been guiding us all along, Gusty," he replied. He pulled her close and they remained in each others arms feeling gratitude to God for the wo n d e rfiul evening and for healing the pain that had come between them today.

After a while, Gustavia murmured. "I need to tell you something, Paul."

"What more can you possibly tell me that could add anything to my happiness?"

"Remember me telling you that there was something singular about Artie Banks?"

"Well, that was a wet blanket," he joked, but half serious.

"Well—guess what?"

"What?" he asked, his curiosity aroused.

"Elder Ream and Elder Larson have that same distinct expression in their faces."

Relief rushed through Paul. "Really?"

"I thought it might be from the church they belonged to, but now I know it's the Spirit radiating from them because they live what they believe."

Paul thought about this for a moment. He, too, saw and felt something exceptional in the elders, and after what Gustavia had just said, the jealousy he felt over Artie Banks left. His heart was completely free. "Thank you for telling me this, Gusty. You did add more to my happiness. He paused, thinking. "I feel we had better listen to everything the missionaries have to say."

Gustavia was thrilled. They had left it open-ended when Elder Ream wanted to set another date. "I do, too, Paul."

⪼CHAPTER 52⪻

Paul set the meeting with the elders at the Martin home for the next evening much to the happiness of the elders. They felt like they had 'golden contacts' at their fingertips, and they thanked the Lord for their good fortune. Both Silvia and Bob Martin felt privileged that Silvia had been the one to answer Gustavia's call.

When Gustavia and Paul entered the Martin home the next night, the elders and the Martins saw a big change in them. Tonight, they were eager and happy, rather than reticent and unsure.

Elder Larsen opened with prayer, and the meeting began. He explained what *The Book of Mormon* was and its purpose.

After his experience the night before, Paul was enthralled with the fact that the book was another witness that Jesus is the Christ, and that it was a record of His visit to the Americas. He turned it over in his hands and paged through it reverently. Gustavia watched in awe. That he was suddenly so open and accepting amazed her because she wasn't quite so accepting. She had to read the book and pray about it as the elders had suggested before she could accept it as a true record like the Bible.

Before she could go any further, Gustavia had to find out what Artie meant when he said that Josiah and Fanny's dreams could be realized. She had wanted to tell only Paul about her dream, but now felt she needed to tell the missionaries. In more detail, she reiterated the events leading up to her grandparents being killed before they could be sealed.

Following the Spirit, Elder Ream began teaching about the temple and its purpose. It was so beautifully expressed and humbly taught that the Spirit testified to Gustavia's heart that is was possible for Josiah and Fanny to have their dreams realized! When she finally understood that she and Paul could go through the temple for them and seal them by proxy, she was overcome. *That's why Sarah and Fanny appeared to me and asked me to help them!* It was then she realized that sometime, somewhere Sarah Sullivan had accepted the Gospel. Maybe in the spirit world where, the elders explained, missionary work continues for those who haven't had the opportunity to hear the truth on this earth. *Had her husband John Sullivan accepted it too?*

Paul put his arm around Gustavia, deeply touched, knowing exactly what she was feeling. It was comforting to learn that God showed his love for all his children, that He had prepared a way for all of them to come back to Him if they chose. He was thrilled to learn that in one year, if they remained worthy, he and Gustavia could be sealed for eternity and that any children they had would automatically be sealed to them.

The elders and the Martins knew that Gustavia and Paul had been given a lot of deeper gospel truth, but knew they needed it and that they were ready.

Gustavia and Paul were quiet and contemplative on the way home. They had agreed to attend church the next day and meet later that night. Their assignment was to read *The Book of Mormon* daily over the next week and pray about it.

When almost home, Gustavia spoke in awed tones. "Paul, I feel so privileged that my grandmothers appeared to me and asked me for help. They were both so beautiful, and I felt such love emanating from them."

Paul looked over at her in surprise. "You haven't mentioned the love before."

"I know. I couldn't put it into words until tonight, but after that beautiful lesson on the temple I'm able to."

Arriving at Ada's, they went over to the garden bench. The moon was full, and the air was cool and fresh. He put his arm around her, and she snuggled against him.

Paul's mind turned to his possible ancestors, Charlton and Evelyn Finch. "Gustavia!" he cried out.

His outburst startled her. "What?"

"Paul Frederick Finch was only five years older than your father, Thomas."

"So it appears."

"Could it be possible that Charlton and Evelyn are still living!"

"Oh Paul, it is! They would probably be in their late eighties or early nineties, but yes, they could be," she exclaimed, jumping up.

He pulled her back down beside him. "If they're my grandparents, could it be that my parents are still living also?"

"Yes. But probably not. If they were, I'm certain they would have come back to get you."

"That's what we'd hope anyway—that they wouldn't have left me there if they were still alive. But . . . if Charlton and Evelyn are still living, they would know whether or not their son and daughter-in-law are living, and if not, what happened to them."

"And what happened to Fanny and Josiah!"

"Yes! We've got to locate them," he stated with finality. "They may still be in London."

"Let's go over there right now, Paul, and see if they're alive and if so whether they're your relatives."

"I want to very much, but we have to finish what we've started."

"Of course! We do." She smiled and kissed him. "I'm so impulsive. You're good for me."

He grinned and kissed the tip of her nose. "And you're more than good for me."

BELFORD, MAINE, JULY 2001:

After attending church one time, and finishing up the lessons, Gustavia and Paul were baptized eight days later on Saturday, July 7th. A sense of urgency had driven them both for different reasons.

Gustavia realized her ancestors had been waiting a long time to have their temple work done, and she wanted to be the one to do it. The year of waiting had to begin as soon as possible! *Could part of the urgency be to find Paul's grandparents before it was too late?*

Paul shared Gustavia's feelings. For his own peace of mind, he needed to get to England and see if he had grandparents and if he did, hopefully find that they were still alive!

The ward members turned out to their baptism en masse, welcoming them into the Church and into the ward with such enthusiasm Gustavia and Paul were overwhelmed. It was a day that would always remain in their memory as a spiritual new beginning.

The previous Sunday when they first attended church, they felt as though they had come 'home.' Their testimonies grew daily as they read and prayed about *The Book of Mormon* and marveled that neither had felt such peace and contentment.

Sunday the 8th, the day after the baptism, Paul was ordained a priest in the Aaronic Priesthood. The awesome assurance of having been given the authority to act in the name of the Lord humbled Paul, but at the same time gave him confidence in his ability to lead and protect his family. It seemed incredible to him that in such a short space of time, he had found the Gospel of Jesus Christ, had been baptized, confirmed, and been given the same priesthood that John the Baptist held!

❧

Her life had been so busy, so full, Gustavia hadn't given Ada any thought. They lived in the same house but went their separate ways. During the time she and Paul were studying with the missionaries, she spent the days working on Ada's biography and the nights reading *The Book of Mormon*. She had finished the biography the day before she was baptized. But it wasn't until the following Monday that she presented it to Ada.

"Here are the last pages of your biography," she said, grateful to have it over with.

Ada reached for them listlessly. It was then that Gustavia really looked at her. She was shocked. Her hair was slightly unkempt, her face thin and pale. Why hadn't she noticed before? Had it just happened or had it come on gradually? She had been too blissfully preoccupied to notice.

A pang of sadness went through her. How had Ada felt as she saw her's and Paul's love and happiness? *Probably more alone and lonely*, she thought.

"You aren't feeling well, Ada."

"I'm feeling fine," she snapped.

"Can we go out into the garden and visit?" she asked, feeling the fresh air would do Ada good.

"We don't have anything to visit about."

"Please, Ada."

"Oh, all right."

When they were seated on the bench, Gustavia breathed deeply of the fragrance-filled air. "I have a lot of happy memories here, Ada."

Ada looked surprised.

"I've finished my grandmother's diaries. You read them too, didn't you?"

"Yes."

"Why did you cut out those pages and keep them from me."

Ada became agitated, her voice rose. "Because—my mother often railed against the wicked Mormons. I didn't want anyone to know that any of my family had anything to do with that wicked church, let alone join it!"

"At first I thought the so-called scandal was Fanny running off with Josiah, but of course it wasn't. That's what you wanted me to think, wasn't it?"

"Yes. I'd rather you think that than for you to know that Fanny joined that evil church! It would have brought disgrace upon the whole family if it were known—and now it's out and . . ."

"So that's the scandal you've been referring to ever since I got here."

"It is! It most certainly is."

After reading Fanny's diary, Gustavia understood why Ada would feel that way. "I'm relieved to hear you say that—for it isn't a scandal at all."

Gustavia saw the whites of her eyes. "If that isn't a scandal, I don't know what is."

"Ada," she said, taking one of her hands. "It isn't a wicked church. It's the restored Church of Jesus Christ."

Ada, shocked at what Gustavia said, promptly pulled her hand away. Gustavia took it again and held it tightly, surprised that Ada didn't try to pull it away again. "Ada," Gustavia began, changing the subject quickly, "you've had a hard life, but God loves you and wants more for you."

"I don't believe that."

"Do you read the Bible?"

"I have done in the past. Why all these questions?" she asked sharply.

A feeling came over Gustavia that surprised her, and she acted upon it. She reached over and put her arms around Ada and pressed her cheek to hers. "I love you, Ada." She felt Ada tremble and, surprisingly, she began to sob. Gustavia released her and let her cry.

When her sobs subsided, Gustavia waited for her to say something.

"My life has been useless, Gustavia. I'm useless. How could you love me?"

"Because you trusted me with your life history. Because I can see a glimpse of the real Ada behind the stiff facade you put up to protect yourself. Because we have the same grandfather, John Sullivan, who loves us both."

There was no response, so Gustavia told her of finding the pockets in the last diary, explaining the pictures she found. "One of them may be Paul's grandmother and grandfather and their children, one of whom might be Paul's father. You know, Ada, he was put into an orphanage as a baby with the message his parents were coming back to get him, but they never did."

"He . . . was there as a baby?" she asked. For the first time, Gustavia saw an emotion for another person on Ada's face.

"Yes. He grew up feeling he wasn't worth loving. That is, until my mother and I met him and fell in love with the darling little boy. And he returned our love. Love is what it's all about."

"It is for you and Paul, anyway."

"We're going to England to see if we can find out if those people in the pictures are Paul's grandparents. I wanted you to know." Gustavia stood up. "We'll be leaving in two days, on the 11th."

❧CHAPTER 53❦

As the plane winged its way toward London, Paul and Gustavia were in a much different frame of mind than the last trip. Paul had done his homework before leaving. He did an Internet search for a Charlton and Evelyn Finch in London. Nothing could describe the feeling that washed over him when he found two people by that name living in the Hounslow area, not too far from the airport.

Wrapped up in each other's arms most of the way, Gustavia could feel Paul take a deep breath now and then to calm his underlying anxiety—his excitement. She would smile and reassure him with a squeeze or a kiss.

Grateful to have his one and only love, Gustavia, in his arms, Paul knew she was all he really needed. He could survive without finding his family, but he couldn't survive without her. The comfort of her touch eased his fear of finding out that maybe their trip might be in vain.

Paul had arranged ahead of time to rent a car. When the plane landed at Heathrow airport, London, they quickly grabbed their carry-on luggage and went straight to the car rental.

Once in the car, Paul pulled out a map of London. He looked up Trippet Street where the Finches lived. He decided to get on Motorway 4 for a distance, take an exit that would lead them to a street called Whittle Gate, and go from there. Taking a deep breath to calm himself, he turned the key and drove toward M4.

"Gusty, I've been thinking. I want you to talk with these people first and see if they are really the friends of your grandparents, Josiah and Fanny."

"Why? I'm feeling more anxious for you to learn . . ."

"If I find out first that these people aren't my grandparents, I'm afraid I'll be so disappointed I won't be able to be happy for you if you find they're your grandparents' friends. Besides, I'm a coward. I'm trying not to get my hopes up too much." He let out a heavy breath. "I'm afraid I have though, and I guess I want to put off finding out differently."

"I understand. I'm a coward too, Paul. I don't want to find out they aren't who you want them to be."

He squeezed her hand, then returned it to the wheel.

"Your hands are cold."

"I know," he said, watching for the right moment to ease into the traffic on M4. "When I'm nervous, my hands get cold."

Sometime later they came to the exit Paul was looking for. He guided the car off the motorway and onto Whittle Gate. Gustavia looked around, trying to imagine in what kind of neighborhood a retired schoolteacher would live.

After driving down several streets, they came to Trippet St. Turning right, they watched carefully for the house number they were looking for while assessing the neighborhood. It was an older area, with semi-detached homes. Paul was glad to see that the yards on this street were nicely kept.

Paul slowed down and stopped in front a of house with the right number. It was a one-story rust brick with large trees and full bushes that looked as old as the house. He looked over at Gustavia "Shall we?"

She took a deep breath and nodded.

Hand in hand they moved slowly up the walk, and as they did so a momentary wave of fear and panic stopped Paul. They gazed at each other, knowing they were sharing the same feelings. They moved on hesitantly, as though they were on the edge of their seats in a thriller, afraid of what the next scene would bring.

"It's a warm, sunny afternoon," Gustavia murmured, trying to lift his spirits as well as her own, "a perfect time to meet a long lost friend or relative, not the kind of weather in which to be disappointed."

"Hope you're right." He pushed the bell. They heard nothing. "Do you suppose it works?"

Just as he asked, the door opened. A tall white-haired man with straight shoulders smiled at them. "Well, if you two aren't a pleasant sight for an old man's eyes."

As they had decided ahead of time, it was Gustavia's cue. "Hello." She smiled at the nice looking man. *Does he look like the picture we have?* He seemed to, but he was so much older, how could she tell? "We're looking for a Charlton and Evelyn Finch."

"I'm one of them," he grinned. "I'm certain you know which. My wife Evelyn is inside. Come on in."

"Thank you," Gustavia said, glancing quickly at Paul's closed expression.

"Come this way." He led them through the tiny foyer into a small living room where a silver-haired woman was arranging some music sheets on an organ. She turned and, like the man, smiled when she saw the striking young couple.

"Evelyn, my dear, these two young people are looking for some people whose names seem to be the same as ours."

The woman walked over to them. "Please, both of you have a seat on the sofa and tell us who you are since, it seems, you know our names."

Does she look like the picture? She knew Paul was also anxiously scrutinizing their faces.

Seeing their hesitation, the woman smiled and asked their names again.

Paul was too agitated to respond. "My name is Gustavia Browne and this is my fiancé, Paul Camden. We're happy to meet both of you." Gustavia plunged ahead, her heart pounding. "Do you . . .did you—uh, know some people by the names of Fanny and Josiah Browne?"

The smiles left the older couple's faces, replaced by shock. They looked at each other asking silent questions. "Why are you asking?" the man asked cautiously.

"Because they're my grandparents. I've been reading Fanny Browne's diaries, and they had some dear friends named Charlton and Evelyn Finch."

The woman put her hands over her mouth, making a tiny mewling sound, then turned to her husband. All he could do in return was shake his head in disbelief. "How can this be?" she asked him. She took hold of his hand and, as if they had silently agreed, both got up and went over to Gustavia, who, seeing the flood of emotion on their faces, rose quickly. The woman took her hands, studying her face, eyes brimming with tears. "My dear, where in the world did you come from? Yes, Fanny and Josiah were our dearest friends."

Gustavia, choking with emotion, pulled her hands away and embraced the woman, who in turn returned it with great affection. The man watched, deeply moved.

No longer able to contain his happiness for Gustavia, Paul blinked back tears of happiness for her.

When emotions were subdued, Gustavia said, "We've come from America to find you."

"You have?" Evelyn asked, incredulous. "We can't believe that we're so fortunate you found us. We never would have found you."

Eventually everyone reseated themselves and Evelyn asked Gustavia how in the world she had gotten hold of her grandmother's diaries?

"It's such a long story. Before I tell you, could you please tell me what happened to my grandparents? Fanny's diary ended on a Saturday, noting that they were going to attend church the next day. I do know they were killed. The neighbors, the Beddows, who were guardians of their son, told Thomas, my father, when he was older, that the police came and told them that his parents had been killed by some men, a mob of some kind."

Evelyn covered her face and cried quietly. Charlton, who was also on the verge of tears, told the story. "It was a terrible time for us, Gustavia. Evelyn's uncle was viciously against the Mormon church. Are you acquainted with that church?"

"Yes. Because of the diaries and some other things we'll tell you later, Paul and I have just been baptized into the Church."

The expression on both their faces was one of total amazement, then joy. "That's wonderful to hear," Charlton said.

"Your grandparents would be so thrilled!" Evelyn exclaimed. Then in an anxious tone she added, "Your grandparents didn't get their temple work done before they died. We've been going to do it for them, but something kept getting in our way. I think it must be that they wanted you, their granddaughter, to do it, Gustavia."

"They do," replied Gustavia with conviction. "But that's another story. Please go on."

"Something began happening that I had never seen before or since that fateful day," Charlton said. "A small mob or group of men had been bothering the church members for a few Sundays."

"Fanny covered that in her diary; you needn't go over it. Just tell us what happened that day."

"All right," Charlton said, relieved he didn't have to relate all the distressing details. "That last Sunday, the mob was unusually quiet. We had no idea they were even around. The hall we were meeting in was getting stuffy and apparently your grandmother, Fanny, who was sitting in the back row with Josiah, got up and opened the door a crack. Immediately, it was flung open by an angry group that seemed to come out of nowhere and shots rang out. Fanny fell to the ground. As Josiah knelt to take her into his arms they shot him.

"By that time, Evelyn and I and others ran to them. More shots were fired. One hit my wife in the fleshy part of her arm, and one grazed my temple. The cowards ran off before the law could get there. In our confusion and grief, no one could identify them. Evelyn's uncle wasn't one of the mob, but we wondered if he masterminded it. However, it could never be proven."

Gustavia covered her face and cried, and Paul put his arm around her. Evelyn and Charlton grieved with her. Finally Gustavia, wiped her eyes. "It's all so terribly tragic."

"Yes. It left us and the whole branch with great scars," Evelyn added. "For a long time I felt responsible because I thought it was my uncle. He claimed innocence, and maybe he was. We don't know."

Charlton continued the narrative. "Evelyn and I were taken to the hospital and kept for a couple of days. We asked a couple from the branch to go see how little Thomas was. As soon as we were released, we went to the Beddows to see him. It was a shock to find they had taken him and moved, leaving no forwarding address. They probably moved out of fear."

"We were able to go into your grandparents' flat," added Evelyn, "but were surprised to find all their personal belongings gone. I knew Fanny kept diaries, but they were gone too. We asked the neighbors if the Beddows had taken their things. They said no, that a strange man went inside and looked around. Shortly after, he and another man were seen carrying the Browne's personal things out to a small vehicle. To this day we don't know who those men were or where they went with the things. That's why we're so shocked that you have the diaries."

"How I got them is an extraordinary story." Gustavia said. She looked questioningly over at Paul, knowing how anxious he was to find out his information.

"Tell them," he urged.

"Yes, tell us, but first tell us about your father, Thomas. Is he living?"

"No."

Disappointed, Evelyn said, "I'm so sorry, Charlton and I would liked to have gotten acquainted with him.

"So would I," Gustavia said, explaining briefly about her parents and her father's early death. She related meeting Ada and Edgar at her mother's funeral. Leaving out the unsavory details of her stolen inheritance, she unfolded the strange story of how she got the diaries, how pressed she felt about getting them read and how, in the end, she found the pocket with the picture of Fanny, Josiah, and their little Thomas and the picture of Fanny and her mother, Sarah. She pulled the pictures out of her purse and handed them to the Finches.

"Yes!" Evelyn exclaimed. "These are pictures of our friends. How wonderful that you found them. And the whole story is amazing. It's obvious that the Lord's hand has been in all of it."

"Yes, Paul and I feel that way too. And now, I want to tell you about a dream I had before I found the pictures. I haven't told anyone about it except Paul and the missionaries." She related the dream, finding that it affected Evelyn and Charlton deeply.

Evelyn turned to her husband. "No wonder we were blocked at every turn when we tried to do their work for them. They wanted you to join the Church, Gustavia."

"Thank you for sharing that with us, Gustavia," Charlton said.

"Yes, thank you," Evelyn reiterated, "We feel privileged. Now—it's supper time, young people. I don't know what your schedule is, but will you have supper with us and stay the night? You see, our children are grown and married with children of their own, so we have two extra bedrooms."

Paul was thrilled that they had been asked to stay, but still nervous about asking his questions, which would now have to be put off until after supper." Thank you," he answered for both of them. "That's very kind of you. We gratefully accept."

❧CHAPTER 54❧

Supper consisted of a delicious left-over shepherd's pie, grilled tomatoes and a fruit pie, topped with hot custard sauce. The conversation was filled with questions on both sides. The Finches wanted to know more details about Gustavia's life, her father and mother and about her education. Then they asked Paul about his family, and what he did for a living.

When the meal ended, they all helped with the dishes, then returned to the living room for the rest of their visit.

Evelyn asked Gustavia how she and Paul met.

"That's another long story," Gustavia said, "one that had better wait until later. Tell us about each of your children," Gustavia asked, knowing it might lead to Paul's question.

"We have two daughters, Sally and Clara who live here in London. They each have four children," Evelyn began. "Charlton, who we call Charlie, lives in Southhampton with his wife. They have five children. We had another son . . ." Evelyn seemed unable to go on. Her husband took over.

"As Evelyn said, we had another son, Paul." Charlton paused, and Gustavia and Paul exchanged anxious glances, each holding their breath. "He was our oldest. He was brilliant. He graduated in 1952 in engineering and was going on into aeronautical engineering and hoped to go to work for Rolls Royce. In his last year of school, he met a lovely girl named Ann Watts, who had just graduated in nursing. She had joined the Church just before they met.

"The Korean War was on when they were married and immediately Paul joined the service before he was conscripted, feeling quite certain the war wouldn't last long. After his basic training, he was sent to Korea. His wife had a baby while he was gone. The long and short of it, he caught a hemorrhagic fever. He got it from a rat or some kind of insect. He and other English soldiers who contracted it were evacuated by plane to the RAF airfield in Lincolnshire, then taken by air ambulance to a small hospital thirty miles from Hull where there were two doctors who specialized in diseases contracted in Korea and other similar areas."

Evelyn took over. "His wife was notified and was told she could see him since it wasn't contagious. She took her eight-and-half-month-old baby with her to the hospital. Ann called us and told us where she was and of Paul's illness, but told us not to worry, that she was going to help nurse him. She related how thrilled Paul was to see his baby boy for the first time.

Gustavia and Paul glanced anxiously at each other, silently asking the same questions. Were Paul and Ann his parents? Was he that eight-and-half-month-old baby?

Evelyn continued. "Ann and an army nurse, Betty Willmont, who worked at the hospital, shared digs in a nearby rooming house run by a widow. Ann paid the widow to look after the baby while she stayed with Paul and helped nurse him. She'd go back to the room only to nurse the baby and care for him at night.

"The doctors had been able to help other similar diseases, but they were unable to do anything for the soldiers with this virus. Some lived, most died of renal failure.

"Ann called us in tears and told us Paul was getting worse. We told her we were coming to see him and help her with the baby. She didn't tell us she was ill herself, and had been for some time.

"By the time we got to the hospital, Paul had died."

Gustavia gasped and glanced at Paul. His face was one of anguish.

"We were devastated," Evelyn went on, unaware of the emotion cascading through her empathetic audience. "Besides that, we found that Ann had checked herself into the local hospital. The hospital staff said that Ann had been ill while nursing her husband, and when he died, she took his death so hard her illness became worse. They thought she had some type of encephalitis.

"When we got to the hospital, we found Ann in a coma. We quickly went to the widow's rooming house to get the baby. When we arrived, he was gone. The woman explained she wasn't able to take care of the baby both day and night, so Betty Willmont, who had been a long-time resident of the area, had taken the baby to a safe place to stay until Ann got well. When we asked where, the woman said the information of his whereabouts had been given to Ann.

"We quickly went back to the hospital and tried to ask Ann questions, but to no avail. That very night she died, taking the information with her. We looked all through her belongings for some kind of a note, but we didn't find any.

"Just before we arrived, nurse Willmont had been sent to Korea so we couldn't ask her where she left the baby. Later, when we were trying to reach her, we learned that she had been killed."

Charlton continued the story. "We had to get back to London with the body of our son and daughter-in-law and make funeral arrangements. Afterward, we returned to Hull and asked the Church members if Ann had contacted them and if by chance had told anyone where her baby was. She hadn't even contacted them. This wasn't like Ann. She must have been so ill she wasn't thinking clearly. We contacted the police in all the surrounding area: Hull, Grimsby and the smaller towns and cities. They looked for the baby for us. We were beside ourselves. Not only had we lost our son and daughter-in-law, but a grandson. To this day we don't know what happened to him."

"You see," Evelyn said, "It's the not knowing that's the hardest." Evelyn wiped the tears away, and Charlton put his arm around her shoulders.

Paul's breathing had turned shallow and rapid. So far, it was still possible that Ann and Paul Finch were his parents! He looked over at Gustavia who was nervously clenching and unclenching her hands. He knew they both should offer some kind of condolences. Gustavia came to his aid.

"We're more sorry to hear this than you know," she murmured.

Paul couldn't wait another moment. "Do you think it was possible your grandson was put into an orphanage near Hull?"

Evelyn looked shocked. "An orphanage? My goodness, no. Ann would never have put him into an orphanage. She was a wonderful girl, a wonderful little mother."

Paul felt as though he had been stabbed in the heart, his disappointment was so great.

"Have you been back to look for your grandson?" Gustavia asked.

Evelyn and Charlton seemed to age before their eyes. Their shoulders sagged and the pain that came across their faces spoke of the many years of suffering they had endured. "Yes we have, over and over. Still—we don't know what happened to him," Charlton repeated almost inaudibly.

"We're so sorry," Gustavia said.

"Thank you for listening," Charlton said. "We hadn't intended to burden you with all this. For some reason it gives us solace to talk about it. We know all our friends and children are weary of hearing about it."

Evelyn added, "They don't want us to go to our graves early over our grief."

"Did Ann's parents try to find the baby?" Gustavia asked.

"We don't really know," answered Charlton. "Ann's parents disowned her when she joined the Church. Though we sent them a note, they didn't even bother to attend the funeral."

"What did Ann and Paul name their son?" Paul asked hoarsely.

Evelyn gazed curiously at him for a moment. "Young man, you look familiar to me. Doesn't he look familiar to you, Charlton?"

Paul's emotions were on a roller coaster, plunging down into disap-pointment, then jerking upward with hope.

Charlton studied him. "Yes, a little."

"To answer your question, Paul," Evelyn said, "They named him after his father, Paul Frederick Finch. Since we called our son Paul, they called him Freddie."

Paul's and Gustavia's hopes rose to a fever pitch.

Paul began slowly, hesitantly, "I'm adopted. Before I was adopted, my name was Paul Frederick Finch."

Both Evelyn and Charlton gasped. "I don't understand!" Evelyn cried. "Are you saying you're our grandson? But . . . but how could that be?"

"I need to tell you more," Paul continued. "I was put into the Hesslewood Orphanage, near Hull, at around nine months old. I was told, when I was older, that there had been a note with me that said: 'This baby is not for adoption. The parents are coming back to get him. His name is Paul Frederick Finch. They call him Freddie.'"

Charlton and Evelyn paled, the blood draining from their faces.

"But, no one ever came to get me," he went on. "I was raised in the orphanage until I was adopted at age ten-and-a-half by a Robert and Sharon Banks and taken to America. Sharon died soon after arriving in America. Robert hadn't wanted to adopt me in the first place and so didn't want to have any more to do with me. With pressure from Sharon's parents, her sister, Karla Camden and her husband Bruce adopted me."

Evelyn appeared to be in shock, clearly suffering over the plight of the abandoned baby. She opened her mouth then closed it. Her head moved from side to side as though unable to absorb what was being said.

"I was fighting the Church for reasons not necessary to tell you at the moment, but might be important to you later on. Gustavia had gone off to a meeting with the Mormon missionaries that I refused to go to. I had behaved rather badly toward Gustavia, and I was feeling very remorseful. Though I had read it, I aimlessly picked up Fanny's last diary, turned to the inside of the back cover and pulled out the pictures Gustavia showed you. Then, something compelled me to continue my examination. I discovered that there was a second pocket concealed beneath the first. I reached in and pulled out another picture. Show them, Gusty."

Gustavia reached into her purse, took out the picture and handed it to them.

"Why," exclaimed Charlton, "that's a picture of us—of Evelyn and me and our four children. Imagine finding that in Fanny's diary."

"In the diary," Paul continued, "Fanny only mentioned your first names, and when I saw on the back of the picture that your names were

Finch, my heart did a somersault. Then when I saw the name Paul Frederick Finch, the same as my own, I was overwhelmed. I wondered if they were relatives. I knelt down and prayed to know who they were. The only feeling that I had was I needed to get to the meeting where Gustavia was. I went and ended up taking the missionary lessons with Gustavia."

Evelyn was still struggling with her emotions. "Oh, I find myself wanting you to be my grandson. Wanting it more than you could ever know. But, we can't imagine Ann allowing anyone to put her baby into an orphanage—even for a short time."

"Evelyn!" Charlton cried out suddenly. "The reason he looks familiar is that he looks like our son! Go get a picture of him grown."

Evelyn left and soon came back with several pictures, handing one of their eldest son to Charlton. He gazed at it, looked at Paul and nodded, then handed the picture to him. Paul and Gustavia stared at it. "It does!" squealed Gustavia.

"I believe it does too," Paul said, trying to control the deluge of emotions that came over him as he gazed at the nice looking man he hoped was his father. "Did you bring in a picture of Ann?"

"Yes." Evelyn handed him one of their wedding pictures and one of Ann alone.

"They're such an attractive couple," Gustavia said. "Both look so happy." Paul nodded, not trusting himself to speak.

Next, they looked at the one of Ann alone. It was a five by seven of her face. She had long brown hair and large blue eyes. She had a slight smile on her face. Her high cheek bones tapered down to a delicate chin. "She's as beautiful as your mother, Gusty." Paul said quietly, as though he believed Ann was his.

Gustavia looked over at him, touched that when only a boy he thought of her mother in that way. "Thank you. I think so too."

Paul looked over at the faces of the two people he hoped were his grandparents and saw an expression of longing in their faces, but also deep weariness from the emotion and confusion they had experienced this afternoon and evening. "You both are tired. Let's all go to bed and talk about it tomorrow."

Evelyn and Charlton nodded gratefully. "But, could we all kneel down together and pray about this before we retire?" Charlton asked.

"We'd appreciate it," Paul said.

When they knelt, Charlton offered a beautiful prayer, beseeching the Lord's help to know the truth concerning their grandson.

As they stood, Paul made an announcement. "As you were praying, I got the strongest impression that Gusty and I should drive to Hull and get a court order to release information about a Freddie Finch who was put into the orphanage around thirty years ago. Then we should be able to get the records from the archives. I've brought all my identification and the records of my adoption by the Banks. In the last five years, the laws have become less strict concerning confidentiality of adoption records. My name being the same as your son and grandson may only be a coincidence, but we need to find out one way or another. You're both welcome to come, but since you've been there so many times, maybe it's best you rest and let us search."

Simultaneously, Evelyn and Charlton said, "Thank you." Then Charlton added, "we'll be praying for your success."

Evelyn said, stepping over to Paul and putting her arms around him. "You look just like what I hoped my grandson would look like."

Deeply touched, Paul returned her embrace.

Next, Charlton gave Paul a hug, then they both took turns embracing Gustavia who warmly returned their affection.

❧CHAPTER 55❧

Early the next morning, Evelyn, with Gustavia's help, fixed them all a good breakfast. It felt a little strange to Paul as they sat at the table together. He felt comfortable around the Finches—as if they were old and dear friends, but there was a feeling of reservation in all of them. Everyone wanted to let go and believe they were family, yet there was still restraint.

Charlton once again suggested they go in the living room and kneel in prayer. This time, he asked Paul to pray. Still a little self conscious about praying aloud, he began stiffly, but soon he was able to express his gratitude for finding and meeting the Finches, asking for help in finding the knowledge for which they were all searching and praying that they would find it quickly.

Seating themselves afterward, Paul spoke to Charlton. "Sir, would it be all right if I used your phone to call a solicitor in Hull? I want to ask him to appear before a magistrate on my behalf and secure a court order to open my file. This could save a lot of time. I hope it can be done quickly, then Gustavia and I will go to Hull and take the order over to the archives. There has to be more information about me, information that would have been collected at the time I was admitted to the orphanage.

"The phone is in the kitchen, Paul. Feel free to use it."

The three remained and visited while Paul made his phone call. When he returned, he was all smiles. "I talked with a solicitor who seemed delighted to be of help to a fellow attorney from America. He said he would do everything possible to get an immediate appointment with a magistrate and secure the court order. We'll leave for Hull when I hear from him.

Charlton smiled. "Though we don't know if you're our grandson, I'm as proud of you as if you were."

It was a compliment that gladdened Paul's heart. "Thank you, sir."

It was then that Charlton brought up a surprising suggestion, one that never would have entered Paul's and Gustavia's minds.

"Since you've both read Fanny's diaries, Evelyn and I thought that you'd like to see something. It will probably be a few hours before you hear from the solicitor, so we could take you there this morning."

"Where?" Gustavia asked, curious.

"The investment bank where your grandfather, Josiah, worked."

"Why would we want to do that?" she asked. "His employer, Simon Sisbee was so unkind to fire him."

Charlton nodded. "We know. It was a painful time for all of us. It was also a painful time for Mr. Sisbee, I understand. I think he loved Josiah like a son."

"It seemed as such, and I felt badly for him too, but still . . ."

"Mr. Sisbee and his wife have long passed away," Charlton went on. "One of his grandsons, James Ruston, runs the bank now.

Paul was intensely interested in seeing it. He turned to Gustavia. "Why don't we? It would be interesting to see where Josiah enjoyed working."

In Gustavia's mind, it was the last place she wanted to see. "All right," she said reluctantly.

"Good!" Charlton said. "Let's go."

In Paul's rented car, Charlton directed him to the banking district and showed them the Bank of England.

"I remember," Paul said, "reading in Fanny's diary that it was often affectionately referred to as the 'The Old Lady of Threadneedle Street.'"

Charlton chuckled. "That's right. It still is at times."

Next, Charlton directed Paul to Mr. Sisbee's bank on Moorgate Street, close to the Bank of England. Paul parked the car. They all got out and entered the stately old building. Gustavia looked around, trying to envision the time when Josiah worked there.

The old-fashioned interior had been modernized, but carefully done so that it would not offend old clients who liked old ways, yet would attract the new clients who would appreciate the conveniences and the feeling of solidity and permanence.

A man came up to them. "May I help you?"

"I believe Mr. Ruston is expecting us," Charlton said, surprising Paul and Gustavia.

"Your name, sir?"

"Charlton Finch."

"He is indeed expecting you. Come this way." He led them to James Ruston's office, explaining that this office had been Mr. Simon Sisbee's at one time. "He's the one who bought and built up this investment bank. He's quite a legend with all the employees here."

The door was open and a man who appeared to be in his early fifties sat behind a desk. Seeing them, he immediately stood up. "Come on in, all of you," he said with enthusiasm.

Gustavia and Paul looked around the office. The furnishings and atmosphere gave them the feeling they were back in Josiah's time.

Mr. Ruston seemed to read their minds. "Yes. The office is almost as Simon Sisbee left it. I wanted to keep the nostalgic flavor of the original. I'm James Ruston," he said, walking around the desk and shaking hands first with Gustavia, looking intently into her dark eyes. "You're Josiah Browne's granddaughter aren't you?"

Gustavia sucked in a surprised breath. "How do you know?"

"You look like the pictures my grandmother, Anna Sisbee, had of Josiah."

James Ruston, still holding Gustavia's hand, said, "I want you to know that Josiah Browne is my hero."

Incredulous, Gustavia said, "I certainly didn't expect to hear that from Mr. Sisbee's grandson."

He smiled. "I can understand why."

"I'm Paul Camden," Paul said, reaching for Mr. Ruston's hand.

"Oh yes," he said, shaking Paul's hand firmly, "you're engaged to this young woman I hear. Please, all of you have a seat." As they found seats, he returned to his own.

Gustavia studied his appearance. From Fanny's description of Simon Sisbee, she felt his grandson resembled him—broad face, blondish-red hair tinged with gray, and blue eyes that twinkled. The main difference between the two was James Ruston was tall and his grandfather, Simon, had been short and rotund.

Mr. Ruston smiled at the confused expressions on the young couple's faces. "I guess you're wondering about a few things."

Gustavia nodded.

"Well, you see, my wife and I have become good friends with Charlton and Evelyn, and we've shared some touching stories. I would like to tell you one now. Charlton told me that you read Fanny's diary and learned that my grandfather, Simon, fired Josiah because he joined the Mormon church."

Astonished, Gustavia nodded.

"Simon was very fond of Josiah. He loved him like his own son, he told us. It was the most difficult thing he'd ever done when he fired him. It was hard on his wife, Anna, also. They suffered tremendously." He smiled at Gustavia's expression.

"About seven months after Simon fired Josiah, he began reading more about the Mormon Church, mainly anti-Mormon stuff, and it began to bother him. In his fervent loyalty to the Church of England, he had been too close to the picture. He said he remembered Josiah suggesting that if he wanted to know the truth about something he should get it from the proper sources. Well, he began doing just that, mainly articles from the *Millenial S t a r* that had some instructive and positive material about the Mormon church. It began to make sense to him. He had Anna read them also.

"Three-and-a-half months passed and Simon and Anna decided to visit Josiah and Fanny. They found that they had moved. They knocked on some neighbors' doors to find out where they had gone and one of them was Charlton's and Evelyn's. They were invited in immediately and told to be seated. It was then they learned of Josiah's and Fanny's deaths. Simon and Anna were grief stricken."

A sadness cut deep into Gustavia's heart. "They were?"

James Ruston nodded solemnly.

"So that's how you know Charlton and Evelyn," Gustavia murmured.

He smiled. " Yes. To make a long story short, Simon felt that if he hadn't worried so much about what other people thought and fired Josiah, that he and Fanny wouldn't have been killed.

"It wasn't long before Charlton visited Simon here at the bank. When Charlton found out that he was blaming himself, he assured him that it wouldn't have changed a thing if he had kept Josiah on. He gave Simon and Anna a *Book of Mormon* and suggested they both read it and pray about it. They did, and believed it."

Gustavia gasped. "They did?"

"Yes. Your grandfather, Josiah, was so staunch, so faithful, so strong in his faith even to the point of sacrificing his job during the depression rather that give it up, that he inspired Simon and Anna."

"Did they join the Church?"

"I'm sorry to say, they didn't. They believed it and told their daughters and sons-in-law to read the Book of Mormon, but they could never bring themselves to break those old ties, to make the kind of changes that would have been necessary to join—but the rest of his family did."

Speechless with amazement, Gustavia could only stare at James Ruston, her eyes pooling with tears. Finally, her voice husky with emotion, she said, "That's almost—too unbelievable."

He smiled. "Yes, it is, knowing the history. Thanks to your devoted grandfather, Josiah, we are members of the Church."

Myriad emotions overwhelmed Gustavia's for a moment. "Thank you for telling me."

"You can also thank your grandparents' friends, Charlton and Evelyn. They did some admirable missionary work with our family. They carried on where Josiah left off."

After they had arrived back at the Finches, Gustavia gave Charlton a big hug. "Thank you for taking us to see James Ruston."

He hugged her back. "It was a joy to Evelyn and me. It was a privilege."

"Just from the written words of the diaries, my grandfather, Josiah, became a powerful person to me, and apparently in life he was to others."

"That's exactly what he was. His strength of character, his integrity were an inspiration to Evelyn and me."

"Yes," Evelyn agreed, "as was your grandmother Fanny's."

"Thank you," Gustavia said, embracing Evelyn. "You've helped us know them better."

After dinner, a call came from the solicitor in Hull, telling Paul that he had arranged an appointment to see the magistrate tomorrow morning at 10: 00 A.M.

Evelyn grasped her chest. "That means we may find out tomorrow night or the next day?"

"Yes," Paul said, slightly breathless himself. "Just as soon as we find the information in the archives, we'll return."

Charlton put his arms around Evelyn to steady her as well as himself. "We'll be anxiously waiting to hear the news. Like my wife, Paul, it seems to me too good to be true for you to be our grandson."

Getting their suitcases together, Paul and Gustavia said goodbye to the Finches and left for Hull. Charlton and Evelyn, clinging together, watched them leave, hoping with all their hearts the futile search for their grandson would soon be over.

By the evening of the next day, Charlton and Evelyn were beside themselves. They kept looking out the window, wondering if Paul and Gustavia were going to return that night, or tomorrow.

Evelyn kept wanting to pick up the phone and ring their children to tell them about their young visitors, but they had decided to wait until they knew the outcome.

They turned on the telly and watched aimlessly for an hour. When they heard a car door slamming, they turned it off and looked out the window. "They're here!" Evelyn exclaimed. "Oh, Charlton, my heart may not stand it if . . ."

"Sshh, relax, my dear," Charlton said, putting his arm around her, as he watched them get out of the car and come up the walk.

They went to the door and opened it just as Paul and Gustavia stepped up onto the porch, then moved aside and let them enter.

None of them said anything. Paul just opened a folder, pulled out a small piece of old stationary, and handed it to them.

Evelyn took it with shaking hands and together she and Charlton read it.

This baby is not for adoption. The parents can't care for him
for a while, but they'll be back to get him. His name is Paul
Frederick Finch. They call him Freddie.
        Nurse Betty Willmont

A groan from deep inside Evelyn escaped. Her chest heaved with unspeakable emotion. She glanced at her husband's dear age-worn face, their tear-filled eyes met, saying more than they could in words. Together, they turned to their long-lost grandson, still unable to move, to speak. All they could do was examine every inch of his face—the face that resembled his father, their beloved son!

Paul gazed back at these two wonderful people who were the first link to his beginnings. He now existed in a time, in a place that made him unique in all the world. He had been loved, not in a cursory way, but his parents and his grandparents had loved him deeply at the time Nurse Willmont deposited him abruptly into the strange world of the orphanage. And that love reached through the years as his grandparents continued to search for him—to grieve over his disappearance. Gone were the tormenting questions that had been his life-long companions.

His grandmother, finally able, opened her arms to him, and he went into them, wrapping his own around her. "Freddie, our little Freddie. How can I take it all in?" his grandmother cried.

Gustavia, choked with joy, stood back and watched the emotion-filled moment, the uniting of a family torn apart by cruel circumstances.

At length, Evelyn was able to let him go so that her husband could have his turn.

Looking into Paul's face, Charlton said, his voice breaking, "This is a miracle, a miracle for which we've been praying for so many years." He took his grandson into his arms and held him, both overwhelmed with such gratitude, neither could speak.

When, at last, Paul looked over at Gustavia's tear-stained face, he went over to her, took her into his arms and clung to her. "I don't know what

I would have done if you hadn't been here by my side, helping me stumble through this, filling in the gaps when my emotions wouldn't let me."

"I wouldn't have missed this for anything, Paul," she murmured.

"Charlton," Evelyn cried, "we haven't greeted our soon-to-be granddaughter!"

When Evelyn acknowledged her as part of the family, Gustavia suddenly realized that through Freddie, of all people, her beloved orphan friend—that she also had grandparents, uncles, aunts and cousins!

More hugs and tears followed.

At last, Evelyn said, "We must all sit down and talk."

Sitting on the couch, holding tightly to Gustavia's hand, Paul said, "The first thing I want to ask you is, what do I call you, grandmother and grandfather, or grandma or . . . ?"

"All our grandchildren and great-great grandchildren call us grandma and grandpa," Evelyn replied, smiling with joy.

"Thank you, Grandma. It sounds a little strange to one who thought of himself as an orphan, but it also sounds great." Everyone's happiness spilled over into laughter.

❧CHAPTER 56❧

"There's something important we have to do," Charlton said excitedly. "Ring up all three of our children tonight and tell them the extraordinary events of the past two days—of our miracle."

"And," Evelyn added, "when they can believe it, they'll be so happy."

"And grateful we won't be grieving as we were," added Charlton "And neither will they."

"But right now, Freddie," Evelyn said, "you must tell us how you and Gustavia got together."

He smiled. "It's a great story. I'm going to let Gustavia begin and we'll take turns telling it because each of our perspectives is important for you to know."

Gustavia began with her mother getting the job with Mr. Fretwell, seeing the charming, freckle-faced orphan boy hop up onto the wall for the first time, their play, his magic stick and the small Bibles presented to them by Alice. She told how Freddie had learned to play the harmonica, performing for the public at the Music Hall on Jarrett Street in Hull.

A sudden thought brought her narrative to a halt. Remembering that, at their first encounter, she had seen Evelyn arranging music at the organ, she asked, "Did your son, Paul, have musical talent?"

"Oh my, yes." answered Evelyn. "I'm of Welsh descent and music and the love of music has been in my family for generations. Our son could play almost any instrument. Also Ann had a wonderful voice. I often teased her that she must have had Welsh ancestry in her to sing so beautifully."

"How marvelous!" exclaimed Gustavia. "You might have a singing voice also, Paul."

Paul laughed. "Well, even if I don't, it's nice to have someone think I might. And thank you, Gusty, for thinking to ask that question."

Paul then took his turn and told them how Alice arranged for him to play in the yard and how he felt loved and part of a family for the first time in his life. How he fell in love with the beautiful little Gustavia, his serenading and declaration of his love, and her firm rebuttals.

Evelyn and Charlton laughed and cried during the narrative, thrilled to hear that there was some happiness in their grandson's life while in the orphanage.

It sounded to Evelyn like a romantic fairytale as Gustavia continued to unfold the story, ending finally with the revelation of her beloved Freddie Finch as he serenaded her beneath Ada Redmore's turret window.

His grandparents were silent for a moment or two, then Evelyn spoke in hushed tones. "I recognize the hand of the Lord in this whole story. He brings about such wonderful 'coincidences' in His children's lives and has especially so in yours. Just think, Gustavia, Freddie's grandfather and grandmother introduced the gospel to your grandmother and grandfather, Fanny and Josiah, who often expressed their gratitude and indebtedness to us. And now we've been paid in full. Through you, Gustavia, Fanny's and Josiah's granddaughter, our long lost grandson has been returned to us."

"Yes," Charlton said quietly, "it's amazing how all the pieces of the puzzle have come together, uniting us."

Gustavia was so moved at the thought, she couldn't respond.

"Weighing it all," Paul said, "It certainly has helped me to understand what the missionaries meant when they said, 'the family is all important to the Lord.'"

After a light and hurried supper, the four gathered again in the living room. The first question Evelyn asked was, "When are you two getting married?"

Paul and Gustavia looked at each other and smiled. "We got engaged, joined the Church, and immediately came over here to find you," Paul said, "so we haven't had time to even set a date."

"I wish we could get married, here, Paul," Gustavia remarked.

"That sounds great, Gusty." The minute he said it, he reconsidered. "But I don't think I could do that to my family in California."

"Of course you couldn't," Evelyn said. "As much as I would like that, it wouldn't be fair to those people who adopted and cared for you."

"Thank you, Grandma, for understanding," Paul said, the familiar name still new on his tongue. Incredibly so!

"Now," Evelyn began, "I don't see an engagement ring on Gustavia's hand."

"She wouldn't let us take time to get one. She was too anxious to finish the diaries, have the missionary lessons and get over here."

"Just a minute," Evelyn said, excusing herself, "I'll be right back."

Paul looked questioningly at his grandfather who shrugged his shoulders and smiled.

Evelyn was back shortly, carrying a white dress in a plastic bag and a small white box. She put the dress over a chair and handed the box to Gustavia to open.

Inside were two identical wedding bands, one larger than the other. "Those are your father's and mother's wedding bands, Freddie. You don't have to use them, but they're yours regardless."

Paul's throat constricted. Here was something tangible, something he could actually touch that had belonged to his parents! He reverently lifted them out of the box and he and Gustavia took turns studying them.

"Let's try them on," Gustavia whispered in awe.

"It fits me perfectly," Paul said in amazement.

"Mine is a little loose, but it can be sized down."

"You mean you really want to use them, Gusty?"

"I would love to!"

He took her in his arms and hugged her, not trusting himself to speak. At last, he asked his grandmother where the engagement ring was.

"Your mother didn't want one. She wanted just a band matching your father's."

"Don't you want an engagement ring, Gusty?" Paul asked.

"No. These simple bands are far more meaningful."

Pleased beyond words, Evelyn opened the plastic bag and showed them Ann's wedding dress. Gustavia shot to her feet to examine every detail. It was white silk chiffon.

It had a wrap-over draped bodice with an embroidered and beaded infill with a high round neckline, three-quarter-length inset sleeves and a floor-length skirt gathered from the waistline. Underneath was a circular-cut silk-taffeta underskirt. "This is elegant!" Gustavia exclaimed. "Much more so than I thought a young woman, just graduating from nursing school, could afford."

"Ann's parents were well-off," Charlton informed them. "They helped her through school. Ann was also very frugal and had saved here and there, so she had a little money."

"This is a 1950s style of dress, Gustavia, so I'm certain you wouldn't want to wear this for your wedding," Evelyn remarked.

Paul, who had been curiously watching Gustavia's reaction to the dress, laughed long and hard.

His grandparents looked at him in surprise and Gustavia tapped her foot, waiting for his amusement to subside.

It was then Paul related what Gustavia was wearing when he first saw her, explaining her penchant for wearing period clothing whenever the mood struck.

Charlton and Evelyn pondered this a moment, then Charlton broke into laughter. "Well, that's what I like—a girl who isn't afraid to be different."

Evelyn smiled. "Apparently we do have a rather unique granddaughter here, don't we?"

"May I wear this dress at my wedding?" Gustavia asked as though she couldn't believe she might have the privilege.

"You really want to?" Evelyn asked, still unsure that Gustavia was in earnest.

Paul laughed again.

"But Ann was not as small as you are, Gustavia. Do you want to try it on?"

"Oh, could I?"

"Come into the bedroom, dear," Evelyn suggested eagerly.

It wasn't long before Gustavia came out, the beautiful dress hanging somewhat loosely on her small frame. The veil with its small silk flowers and pearls fit nicely over her dark hair.

Paul hadn't expected to feel emotional, yet through misty eyes he could almost see his own mother standing there. Then his vision focused on the beauty of his wife-to-be.

"What do you think, Paul?" asked Gustavia, her eyes sparkling with excitement.

His eyes still moist, he said softly. "You look like an angel."

"But it's too large, Gustavia," Evelyn said, "and it's so intricate, it would be difficult to remodel."

"Not for Gustavia," Paul said.

The next day on their way to a special Finch family reunion celebration that Evelyn and Charlton had arranged the night before, Charlton directed Paul to the cemetery where his parents were buried.

Paul knelt and with his finger traced the words on the double-sized headstone before him:

IN LOVING MEMORY
JOINED TOGETHER FOREVER
PAUL FREDERICK FINCH   ANN WATTS FINCH

He got no further. Touching the hard granite surface sent a shock of recognition throughout his body, carrying with it a great relief as well as great sadness. His eyes were blinded by tears.

Evelyn and Charlton watched him, their hearts aching that this had to be the introduction to his parents. Freddie needed time to accept, to grieve, Evelyn thought, her throat tight with emotion.

Before they left the cemetery, Charlton took pictures of Freddie beside the memorial of his parents, then one of Freddie and Gustavia standing together behind it. Promising to send them copies, he led the group back to the car.

❧

Later that night, driving back from the joyful Finch family gathering, Charlton and Evelyn were exhausted. They had rented a building in London large enough to house the whole clan—children, grandchildren, and great-grandchildren.

Gustavia and Paul were overwhelmed with such a large group but thrilled by the joy everyone expressed at the discovery of the long lost grandson, nephew, and cousin.

Paul's Uncle Charlie, Aunt Sally, and Aunt Clara gave Paul hugs that threatened to end his life. They hugged Gustavia a little more gently but with just as much enthusiasm.

The once orphan-boy was in a state of disbelief. That all those people were actually his relatives was beyond his comprehension! It was difficult to remember all the faces, and other than his uncle and aunts, he definitely couldn't remember names. Evelyn had taken pictures of everyone and promised to label each one carefully for Paul, so he would know who he met and learn their names.

He did remember, however, what good-looking people his uncle and aunts were, as well as their children and grandchildren. Very aware of their countenances, he saw the gospel light in them, making him feel even more grateful to be part of the family. They seemed to be intelligent and cultured people, people he would be proud to present to his mother, Karla.

❧

The next morning, with the wedding bands securely in her purse and the wedding dress in her garment bag, Gustavia joined Paul as they prepared to leave.

His arms around both, Paul asked his grandparents if they could possibly come with their three children to the wedding, which would most assuredly be in California.

"We'll do our best to be there, Freddie," Charlton said. "Just let us know when and where."

The goodbyes were difficult for all of them. It had been far too short, but Paul had to get back to work. Nevertheless, they parted with the full expectation they would see each other soon.

During the flight to New York, then to Augusta, Gustavia and Paul thought about and discussed the amazing changes that had occurred in their lives as a result of Fanny's diaries. Because so much had happened in such a short time, they had to talk about it, discuss every detail, fix it all forever in their memories so they could record it accurately and permanently.

When they finally reached Ada's, Paul took Gustavia in his arms and kissed her, not wanting to let her go. "Let's get married soon, my sweetheart," he whispered in her ear.

"Oh, let's do, love. It's all up to you and your family now."

"Tomorrow I'll call and talk with them about it."

He walked her to the door, kissed her again, and said a reluctant goodnight.

❧CHAPTER 57❧

The next night, Paul arrived shortly after dinner. Gustavia waited for him in the garden. It felt to her as if they had been apart for three days rather than one. She ran to him as he opened the gate and threw her arms around him, kissing him passionately.

"Wow! That's the greeting I expect every day after we're married, Gusty."

"That's the plan. Now what is yours?"

"Mine?"

"Did you talk with your family last night?"

"Oh." He grinned, pulling her to the garden bench. "That plan. Mother is in her element planning lavish weddings and wedding receptions. The only problem I presented her with is I wanted to get married August 8th, if that's all right with you, Gustavia. That's only four weeks away, but it would give Grandpa and Grandma Finch and their children time to make plane reservations. Mother finally agreed that she could do it."

Gustavia clapped her hands. "Four weeks? That's wonderful. I missed you last night and today so much, Paul, I'd be willing to marry you tomorrow, almost."

"Great!" He squeezed her till she protested with a squeal.

"Now, where are we going to live? My one-bedroom with one small closet won't work. I'm sure you need a big closet for all your clothes."

"I'm afraid I do. I have a small storage room in Boston that has some more period clothes, all my design paraphernalia, and my sewing equipment."

"Oh-oh," he smiled. "What do you have to do in the next four weeks?"

"I have to go to Boston and bring back my sewing machines, so I can take in the wedding dress. After that I need to do a little shopping."

"Maybe we can squeeze in some time to go looking for a home."

"Oh! How exciting! But we can live in your apartment for a little while. I'll only bring over a few things and store the rest in the turret room until we find a home. Now, let's go in and tell Ada our plans, and if she seems interested we'll tell her about our discovery in England."

Paul shook his head. "You know, my sweet Gusty, I don't know why you keep trying. You have more patience than Maine has blueberries. Okay, let's go on in."

Gustavia found Ada in the library and motioned for Paul to enter. "Ada, Paul and I have something to tell you."

"I'm rather busy right now."

"Come on, sit down and let us tell you."

Ada sighed impatiently, but got up and sat in one of the chairs while they seated themselves on the couch. Gustavia studied her. She definitely looked better. Her hair was styled the usual way and she had a little more color in her face. "You look as though you're feeling better, Ada," Gustavia remarked.

"I don't know why you would say that," she responded briskly. "I always feel fine."

Gustavia was undaunted. "I'm glad. We wanted to tell you that Paul and I are going to be married in four weeks, August 8th. We'd like you and Edgar to attend if you can. It will be in California."

"There's no way I can take time off for that."

That was it, no congratulations or anything. But then she hadn't expected it.

"I'm sorry, some other special people are coming from England. Paul and I have had some miraculous things happen to us when we were over there. We'd like to share them with you."

"I don't know why you think I would be interested, Gustavia,"

It was like a sharp knife to Gustavia's heart. The progress she had made with her just before they left for England had taken a giant step backward. She stood. "Well, in that case, we'll go tell Edgar. I'm sure he's interested." She took Paul's hand, and they walked out.

When they were in the car, Paul took her hand and kissed it. "I'm sorry, Gusty. Ada can be very cruel. I hope this last episode will convince you to quit trying."

Gustavia didn't answer.

When they entered Edgar's office, it was a whole different atmosphere. He was delighted to see them and was happy to hear they were getting married. When they invited him to the wedding, he shook his head, already knowing Ada wouldn't attend with him.

"By Jove, I would like to go—but I can't leave Ada."

"You're a wonderful brother," Gustavia said. "Now we have something quite astounding to tell you."

Edgar's rapt attention, and his reaction to Paul finding that he wasn't an orphan after all, was satisfying to them both. When they got up to leave, this lonely man thanked them profusely for sharing their lives with him.

❧CHAPTER 58❧

SAN DIEGO, CALIFORNIA, AUGUST 7TH, 2001:

It was late, and everyone had gone to bed. Gustavia and Paul, out on the lovely patio of the Camden home, were sitting on the porch swing, enjoying the pleasantly cool evening air.

They had spent the four preceding days with family, the last two with Charlton, Evelyn, Paul's uncle Charlie, and his wife and his two aunts and their husbands. Their reunion was wonderful. Paul rented a touring bus and treated them to a deluxe tour of San Diego and the surrounding cities. They were intrigued with California in general, the beach, and the weather in particular.

Paul had reserved rooms for them in a hotel as close to the Camden's as possible.

Gustavia had completely won over Paul's family, even his mother. And to Paul's great relief, the Camdens were impressed with Evelyn and Charlton and their family.

Karla confided to Paul that they seemed to be an outstanding family and that he had certainly come from good blood. Paul had kissed her on the forehead and replied, "Thanks, Mother." *The taint of being adopted is gone,* he thought, smiling.

"I love your family, Paul," he heard Gustavia saying.

"You do?"

"I do."

This was the last hurdle for Paul and his heart was at ease.

They rocked silently to-and-fro, thinking of what was ahead for them tomorrow. A wedding in the elite Community Church, a wedding luncheon at the country club where the families could visit with each other, then that evening, a large wedding reception for four hundred invited guests.

"You know, Gusty, alcohol will be served during the reception, don't you?"

"I know that. I've been around it often enough to know what to expect."

"I've told my grandparents and uncle and aunts to expect it. They know that none of my family are members."

Gustavia smiled at him, leaned her head on his shoulder and sighed. "I guess we have a lot of missionary work to do here in California—and in England."

"In England?"

"You know. Your mother's parents, even though they wouldn't have anything to do with her when she joined the church. That is, if they're still alive."

"You're right! Maybe I have *another* set of grandparents living, or at least aunts, uncles and cousins. Wouldn't that be something?" His face turned solemn. "But it sounds a little hopeless since they wouldn't even come to their daughter's funeral."

"It does, but look at Simon Sisbee. One can never tell."

"You're right, Gusty. We can never judge who will and who won't join." With that he leaned over and gave her a lingering kiss. Breathless, they parted, anxious for tomorrow.

❧

AUGUST 8TH:

Accompanied by lovely organ music, Paul's sisters—the bridesmaids—preceded the bride. When Gustavia gracefully moved down the aisle of the church, she heard murmurings from both sides—from the Camden's select group of friends, from the Camdens themselves, and from Paul's family from England. All were entranced by the beauty of the bride. Neither Karla nor her friends could have guessed that the dress she wore was a 1950s creation worn by Freddie's own mother on her wedding day.

Paul watched her move toward him—a vision of loveliness. The woman he had loved almost all his life would actually be, in the next few moments, his wife. His thoughts, like a fast moving current, rushed through his mind. *Am I worthy of such good fortune? Yet didn't Grandmother validate what Gustavia and I have said to each other—that the Lord has guided our lives—guided us back to each other? How else, out of the whole world, could I have been in the right place at the right time—and sought out the Redmore's account when I did?*

And now, in that dress, it was as if his own mother was leading Gustavia by the hand—to stand beside him. Through misty eyes he beheld her upturned face, her radiant smile and dark eyes—reflecting his own happiness.

THAT EVENING, 9:30 P.M.:

As Gustavia and Paul were getting ready to leave the reception, Rick gave him a hug and a clap on the back. "You've got a great girl there, brother."

"Thanks, Rick. That means a lot to me."

"And thanks for telling us, at the wedding luncheon, the amazing story of how you found your grandparents. Our whole family was fascinated and very happy for you."

"When we get settled in a home," Paul urged, "you've got to come out to see us—you, Melanie and the children."

"We will, but not in the winter," his wife, Melanie said, smiling.

Since he and Gustavia were leaving for Augusta right after a three-day honeymoon, Paul embraced his mother and thanked her for the luncheon and the lovely reception.

"We're happy for you, Freddie," she said.

"Yes, thank you, Mother," Gustavia added. "We appreciate all you've done for us."

The judge embraced them both, congratulating them heartily.

Paul's sisters and their husbands and children affectionately hugged them goodbye, and his heart swelled with love for his Camden family.

With more gratitude than he could adequately express, Paul thanked his English relatives for coming, and he and Gustavia got a round of affectionate hugs. It was heart wrenching to say goodbye to his grandparents.

Charlton said, " Freddie, your grandmother and I have marveled many times that after searching for you for so many years, it was *you* who found *us*."

"And," Evelyn added, "to be able to witness your marriage to our dearest friends' granddaughter has been a blessing we could never have imagined."

"Me neither, Grandma," Paul said, clasping her in his arms.

It was a tearful farewell for them, all promising to visit as they could. Secretly Paul was fearful that Charlton's and Evelyn's advanced age might mean that this was the last time he would see them on this earth.

At last, Gustavia and Paul were alone, heading for their hotel. Still marveling that after searching for each other for twenty-one years, they were in fact married! They clasped hands until Paul had to take the wheel.

Gustavia had no idea where Paul was taking her. She knew it would be a nice hotel, but he was keeping it a surprise. All he said before they left for California was, "Bring your swimming suit."

It wasn't long before they crossed a bridge—a soaring silver strand from San Diego to Coronado Island.

"How impressive." She sighed. "I love California."

"I do too. It would be nice to live here someday." Just then Paul said, "Here it is Gusty, the Del Coronado Hotel."

"What a magnificent place!" she exclaimed, taking in the large white, structure and peaked red roof, which spoke of the age of classic Victorian architecture—a gentler, more elegant era.

"It's a historic old place with a lot of stories connected to it. Though it's old, it's kept in excellent condition, and it's right on the beach. It has great restaurants, so we don't have to go out anywhere. We can spend our three days together without any interruption."

"Sounds wonderful," she murmured.

They parked and went into the lobby where Paul registered while Gustavia looked around.

"It's such an interesting place," she said, following him to the elevator.

They arrived at their room, and immediately Gustavia went to the window. "Oh, Paul," she burst out excitedly, "this room faces the beach and the ocean."

He was pleased at her reaction. "That's what I requested."

She turned to see Paul taking off his coat and tie. The full impact that they were now man and wife caused her heartrate to escalate. It was the culmination of many years of romantic dreaming—many years of anticipation. Her mum had taught her to save herself for this very moment, telling her how much more wonderful and exciting it would be if she did. And that moment was actually here—with the man of her dreams, her best friend, the man she was desperately in love with—Freddie!

Paul placed a 'Do Not Disturb' sign outside the door and locked it. He walked slowly toward his bride, his smiling eyes full of ardor—ardor that was meant solely for his childhood sweetheart, Gustavia.

"Words can't express my love for you, Gusty," he whispered huskily. Taking his time, he tenderly kissed every inch of her beautiful face until he reached her lips, his tenderness remaining throughout the rising passion that engulfed them both.

Reluctantly, Paul glanced out the window. "Wait here," he said, going over and turning off the lights. He went back and took his bride's hand in his and together they gazed at the scene before them, lit by the full moon—people sitting on beach chairs, others walking together along the glittering sand.

Paul's eyes were drawn to the ocean. Moonlight reflected off the rising tide, transforming the tips of the waves into bubbling, frothy silver, leaving the underside dark and frightening. The stark contrast between the pale moonlight casting its dark shadows and the bright sunlight of morning dispelling those shadows, reminded him of his life in the orphanage before he met Gustavia and her mother—and his life thereafter.

He vowed that beginning now, he would do everything in his power to make Gustavia's life one of sunlight as she had his.

❧CHAPTER 59❧

THREE MONTHS LATER, NOVEMBER 2001:

The anticipation of helping Fanny and Sarah as they had requested in her dream made the year of waiting seem long to Gustavia. But already, over four months had flown by since their baptism.

Right after she and Paul had returned from their honeymoon, they moved a small amount of her belongings into the tiny apartment. She felt as though she was in heaven 'playing house' as Paul teasingly referred to it, for their small crowded place did seem rather like a play house.

And almost immediately, they began looking for a home to buy. This had been exciting to Gustavia. They wanted one large enough to make extended family comfortable when they visited and still have enough room for all the children they wanted.

At last, they found the home. It was salmon brick with white shutters around each window. It spread out on a large lot with tall full-grown trees. Only one portion of it was two story. She concentrated on furnishing their home with a combination of antiques and traditional furniture, which pleased Paul.

The colorful leaves of fall had fluttered to the ground and had been gathered up. Though most of their trees were bare, with the few evergreens on their lot and on the surrounding areas and country side, Maine was still beautiful.

That evening, she remembered a promise she hadn't kept—a call to Artie Banks with the results he had asked for. She broached the subject tentatively to Paul, and to her amazement, he was perfectly agreeable and even wanted to get on the extension phone to thank him for his part in their conversion.

Artie was silent a moment, then congratulated them enthusiastically and told them how happy he was to hear it. Then, to their surprise, he told them that he had just gotten engaged. Happy and relieved to hear this, Gustavia congratulated him, and Paul added his congratulations, perhaps with a little more exuberance than was necessary.

Paul had been ordained an elder in the Mechizedek Priesthood. They both had Church callings and had rapidly become acquainted with the members, feeling as though they belonged in this ward full of brothers and sisters.

❧

The only thing that marred Paul's happiness was Gustavia's recent and unfamiliar moodiness. Several times he had caught her looking troubled. One evening he finally pulled her over to him. Tilting her chin with his fingers, he gazed into her dark pensive eyes. "What is it, Gusty?"

"What do you mean?" she asked, evading his question.

"I've seen the troubled look that comes across your face when you think I'm not watching. What's bothering you?"

"I haven't wanted to spoil your happiness, love, but I'm wondering why I haven't gotten pregnant."

Paul had wondered about that himself, but had put it out of his mind. "I guess it isn't the right time yet."

"You think so?"

"What else could it be?"

"You know what else it could be."

"We can't allow ourselves to think like that. We'll just have to pray for faith that it will happen in the Lord's due time."

"But we're both older than most couples when they start having children."

"I know, my darling, but it isn't our fault. The Lord knows that."

The pensiveness left her eyes and she smiled. "All right, I'll do my best not to worry about it."

The cold winter evenings passed with Gustavia working on the genealogy records of John and Sarah Sullivan, and Fanny and Josiah Browne, and her own parents.

They had to be made out as accurately as possible and submitted for ordinance work at the Boston temple. With the correct names, dates, and places, she had found everything she was looking for in the genealogy library at church.

❧

MAY, 2002:

After a long winter, May brought spring in its fullness. Paul called his Uncle Charlie and told him that if they could arrange it, he would send four round-trip tickets for them to bring his grandparents to visit. Uncle Charlie and his wife, Mary, accepted eagerly.

Reveling in their home, Gustavia planted flowers and tended the bushes while Paul fertilized the lawn and mowed. A sense of satisfaction settled upon them, adding another dimension to their happiness.

The first of June, one month later, the beautiful Maine summer arrived at the same time as his family. Paul was shocked to see how Evelyn and Charlton had aged. It was is if they had been holding on to their vitality until they found their grandson, saw him married, then let go, feeling that the last part of their mission in life had been fulfilled. Nevertheless, their reunion was wonderful.

Paul was elated over the box full of pictures they brought to him. He and Gustavia pored over the pictures of his father growing up, then over his parents' wedding pictures. Included were pictures of his uncle, aunts, cousins, all properly labeled as Evelyn had promised.

Paul drove the six of them around the beautiful state as much as his grandparents' strength would allow. He also took them to Belford to see Ada's courtyard where Paul had revealed his identity to Gustavia, then took them to meet Edgar who warmly welcomed them and expressed his happiness at the reunion with their grandson and nephew.

Paul affectionately thanked his Uncle Charlie and Aunt Mary for bringing his grandparents over, and in turn they expressed their pleasure in doing so and in seeing them and the beautiful state of Maine.

When it came time to say goodbye to his beloved grandparents, Paul was again fearful that this might be the last time he would see them. Charlton and Evelyn tearfully expressed their joy at seeing him married, and secondly, seeing where he and his bride met, where they lived, and where he worked.

"It all cements in our minds that finding our grandson is indeed real and not a fleeting dream," Evelyn murmured with tears in her eyes.

"It does. Thank you, Freddie and Gustavia for allowing us to have this privilege," Charlton said.

"It's our privilege," Paul said, embracing them both, wishing he could enjoy their company longer.

☙

July arrived at last! The records of their ancestors had been approved and the date to attend the temple in Boston Massachusetts had been set for the 10th, three days after they would receive their recommends.

As the time neared for them to leave for Boston, an excitement grew within Gustavia's heart that was difficult to put into words. Looking back over the many years and experiences she and Freddie had had, they seemed to have been led purposefully, step by step to the temple—God's

House—to partake of the covenants which would lead them to life with their Heavenly Father and His Son—to be together as a family forever. These thoughts brought to her mind phrases from the present-day prophet: ". . . this phase of mortal life through which we pass is part of a continuous upward climb . . . to the temple . . . Through the Atonement of the Savior, the temple becomes the bridge from this life to the next."

She wished she could tell Sarah and Fanny that they would have their work done very soon. But then, maybe they already knew. From what she had learned this past year, those on the other side at times help those on the earth find the names and facts they need in order to get their work done.

✣CHAPTER 60✣

The 9th of July, Paul and Gustavia left for Boston. The long year had finally ended and they, at last, were going to do what Fanny and Josiah had scrimped for, saved for, what they had longed for—to be sealed as man and wife, to be sealed to their little Sarah and Thomas, so they could be together forever as a family. But first, they themselves were going to be sealed—to experience that divine privilege which was denied to Fanny and Josiah in mortality.

Arriving at the hotel nearest the temple where Paul had reserved a room, they freshened up then went downstairs to the dining room and ate dinner. They retired soon after because they wanted to leave for the temple early.

The following morning, when they went down to breakfast, Gustavia murmured, "I'm so excited, so nervous, I don't know whether I can eat."

Paul reached over, took her hand and kissed it. "It's a momentous experience we're about to embark on. I feel the same."

When they arrived at the temple, they gazed at its beauty, its one spire reaching toward heaven with the angel Moroni on top.

Paul found a parking place and together they walked toward the entrance of the temple, feeling grateful that the bishop had prepared them, so they knew what to expect. They had planned that on this first day to only do their own temple work and start tomorrow on the others.

Hours later, Gustavia and Paul silently left the temple. Outside, they were greeted by their loving friends from the ward who had traveled from Augusta to attend and assist them through the endowment and witness their sealing.

After pictures and a round of warm embraces and congratulations, their friends left.

Hand in hand, Gustavia and Paul walked the temple grounds in deep contemplation. Finding a place to sit, Paul put his arm around her and drew her close, his mind on the profound experience in the sealing room:

Their eyes moist, he and Gustavia had leaned across the alter and kissed for the first time as man and wife, sealed for eternity. Afterward, as he glanced over his bride's shoulder at the mirrors, seeing their image reflecting and multiplying in ever increasing waves, he imagined he could see his descendants multiplying in this same way—unnumbered, infinite, into eternity.

In soft and reverent tones, Gustavia reinforced his thoughts. "I can't even describe the glorious experience we had in the temple."

"I can't either, Gusty."

"I can scarcely take it all in." she murmured. "I've learned so much, but I need to understand it better."

"I suspect it will take a lifetime of attending the temple to learn and understand it all," Paul mused as if he were talking to himself.

The following morning, they entered the temple without the nervousness they felt the day before. Instead, they were anxious and thrilled to begin the work for their family, as well as enjoy the experience all over again for themselves.

Paul's grandparents, Evelyn and Charlton, told them that they had done his parents' work for them, but had not had him sealed to his parents. Their faith had led them, rightfully, to believe they would eventually find their grandson, and they had hoped he would have the opportunity of doing it himself.

First, Paul was going to do the work for Josiah Browne, John Sullivan and Thomas Browne. Gustavia, of course, intended to be proxy for Sarah and Fanny as they had asked her in the dream. Her heart was in her throat as she thought about the dream. Sarah and Fanny would finally have their desires realized this very day.

Gustavia had decided to do Fanny's endowment first because she felt so close to her after reading the diaries. Also, because if it weren't for Fanny, Freddie wouldn't have found his grandparents! And last, but not least, she would do her dear mother's work, feeling certain because of her humble and loving nature she had already accepted the Gospel.

After the first ordinances were performed, they were ready to go through the endowment for Fanny and Josiah Browne. Before it even began, Gustavia felt the presence of her grandmother, Fanny, and from then on and all during the endowment as she continued to feel Fanny near, she was a bundle of tears. The temple workers kept supplying her with tissues. In the Celestial room, the Spirit was still so strong, they sat down and clung to each other, their hearts too full to speak.

At last, they were able to look around and again admire the beautiful room with its magnificent chandelier hanging from the tall ceiling. They gazed into the mirrors on opposite walls, which so profoundly portrayed their images holding hands for eternity. Not only had they found each other, but they could be together forever.

Gustavia whispered in awe. "How God must love his children to provide such blessings and give us such beautiful places in which to worship and learn."

Paul nodded, agreeing wordlessly.

After lunch, they began the second session. Gustavia was proxy for Sarah Sullivan and this time, Paul was proxy for John Sullivan.

Gustavia felt a sweet spirit with her, not as powerful as Fanny's, but she knew that Sarah was aware of her work being done.

❧

Another session began early the next morning. At last, Gustavia could do her mother's work and Paul would be proxy for her father. The Spirit was felt simply because family was being taken care of, but in Heaven's economy, powerful revelations are not always needed, so not given. Therefore, Gustavia didn't feel her mother's presence as she had Fanny's. She simply remembered her mother's sweet and dear qualities as she lovingly did her work.

After the endowment, they were ushered into a sealing room to take care of all the sealings. The sealer introduced himself and talked with them for a few minutes. Then he paused for a long time, his eyes staring beyond them in deep contemplation. "Before we begin," he said quietly, "I feel a great many spirits in this room, spirits of those for whom you are doing the work, and others whose work also needs to be done." His eyes moistened. "It has been a while since I have felt this so powerfully."

A feeling of great reverence came over Gustavia and Paul.

"Thank you for telling us this," Gustavia said softly.

He smiled. "You're more than welcome."

With the help of Gustavia and a volunteer male patron, Paul was sealed to his mother and father. As the sealing progressed, Paul felt his parents presence, almost as if their arms were around him. He was choked with tears of gratitude and said a silent prayer of thanks to his Father in Heaven for allowing him to feel their love.

Gustavia and Paul were then proxy for the sealing of Josiah and Fanny Browne. *At last, Fanny's work was nearing its end!* thought Gustavia. Then with the help of two patrons, their son, Thomas and their little Sarah were sealed to them. *How they longed for this moment when they were living,* Gustavia recalled. *Now it's here, my dear grandparents,* she told them tearfully.

With Gustavia and Paul taking their places at the altar, Sarah and John Sullivan were sealed next. Then with the help of two female patrons, John and Sarah's two daughters, Fanny and Melissa, were sealed to them. With great relief, Gustavia spoke to them silently, *I've done as you wanted, grand - mother and great-grandmother. And I promise I'll continue to do the work for your parents and ancestors as I can.*

Lastly, Paul and Gustavia were proxy for the sealing of Gustavia's own parents. Then with the help of a patron taking Alice's place, Gustavia took her own place as a daughter and was sealed to her parents. It was during that moment she felt her father's arms around her. Tears of joy flowed. She, like Freddie, had been deprived of a father and had felt such a need for him throughout her life—and now she had him!

❧CHAPTER 61❧

TWO MONTHS LATER, SEPTEMBER 2002:

It was a beautiful fall day when Paul arrived home from work at 5:30. Coming into the kitchen from the hall, he saw that dinner wasn't ready as it usually was, no Gusty to greet him. He called out to her. No answer. He went through the house looking for her and calling her name. Still no answer. When he came to his bedroom door he found it closed. He could hear movement inside.

He opened it and saw a sight that shocked him into immobility. Gusty, putting her period clothing in plastic bags—for storage he presumed. Why else?

When Gustavia saw him, she ran to him, threw her arms around his neck and kissed him on the lips over and over. "I'm so glad you're home, darling."

"Now that's more like it. I felt as though I had been abandoned when I entered the kitchen. No Gusty. No dinner."

Gustavia laughed. "Sorry," she said, not sounding a bit sorry.

"What in the heck is going on?" he asked.

"Sit down, love, and I'll tell you," Gustavia said, patting the bed and moving things so he could.

Gustavia gave him a glowing smile. "Well, when we came home from the temple, I continued to periodically wear my 1890 to 1920 clothes as I've been inclined to do of late. It wasn't until this afternoon that I realized I had been wearing them simply out of habit—that I no longer had any desire to wear them."

"Really?" Paul asked astonished.

"Really," she repeated. They gazed at each other questioningly, wondering. Shrugging her shoulders, she smiled. "It will certainly make life a little simpler if I don't have to explain to people why I'm wearing such out-of-date clothing."

Paul chuckled. "I guess it will."

"And," Gustavia began, tenderly gazing at Paul, "my insight came just in the nick of time. The clothes would all soon be too tight."

Paul looked at her puzzled, then it sank in. "You're pregnant!"

"Yes, Paul!" She stood up and danced around, her face shining as bright as the sun. "I'm pregnant! I really am. I went to the doctor this morning, and he confirmed it."

Paul took her in his arms, overwhelmed with emotion. "I'm so happy, Gusty," he said huskily.

Gustavia and Paul, smiling and crying, realized their small circle of love now included three.

THREE MONTHS LATER, DECEMBER 2002:

The large fluffy flakes of snow were gently floating down from the sky, covering every limb, every housetop, every bush, turning the world into a white paradise. It was a time Gustavia would have loved to take her sweetheart's hand and go for a romantic walk. Instead, she had asked him to drive her over to Belford this Saturday morning, so they could tell Ada and Edgar the news.

Paul shook his head, puzzled. He could understand going over to tell Edgar, but Ada? One moment he wanted to shake Gustavia for her persistence with Ada, a woman whose ways seemed to be set in stone, and next he wanted to cover her face with kisses for her patience. This, he hoped, meant she would have patience with him when he needed it.

As they arrived, Paul said, "I think you should visit Ada alone, Gusty. She wants me around even less than she wants you."

"I know. But I need you with me, and though Ada doesn't know it, she needs you too."

Paul looked askance at her and shook his head. "I give up."

Parking in front, Paul opened the door for Gustavia, held the umbrella over her head, and they walked through the falling flakes. Gustavia gasped when she looked into the patio garden. "Look, Paul, our garden has been magically changed into a wondrous fantasy world."

Paul was feeling too irritated to comment on her remark, and pulled her along up the steps to the door, wanting to get this over with as soon as possible. He pushed the bell hard and long.

The door opened and Ada's angry face appeared. "There's no need to ring the bell like that. I'm not deaf."

"Oh, excuse, me Ada," Paul said acting a little surprised. "My thoughts ran away with me as my finger pushed the bell."

Ada waited for them to tell her the purpose of their visit. Paul and Gustavia kept silent. Impatiently, Ada finally said, "Well, are you just going to stand there and let the cold air in all morning?"

"No. As soon as you invite us in, you can close the door," Gustavia replied cheerfuly.

"Why are you here?" she asked abruptly.

"We'll tell you as soon as you invite us in," Gustavia said, smiling.

"Well, shake the snow off your feet and come in."

Gustavia stepped in while Paul shook the snow off the umbrella and set it in the stand.

"Isn't it a magical day, Ada?" Gustavia remarked.

"It seems no different than any other day," Ada replied curtly. "Would you like to come into the parlor?"

"We would. Thank you, Ada," Gustavia said, smiling and eager.

When the three were seated, Ada asked, "All right, what's all this sunshine and happiness about, Gustavia? Let's get it over with."

"Well," Gustavia began, smiling broadly "We have some news, and I have a favor to ask you."

"I'm too busy to do any favors right at the moment."

"Oh, but you don't know what the favor is."

"Well then, what is it?" Ada asked impatiently.

"First, we want to tell you the news. Paul and I are going to have a baby."

This news left Ada speechless.

Gustavia and Paul watched the irritation leave her face. Only a surprised expression remained, one that was almost pleasant.

Her mouth moved, but no words came out. Finally, she managed to say. "That's nice."

"We went to the doctor yesterday and found out we're going to have a little girl."

"A girl?" Ada's expression was infinitesimally more pleasant.

"Yes! We're so excited. Before I tell you what we would like you to do, I must say this. As you know, I only had my mother. I longed for grandparents, for aunts and uncles and cousins. I'm grateful that our little girl has the relatives she has in California and England, but they're so far away. Here she has two cousins, you and Edgar. Now for the favor, Ada. I was hoping that you would consider being part of her life."

"Me?" She asked incredulously. "You want me to be a part of her life?"

Paul was just as incredulous at what Gustavia was saying.

"Yes. You haven't let me in your life, but would you let your baby cousin into your life?"

"How do you expect me do that?" she asked, puzzled.

"By coming to see her and spending time with her. Letting us bring her over here and spend time with you."

Ada swallowed hard. Her lips trembled slightly. "I've never been around babies or children." It was obvious to Paul and Gustavia that Ada was trying unsuccessfully to recapture the edge to her voice.

"It won't take long to learn how, they're so loving, so accepting."

"I . . . I need time to think about this, Gustavia. I have many things to do."

"All right. All I ask is for you to think about it. There's one more thing. You will be a cousin to our little girl, but since the age difference is so great, could she call you 'Aunt Ada?' 'Cousin Ada' could be more confusing to a little child."

Ada nodded her head before she thought. "I . . . suppose so. Aunt Ada is . . . easier."

Gustavia stood and Paul quickly followed. The baby is due in four months. We'll bring her over to see you. You can tell me then if you'll be part of her life."

Ada, so surprised about all this, felt unnerved and couldn't quite respond in her usual way. She felt irritated with herself for being soft. Nevertheless, she couldn't seem to help it. When Gustavia and Paul left, she watched them through the parlor window, the feathery flakes falling lightly onto their umbrella as they walked to the car. They drove off and all that was left to look at was her patio garden which had been transformed into something rather amazing—something enchanting. She hadn't contemplated such a thing since she was a child.

Before they got out of the car at Edgar's, Paul took his wife into his arms and kissed her. "You're amazing, Gusty. I think I witnessed the first softening of Ada—something I thought I'd never see."

Gustavia nodded, smiling. "Babies can do that, even before they're born."

"I don't want you to be disappointed though, Gusty. She was taken off-guard this morning, and when she thinks about it, she might be right back to her old stubborn, unbending self."

"I know. I'll finally accept it if she does, but until I'm sure she won't soften, I have to keep trying. And we can pray for her. She's the loneliest person I've ever known in my life."

"I know, Gusty. Let's go tell 'Uncle Edgar' our good news. You'll be much more satisfied with his reaction."

❧CHAPTER 62❧

As the time of the birth neared, and Gustavia's excitement increased, a jarring idea came to her. It was astonishing to her that such a thought would even enter her mind. The big question was how would Paul take it? She knew this much, he would be shocked, then adamantly put his foot down.

She prayed and tried to forget it, but it kept coming back to her more forcefully everyday it seemed. Finally, after praying for courage, she broached it to Paul. He reacted even worse than she thought he would.

He stared at her in shock. "You can't mean it, Gusty."

"But I do," she said in a small voice.

He stomped around the room for a few moments and then stood before her and practically yelled, "No! No way."

"Please, Paul, just think about . . ."

"I don't need to think about it! The answer is no." With that, he left the room, and once more a rift came between them, Gustavia feeling strongly one way and Paul another.

As the baby's birth date drew near, they tried to forget the rift for her sake, but to no avail. One day, Gustavia said, "Paul, I can't go into labor with us feeling so apart. If I didn't feel as strongly about the idea, I could let it go for our sakes, for the baby's sake, but I can't."

"And I feel just as strongly."

"Have you prayed about it?"

"No."

"Will you?"

"I don't want to."

Gustavia said a prayer in her heart. "If you pray about it with an open heart and if the answer is no, I'll accept it. But if it's yes, will you give in?"

Paul's jaw rippled as he thought about it. "I guess."

"Gracefully?"

"I can't promise that. It's a terrible idea."

❧

MID-MAY 2003:

Paul was sitting in the front seat of the car and Gustavia was sitting in the back seat with their month-old baby girl in her new car seat. She was a beautiful baby. Gustavia was thrilled that she took after her husband in features and coloring.

Paul wondered how life could get much better. The only way, he decided, was to have more children. At the moment, his heart felt so tender toward his beloved wife as they proceeded on this *special* errand, he wondered how he could possibly live up to and be worthy of her. This he did know, he was one smart little boy back there in England when he asked her to marry him!

They parked in front of Ada's house and got out. This time Ada was expecting them.

When she opened the door, she smiled ever so slightly. "Come in." She led them into the parlor and invited them to be seated, her eyes never seeming to leave the bundle Gustavia held. "So, this is your baby girl," she remarked stiffly.

"Yes," Gustavia said, beaming.

Edgar stood up as they entered. He smiled broadly. "Congratulations to both of you," he announced with gusto.

Paul returned his smile with a broad one of his own. "Thank you, Edgar."

"And thank you for coming over as we asked," Gustavia added.

"I wouldn't have missed it for the world. I've been rather anxious, I might say, to see that new little cousin of mine."

After everyone had seated themselves, Gustavia unwrapped the infant, and went over to show her to Edgar.

He stared at her, marveling. "She's rather a tiny little thing, isn't she?"

"She is. She was only six-and-a-half pounds when she was born."

Next, Gustavia went over to Ada, kneeling before her while holding the baby closer for her to see.

Ada gazed at the little face. "She's beautiful."

"Thank you, Ada," Gustavia replied.

"Yes. Thank you, Ada," Paul said barely believing his ears.

Ada studied the baby. "She certainly doesn't have your dark hair, Gustavia."

"Would you like to hold her, Ada?" Gustavia asked.

"Oh . . . uh, I've never held a baby. I'm afraid I wouldn't know how."

"It's very easy, here," she said placing the baby into her arms.

Ada looked a little frightened for a moment, then her face relaxed at the feel of the soft, pliable little body. She gazed at the baby, then miracle of all miracles, Ada smiled at her. The baby's wide eyes seemed to gaze back. "I . . . I believe she's looking at me. Can she see yet?"

"A little," smiled Gustavia. "Have you thought about being part of her life?"

Ada looked down at the baby. "I don't know how to be part of anyone's life," she said through tight lips.

"Would you try?"

Her nod was almost imperceptible. "I've always wanted children," she said almost to herself, her eyes gazing longingly at the tiny, dainty face.

"Would you like to know her name?"

"Yes."

"We haven't had her christened yet. In our church, it's called a blessing. Paul will give her a name and a blessing tomorrow. We're naming her after you—'Ada.'"

Ada was so startled, so shocked, she was certain she hadn't heard correctly. "What did you say?"

Paul replied. "We're naming her after you, 'Ada.'"

"Me? Why?"

Paul continued. "Because, to be frank with you, Gustavia badgered me into it. We disagreed for weeks until I finally gave in. Actually now—believe it or not—I'm fond of the name."

Ada was speechless, especially at Paul's candidness. "Gustavia mentioned you had relatives in California and England, wh-why would you not want her named after one of them?"

"Because I like the name Ada," Paul replied. "However, she has a middle name, Ann, after my mother."

"Your mother? I thought you were put into an orphanage when only a baby."

"I was. The story of miraculously finding my grandparents, and subsequently finding out what happened to my mother and father who died before they could come back to the orphanage to get me, was the story Gustavia came over to tell you—the one that you weren't interested in hearing, remember?" Paul was surprised to see in Ada's face a fleeting moment of regret.

"But, since Ann was your mother's name, why don't you call her Ann?" Ada persisted.

"Because we both want to name her after you. Most of the time we'll call her Ada, but sometimes we'll call her Ada Ann."

Ada repeated the name several times. "Ada Ann."

"It sounds musical doesn't it?" Gustavia asked.

Ada nodded. Suddenly tears filled her eyes. At long last, her hard shell started to crumble. She lifted little Ada Ann onto her shoulder, and gently laid her cheek against the baby's soft one whispering, "Little Ada Ann, I'm your aunt Ada. We have a lot of getting acquainted ahead of us." She kissed her soft little cheek and handed her back to Gustavia with a barely audible whisper. "Thank you, Gustavia."

"You know how you can best thank me?"

Ada looked slightly wary. "How?"

"Two ways. First, you and Edgar come to church with us tomorrow and hear Paul bless our little girl and give her your name."

Edgar smiled and nodded, his eyes misty with gratitude that, as he had hoped from the beginning, Gustavia was healing the breach in the family.

Ada could only nod.

"Have you sent a copy of your biography to the Archives in Grimsby yet, Ada?" Gustavia asked.

Surprised at the question, she shook her head. "Not yet. It has to be proofread."

"The second way you can thank me is after you send a copy to Grimsby, would you add touches of your personal life to your biography— your sorrows, your happy times, your personal feelings? Little Ada needs to know about your life, so she can always remember you after you're gone. She needs to have it written, so her children can know you too, and their children. They all need to know your accomplishments, but especially, to know you personally. You need to leave your legacy behind for them."

For the first time in her adult life, Ada allowed herself to be vulnerable. She nodded slowly, her chin trembling. Covering her face, she sobbed quietly. Though she couldn't articulate it, for the first time she felt as though her life might be meaningful to someone, that maybe someone might remember she had lived. And more importantly, that she might add something to someone else's life—little Ada's.

Paul and Gustavia looked at each other. Never had Gustavia looked more beautiful to Paul than she did at this very moment.

ABOUT THE AUTHOR

ALENE REDD ROBERTS was born and raised in the small town of Monticello, Utah. One of her happiest memories as a young child, before she could read, was the daily ritual of sitting on the floor in front of the bookcase looking through the books, even loving the smell of them. When she was older, reading a book was like eating candy.

At ten years old, she contracted polio and had to spend a year in the hospital. During those long months, three hundred miles from home, she discovered the joy of communicating her thoughts through her letters. She wrote every day to her family, to her friends, her relatives and anyone else she could think of—even her beloved dentist.

Born a hopeless romantic, she wrote a truncated love story at the age of twelve. She always had a secret yearning to write, but never thought she could until her advanced creative writing teacher in college told her she should seriously consider writing.

Though thrilled at the professor's confidence in her writing ability, she decided to table her desire to write seriously until her children were raised. She did, however, write a lengthy children's book while waiting in the car for her children at seminary. Also, she wrote an extended life history for each of her five children. Now, with her seventh book published, she says, "You're never too old to accomplish your dreams!"

Alene graduated from Brigham Young University with a bachelors degree in Drama, a minor in English, and a teaching certificate. She has made a study of behavioral genetics, neurological reading problems, and nutrition. Spending time with her husband, Elliott, is her joy. Family, friends, reading, enjoying nature and going to musicals are a few of her passions. She and her husband have five children and a slew of grandchildren. They have lived in Arizona and Texas, and now reside in Utah.